Praise for the
Red Dog Conspiracy

"Melancholy and loyalty. Blood and love. Violence and tenderness. They're all tangled together in this powerful series ..."

— OLIVIA WYLIE

"This very well thought out world is created with incredibly believable and realistic scenarios based on the best of steampunk, mafia family organisation, 19th century English living (not the nobles, but the real world of real people, similar to Dickens or Swift) and an intriguing dystopian future."

— LIN CRAN

"Rival gangs, dishonest wealthy, and the grubby poor — all trying to make a living amidst a life-style that has fallen into ruins."

— MARILYN COATES

"Although it's an easy read there are twists and turns, dead ends and hidden meanings that help provide a wonderful dangerous complexity. For me the greatest meanings are in relationships and cultural distances. Things that are the heart of Jacqui's problems. That and love. A brilliant portrayal of flawed people caught in their own suspicion-based traps."

— KAY MACK

"Even if you aren't a fan of steampunk, this series is a fun read! The author has created a unique world set far in the future where Victorian culture and steampunk technology are the norm. It is in this world that Jacq must try to make her way. Surrounded by enemies, married to a man she doesn't love, and every action by any person in her world could be an act of betrayal that will cost Jacq her life!"

— KEVIN SIVILS

For clues, backstory and more, visit JacqOfSpades.com

FICTION BY PATRICIA LOOFBOURROW

RED DOG CONSPIRACY

Part 1: The Jacq of Spades
Part 2: The Queen of Diamonds
Part 3: The Ace of Clubs
Part 4: The King of Hearts
Part 5: The Ten of Spades
Part 6: The Five of Diamonds
Part 7: The Two of Hearts
Part 8: The Three of Spades
Part 9: The Knave of Hearts
Part 10: The Four of Clubs
Part 11: The Jack of Diamonds

THE PREQUELS

Gutshot: The Catastrophe
The Alcatraz Coup
Brothers
Vulnerable

THE COMPANIONS

Drawing Thin

OTHER FICTION

Weird Worlds: Science Fiction and Fantasy Flash Fiction

The Jack Of Diamonds

Part 11 of the Red Dog Conspiracy

Patricia Loofbourrow

Published by Red Dog Press, LLC
Printed in the USA

The Malady

I have an interesting malady: I seem to recall most everything I've ever heard, ever read.

Yet for the first month after the meeting atop the Grand Ballhouse, I don't recall much of anything.

The city, like me, lay stunned, quiet.

I believe we all needed those calm days of rest. Those soft morning mists. Those gentle overcast skies.

In the past two years, Spadros quadrant had lost two Inventors. Hart quadrant had lost their Inventor and Heir. Spadros and Clubb had both lost their Patriarchs. Diamond had lost their Keeper of the Court.

But along with sorrow, the Four Families of Bridges had hope. For the first time since the Coup, my husband Tony had collected the Families together to defeat our common enemy.

We had hope that Bridges might return to peace under the Four Families' rule.

Well, they had hope.

I had pain.

Confusion.

Grief.

My butler Alan Pearson brought fresh flowers from my gardens every morning, trying to cheer me. My servants brought me food, urged me to bathe, to dress, to eat. Took me wherever in the house I was meant to be.

I drank my tonics: once in the morning for my ruined liver, the second in the afternoon for my general constitution.

My mind ever swam — with images, with words, so much so that I might hardly see.

So many dead. So much betrayal. The names, the faces, constantly in my mind. So much revealed at that meeting, so much that threw every word, every deed from those around me into question.

I didn't know what to do with it all. I felt so lost, so bereft, so lacking in the hope that I would ever grasp what to do. What caused all this pain, this turmoil?

All I wanted was to understand.

But I couldn't.

The pain from Joseph Kerr's ministrations, low in my belly, never left me. Dr. Salmon offered salicylate, saying anything stronger might interfere with my bowels, make the matter worse.

Yet the salicylate did very little, and I quit taking it.

I suppose I could've had more useful remedies had I lived in Azimoff, Nitivali, or even Tollkeen. But though our Magma Steam Generators produced limitless power, our city was under an "Edwardian" tech charter (whatever that meant).

All I knew is that "Edwardian" meant children died of measles, men died of a wound, and my baby suffered, when a mechanism in his hip might heal him.

Five hundred years earlier, Benjamin Kerr set us on this path, and the Cultural Correctness Committee was implacable in its desire to keep Bridges to his word.

And so we suffered.

***

At times, the pain discouraged me. Joseph Kerr had to have known something was wrong with him. Why didn't he care enough to protect me? Had passion blinded him to all reason?

I didn't know.

But the aftermath of our few minutes of not-quite love was too much. The horrible look in his eyes, the way he dismissed my fears. I could never trust him again. And that grieved me more than anything.

Yet I had to keep going. I still was Acevedo's mother. I loved him. He was my baby. I had to survive, for him.

I'd write notes. I'd send up sweets. I'd take steps towards his rooms.

But it seemed too much. To go into that horrible bedroom where Roy had been tortured? I'd find myself weeping on the stair.

So Daisy brought him to my study, every day.

The sight of my baby. crippled and in pain because of me, would bring me to tears.

Now fourteen months old, little Ace became confused, would cry.

Eventually, Tony made her stop.

There was no way around it: I had to keep going. I was still Queen of Spadros quadrant.

Every day, I sat at my desk. My Queen's box, with its piano black construction and silver embossing, stared back at me. I tried to make sense of words on pages. It felt as if I pushed neck-deep through mud.

After the attack on the Manor a year prior, Tony had ordered street access limited to those on our block. Every time a carriage came past, I heard Acevedo's terrified screams all the way to my study.

My son loved carriages — until the day they produced bullets and death and blood.

His screams broke what little concentration I had; I'd begin again.

It took me an hour to read a simple sheet. Another hour to come to some decision on it.

The unread pages piled up, leaving my secretary Mr. Eight Howell to make sense of the urgent, to make decisions for things I couldn't.

***

I didn't suffer alone. All our emotions were very close.

Despite his words outside the Ballhouse, Tony seemed devastated by Alexander Clubb's death. He spent hours on the veranda, pen and ink and notepad before him, his cane beside him, just staring at the garden.

Our bomb-sniffer dog Rocket would often lay beside Tony, his head upon Tony's foot. Rocket was getting older; white hairs dotted his sleek black coat. Rocket's brood of pit bull terrier pups, now several years old and well-trained, had taken over much of the work, guarding the homes of Tony's Button Men.

During the day, Tony sat on the veranda. I sat in my study. I opened my Queen's box. I tried to work.

During the night, Tony and I lay facing each other, holding hands as we cried.

I never asked why he cried, nor did he ever ask me. But I think we both felt overwhelmed by the magnitude of what we'd learned.

He had good reasons for grief: his sister Katie's murder, made to look like suicide. His son's injury, and perhaps even his own. His mother's betrayals. Her lies.

The deaths of so many of his kin, some at his order. Some at his hand.

Tony had always hated and feared the Business. Now he'd found himself leading the thing.

I wish I'd been able to give him even some small comfort.

But I was drenched in grief, choked in it. I'd cry myself to sleep, then wake in terror. A shadow of a man with a knife, behind me, or to one side. I never knew who he was, when he would grab me, how it would happen.

Sometimes Tony or little Ace lay dead in the street. Other times, all the hundreds dead because of me were there, eyes accusing.

I almost wished the dark shadow would kill me, if only to make the dreams stop.

***

Through this time, huge boxes of documents, letters, and ledgers about the Red Dog Gang and Polansky Kerr IV came in every day, sent by the other three Families.

My bedroom filled first, then my study. When the boxes continued arriving, I had my butler Alan Pearson use the now-empty basement room his father had used to store his many ledgers.

Tony had given me the idea to use the basement room. Tony had sent what he'd collected down there as well.

But on the day that the last box was placed, as though an electrical light switched off, Tony no longer cried.

On that day, he turned distant, bitter.

Every time I made a move to go down there, he'd make some cutting remark. "Go in," he'd say, voice dripping with sarcasm. "Not that you'll ever do anything with it."

I didn't know why he felt so angry. He'd volunteered to gather the information. He seemed pleased that I volunteered to help.

One day, I asked. "Are you angry with me? Or have you learned something that troubles you? Please, my love. Speak to me."

But he'd snap, "You know what you've done." Then he'd pull away, storming down the hall.

On the steps to the Ballhouse, he'd asked if we might try to love each other again. He desperately wanted to, or he never would've asked. But since then, he'd only grieved. And now he blamed me for something.

You know what you've done.

Did he mean me bedding Joe? That had been over a year past, and we'd spoken of the matter in detail. He knew what a terrible experience that had been, how I regretted it, what it had cost me.

What did that have to do with all this?

Yet even though he came to my bed that night, he wouldn't answer. "If you don't know, then nothing I say will help." Then he'd turned away to lie staring in silence.

I thought: *perhaps he feels I won't help, as I promised. Perhaps he's lost faith in me.* So the next day, I made myself get up, go to the stairs, ignore his bitter words.

The boxes of information from the Four Families sat along the walls, reaching from floor to ceiling. A table sat in the center. The room was lit by a bare electrical bulb overhead.

I stood in the doorway in dismay. It was all too much. It reminded me too much of the room full of Court cases when we thought Jonathan Diamond had been taken.

Jon was dead.

Master Blaze Rainbow (who I always thought of as Morton) had helped me. He was dead, too.

I ran from the room weeping, passing my servants, throwing myself onto my bed.

When would this ever end?

***

Duchess Sophia Whist, one of our few friends in the aristocracy, gave a Midsummer Night's Ball in honor of Tony's twenty-seventh birthday. The attendance was half of what she'd hoped. Tony didn't seem to care.

Perhaps intending to brighten the tables, Duchess Sophia had included pressed daffodils in the circle of decoupage that sat upon each center. They reminded me too much of Jonathan Diamond.

Fortunately, I didn't notice them until we'd finished our meal. We left early; I couldn't stop crying.

After that, I began saying no to every event. I just couldn't make myself go to them.

But I felt desperate to do something, anything, to make the words and images and feelings stop. I'd try to play our grand piano, then find myself weeping upon the keys. I'd sit in my garden as my lady's maid Shanna tried to console me.

Each night, Tony lay facing away. Silent, sullen, as I cried.

Each morning, I felt tormented by grief, flooded with grief.

I felt in a truly desperate despair, one I never felt even in my darkest days of the trial.

I knew I must get up. I must do these things. I wanted to do them. Each was so vitally important!

Yet I could not.

I felt that I failed at every turn. I hated myself for it.

The Heat

Then came July. By our Blessed Dealer's mercy, 1903 years after the Catastrophe. On the third day of July came the full force of summer. And that summer was dreadful.

Sweltering heat overtook the city. It was an unnatural heat, stifling and moist, without so much as a breeze. And the Inventors couldn't explain it.

Tempers rose. Old people died. Babies wailed up and down every street as their exhausted mothers doused them with water.

People took to their basements to escape the heat. Doors and windows lay open, wet sheets hung across them to keep out flies. The sale of mechanical fans skyrocketed. Ice vanished from the city.

Perhaps Tony'd had some premonition: he'd asked our housekeeper Jane to buy double our usual ice order at the beginning of the season. Which was fortunate for us: we had some at the end, where even the other Families ran out.

It wasn't the worst summer of my life, even so. It was perhaps the second worst, or maybe third. I didn't know it yet, but those terrible days were soon to come.

I felt so very grateful for Tony's foresight, yet the relative cooling in Spadros Manor seemed the only comfort I might have.

I walked the halls, numb. I couldn't think.

Mrs. Regina Clubb said at the meeting that I was a Memory Girl. Back then, I saw no benefit in it.

I felt like a pillow so full that it strained at the seams. Names, faces, dates. The movements of so many people, I couldn't follow them all. I walked the halls, numb. I couldn't think. I could hardly see.

And grief, grief, for the people who'd died because of me. Air, Nina Clubb, Herbert Bryce, Stephen Rivers, those hundreds in the zeppelin bombing. The guards outside the Courthouse. Madame Biltcliffe, Maria Athena Spade, the men who left Roy for the Ten of Spades. Inventor Maxim Call. Anna Goren. My great-grandmother, who to this day I only know as the Cathedral's Eldest. Major Wenz Blackwood. The Major's lawyer Hambir Dashabatar and his family, betrayed by their own driver.

Morton.

Had Morton ever been my friend? Or all the time he lived in my home, worked beside me ... had he only been plotting my ruin?

And rhen there was Jonathan. Jonathan Diamond had loved me. He'd loved me! How did I not know? How did I not see? Why could I not understand?

He'd begged me. **Begged** me.

The way his hands had trembled! The way he'd pleaded! How did I not see it?

"Come with me," he'd said. In my folly, I'd turned him down.

Jonathan saved me, and my son, and that night he lay dead.

I don't know if I can ever forgive myself.

The only positive thing about the situation was that it felt decidedly cooler in the basement. Many of the house servants took to their rooms there during the heat of the day. And to my surprise, Alan — and more to the point, Tony — let them. "We must keep our servants well. If the house is presentable and the meals on time," Tony said, "that's all I ask."

There was so much I didn't know. So many questions that I felt desperately needed to be answered. So much I didn't understand.

Where was Joseph Kerr? Had he decided to remain in Azimoff? Was he safe? Was he well?

Did he ever think of me?

I didn't see what he might do there. So far as I could tell, he had little schooling and less skill in trade.

He needed me. Why had I not gone with him, when he asked?

Did he plan to return, to resume his goal to become Mayor? I hoped so. With him gone, whoever the Red Dog Gang had chosen for their Mayoral candidate was one step closer to taking over the city.

And where was Joe's twin sister, Josie? I'd not heard anything of her whereabouts.

I worried for her so, alone with her grief. She'd been maimed during her kidnapping, her wrists rubbed beyond raw by the heavy iron shackles placed too tightly upon her delicate pale skin. She'd lost her betrothed, her brother, and her home.

Had she healed? Was she safe? Was she with her grandfather? Or had she finally decided to escape with Joe?

I missed her so much. Would I ever see her again?

I didn't understand why everyone seemed so against Joe and Josie. It had to be their grandfather's doing.

Yet even then, the things Mr. Polansky was accused of seemed inconceivable. Could Polansky Kerr IV possibly be as evil as everyone made him out to be?

When I went to see Joe after his terrible accident, he'd told me: *My grandfather is a monster.*

Yet Tony and I had spoken to the man. He'd had us in his home. Tony felt alarmed by him, fearful even.

Yet to me, Mr. Kerr seemed merely old, even kindly.

I felt hesitant to believe evil of the man. Something about all this didn't seem right.

My enemy Jack Diamond believed Joe and Josie had been doing their grandfather's bidding this entire time. That they were plotting against me and my Family.

I didn't know what to believe.

I had to talk to Joe about this. If I could only speak with him, then I would know the truth. I felt sure I could see it in his eyes. At the time, it was the not knowing what to believe that grieved me so.

But where was he?

And what could we possibly do about the Magma Steam Generators? Were the Generators somehow responsible for this terrible heat, or was there some other cause unknown?

I went round and round in my mind, just as I stumbled round and round in the Manor, unable to understand anything. All the thoughts, the memories, they weighed on me. I couldn't sleep, I could barely eat.

Yet somewhere in that horrible summer, when I did sleep, the terrible nightmares that had plagued me became lost in my exhaustion.

In a way, it was a blessing: I was free of Jack Diamond in my dreams.

The Kin

Sometime in the midst of this, Alan's youngest brother Rob (now our night footman) roused us in the dead of night.

Tony and I put on our robes. Tony took up his cane, and we went downstairs.

Charles and Judith Hart stood in our parlor: all in black, hooded and cloaked. They were in their seventies, their hair mostly silver, although with streaks of red here and there. They'd both lost weight. Mrs. Hart couldn't stand to lose much more.

Mr. Hart had implied his wife faced some dreadful illness, but at the time, I didn't know what it could possibly be.

The last time I'd seen Judith Hart was at the meeting. She'd stormed out with threats to take her husband to court for his infidelity with (for one) my Ma. So I was completely astonished to see them here together.

Tony seemed as surprised as I was to see them. "How might we help?"

Mrs. Hart looked terribly pale. She smiled weakly. "We'd like to see your son, if we might."

Tony nodded. "Of course."

We moved into the foyer; Rob stood at the top of the wide sweeping staircase at parade rest, a pistol strapped to his side.

Mrs. Hart hesitated at the first step; Tony and Mr. Hart helped her ascend. We passed Rob without a word.

Tony's first cousin Ten Hogan (who we all called Sawbuck) sat dozing at the antechamber to Ace's room. A lit candle sat on the table beside him.

A huge, formidable-looking man, Sawbuck stood quickly, took up the candle's holder, went to the far door, and gently knocked.

A few moments later, Acevedo's nursemaid Daisy peered around the door at us, her long blonde hair tied in a kerchief. "Oh," she said, then opened the door wide, curtsying to the floor.

I took the candle from Sawbuck and led the rest inside.

The window was cracked open; a slight breeze stirred the room. Acevedo Spadros III lay curled up on his right side asleep, facing us in the candlelight, sweat plastering his wavy brown hair. His crutches — long canes, really, with straps to go round his upper arms — stood leaning on the end of his little bed.

Mr. Hart said, "He's beautiful."

Mrs. Hart's eyes were full of tears. "He looks so much like Etienne did at that age."

My half-brother, the former Hart Inventor. He'd been some thirty years older. I'd never really known him, other than a few strife-ridden words.

Now he lay dead.

He'd been about to reveal something that his allies the Red Dog Gang didn't want known, and his most trusted man shot him from behind.

The Hart Inventor's most trusted man murdered him on the word of Polansky Kerr? How had one elderly man inspired such blind loyalty?

Mr and Mrs. Hart gazed at my son for some time, then Mr. Hart took his wife's arm. "Let's go back down."

I turned to Daisy. "We were never here."

Handing the candle back to Sawbuck, Tony and I led the Harts downstairs to sit in Tony's study.

Mr. Hart said, "Your home is remarkably cool."

Tony smiled. "We store our ice in the rafters."

It'd been our newest Inventor's idea, and it worked remarkably well.

Mr. Hart gasped. "Like a giant cold box!" He turned to his wife. "Judy, we must do this at once."

I felt surprised at him using her private-home name in someone else's, but Mrs. Hart smiled fondly at him.

Tony set his cane beside his chair. "We're as safe from listening as humanly possible. How might we help?"

Mrs. Hart stirred. "I'm dying."

I realized my mouth lay open, and shut it. "I don't understand."

Mrs. Hart glanced at Tony, then back at me. "It's ... a woman's sickness. The doctors say it might be time to seek help in Azimoff —"

I gasped. Azimoff had the best medical tech in the world, but for many, it was a last resort. Most either didn't — or if they needed tech not authorized in Bridges, weren't allowed to — ever return.

Mrs. Hart's shoulders drooped. "But I've decided not to go. I've lived to see my boy die." She shook her head. "What else is there for me?"

My immediate thought was: *What about your granddaughter?* Ferti Hart might only have the mind of a child, but ... she was Etienne's blood.

Then Mrs. Hart smiled, putting her hand on her husband's. "But I've also lived to see my Charlie finally happy. The plans he's making for your boy's future!"

For some reason, I felt touched; my eyes stung.

Tony stirred. "What plans?"

Mr. Hart leaned forward. "That's what we're here to talk about."

Mr. Hart planned a tour of the whole of Hart quadrant, visiting every village, spending at least a day in each. Speaking to the people, taking note of their concerns. "I've spent my entire life ignoring them," he said. "That's how Polansky Kerr wooed them away." Then he hit the armchair with a meaty fist. "I must have my quadrant behind me. Otherwise, they'll have no love for my Heir."

I nodded. *Acevedo.*

He turned to Tony. "With your permission, I'd like to add my guards to yours in the protection of your wife and son." He gestured towards the door. "You can't have your right-hand man play guard at night, not if you expect him to run your quadrant during the day."

Tony blinked, drew back a bit, then nodded.

"These are my most loyal men," Mr. Hart said. He turned to me. "Your kin. They'd die before allowing any harm to come to me and mine." He said to Tony, "But you're welcome to investigate them yourself before allowing them into your home."

Tony nodded.

Etienne thought the man who shot him in the back of the head was his most loyal man. The memory of my brother's eye exploding has never left me to this day.

"The Four Families are being pushed out." Mr. Hart took a deep, shaky breath, and I realized: *he's afraid.* Why? "Julius and I are all that's left. If anything happens to either of us ..."

Tony's jaw set, and I could see the mix of emotions cross his eyes: doubt, shame, anger, fear. His hand shook, just a little. "Let's hope that never happens."

Mrs. Hart surveyed Tony with new respect.

Even though Mr. Hart was the first to acknowledge Tony as Patriarch, he clearly didn't think Tony was ready to do what might need to be done.

And I wondered: *is Lance Clubb ready? Is Cesare Diamond ready?*

Am I ready?

For better or worse, I was both the Spadros Queen and the Hart Heir.

But I was, as they say, a Pot rag. Hart quadrant probably despised me.

Besides, it was probably safer to say that my Acevedo was the Hart Heir — he was male, after all.

Yet Acevedo was just a baby. Merely a name on a page.

Not only that, he was a Spadros baby, the grandson of their Patriarch's most hated enemy. It would take a lot for Mr. Hart's people to accept him as their own. If Mr. Hart died before Acevedo had enough loyal men to seize power, Hart quadrant could fall into chaos.

Was that what Polansky Kerr wanted? Kill me and Acevedo, leaving him to pick up the pieces?

But he was over ninety. He had to have someone in Hart quadrant. Someone already known and entirely trusted. Someone the quadrant would surely follow. "Do you know the names of Polansky Kerr's men in Hart quadrant?"

Mr. Hart fixed his gaze upon me. "I believe so."

I sighed. "Assume there are double the number. Even triple. We found several here upon the Spadros Manor grounds."

Mr. Hart's heavy-lidded eyes widened, just a bit.

I said, "My own lady's maid and her husband — our stable-master — gave aid to our enemies the day we were attacked."

Tony flinched.

I shook my head, feeling exhausted. Details, information, pictures, faces of the dead. They never stopped. "If these people can get into the midst of this Manor, they can get into yours. Trust as few as you can. Put spies on the rest." I peered at Mr. Hart. "What did you decide about your granddaughter?"

The Harts looked at each other, evidently surprised by the change of topic. Mr. Hart shrugged. "In what regard?"

"Is she well? Are you keeping her a spinster? If not, have you chosen her ..." I wasn't sure how to phrase it.

Mrs. Hart said, "We're not forcing her to marry." She took a deep breath, let it out. "Some days she's distraught, asking where her Daddy is, when he's coming home. Other days, she plays quietly with her toys." Mrs. Hart looked away, sadness in her eyes. "Ferti's days of crying come farther apart each week." She sighed. "I suppose I shouldn't blame her; it's been over a year since Etienne's death. But I fear she'll soon have forgotten him."

"I'm sorry," Tony said quietly. "I truly am."

We sat silent for a moment, then Tony said, "What is your plan? Other than guards? How can we possibly heal this ... **rift** between our two quadrants my father's made?"

I felt uneasy hearing Tony refer to Roy as his father once more.

Perhaps Mr. Hart felt the same, because his eyes widened. "I must continue to act as if nothing has changed until we can secure our Manors. But ..." He seemed at a loss.

What would make people turn from hatred to love? "Perhaps your local news might help. I know the editor of the *Bridges Daily*, and —"

Mr. Hart leaned forward. "Yes! Stories of human interest." His manner turned downcast. "I fear the museum for your father was a mistake in that regard. My people leave there with an even greater hatred of the man."

Tony let out a laugh. "So why not **use** this? These newspaper stories might speak of the ways this quadrant moves past my father's," he let out a breath, "grisly legacy. How we aim to come to the truth, move forward."

My imagination of the terrible reports I'd received swam before me — hundreds found dead in the pit below Spadros Castle, each sprinkled with lime. I thought I might be sick. "Why did he **do** these things?"

Tony sighed, staring over at his desk. "I don't think we'll ever know. Some need ... compulsion, maybe. Something drove him. I recall as a boy, he'd become more and more irritable. Angry. He'd lash out at the slightest wrong breath." Tony turned his head to look at us. "Then, after a few nights — well, sometimes weeks — away, his mood would change. He'd become almost happy."

Mr. Hart shuddered.

Tony shrugged, his gaze far away. "Those nights, he must have been doing what he most wished to."

Mrs. Hart said, "Mr. Spadros, what he did wasn't your fault." She took a deep breath, then nodded, as if to some inner voice. "Perhaps my people can be of help."

Tony froze.

Mrs. Hart had to mean the Bridgers: her father was the Bridgers Grand-Master. But how could the head of the most despised religious sect in the city be of any help with public opinion?

Then I recalled their love of printing anonymous pamphlets.

"Speaking of the truth, sir," Mr. Hart said. "There's something you should know."

Tony twitched, as if he'd been thinking of something else. "Oh?"

Mr. Hart took a deep breath. "Your father kept a private journal. We found it in his torture rooms." He hesitated, just a bit. "It's gone missing."

Tony and I both drew back. "Oh."

This was bad.

Tony said, "This has to be the work of our enemies. No one would want this, or even care about it, if it weren't intended to harm us."

Mr. Hart nodded. "I thought the same."

Tony took a deep breath and rose. "Well, I wouldn't fret much over it. When they use something in it, we'll know who they are."

I hadn't considered that.

Mr. Hart helped his wife up, then shook Tony's hand. "Thank you for seeing us."

"Not at all," Tony said. "You're welcome here anytime."

As Tony and Mr. Hart moved away, Mrs. Hart took my hand. "I know what it's like to be in a home with ways very different than yours. Keep your eyes on the path in front of you, and you won't go astray."

This sounded a bit too much like Bridger rhetoric, but I gave her my warmest smile and squeezed her hand as I walked her to the front door. She meant well, and who might blame a dying woman for giving her last bits of advice? "Thank you."

She stopped, facing me. "My father can be fearsome. But he's not evil. He could be a formidable ally."

Ally with the Bridgers? Things would be more desperate than we thought, if we had to take them on as partners.

Mrs. Hart smiled. "I only meant that he would be glad to see his great-grandson." She let out a breath. "He's old, Mrs. Spadros. Sometimes, when you get really old, petty differences mean less than they once did."

I nodded, not really understanding. "I'll think on it."

Mr. Hart returned to her side.

Mrs. Hart said, "That's all I ask." With that, she pulled up her hood and let her husband lead her away.

The Test

After they left, grief filled me again. I lay in bed unable to sleep, seeing the death. My brother's murder by his own man, his blood and brains spattering me. Marja's face in the twilight as the blood pooled around her. Little Ante, Duck's brother, so pale and still, his hands still clawing at mine. Maria Athena Spade's dead eyes, staring.

My front porch, dripping with Roy's blood. With John Pearson's blood.

Days passed, weeks in the steaming heat, without any relief in sight. The names, the faces, the images, lying dead. Nightmares of my Tony, of little Acevedo, even of Joe and Josie, dead.

Dead, because of me.

I lay weeping on my bed after dinner one night — oh, I'd say it was sometime in early August — when my lady's maid Shanna came to me. "Mum, your husband wishes to see you in his study."

Fear spiked inside me: *what happened?* I wiped my face, put on my house shoes and shawl, and hurried out, dreading whatever news he had.

Tony's study was in the middle of the hall, so I descended the back staircase. The gray-white marble felt cool against my bare fingers, the one bit of comfort in this great lonely house.

Of course, in all this heat, the electric lights lay quiet; only a few candles lit the edges of the room.

Tony sat in his chair beside the unlit fire, and when I entered, he gestured to the chair across from him.

A figure, hooded and cloaked, head bowed, face hidden.

I laughed, despite how awful I felt. "Is this some test?"

Tony smiled. "It's good to see you laugh. It's been far too long."

When was the last time I'd laughed?

Ah, it didn't matter. First, the puzzle before me.

The figure was of an adult, but hunched a bit, smaller. A woman?

The cloak was of a thin dark linen that I'd thought was black, but upon moving closer, I saw it was actually dark brown. Gold embroidery lay upon the medium brown cloth peeking through the opening of the cloak, far down at the hem touching fine leather boots. More embroidery, dark brown, covered the cloak's edges.

The skirts, the embroidery, the cloth ... all were of **very** fine make.

I took a step back. "This can't be."

A wry laugh came from the cloak, and I knew.

Mrs. Regina Clubb cast off her hood, the straight golden hair piled atop her head shining in the candlelight. "Very good, Mrs. Spadros."

Since Roy's death, Clubb quadrant had distanced itself from us. Mr. Alexander had said this was to help smooth the way for his son Lance's marriage to Gardena Diamond. So I never expected to see the Queen of Clubs in Tony's study.

Mrs. Clubb's oldest daughter was almost sixty, so Mrs. Clubb had to be close to eighty! But it was clear Regina Clubb took illegal treatments from Azimoff. Her skin had barely a line, her hair not a strand of silver. But her eyes ...

I went to her, took her black-gloved hand, and curtsied low. "You do me great honor." One only had to look in her dark blue eyes to see the story of great age. Of having seen much, much too much.

"The honor is mine," Mrs. Clubb said. "Please, sit beside your husband. There's much work to do."

I sat. "I don't understand."

Mrs. Clubb said, "I owe you an apology. I should've arrived sooner. You have your husband to thank for my coming here." She peered at me as if she saw my soul. "Yes. I've never trained one this late, but —"

Trained one this late? "I don't understand."

She sighed. "Too much memory is a dangerous thing."

Alarm spiked through me. "Dangerous? How?"

Tony placed his hand on mine.

Mrs. Clubb said, "There's a reason most people don't recall things too terrible to face. Or their minds change their recollections to give them the best chance to survive." She shook her head, her gaze downward. "True, unvarnished memory ... now, that gives you nowhere to hide." She raised her face to peer into mine. "Nothing to protect you." She let out a sigh. "There's a reason we grant such rare gifts to the families of our Memory Children. By your age, most untrained Memory Girls are either dead by their own hands, or completely mad."

I felt entirely taken aback.

Tony exclaimed, "Good gods."

Mrs. Clubb nodded.

The Eldest, my great-grandmother, had told me of the sack of the Cathedral: *they say some women don't remember. But I remember every man. One hundred and one years later, I see their faces before me.*

How had she survived it?

My husband's voice shook. "Is there a way to help her?"

Mrs. Clubb raised her hands, her cloak falling aside: a thick sheaf of paper lay in them. "There is." The sheaf was bound on one side with a stout golden cord. "I want you to read this before anything else. Tonight, if you can. This is more important than anything you must do."

I suppose as Queen of Spades, I should've stayed seated. Let her come to me.

But she was so much my elder that I rose, took the book from her. Stood peering at it. It held an unusual odor. "What's inside?"

She gave me an amused smile. "You'll have to read it and see."

Mrs. Clubb rose then.

"Wait," I said. "Ariana Spadros. I thought she should be tested. As a Memory Girl —"

Tony gasped, taking a step back.

"— Have her parents contacted you yet?"

Mrs. Clubb stopped, staring into my face, but at nothing. Then she focused on me. "They did. She's in the books," at that, she frowned, "but her testing date hasn't been set." She gave a definite nod, glancing away, then back at me. "Tell me what you saw."

"She's only two, but she's smart. She remembers things." I shrugged. "I don't know any of your lore, but even if she's not ... even if she might only go to school, her parents would be so happy." I glanced away. "I'd pay for her testing, if need be." I took a deep breath, eyes stinging. "If she is ... like me ... I don't want her to go through what I have."

Mrs. Clubb placed her hand on my upper arm. "I'll see to it myself."

***

After Mrs. Clubb left, I sat reading in bed, more out of curiosity than anything else. Much of the book was filled with exercises intended for very small children.

Tony peered over my shoulder, helping me with words I didn't know.

I asked, "Why does this smell so?"

"Ah," he said. "It's a new mechanism for printing ... I believe it's called the Automated Mimeograph? One of my Button Men has the mechanism in his office; it smells just like that."

"Oh." I loved the warmth of Tony's body next to mine. He hadn't shown such interest in my welfare since I recovered from womb fever. I had a great desire to put the book aside and kiss him.

"Astonishing," said Tony.

I'd lost focus. "What?"

Tony pointed at the page. "See here?" He began to read aloud. "'We don't know exactly how the phenomenon came forth. The religious call it miraculous, or cursed. Tollkeen calls it a mutation of their Sacred Code; Azimoff in their arrogance names it merely the product of training. That last we deem wrong, because tiny children with no training at all can recite an entire book they've barely learnt to read.'" Tony sat straighter, turned to face me. "That must be why your mother set you to messenger duty as a girl."

Some pain loosed within me. I wasn't being punished. I wasn't deemed unworthy. "I could recall everything, even to the conversations going on around me at the time."

The implications of this disturbed me. Why had I at times been unable to remember **anything**?

Dr. Salmon had thought it to be protective, but Mrs. Clubb had implied that a true Memory Child had no such protection.

I shuddered.

"What is it?"

I shook my head. "A feeling, that's all."

Tony took a pen from the bedside table and placed it as a bookmark. "Enough of this then. You'll have all day tomorrow to read."

I let him take the pages, place them on the table beside him, cover me and kiss my hair. "Now rest," he said. "You've been too long a-crying, too little asleep. You **must** rest, if you're to truly get well."

I turned to face him. "I need you, Tony. I need you. Please. I love you. You said you wanted to love me." A sob burst forth. "Will you hate me forever?" I reached out to him. "Am I to become one of the Dealers, here in my own home?"

He flinched, drew back.

I repulsed him? I began to cry. "I can't go on like this."

Tony shook his head. "Do you want me to go?"

I grabbed his arm, sobbing. "No. Oh gods, no. Please don't leave me."

Tony took me in his arms then, but kept most of himself far from me. "I won't leave you, Jacqui. I promise." He drew the covers over my shoulders. "Here. Just rest."

He held me as I cried.

***

Tony took over my work for the next few days to let me rest and read.

I felt better the next day, and more so the next. I continued reading the sheaf — part instruction manual, part treatise on the knowledge gleaned about the Memory Children — and began to do the exercises in it.

"Close your eyes," it said, "breathe deeply, and sit still. Picture your home, empty in your mind. No furnishings, no pictures, nothing to distract or recall. See each room clearly in your mind, as if you stood there. Now in your mind, go to your front room. Picture enough baskets to fill the room from floor to ceiling, from wall to wall! There should be enough baskets so that there is not even room to crawl inside.

"In your mind, take any piece of information and put it into one of the baskets. There is no wrong piece! There is no wrong basket! Sort the information in any way that pleases you. If you don't know where to put a piece, give it its own basket until you find a piece that goes with it."

I had a large, overflowing basket of information that I wasn't sure what to do with still sitting in the corner of my bedroom.

"When you can find nothing more for a basket, bring it to one of the empty mind rooms in your home. You may choose any room you like. Put it there, note it, and leave it. Free your mind from it, except for its location, until the basket is needed again."

I gasped. Free your mind from it? Oh, what a blessed relief!

I rushed then to look at every room in the Manor. I'd forgotten to tell Alan what I was doing, so suppose I must have startled the servants when I went downstairs, into the kitchens, along their private hallways.

But I had so very much in my mind. I had to see it all.

I even took the winding metal stairs beside the kitchens. Down, down, to the area the Inventors once worked, now dark, quiet, empty. I lifted a lantern before me. The ray cannon that the man who had become our newest Inventor once worked on now lay upstairs with the rest, dead hunks of mechanism until we might learn how to best repair them.

A few books lay scattered here and there upon the dusty shelves, old notes and a well-used pencil upon the bench. The lift to bring me to the chambers far below was locked shut.

I could find neither a mask to protect from the foul air in the depths nor the key to open the lift door. Yet I recalled what the chambers far below looked like: that would have to suffice.

Returning to my rooms, I started in on the first exercise, in what would occupy my time for many an hour.

I believe it saved my life.

Yet there, that day, alone in my bedroom, I felt confused. What should I sort first?

There is no wrong piece! There is no wrong basket!

I first decided to make mind-baskets of the dead.

Two baskets contained those that I felt certain the Red Dog Gang had killed. In the first went people I knew: Marja, the Bridges Stable-Master, Madame Biltcliffe, Herbert Bryce, Army Major Wenz Blackwood, his lawyer Mr. Hambir Dashabatar, Stephen Rivers, Inventor Montgomery Arrow, Morton.

After some thought, I put Jonathan Diamond in there as well. I pictured his face as he lay dying in that alley, so unnaturally pale. His lips, bluish. The way he gasped for air. The Red Dog Gang may not have pulled a trigger or thrust a knife, but they'd hounded my poor brave Jon to his death, as sure as if they'd choked the life from his body themselves.

Then, a second basket of the people I'd never known: Joe and Josie's uncle Mr. Shigo Rei. The man who sold the jacket that Frank Pagliacci wore whilst moving David Bryce around. Mr. Dashabatar's wife and children. The Detective Constable turned Family man Albert Sheinwold. The rogue Spadros men calling themselves the Ten of Spades, who the Red Dog Gang had used then murdered as they fled to what they thought was safety.

Maria Athena Spade.

I felt it a triumph that I was finally able to let Maria Athena Spade rest in the basket of those killed by the Red Dog Gang. I'd shot her, though she was unarmed. But I had to make myself see the truth: both Morton and little Tim made it clear that when I fired, she'd already been dead.

I had a third basket for Anna Goren and Inventor Maxim Call. Both killed, it seemed, by the same person, but not, so far as we knew, anyone from the Red Dog Gang. A woman, brown of skin with eyes of blue, who Jack Diamond claimed to be with the Dealers.

At the time, I wasn't sure I trusted Jon's possibly-mad twin to have told the truth on that account.

I put those three baskets in the empty bedroom of my mind. I wanted to keep them close.

A fourth basket was for those the Red Dog Gang had tried to kill, yet failed: Dame Anastasia Louis, her "great-nephew" Trey Louis, my Ma. Those went into my bedroom as well.

And then I needed that second basket again, for the hundreds of people on the zeppelin, exploding in front of my eyes as it rose to its doom. All the young men who the Bridges Strangler had killed, before and after then-Mayor Chase Freezout had covered up the murders. The men who rebelled against Alexander Clubb, probably at the behest of the Red Dog Gang, and had been executed for it.

One of those had been my friend Karla Bettelmann's father.

Frank Pagliacci, who I felt sure was the Strangler, was deep in the Red Dog Gang, and I put his atrocities at their doorstep. The Red Dog Gang had to have known him for the fiend he was, and did nothing to stop him.

Then I needed that first basket again. There was enough evidence in my eyes that Frank had killed Tony's sister Katie, arranging it to look like suicide and getting the police to agree. Whether the Red Dog Gang had sent him to kill her, or if he'd done it on his own, didn't matter. They were going to pay.

I placed Duck's little brother Ante in a separate basket. I'd killed the boy with my own hand. But then there was also that driver who tried to violate me as I left Spadros Manor, and I shot him for it.

That basket I put in the back of the empty closets of my mind, and let it sit alone.

Filling these baskets drained my strength, yet left me feeling a great vastness inside. I lay on my bed, my feet still in their house shoes dangling over the side, weary.

Words from the Memory Sheaf (as I called it — no title lay upon the pages) came to me:

Filling your baskets is only the beginning. Keeping your information in their baskets will become your main test. You must continue to direct the information to their proper baskets as the memories come forth. Only then will your mind be free for other things.

I felt daunted.

Yet I felt hope. If small children could learn these things, I could too.

And I had to. I had to understand the connections between these things I'd learned, if only to root out those who had tormented my Family, murdered my friends. It was the only way to keep from going mad from grief, from pain, from all these memories.

Dame Anastasia said the Red Dog Gang wanted me broken. So I must not break. I had to fight. I had to live. I had to learn the truth. This was the only way I could defeat them.

The Protection

These exercises had taken me some time. Yet Tony was far from idle. Over the course of several days, Hart men came to call in small groups, brought by our plain carriage. As I gained my strength, I spoke with Daisy, which was how I learned of these meetings.

Tony called the Hart men in one by one, presumably to discuss their qualifications and feelings about the Spadros Family. Tony greeted the men in his study. Daisy sat off far to one side, Ace playing with his toys on a quilt at her feet. Sometime during this meeting, Tony would introduce Ace.

The man would usually tip his hat to the boy and go back to the conversation.

"You should've seen it," Daisy said. "The minute Master Shengji walked in, Master Acevedo picked up his canes and stood." She put her hand to her chest. "And oh, the way the little master went to him! It touched me so to see the man stop and crouch to greet your boy, before he even acknowledged your husband."

"Master Shengji?" I felt confused, not recalling such a name.

"Oh, yes. Shengji ... what was his last name again ... Forbus? Yes, that's it. I believe he's Mr. Hart's third — or maybe fourth — cousin, on his mother's side." She brushed lint off her apron. "He claims you've met. He's younger even than me." She smiled fondly, cheeks reddening. "The men all call him Chipmunk."

"Yes! I remember him." A young man, perhaps twenty or so by now, not fat, but giving the impression of softness, with a round face and a bright smile. "So now my boy has another companion."

Daisy nodded. "He's wonderful with the little master." She let out a sigh. "To be honest, I'm glad he's here."

"Why do you say that?"

She looked away. "I feel he truly likes children." She faced me. "Master Ace loves everyone. It's best for children to be around those who love them in return."

***

I felt so relieved that Ace had someone he loved guarding him that I felt a burden lift from me. My baby would be safe.

As I continued the exercises, my mind became clearer. I still grieved for everyone I'd lost. At times, I even wept. But the crushing melancholy which had plagued me for so long began to lift.

And I began to consider my questions.

I couldn't learn much about Joseph Kerr or his sister Josie until one of them contacted me. The Four Families were already searching for their grandfather; someone would tell me if any of them had been found.

To be honest, now that I'd regained my senses, I really didn't care to see Joseph Kerr. He didn't need me. He didn't love me.

I had to focus on today, on dealing with what I could, on understanding what was happening to us — me and Tony, the Four Families, the city's mechanisms.

Most of it I had no idea how to solve. But I might be able to help with Mrs. Hart's request.

The Bridgers were dangerous, her father their Grand-Master even more so. But I knew a woman, Gertie Pike, who seemed to still have contact with the man.

But I didn't dare do anything without speaking with Tony. Something about the situation frightened him. Until I knew what that was, I might find myself making matters worse.

***

A few hours later, I sat at the table in my kitchen at my apartments on 33 1/3 Street, Spadros quadrant. The meeting was with Blitz, Mary, and my secretary, Mr. Eight Howell. I both loved being there and felt Mr. Howell's Backdoor Saloon at the end of the street was much too close.

But I had to attend: the discussion was about my building.

This was one of the safest places I might be, apart from Spadros Manor. Blitz and Mary Spadros were the butler and housekeeper of my apartments. Blitz was also Tony's distant cousin, born "under the table," as it were. Both Blitz and Mary were well-versed in firearms and sworn to protect me.

Mr. Howell, a short man with a big, bushy beard, had been a Spadros Associate before becoming my personal secretary. He had rented the use of every rooftop around; when I came here, snipers sat upon each, rifles in hand, scanning for danger.

My own footman and driver stood out front. Men guarded the apartment on the other side of this duplex, both inside and out. A host of armed horsemen stood ready at the Backdoor Saloon; Blitz need only whistle and they were minutes away.

So why did I feel uneasy?

A mechanical fan blew right at us. Tony had sent a chunk of ice to place behind it, yet even so the room felt stifling.

Blitz had located the blueprints to our building, which were laid out on the table. We held the edges to keep them from flapping.

"I don't know what else to tell you," Blitz said. "All appears quite ordinary, on both sides of the duplex."

"Hmph." Mr. Howell scratched in his big bushy beard. "So they had to have made the modifications after filing this." He pointed at the area depicting the back room. "Because nothing of what you've already found shows here." He leaned back. "There's got to be a second set of drawings. Besides telling the laborers where to place what, you'd need correct blueprints, if only in case something doesn't work as you hoped."

Blitz shrugged.

Blitz and Mary's daughter Ariana sang in the distance. It sounded as if she were playing in my old rooms again. "Is there anything to indicate a false ceiling? Or a place where a crawl space might've been added?"

"I haven't seen one," Blitz said. "The foundation is solid concrete. I've tapped it for hollow areas, measured inside and out ... I haven't found so much as an inch of difference." He sighed, looking at Mr. Howell. "I don't know where else to look."

Mr. Howell gave several quick nods, mouth pursed. "Not to fret. I don't see anything either. It's just ... I have a feeling. Something isn't right about this place."

Blitz said, "The men in the back said they thought they had mice. No one's found droppings, but one of the kids said he heard scratching." He shrugged. "I'll set traps on both sides, see what we find."

I stood, so they did as well. "Thank you for your work," I said, feeling morose. Not at the idea of mice; I too felt something bigger was wrong here. "I truly appreciate it."

We all walked Mr. Howell to the door. Mary had a loose house-dress on, but even so, her third pregnancy was starting to show. I'd have to hire help for her soon, if only someone to do the shopping once she was too big to hide her condition.

Ariana sat in my old bedroom with the door open, dolls everywhere upon the tight-laid hardwood floor, singing, "The only solution is truth!"

This pregnancy had definitely shortened Mary's temper. "Ariana Spadros," she snapped. "You pick that mess up this instant!"

Ariana crossed her arms. "No."

"Get up and do it. Right now. You know you're not supposed to play in there!"

Ariana scowled. "No."

Ariana was almost three, and we'd hoped she'd go right past the "no" stage. But in the last few weeks, "no" had become her favorite word.

I laughed. "What's that she's singing?"

"Some slogan," Blitz said. "One of the Mayoral candidates says it."

Mary said, "She must have heard it from the kids out front." She went to Ariana and took her arm. "Up with you, right now."

"No!" Ariana pointed at the the floor; dolls lay scattered there. "I wanna talk my friends!"

Mr. Howell laughed, shaking his head. "Looks like you have your hands full with that one." He tipped his cap. "Enjoy your day." Off he went down the front steps and to the left past my plain carriage.

A messenger boy raced by, the little bell on his bicycle jingling.

As Mary tried to make her daughter stand up, Ariana screamed, "No! No!" and collapsed upon the floor, wailing in a most dramatic manner.

Blitz and I still stood inside the front door. Blitz said, "There's something I meant to ask. You haven't had a case in some time."

Mary knelt beside Ariana, giving Blitz a "what the hell are you doing?" sort of look. Then she hoisted the girl over one shoulder.

Blitz ignored her. "Should I take down your signs, or leave them?"

I stepped outside and turned to look at the signs:

> Kaplan Private Investigations
> Discreet Service For Ladies
> Studio For Hire — Inquire Within
> Room for Rent

I understood why no one had come to see me. Could anyone dare to ask the Queen of Spades to act as their private investigator?

I'd never wanted this life, or this title. All I'd ever wanted was to become an independent woman of means. Have a legitimate business, to support myself so I could travel. Live how I wanted.

So I could get out of this city.

In my present situation, a paying case seemed too much to hope for. But to take my business sign down felt like surrender. "No, leave them."

Mary had moved to stand beside Blitz; Ariana lay over her shoulder, sobbing. Mary gave me a thin smile. "It'll work out, mum. Maybe you should advertise at the Stations. Some outsider might need your help."

I hadn't considered that. "It's a good idea." I had money saved up; surely I could spare some for advertising. "I'll have Mr. Howell order more business cards."

Mary took Ariana off her shoulder and placed her on her hip. "That sounds good, mum."

Ariana wrapped her arms around her mother's neck, her face buried in Mary's shoulder.

My day footman (and Queensman) Skip Honor stood by my carriage, waiting. Tony was to meet with the Spadros Inventor and his men, and wanted me to be present. "Well, I best be off." I rubbed Ariana's little back, feeling a great fondness for her. "All will be well, little one."

Ariana turned her head towards me, face pink and sleepy, her blonde hair plastered with tears and sweat. She rubbed one eye with a chubby fist. "Bye."

The door closed behind me. I stopped on the stair — as I often did — to look at the flat stone where my little bird lay. My bird needed to go in the basket of those I'd killed. I let it loose into a world it had no defense from, unaware it even needed protection.

Did it even know it was free? Had it been able to fly, even for a moment, before being ripped by a claw?

My driver Zeus called out; his voice startled me. "Mrs. Spadros?"

I smiled at him. He was a kindly old man Jonathan Diamond had picked for me after my former driver's murder. "Yes, here I come."

As we drove to Spadros Manor, the exchange with Blitz and Mary nagged at me. What had they really been trying to say?

Melancholy filled my chest, tinged with fear.

Maybe I should give up this business, or at least, move it somewhere else. Every time I went to my apartments, it pointed to Blitz and Mary. It shouted out where my enemies — the aristocrats, the Red Dog Gang, the tabloids — might best hurt me.

I'd been using the plain carriage to hide my movements, but it clearly wasn't enough.

Hmm, I thought. An actual office somewhere might do me some good. If I weren't going to my apartments anymore, we could finally use those rooms Mr. Howell always balked at renting.

I'd miss seeing my friends there, especially little Ariana. But if moving helped protect them, it'd be worth it.

The Enemy

Two hours later, my husband Tony and I sat behind his desk in his study at Spadros Manor. The most recent Spadros Inventor and his eight Apprentices, dressed in linen, sat sweating in Tony's stuffed black leather armchairs. It was almost a circle.

Or a horseshoe.

The afternoon with Joe, the horseshoe tattoo on his belly, the horrible look in his eyes ... it all flashed before me.

Keep your eyes on the path in front of you ...

Just the week prior, we'd buried our second Inventor in as many years. Tony had summoned the Inventor and his men to report on their investigations. And for some reason, Tony wanted me to attend.

Inventor Piros Gosi was a swarthy man of medium height. A rather odd one, I should say. He would either not look at you at all, or fix his gaze directly into your eyes without moving. It was most unsettling.

And his voice was strange, too: not particularly high or low in pitch, but quite nasal. "Yes, well," the Inventor was saying. "Our Inventor had been most secretive since Maxim Call's murder. Inventor Arrow would be gone for hours, giving no explanation for where he'd went. But he'd been punctual, and consistent in our daily reporting." He stopped, staring at nothing. "We were having our afternoon meeting. Before tea, to report on our day's work. Then the woman arrived." He then turned to Tony. "The one he'd been seeing. Miss Cashout."

Zia Cashout: Traitor. Murderess. Fed.

I wasn't sure which was worse.

The woman was an utter fiend. She'd betrayed the Feds. I felt sure she'd murdered both her partner Agents. Morton claimed she'd murdered scores of informants. We suspected she'd killed many more. I suspected she lured little David Bryce from his back step over four years earlier.

I realized I hadn't been listening to Inventor Gosi's story.

"But then Inventor Arrow ordered us to leave. Right in the middle of the meeting!" The man seemed put out. "He called for wine. A Tollkeen gold, if I recall. Quite expensive; we'd been saving it to celebrate the last of the piling explorations!" He composed himself. "We sat out in the hall in case he might wish to resume. I could hear them whispering. Laughing. Giggling!" He seemed scandalized. "I felt unsure what to do, so as Senior Apprentice, I conducted the meeting there, in the hall, without him."

Inventor Gosi took a deep breath, let it out. "A man came in —" He fixed his stare upon me. "The man you described, all in brown. Master Rainbow, I presume."

Tony nodded.

I always thought of Master Rainbow by the name he'd first given me — Morton — so hearing his true name felt jarring.

Inventor Gosi continued. "Several men came in after him. New men, ones our Inventor had hired. 'For his own protection,' he said. As if the Family wouldn't keep him safe!" The thought seemed to dismay him. "We tried to stop them, but Master Rainbow pushed past us all."

I leaned forward. They might have been among the last to see Morton alive! "How was Master Rainbow? Was he well?"

Inventor Gosi shrugged. "Clean, but disheveled. Recently injured to the face. And he had a wildness in his eyes." He glanced up at us. "Not to offend, sir, mum. But he had the air of a man who no longer cared about his own safety." He shuddered.

This Inventor might be odd, but he seemed remarkably observant.

Tony leaned back, face stunned. "Good gods."

Inventor Gosi continued. "Most of those new men followed Master Rainbow in, but two stood guard, facing us in the hall. We heard the sound of their voices, but little of what was said. Master Rainbow sounded most displeased to see Miss Zia there."

This didn't surprise me.

"There was quite a commotion; arguing, fighting. The men on guard wouldn't let us enter, even though we commanded them to. We felt in fear for our Inventor's life! By the time we joined together to overpower the men, the room was empty." He seemed dismayed. "I don't know how they left. There were no windows, and that hallway was the only exit."

Tony said, "Thank you for your time."

The Inventor and his Apprentices stood.

Tony reached up and behind him to pull the bell-cord.

Our butler Alan Pearson came in as if he'd been standing right outside the door.

Tony said, "Send a dozen men to search the Inventor's home." He nodded to Inventor Gosi. "Pay particular attention to the room our Inventor indicates. There must be a hidden way out of the building."

Alan said, "Yes, sir."

I felt stunned. A hidden way out?

Tony smiled at me as you might smile at a child. "Many of these old mansions have them. Hidden doors to the outside, or rooms kept behind a bookcase or pantry." He shook his head, looking aside. "Blaze Rainbow was in the Inventor's home. Why did he go there, of all places?"

"He didn't know Miss Zia would be there," I said. "Otherwise he surely wouldn't have gone."

"No," Tony said softly.

The Inventor and his Apprentices were still standing awkwardly, caps in hand, as if not sure what to do.

Tony gestured at them with his chin. "Did you see Inventor Arrow after that time?"

"Well," Inventor Gosi said. "Yes. He returned late, after dinner. He'd not answer any of our questions; he just went straight up to bed. And that was the last time I saw him alive."

A intense surge of grief overcame me, and without explanation to anyone, I rushed to my rooms.

I knew Zia and Monte had been close. But Morton had gone to Inventor Montgomery Arrow for help, and then instead been **taken!**

Murdered!

I managed to keep from crying until my door shut behind me.

Morton had come to the Spadros Family for help, and been betrayed.

I threw myself upon my bed weeping. Sure, he was a Fed. Sure, he probably only came to my home to find ways to betray me.

But he'd been my friend.

He'd lived in my home. He'd saved my life. Whatever his intentions, he'd never actually done me any wrong.

On the contrary! He'd offered good advice, given his support, and never asked for anything in return.

Well, other than his share of the cut. And who wouldn't want that?

Morton sent me a message when he was in trouble. He trusted I could save him.

And I failed.

A weight upon the bed beside me; Tony put his hand on my shoulder. "I thought I'd find you like this." He smoothed my hair. "Master Rainbow's death is not your fault."

"He came to us," I sobbed. "You asked a month or so back why he didn't come to us. But he did."

Tony let out a quiet breath, moving his hand back to my shoulder.

I couldn't stop crying. "He had to feel like we betrayed him. Our Inventor, in league with his enemies!"

"Hush," Tony said gently. "We don't know what he thought."

I rolled away to face him. "He sent a message to me for help. He went to our Inventor for **help**. How could he feel otherwise?"

Tony took my hand. "This is something we'll never know. And it helps nothing to berate yourself. You want to know what happened, and why. Am I right?"

I nodded.

"After you left us, one of the Apprentices said he visited a friend who works the ticket counter at the zeppelin station. The man told him he'd seen Inventor Arrow in line."

I leaned up on an elbow, shocked. "Our Inventor tried to flee the city?"

"It looks that way. The ticket-man didn't realize we were searching for the Inventor. But Inventor Arrow must have realized he'd been recognized: he left in a hurry." Tony shook his head. "This was well after

Master Rainbow's murder — just a few days before we found Inventor Arrow's body."

I sighed, feeling dejected. "Miss Zia turned on him, too."

"Yes," Tony said. "So let's stop moping about what we can't change."

This angered me. "She's still **out** there! How many of your men will she **kill** before you **do** something?"

Tony leaned back on one arm. "What would you have me do? My men are searching for her. All four Families are searching for her. It sounds to me like you've searched for over four years." He sighed, looked away. "I know you're frustrated, angry. Grieving too many friends. But as little help as I might seem, I'm on your side. I want to find who murdered Master Rainbow, whether it's this woman or someone else. Yes, even though he was a Fed. Whether he was false or not, for a time he was my man. That makes his death a Family matter."

I peered at him. "You think the Feds had him killed."

"I don't know what to think. But something about this doesn't make sense. Why would an experienced Federal Agent murder her own men? You said once that she killed the partner she had before Master Rainbow."

"Master Rainbow believed she had."

"So why return? Why bring another man to the slaughter?" He sat for a moment, hand to chin. "Unless she saw this as some game. And why did the Feds send her back? Surely they'd suspect her."

I hadn't considered this. "I have no idea."

"Why kill Master Rainbow? Why kill him now? And why did he go to Inventor Arrow?" Tony stopped for a moment, eyes distant. "He'd just escaped his cousins' imprisonment at Clubb Manor. He could've gone anywhere." He let out a breath. "I don't think he went there for help. I think he went there to get something, something valuable enough to risk his life for."

I thought about this for a moment. "All Master Rainbow ever wanted was to clear his name with the Feds. It must have been something — some document, something he could show them. Something that proved Miss Zia was false."

"Hmm," Tony said. Then he sighed. "I fear his mission. Why was he even **here**? No one's asked that yet."

I don't know why, but I laughed. The whole thing was too absurd. "He once said he had interest in the Pot. And then there were —"

"The Generators," Tony blurted out. "He never seemed to care about much else. But mention those, and he was immediately interested."

"This makes sense," I said. "And who else would know about them but an Inventor?"

Tony seemed puzzled. "But why go to Inventor **Arrow**? By all accounts, Inventor Cuarenta was Master Rainbow's cousin. Why not speak with **her**?"

Clearly, Tony didn't understand how things worked. "If he showed too much interest in the Generators, Mr. Alexander would've been instantly suspicious. And he couldn't have spoken with their Inventor directly. A distant cousin wishing to speak alone with ... a younger, unmarried woman ...?" I shook my head. "Unless he signed Intent to Courtship, that would go precisely nowhere." I felt amused. "Even if the Inventor wished to defy the proscription on marriage — and had feelings for the man — I doubt Master Rainbow would be false in that way."

Tony shook his head, appearing deflated. "I'm sorry; you're right." Then he said, "Why come to **us**? Why not go to the Diamonds? Inventor Jotepa might've had what he needed."

I lay back, thought about this for a while. "Master Rainbow's just escaped capture by the Clubbs. He made it to Tenni's shop in mid-Clubb quadrant and sent a message to me. Now what? He knows the Clubbs and Diamonds are soon to ally. Does he go to Diamond, hoping he won't be returned to the Clubbs as proof of Diamond loyalty? Or does he go to someone in Spadros that he believes he can trust?"

"I see now," said Tony. "Whether he went through Market Center or fled across the river, the Inventor's home would be closest. The Inventor would be sure to have information about the Generators, if that were Master Rainbow's goal."

"Hmm," I said. Had Master Rainbow been sent here to find information? Some cause strong enough to allow the Feds to take the city? Proof that the Magma Steam Generators were failing — and that we had neither the plan nor the ability to stop it — might be enough. I fanned myself with a small pillow. "We must find Inventor Arrow's men."

Tony shifted himself on my bed. "I asked for them the day we found his body. They seem to have escaped. One of them had been friends with my father's man who'd been patrolling the grounds here."

After Tony dismissed his entire Spadros Manor patrol, a few of the men disappeared. It seemed at least one had been in the pay of Inventor Arrow. Which meant loyal to Zia and the Red Dog Gang.

Which, according to everyone else, meant Polansky Kerr.

The very night we left the meeting we'd had with the Patriarchs atop the Grand Ballhouse, Mr. Hart sent men to Mr. Kerr's brownstone to invite Mr. Kerr to dinner. The house was just as I'd described it: a lower-card home that had seen better days. Mr. Polansky, Joe, Josie, and their servants, however, were gone.

Why did they suddenly leave? "Cards are moving that I can't see." Had something happened? "Do you think Mr. Polansky seized his grandchildren? Took them somewhere?" Mr. Cesare had done the same to his parents and brothers when he thought there to be danger.

Tony shrugged. "It sounds like he has enough men to do it." His voice took on an edge. "But what if Master Joseph and Miss Josephine left willingly?"

I feel like he expected me to be angry. But I wasn't. "They could have." I scooted up in the bed so my back was against the headboard. "If they learned what their grandfather was doing, it could be why Joe is running for Mayor. Or was." I hoped he hadn't given up.

Tony didn't speak. He didn't look at me.

"I can't believe either of them would countenance the things Mr. Kerr is doing. Joe may be more than a little stupid and terribly reckless, but he's not evil!" I sighed, hugging my knees. "And Josie's the smartest person I know. She can't possibly support this."

"I've looked at what Master Jack has from his lawyer."

Ugh. Jack Diamond, I thought. *Horrible man.*

How could I refute Jack's allegations? The man seemed determined to ruin them. "And?"

Tony hesitated. "The brownstone in Hart quadrant is owned by a Mr. Lans Pasha."

"And?"

"Lans Pasha owns many companies, which are in turn owned by another, named Monarch. This —"

"Wait," I said. "Monarch —?"

"Yes," Tony said. "Mr. Monarch, the Spadros man for your street. The one who was left murdered on the doorstep of your apartments before your trial? He was a distant cousin of the Kerrs." Tony shook his head. "It somewhat explains how he ended up on your porch, somehow 'unseen' by a half dozen Constables."

We'd learned many on the police were in Polansky Kerr's pay. But why kill Mr. Monarch? Had he offended them somehow? And how had he gained Roy's trust enough to be in charge of my street?

"But what I wished to say," said Tony, "is that this Monarch company oversees them all. Its chief financial officer is a Miss Finette Pasha."

"I don't understand."

"Birth certificates are private. But company holdings — with the names of their officers — are public knowledge. I had Ten visit the City Clerk. It's all there."

"Okay ..." I still felt confused.

"The check paying off Stephen Rivers' family after his murder by the Bridges Strangler. The checks to Monarch company holdings. They're all signed Finette Pasha. Did you not say at the meeting that Miss Josephine has gone by the name Finette Pasha?"

I sighed. "She has. Once. She came to my apartments a few years back, after you caught her brother."

"How could the financial officer of a company **not** know what the company was doing?"

"For gods' sake, Tony! All this time, she's thought her grandfather was dying! And she was planning a wedding. Not just any wedding, but to the Hart Heir — the biggest wedding in their quadrant in fifty years. She was unbelievably busy. Couldn't she possibly have signed those checks to help her grandfather? If she trusted him, would she have asked 'why do you need the money?' to every one?"

"I can't answer those things, Jacqui. I'm just telling you what I saw." He hesitated. "It's because she's so intelligent that I ask. Surely if she thought they were poor, she'd wonder at the size of these checks. Where was he getting all this money, and why wasn't any of it going to them?"

"I don't know. I can't guess what he told her. If she was given a pile of checks to sign, she might not have read each one."

"But that's just it," Tony said. "Unless she hired an accountant, she'd have had to enter each one into the books herself. And if they had money to hire an accountant, they'd have had money for her grandfather. This literally doesn't add up."

As much as I might have normally appreciated the joke — and wondered at Tony, of all people, making one — I didn't find any of it funny. "There are many reasons why a businessman might be poor." I recalled Jack Diamond's assertions that Polansky Kerr had several wives who'd died. Was he still supporting their children? "Her grandfather could have fallen into debt, or play the horses, or have obligations we know nothing about. Josie is **not** involved with the Red Dog Gang, and that's final. I plan to prove it."

"I truly hope you can, Jacqui. I really do. Because it looks bad."

"What do you mean?"

"We know her grandfather has been taking in huge amounts of money, both from his companies and from blackmailing Mr. Hart —"

I'd forgotten about that.

I didn't know everything about how illegal enterprises — for example, brothels — were run. But I knew enough. "Then her grandfather may not keep — I mean, he likely has two sets of books. So they don't have to pay Family fees. Just like I'm sure we do, in case the Feds come knocking."

Tony twitched.

"One, she holds. The real set of books might be held by someone else, whoever knows what's really going on with the company." I considered this for a moment. "If that's the case, then she may only know what they want her to."

"I suppose that could be true." Tony didn't seem convinced. He looked like he wanted to say more, but decided against it.

"Could someone have forged her signature on the checks?"

Tony shrugged. "I suppose anything's possible."

I leaned forward. "How could she possibly agree with her grandfather blackmailing her future father-in-law? It sounds like you're saying Mr. Charles Hart was coerced — no, coerced Inventor Etienne — into marrying Josie." I shook my head. "And I spoke with my —" I hesitated, not knowing who listened. "— the late Inventor the night Josie was so sick with the women's fever." I pictured how distressed my half-brother Etienne was at the thought that Josie might die. "He really loved her."

Tony didn't answer.

But then, Tony thought they deserved each other. "What do you have against Josie, anyway? She's done nothing to you."

Tony looked incredulous. "She pretended to be your friend, whilst drugging you so you might be violated by her brother!"

"She couldn't have known —"

"Not to mention arranging for you to betray me with him before that."

I felt defeated, ashamed. "She was only trying to help. She even said so. Our ways in the Pot are different than yours. We don't have marriage like you quadrant-folk do. There's no ... law there about who you can love." I sighed. "She was only trying to help."

His eyes narrowed. "Which is one reason I haven't had her killed myself. Or let Mr. Hart do so. She's your friend. Your ways are different than ours." He looked aside, just a moment, then back. "But are they really? You never told me the truth —"

"I was afraid —"

"Of who? Me?"

I shrugged.

"Oh, so my father. Or ... whatever."

Yes. I'd been terrified of Roy Spadros, and that fear had led me to this.

Tony said, "I listened to what you said in the meeting. How was this going on in my home and I never knew?"

"They didn't want you to know. Roy said if you learned the truth, he'd kill me."

"Which is why, I suppose, you never told me you knew how to shoot, or about being told to take over if I became injured, or any number of things I might find needful to know."

I nodded, feeling glum.

"You said 'they' didn't want me to know. So my mother was in on this as well. Did she beat you, too?"

I shook my head. "But she never had to."

"Ah. Of course." He shook his head. "I should've seen it."

I gaped at him. "This is how you grew up."

He shrugged, looking away.

The bed squeaked a bit as I leaned forward to take his hand.

Tony sighed. "Roy Spadros was my true-born brother. Why —? No, I see now. When he saw me, he saw his father. He saw my mother's betrayal. If he had any goodness in him, if he was ever even capable of remorse, he probably also saw my older brother, whom he murdered before my eyes." He stood. "Why did he **do** these things?" He raised a hand to stop me from speaking. "Yes, I know his mother was a fiend. And despite my mother's words, I've yet to meet anyone else who knew my grandfather — um, father, I suppose — who believed him to be particularly special, or even good at heart."

"Oh, Tony ..."

He shook his head quickly. "It doesn't matter." He took a few steps away, then turned to face me. "I'm not them. I don't even want to **be** them. And I don't understand why my — why Roy — oh, gods, I don't even know what to call the man. Why he did such monstrous things." He put his hand to his forehead. "And why did I not see he was so ill?" He began to pace. "I had no idea what he was going through. His life must have been utter torment at the end."

I nodded. "Your mother told me that after he was shot, she thought that he got up choosing to die. That day on the front porch."

Tony stared at me, mouth open.

"But from things he's said, I think his main worry was for the Family to continue. Didn't you say he wept when he learned about Roland? Perhaps that's why. Perhaps he was relieved."

Tony nodded slowly, eyes distant. Then he sat on my bed. "Despite everything, he feared for me. That I couldn't do what needed to be done." He smiled wryly to himself. "For most of my life, he was probably right."

"What's changed?"

He let out a breath, gently chewed his lip. "I'm not sure. I came to believe that no one would rescue me from this duty." He threw his arm out to encompass the room. "This Family. I'm the only hope we have of not being overrun, either by the other Families, the gangs waiting to pillage our home, or the Feds themselves. I alone stand in the way."

I took his hand. "Not alone."

He let go of my hand and chuckled, but it seemed bitter. "Until you go out of a window to bed my enemy."

He called Joe his **enemy**? Gods, my not being at the 500th Celebration with him must have hurt, my bedding Joseph Kerr must have **hurt**, for him to say this to me. "I regret that what I've done has harmed and upset you. Deeply. But I don't regret going to the Old Plaza that night. If I hadn't gone out of that window, your cousin Ten would be dead today. Or did he not tell you?"

Tony sighed. "He did."

I crossed my legs, sat up tailor-seat. "Whatever you believe, I love you. I'm on your side. I want you and our son to prosper. I want the Family to prosper." I took a deep breath. Tony wasn't going to like this. "But I will not believe that Joe and Josie are our enemies! I've known them since I was born, and they just don't have it in them to be this cruel, particularly to me."

Tony shook his head. "You need to choose, Jacqui. Me or them. And until you do that, I can't trust you."

A wave of grief came over me. "What you're asking is like me asking you to choose between me and Jon. Me and Ten." Despair came over me. "How can you ask this? Joe and Josie are the only friends I have left."

Tony shook his head. "Master Jonathan never trusted them. Ten doesn't trust them. And you're wrong, Jacqui. You have other friends here, better ones."

Ma and the Eldest and Benji had all placed me as their enemy, said I was on the side of these quadrant-folk. Dame Anastasia had betrayed me. Madame Biltcliffe was dead.

Who besides Joe and Josie could I possibly have left?

"You don't need them."

I shook my head. "I do need them. We need Joe and Josie on our side if we're to overcome their grandfather's plotting. Don't you see? If they've learned anything about what he plans against us, that could give us the advantage."

"Do you really think they oppose him?"

"Why else would Joe want to run for Mayor?" A laugh burst from me. "Ruling over quadrant-folk? He cares nothing about such things. Every time I've spoken to him at any length, his goal has been to get out of here." I took a deep breath, feeling shaky. Joe wanted me to come with him. "The only answer which makes any sense at all is that he's learned what his grandfather is doing to me and wants it to stop."

Tony hesitated, face uncertain.

"If I can bring proof of their innocence in Mr. Polansky's schemes, would that be enough to sway you?" I didn't want to say what I thought: *or do you just hate them for no good reason?*

Tony sighed, looking away. "I don't think you'll be able to do that. If you can, really can, then ... yes, I suppose I'd have to reconsider."

I felt relieved. Too much was going on for him to continue focusing on Joe, when he could be spending his energies elsewhere.

Tony rose to go, but I stopped him. "Oh. I forgot. It's time I found an office for my business elsewhere."

He faced me. "Really? Why?"

"It'd be safer for your cousins if I stopped going to my apartments."

Tony nodded.

"But ... I don't know of a good place. Market Center's out of the question. Mrs. Mary thought catering to outsiders might work better, but I can't see setting up shop in Clubb quadrant —"

A laugh burst from Tony. "Surely not." He stood still for a moment, then said, "Let me consult with your Mr. Howell. Surely he knows a place or two that might suit."

"Thanks." I felt humbled. "I know it might not seem like much to you, but it means a lot to me that you'd make the offer."

The Motivations

Once he left, I fell back into thinking. Grieving. Going to my apartments had been a happy time for me, and now I'd have to let even that go.

I drew my knees up to my chin, there on the bed. The exchange between Tony and I pained me. He hated Joseph Kerr, a man that (at the time) I loved more than life itself.

The more I thought about what Tony had said — particularly the part about Josie and those checks — the more his view of her made sense. And yet I couldn't bring myself to believe his allegations.

Joe and his twin sister Josie were a year older than me. They'd run our childrens' street gang. Joe and I had loved each other since I was fourteen, and had pledged to each other when I was sixteen, just before I'd been dragged to Spadros Manor.

I knew Joe. He could not, would not have anything to do with the Red Dog Gang. And neither would Josie!

I had to prove it.

I clung to these thoughts in that terrible time, when I feared I was going mad in my grief. I had to do something.

David Bryce had yet to speak one word about what happened to him. And from everything I'd seen and heard so far, the boy had no special skill in remembering. His memories of the several weeks he'd been held captive, over four years earlier, had to be fading.

Would we ever know the truth?

If I could speak with Joe and Josie, learn where they'd been those weeks, find proof that they weren't involved ... this would help when their grandfather's crimes came to light and they were implicated.

Perhaps they were with others at the time of the abduction. Perhaps ...

It didn't seem like enough, but it was the best I might do.

At the meeting, everyone seemed to believe their grandfather, Polansky Kerr IV, was the leader of the Red Dog Gang.

But I'd seen little proof, so I still felt as if there might be some doubt as to Mr. Polansky's motivations. He was the rightful heir to the Kerr Dynasty. Could a man be faulted for buying up the city he should be ruling? What if his purchases were just that, a way to regain what he felt had been stolen from him?

It wasn't that I didn't believe Mr. Hart when he said Mr. Kerr had been blackmailing him. I completely believed Mr. Hart. But Julius Diamond had been blackmailing Tony for over a decade, and no one had set out to ruin **him**.

So why had Mr. Kerr fallen under all this scrutiny?

Major Blackwood, of all people, had been investigating him. Jack Diamond had been investigating him. Why?

Then I recalled the letter I'd received some time back from one of my informants, who believed a wildcard was in play in Hart quadrant.

Some don't believe in the wildcard, but the Dealers did. When at a child's blessing their divinations revealed a wildcard, they'd have the child quietly put to death.

Yet since the Coup, unless you were wealthy enough to pay the bribes for it, no one brought their child to a Blessing anymore.

Could Mr. Polansky be the Hart wildcard? Had he murdered dozens of our men, attacked all four Families, instigated a trial against me for murder, and killed a score of my friends? Was he truly the Director of this Red Dog Gang that by all accounts planned to take over Bridges?

If so, why was he tormenting us **now**? What had I done to make him terrorize me? What event four and a half years back had caused him to start this madness against us? And why had he allowed the Bridges Strangler to run free through the city?

I had to speak with him. Perhaps if I could just understand what this was about, we could negotiate with him, learn what he wanted, come to a some sort of truce.

***

Even with Mrs. Clubb's exercises, the grief never stopped, day or night. Nor did my thirst.

The desire to drink stayed strong with me each day. I even had the exact drink I wanted in my mind. Not bourbon, not anymore, not after the nauseating time having been weaned off it. No, I'd pick a good dark rum, neat, a whole bottle-ful.

I pictured it all. The taste as it went down ... the color in the glass ... the ease it gave to me as this life's troubles slipped away.

I came much too close to ending my life in those days. It was only my need to learn why these men, this Red Dog Gang ... why they targeted and tormented me so ... that kept me from running to the nearest bar and drinking until I died, just to escape it all.

I knew I had to do something, or I would die. And I couldn't die yet.

Mrs. Hart had been right: I had to focus on the path ahead. The steps right in front of me.

So one day, when the glare of afternoon began to soften into evening, I sat at my tea-table overlooking the courtyard and made a list. What was it I truly wanted?

I needed to learn who took little David Bryce from his back stair. But I'd learned little in the last four years. What could I possibly learn now?

No, I wouldn't think that way. I couldn't. Too much was at stake here.

The boy had been fed, clothed, moved, guarded. Someone had placed him into Jack Diamond's factory and held him there without the workers' knowledge. Seven of those men were now dead, but I hoped some of the others still lived. If I could find them, I might get a better description of Frank. Learn who was involved. What they were trying to achieve.

This might lead me to understanding more about the nature of this Red Dog Gang and what Mr. Polansky Kerr IV — if he indeed was their Director — really wanted.

Mrs. Clubb believed him to be driven by pure revenge. I'd gone round and round about this. Tony thought that Mr. Kerr might want revenge on him personally. Tony (and our little Acevedo) were the descendants of the man who'd orchestrated the downfall of the Kerr Dynasty over 100 years earlier. Mr. Kerr's grandfather (and namesake) King Polansky I had ended up with his head on a spike.

I could understand revenge on the Spadros Family. But why target **me**? My **family**? My **friends**?

I had no answers.

I thought I understood who backed the Red Dog Gang. Most of the Bridges aristocrats had made their views obvious when they refused to attend our Grand Ball this past New Years' Eve.

According to Mr. Hart, Polansky Kerr had the Chief of Police in his pocket. So the police either stood against us, or if worst came to worst, would have to choose who to attack.

Even my homeland in the Spadros Pot opposed me. A woman with the Red Dog Gang calling herself "Black Maria" and the "Death Card" had taken over. And whilst the Cathedral seemed more or less neutral in the matter, when I gave Inventor Call the map of the pilings under the city which lay upon the Cathedral's ceiling, they named me traitor.

The now-deceased Mayor, Chase Freezout, had been an implacable enemy. Whether his mousy little Acting Mayor felt the same way was unclear. But it was safe to say we'd find no help from the city.

What could I **do**? What did I **need** to do?

I needed to focus. Put everything back in its baskets. Clear my mind.

I had to clear Joe and Josie for David Bryce's kidnapping.

To do that, I had to prove where Joe and Josie were at the time David disappeared. When I knew that, well, it would show everyone that Joseph and Josephine Kerr couldn't possibly have been involved in whatever plot their grandfather had used the boy in. Plus, it would at least cast some doubt on Tony's theory that they were working with their grandfather against us.

But I had very little time. I had to find whatever I could before Jack Diamond found his proof of Mr. Polansky Kerr's crimes. If the old man's crimes came out publicly, Josie would be drawn right into the center of it.

Tony was right: everyone would ask what she knew. And if her grandfather had truly kept her in the dark, no one would ever believe her!

I cursed myself for my weakness, my melancholy, my distraction, and the advantage it'd given the man who I felt sure still was my enemy. Even now, Jack Diamond would be instructing his lawyers (and whoever was helping them) to find proof of Mr. Polansky's crimes that no one could gainsay.

The Distrust

Even so late in the day, the air radiating from the courtyard steamed. My house dress was damp with sweat. I called for my lady's maid Shanna, and after undressing, being doused with cool water, and redressing in fresh clothing, I felt somewhat better.

As Shanna braided my thick wet curls, I pondered it all.

Who might know the facts about David Bryce's case?

Jake Bower had confessed to helping Frank Pagliacci move the boy, going so far as to impersonate Jack Diamond. But I could learn nothing about his associates. I'd sent a messenger with a letter to Mr. Bower's wife Reina, but the two Constables standing guard over the apartment building took the letter from the boy. I never received an answer.

Constable Hanger had visited Spadros Manor over four and a half years earlier. He'd been inquiring about the boy Stephen Rivers, who I'd sent to look for David. But the Constable's visit indicated that he'd been at least somewhat involved in the investigation. "Once you're done, Shanna, might you find Mr. Pearson and ask him to join me in my study?"

Shanna curtsied. "Yes, mum." She pinned up a last braid. "That looks quite cooling."

"It is." I suppose it was, at least more than having my hair puffed out around my head. "Thank you."

When Shanna left towards the back stair, I went down our grand sweeping main staircase. Master Alan Pearson wasn't at his post, which was, I suppose, one reason Shanna didn't go that way. But servants didn't often take the main stair, and now Alan was to be called Mr. Pearson, his title as Spadros Manor's butler.

How things had changed.

When I went to my study, I drew the curtains to my side gardens closed and sat. Tony's portrait hung on the wall to my right. I whispered to the portrait, "I love you."

And I felt moved.

Tony didn't trust me.

I remembered his words to me almost two months earlier on the Grand Ballhouse stair, as we watched Mr. Clubb's body being raced away by his men. He wanted to try to love me again.

Was he failing?

I just didn't understand any of it. Why had he'd pretended for so long to be having an affair with Gardena Diamond? Why did he hate Joe and Josie so much? Why would he ask me to choose between him and my dearest friends?

A knock at the door. "Come in."

Alan Pearson peered around the door. "You asked for me?"

I gestured for him to come in. "Yes. I need to speak with a Constable Paix Hanger — without anyone knowing of it."

He looked uncertain. "Where is this man based? What quadrant?"

"Last I recall, he was restricted to Market Center." I shrugged. "So ..."

Alan bit his upper lip. "Hmm. Let me see what I can do."

"And did you ever find the information your father was gathering on Mr. Roy's grandparents? His mother's parents."

Alan shook his head. "As you asked, my brothers, Master Ten Hogan, and I have read through my father's ledgers for an hour each day, looking for any insights we might gain on what he knew." He looked daunted. "I fear my father was more cunning than I'll ever be."

I snorted. "He had to be, to survive around Mr. Roy." Then I had a thought. "Did he have any private notes? Things he didn't want anyone to walk in and find?"

Alan blinked. "I don't know, mum. I'll ask my mother."

His mother Jane was the housekeeper for Spadros Manor. Ever since her husband died keeping my infant son safe with his body as Tommy-guns were loosed on our people, Jane had kept to deep mourning.

I said, "Thank you. Please assure her that we're not interested in anything which intrudes upon their private lives. I'm looking for information we can use against our enemies."

Alan gave three tiny quick nods. "I'll let her know, mum."

I hurried to finish my Queen's box before Mr. Howell came to fetch it. I put a note in for more cards, attaching one of the old ones and making a notation to add the new address once a suitable place was found.

Then I began reading the tabloids, setting each to one side after reading the articles circled there. Letters to answer. Invitations. Events.

Tony's bitter words and sullen silence over the past few days nagged at me. It hurt that he distrusted me. How could I prove I was on his side?

Perhaps encouragement for those who still supported us might help. I left a note for Mr. Howell to compile a list of the birthdays of the wives and children of Tony's main men, along with any needs or likes.

The next item in the box was a list of the current Mayoral candidates, which I'd asked Mr. Howell to prepare. The list was several typed pages long, well over a hundred men.

I sat back, peering at it. One of these men running for Mayor had to be Frank Pagliacci, the man I felt certain to be the Bridges Strangler. Tony had thought it, and so had Jonathan Diamond.

The Director of the Red Dog Gang was too smart to run Frank Pagliacci under his real name. Joe was the one man running for Mayor that I knew couldn't be the Bridges Strangler. So it had to be one of these others.

But Joe's name was gone!

So he'd dropped out. Or he couldn't get verified by the City Clerk.

As far as I knew, he was still in Azimoff. But when Joe tried to find a job, he learned people from the Pot couldn't be registered in Bridges. That left us Pot rags without a city, a country, a home — other than inside the Hedge that kept us trapped there.

Perhaps Joe left for Azimoff to find work. But why lie and tell me he was taking his grandfather with him?

I shook my head; it didn't matter.

I needed to find Joe, see what he knew about what his grandfather was doing. Learn what he knew about the other candidates. He could've heard something we could use.

And there remained only a few months until the election. If the Red Dog Gang got the Bridges Strangler in the Mayor's office, well, he'd be nigh impossible to get out. I didn't want to think of what might happen.

The one thing that I hadn't looked into yet was the idea of there being a wildcard in the city. I'd never spoken with my informant to understand why she thought so, how she got her information, or who she thought it might be.

But I had to be careful. Everything I sent was scrutinized, every messenger followed, every letter, opened.

After some thought, I wrote:

Dearest Madam:

Please forgive my delay. The business of my new position is wildly different from what I imagined. So much to do, so many tabloids and pamphlets to read, so many cards to answer for one Hand.

The ideas put forth in your last message are entirely sound! I would be pleased to discuss them more thoroughly. Please consult with my secretary to schedule an appointment.

In all sincerity,

Sir Q. Jack von Hamm, Hub Importers

Hart, Bridges

I smiled at that signature. My informant and I had first met at a bistro outside the Records Hall. We sat at nearby tables, discussing the virtues of their establishment's roasted ham.

I put the message in a sealed envelope and addressed it to my informant. I then put that inside another sealed envelope and addressed it to my dressmaker, Tenni Mitchell, who had a shop in Clubb quadrant. That envelope I put inside a third and brought it downstairs.

Alan Pearson, Spadros Manor's butler, stood at his post. A podium and lectern, the Telephonic Telegram in a panel beside him, an array of bell cords, each with their own handles, on the wall beside that. Behind him, cubbies with various keys in them and a counter containing baskets for outgoing and incoming mail. He smiled when I approached. "What can I help you with?"

"Might you stop by tonight and see how your sister fares?" I handed him the letter. "And give this to Blitz while you're there."

He smiled to himself. "Anything else, mum?"

I lowered my voice, not sure who listened. "Let Mary know Mr. Anthony agrees with them. About my office. He's having Mr. Howell look into it."

Alan seemed surprised. "Oh! That does sound good. I'll let her know."

***

The next morning's edition of the *Bridges Daily* had a horrifying headline:

SPADROS AND CLUBB ALLIANCE RESTORED

Protests in Diamond quadrant

I grabbed the paper, went through my closets, and banged open Tony's door. He was in the midst of dressing, and he and his manservant Jacob Michaels both stared at me.

Tony said evenly, "Mrs. Spadros. Good morning."

I shook the paper at him. "How could you do this? Mr. Clubb made it plain that he kept from the appearance of an alliance to make things safe —!" I almost said, "for your son," but I didn't know who was listening.

Tony seemed unaffected. "First of all, I am your Patriarch; I don't need to explain myself to you. Second, even if I felt an explanation was necessary, this is neither the time nor place for such discussion."

I felt abashed, and I curtsied low. "Forgive me. I ... I just ... didn't understand."

"No," Tony said, "you don't. Nor do you need to. Now please," he flicked his hand at me, "make yourself presentable next time you wish to leave your rooms, and stop flaunting yourself in front of my men."

I gaped at him. Is **that** what he thought?

Michaels had turned his face away.

I looked down. I wore my nightgown, my robe. But my robe was open. My nightgown was cut low, and my bare feet peeked out. I sighed. "As you command, sir."

Had he really needed to reprimand me in front of Michaels? Had he guessed that Michaels was one of my Queensmen, and wished to assert his power?

I slumped into my chair at my tea-table, throwing the paper on the floor. No matter what Tony said, nothing good could come of this. I feared he was making a dreadful mistake.

The Children

Breakfast, in its special room with windows on all sides overlooking the gardens, was a quiet affair.

I sat to Tony's right at the round table. Alan Pearson stood beside the buffet. Our newest housemaid, Millie, stood by the door. She was fourteen, a former scullery maid who Tony had recently promoted.

Neither of the servants looked at me, but I imagined the whole household knew of Tony's reprimand. I pitched my voice so only he might hear. "I can't believe that the Clubbs agreed to this."

Tony put down his fork and turned his whole body to face me, speaking so anyone might hear. "I can't believe that you'd assume they **didn't**." He said sternly. "Is that **enough**? Or do you feel **further** need to question me?"

I felt taken aback. Why did he feel the need to humiliate me in front of my staff?

His face softened then, and he spoke quietly. "Just know it was done out of friendship. I'd not leave any man to suffer alone as I had, no matter how his father might have felt about it."

He went back to eating as if this explained everything. But I still felt angry — both at his actions and his treatment.

That day went on as usual: the morning meeting, then to my study.

Alan stopped me in the hall. "Oh, mum, your husband wished me to give this to you." He handed over a white envelope — already opened — edged in silver entwined with gold.

I brought it to my study and opened it. A card lay inside, embossed in deep brown:

MRS. ALEXANDER CLUBB
REQUESTS THE HONOR OF YOUR PRESENCE
AT THE WEDDING OF HER SON
MASTER LANCELOT ALEXANDER CLUBB
TO
MISS GARDENA RACHEL DIAMOND
DAUGHTER OF
MR. AND MRS. JULIUS DIAMOND
ON THE FIRST OF OCTOBER
IN THE YEAR OF OUR BLESSED DEALER
NINETEEN-HUNDRED AND THREE
PLEASE ARRIVE AT ELEVEN O'CLOCK AM
RSVP

So it was finally happening! I felt excited for Gardena and Lance. What might we get them?

I had some time to consider it, but I felt dismayed that I couldn't think of anything off hand.

This reminded me, of course, of Tony, of his feelings for Gardena. My husband surely had Alan give this to me because he didn't want to deal with it.

I put it in a drawer and began work on my duties as Queen.

I was "at home" that day, and I had the usual few visitors, all people I'd reached out to before I became Queen.

They visited, I think, out of a desire to show they were still loyal. But they often brought news.

"I'm no longer invited to the parties," Duchess Sophia told me. "Countess Victoria said I was 'sniffing at the dogs.'"

I sat back, surveyed her. I shouldn't have been surprised. Countess Victoria Welli Von Schafkopf detested me, once calling me a "Family Pet" to my face. As punishment, Tony had taken her mansion and given it to Inventor Call, forcing her to move to smaller (yet almost as opulent) accommodations. "Thank you for telling me."

Duchess Sophia seemed reasonable. But I wondered if she were too trusting to come here so often, so openly. "What do you think happened? To bring us to the situation today?"

Duchess Sophia drew back, just a bit. "I don't know! Might I consider the matter, mum, and bring you an answer when next we meet?"

I hoped my smile appeared warm. "You may." I rose, signalling the end of our talk, and the woman left.

Then I sat, disheartened. How had Roy lost the aristocrats so badly? Surely they couldn't **all** blame him for his mother's disappearance!

But then I recalled what Tony had said: *despite my mother's words, I've yet to meet anyone else who knew my grandfather who believed him to be particularly special, or even good at heart.*

So perhaps this went back further than Roy.

***

At dinner I sat in my finery, as we did every night, at the opposite end of our long dining room table from Tony. Our servants all round. I had to do something, so I ate.

My life was an utter ruin.

My husband didn't trust me. My friends had suffered and died because of me. I'd brought the threat of ruin upon my Family. Upon even the Cathedral!

And I could find nothing to do about it.

Tony said nothing. The servants, of course, said nothing.

At that so finely arrayed, so beautiful table ... all I saw were the people I'd killed. I saw Maria Athena Spade's empty eyes, little Ante lying so still after I smothered him, Jake Bower pleading with me to save his life.

I screamed, inside my head: *Get back into your fucking baskets!*

Had I done anything good?

I took a drink of water, wishing to all the gods that it was wine. There had to be someone I could save.

I decided that the only thing that mattered were the children.

Acevedo. Roland.

David.

I sat up straighter, focused on Alan Pearson, who stood his post be: and behind Tony's chair. "I must speak with you after dinner, sir. On matter we discussed."

Alan grew pale. "Yes, mum."

Tony turned back to peer at Alan, then at me, face amused.

It didn't matter. I had to speak with Constable Hanger, and soon.

***

Alan had set up a meeting with Constable Hanger in a rather disreputa pub in the servants' area on Market Center.

The plain carriage sat out front of Spadros Manor: Shanna and I w inside. I wore my normal clothes — a fine green walking dress, with l and full jewelry. I carried my green-and-gold Paisley carpetbag; Shan held a basket covered with a gingham cloth.

When we arrived at my apartments, we strolled up through the fro door, which Blitz held open for us.

Ariana came barreling around the corner, throwing herself onto n legs. "Jacqui!"

I squatted down to hug her. "How's my girl?"

"Good." She batted at my shoulder. "Unca Teddy here."

I'd pondered who to bring along. Tony had asked Mr. Theodo Sutherfield to meet me at my apartments.

Blitz was Mr. Theodore's youngest half-brother, and Mr. Theodo lived close by, so choosing him made sense. "Oh, well, that's good! Go se your Mama; I need to get my other clothes on."

"Okay." She went running off down the back hall and into the kitche "Jacqui here!"

I laughed. "Come on, let's get this done."

Mary had closed the drapes to the front bedroom and set up a cha and mirror.

My carpetbag held clothes I'd borrowed from one of our maids, an my hooded cloak. Shanna got me dressed, braided my thick curls in row tightly back, then took the long straight blonde wig I'd bought long ag from her basket, its combs sliding their way under the front of my braids

The hair reminded me of the woman's portrait in Jonathan Diamond desk that I found the day he went missing.

He'd gone missing on purpose to help his brother Jack feign his own death. But I don't think Jon meant me to see the portrait, and since then I'd wondered why.

I'd asked him, and Gardena, and Jack, yet no one ever really told me. A girl he knew.

Last I knew, she was in Azimoff.

But something lay beneath Jon's words, something important. Something deep.

Something I'd probably never learn.

The woman had meant something to him, and I don't to this day know why that bothered me so. It wasn't jealousy — no, it was ... a feeling. A feeling that he'd feared to tell me she even existed.

Why?

Shanna did up my new hair and pinned on a plain hat with an even plainer veil. "Turn round, mum."

I'd also brought the stage makeup book that Dame Anastasia Louis had given me several years ago. While I took off my makeup, Shanna held the book, peering at the pages. "How do you want your face done?"

"How would a servant do theirs?"

Shanna looked embarrassed. "Most can't afford makeup, mum. Maybe a little rouge if they go out with a gentleman they fancy. But usually?" She shook her head.

"Then we'll leave it off. I'll go as Miss Jacqui Kaplan of the Spadros Pot, in the face the gods gave me." I grinned. "I'll never be recognized."

The Portrait

Mr. Theodore awaited me in the kitchen. A middle-aged, brown-skinned man of a medium height, Mr. Theodore wore workman's brown, replacing his usual gray tweed coat and cap for shabby brown linen ones, along with well-worn leather boots. We looked a pair of day-hire workers on an outing, which was my intent.

Mr. Theodore and I exited the side door from the kitchen to the narrow alley and turned left, making our way to the taxi-carriage on 32nd Street.

Tony hadn't wanted me to go by taxi. But it seemed everyone knew I used the plain carriage. If someone were indeed following me, the black Spadros horses and silver tack marked it as ours. Leaving the carriage parked on 33 1/3 Street in Spadros Quadrant along with my snipers and guards in position would suggest I still remained at my apartments.

I hoped it worked. For Constable Hanger's sake, I didn't want anyone to know about this meeting that didn't have to.

As we exited the taxi-carriage on Market Center, I glanced around. A Family man rode past on horseback; another, also on horseback, went by the other way. A third strolled along across the street with his wife, to all appearances on promenade.

Clever, I thought. I took Mr. Theodore's arm and went inside.

Constable Hanger, a lightly-tanned, dark-haired man in his early forties, sat at a booth in the back. He glanced up at Mr. Theodore when we approached. "May I help you, sir?"

"Thank you for meeting us here," I said.

For an instant, confusion lay on the Constable's face, then he pointed at Mr. Theodore. "Wait, I remember you. You were at the apothecary shop with Mrs. —"

"Stop," I said. "May we sit?"

He'd really not looked at me up until then. But recognition dawned in his eyes. "My gods, it's **you**!" Then he recalled his manner. "Please, yes." He made to rise.

But I waved him off. "No need, sir. I'm just a servant, nothing more."

We sat across the table from him.

Constable Hanger sat blinking. "You should've been using this disguise the entire time."

I smiled at him, feeling amused.

Constable Hanger shuddered. "I'm serious. Too many people know your movements. Too much is being said." He glanced around, then leaned forward. "I've paid the owner for the booths on each side to stay empty so long as I'm here. But I don't want to push my luck. What is so urgent for you to meet **me** ... **here** ... dressed like **that**?"

I leaned forward as well. "I need everything you have on Master David Bryce and his abduction."

Constable Hanger sat back. "That was over four years ago! When we last spoke on the subject, you claimed to know nothing about it." He glanced at Mr. Theodore, then back at me. "What's your interest in this?"

Should I tell him? I decided against it. "A friend was implicated in the matter. I only wish to clear his name. If I might see the findings, particularly any physical evidence, then I could match them to his known features and whereabouts ..."

Constable Hanger nodded slowly, just slightly leaned forward, a wary look upon his face. "Might I ask who this 'friend' might be?"

Mr. Theodore froze.

I glanced around. "I shouldn't say. Can you help me or not?"

Constable Hanger leaned back and crossed his arms. "I no longer work in Spadros quadrant. By your husband's command, I might add, simply because I wanted to learn the truth." He took a deep breath, looked away. "One of my oldest friends tried to learn the truth. He fell into despair by what he learned, into disgrace, then was murdered for it." He leaned forward. "I've spent four and a half years trying to find the only possible witness, without success, whilst people die in my wake. Not only do I no longer have access to the evidence, a good man died during an attempt by the city to destroy it."

I realized my mouth lay open, so I shut it. "I'm sorry."

"So no, I can't give you anything. But I can tell you what I know."

Constable Hanger had been called to Eleanora Bryce's home the day after Yuletide Center, 1898. The only thing he found in that dismal back alley was what I did: the stamp of a red dog upon the alley wall. "It seemed to me that an adult made the stamp at the height of a child, so as to disguise the person behind the mark."

I felt surprised: I'd never considered that.

"I've never thought that children took the boy. First, abduction isn't something children do. And to intentionally disguise the one clue they intentionally left behind? This never comes into the mind of even the worst child." He shook his head. "I've arrested hundreds of children, for crimes from petty theft to murder. Not one has shown this kind of ... I don't know, complexity."

I said, "This makes sense. I suppose I'd always assumed it to be an adult. Possibly a woman."

Constable Hanger nodded. "Yes, an attractive and kindly woman would dazzle a boy that age. He might go with a woman without a shout, where a man might frighten him. But he'd just moved there with his mother." He glanced at me. "Has he yet spoken?"

I shook my head. His outburst the night I left Spadros Manor hardly counted. Then what he said hit me. "Why do you think I might know?"

He shrugged. "You must know her: she went to your apartments to help during the auction." Constable Hanger looked glum. "Until the boy speaks, we might never know what happened that afternoon."

He had to have sources here: he'd been banned from the quadrant, after all. "So what did you learn?"

"Not much. You knew nothing. Or rather, it seemed to me you might know much, yet couldn't — or wouldn't — speak."

I nodded.

"For which I don't blame you, living there." He glanced round, apparently unwilling to say more. "But if you know anything which might help ..."

I shrugged. I didn't think I'd learned much of anything either.

"Very well," Constable Hanger said. "A woman was implicated. It seemed to me that she was doing her own investigation of the matter, possibly hired by the mother. Yet I've never found her. A boy named Stephen Rivers had met with the woman —"

Stephen's little face swam before me.

"— and he was murdered by the Bridges Strangler. To this day, I don't have proof the two are related. Yet I have a feeling that they are."

Mr. Theodore glanced at me. How much had he overheard at the meeting atop the Ballhouse?

I felt confused, and more than a bit concerned. "You think this woman trying to investigate the kidnapping is in league with the **Strangler**?"

"I don't know what to think. It crossed my mind that if she were, offering to investigate the crime might be a decent swindle. Yet the mother had no money." He shrugged. "Little of this crime has made sense to me."

Yet he himself said ... "The city tried to destroy evidence around David's **abduction**?"

The Constable looked away. "It's complex. Stephen Rivers said a man was following him. The boy was as terrified as I've ever seen a child." He took a deep breath, eyes on his hands clasped on the table. "We got a portrait from him. My Detective thought the portrait resembled a young man who'd been accused of following before. One of your husband's men, by the way. When we brought the man in for questioning, he claimed he'd also been taken by the man in the portrait." He glanced around, then faced me. "I knew this young man. I'd interviewed him at least a dozen times. He was legitimately frightened. My Detective didn't believe him, but I did." He bit his lip. "Then something happened, oh, at least a year ago. Maybe two, I don't rightly recall. It was before that exposé in the papers about the Mayor's office. A woman came forward and said she could identify this man. We produced a portrait."

"Wait," I said. "Who?"

Constable Hanger drew back, face pale. "I promised no one would know her name!" He shook his head. "No one but me ever knew who she was." He glanced away. "She's left the city, and now I'm glad of it."

I said, "I don't understand. Why?"

"I'd had all the evidence on this case moved to the Market Center station. We suddenly got a summons to surrender the evidence on this case to the city." He shook his head. "It's unprecedented; there was no reason the Mayor needed that information. But a week later, the Mayor's office seized the portrait the woman had given us along with some others, including the one your man gave. The artist who'd done the portraits was fired without cause, and was later found hanging in his home. He was a good man, a bright and promising man with a wife and small children." He frowned, face set. "Neither I nor his family believes it was suicide."

I felt appalled. "Good gods." But the story sounded familiar. Someone had already told me about this.

"But do you sees? Stephen ended up dead. Other boys, including little David's brother — were taken and murdered by the same hand. And I go to see your man at your Manor, only to find him dead."

"Wait. Crab?"

Constable Hanger nodded. "The same."

Crab, my husband's Associate, had killed himself. At the time, I'd thought it was out of grief for his lover's death, and possibly to avoid being tortured by Roy for betraying the Family. But what if it were partly out of fear of this other man?

Constable Hanger sighed. "The witnesses, either dead or vanished. Then the only physical evidence — the portraits — are stolen, with the only other place they might be found," he tapped his head, "the artist's mind, destroyed. This can **not** be a coincidence."

No, it couldn't. But I didn't know what it meant. The city, one or two years ago, meant Mayor Freezout.

Why would Chase Freezout care about David Bryce's abduction?

"Who's Eunice Ogier?"

The Constable's question threw me off guard. I shrugged, unable to meet his eye. "The only person I know by that name was a woman who was kind to me." I looked at him. "A servant. She died when I was small."

He nodded, face uncertain.

I glanced around. We couldn't stay too much longer. "Have you learned anything else?"

Constable Hanger leaned forward. "This boy's case is linked to the Strangler cases. Stephen Rivers and Herbert Bryce. Albert Sheinwold. Plus several other boys and young men that I know of." He let out a breath. "I no longer have access to the Strangler cases, but there are hundreds more. As I told you when we found Albert Sheinwold dead in that alley, they were all done by the same hand. The real thing I don't understand is why he didn't kill David Bryce."

He took the boy to capture me.

But to say that would be to expose myself as the very Eunice Ogier he thought was in league with the Bridges Strangler. "If you think of anything else, send it to my apartments. To Mrs. Mary Spadros. Make up a sending name, or have someone else send it for you." I couldn't have Blitz and Mary linked with the police, not in Bridges.

Constable Hanger nodded. " If I think of anything, I'll have my cousin Lane send it. She's reliable."

I gestured to Mr. Theodore with my chin, and he rose from the bench so I could as well. "Thank you for meeting us here. Was it very costly?"

The Constable rose. "Don't worry for that. I'm doing some work on the side that more than covers it."

I felt surprised. *He's as straight-arrow as they come*, Sawbuck had said once. Where was he getting the money? "Well, good for you, sir."

Once inside the carriage, I said, "What do you think?"

Mr. Theodore glanced aside. "I think he's hiding something."

The Division

I thought Constable Hanger was hiding something, too.

Morton had said he thought the man was hiding something. He thought Constable Hanger didn't trust him. But had the Constable known that Morton was a Fed, all this time, and never told me?

I went by my apartments, to collect Shanna and my belongings. Mr. Theodore went his way, while I sat in the parlor and let Shanna comb out my hair.

It was late afternoon, and all the windows lay open. Blitz had the fans on; the air, though very warm, felt pleasant.

Ariana, ever unrepentant, sang her little tune in my rooms, every so often saying "hi," or "uh-huh," presumably to her dolls.

The jingle of messenger boys, the sounds of people trundling carts. Far off, a guitar played. A woman laughed.

I liked it here. I didn't want to leave forever.

But what if someone had decided — when they thought I was here — to attack?

I had to make sure this little family — particularly my little Ariana — was kept safe, even from me.

Blitz stuck his head in from the kitchen. "Will you be staying for tea?"

By this time, Shanna had put my hair up for me. "Done!"

I stood. "I best not. My husband will worry."

Blitz smiled. "I'll let Mary know."

After tea back at Spadros Manor, I went to my rooms and retrieved my earlier notes from my locked dresser drawer. The letter from Morton, my list of clues.

Everything I knew about Morton was thrown into question. Everything he'd said, everything he'd done.

Why become my tenant? Did he even really have a home in Hart quadrant? And a secret compartment — in his shoe? Every time I thought of that, I felt both amusement and dismay.

Master Blaze Rainbow had tricked me, fooled me. Got my husband to take him on as one of his men! And by doing so, had likely earned the trust of dozens of others. What had he learned? What had he told the Feds before the Clubbs caught him calling out of the city?

And as I'd done each time I tried to make sense of it all, I wept.

Morton was my friend. I loved him as a brother. As a father.

And now he was dead.

This was what the Red Dog Gang wanted. They wanted to take everything and everyone from me. What had Dame Anastasia said? *They had this entire plot: isolate you, break you down to have you under their control. And if that didn't work, kill you.*

Why did Polansky Kerr IV think I'd join him, though, after everything he'd done to me? Could he be that delusional?

No. Polansky Kerr's actions weren't that of a delusional man. Buying up half the city spoke of decades of planning. Suborning the aristocrats after growing up in the Pot was something only a extremely charismatic, diplomatic, and astute fellow might do. He had to been well-trained by someone, someone there in the Pot. He had to have started as a very young man in order to have accomplished so much.

These deeds indicated great determination, along with a good mind. A cunning mind. A strong mind.

I recalled the well-used chessboard in Mr. Kerr's brownstone.

I'd tried playing chess once, with Roy, long ago. But I could never get very far. Roy told me I thought too much in straight lines, and too few of those ahead.

Roy told me I was too reckless, too rash. From what I'd seen so far, Mr. Kerr didn't seem like a man to make rash actions.

Well, all but the kidnapping of David Bryce. I still couldn't figure out what Mr. Kerr wanted to lure me to that basement for. And why use Frank Pagliacci and Jake Bower, of all people, to do it?

David Bryce's kidnapping and torment made no sense. It achieved nothing other than to ruin a child and upset me.

And then there was Morton. He'd gone along with this scheme unwittingly, trusting the word of his partner Zia. But then he could identify the conspirators, which meant he'd become a liability.

Several things bothered me about Morton's story. But the main thing that bothered me was this: if the plan to kidnap David originated from Mr. Polansky, why wasn't he at the meeting? Did he really trust the multiple murderer Frank Pagliacci, the disgraced former detective Jake Bower, the rogue Federal Agent Zia Cashout, and the murderous leader of a Pot gang calling herself the Death Card?

And if he really did trust them, why?

Then I had a thought: Could he have been blackmailing **them**, too?

It was surely possible. Polansky Kerr seemed to be a master at it.

Which brought me back to: why? If Polansky Kerr's goal in bringing me to that basement in Diamond quadrant was to capture me ... why go to all that trouble? He could've captured me at any time. Back then, I'd been only lightly guarded. And if he'd done so, Charles Hart — my true-born father — was already being blackmailed by him. Mr. Hart would've done anything to keep me away from Mr. Kerr.

Polansky Kerr could have achieved a lot more with the vast wealth of Hart quadrant at his fingertips. He might already own the entire city, if he'd done so. It was almost like the kidnapping was done by someone else, someone not associated with Mr. Kerr.

Or perhaps, not authorized by him.

I sighed. It did fit what I'd thought back in that warehouse when Frank Pagliacci shot at me. Frank had sounded like a raw amateur, with a wild idea that he thought would be daring. He'd recruited Jake Bower (who'd said himself that he felt Frank blinded him to reason), getting Mr. Bower to go so far as to disguise himself as Jack Diamond! Somehow, he'd even persuaded the Federal Agents Zia and Morton to aid him.

He persuaded **Federal Agents** to do all this.

I shuddered. Gods, what charisma Frank Pagliacci must have!

I felt certain Frank was the Bridges Strangler. Frank had murdered hundreds of young men and — as a child — at least one young girl.

And yet Mr. Kerr had covered for him, even persuading then-Mayor Freezout to have another man hanged for the crimes. Which made no sense. Who was Frank Pagliacci to Polansky Kerr? Why was Frank, of all people, so important?

The biggest mystery was that Mayor Freezout had gone along with this, despite the fact that Mr. Kerr had let him be beaten half-dead by Roy Spadros on the Courthouse steps whilst the police stood by and watched. This made no sense whatsoever.

Had the beating been Mayor Freezout's punishment? He'd failed to have me convicted of the crimes they'd framed me for, and that must have spoilt some of their plan.

But what **was** Mr. Polansky's plan? I still couldn't deduce it.

It did seem, though, from what Dame Anastasia and her "nephew" Trey Louis had told me, that Mr. Polansky's minions were divided. Which seemed a good thing.

What had the man said? I focused, trying to recall it through the glare, Jack Diamond's arm coming out of nowhere to strike the man. The blood.

Something about Frank thinking I was in danger.

But why would Frank Pagliacci, of all people, care? Didn't he **want** me in danger?

I felt so tired. I felt so jumbled-up, like a vast puzzle lay unstarted in my brain, pieces lying everywhere.

Morton had been with Frank, at least for a time. Morton had been with the Feds. Yet he'd been in my home! For **years**!

I put my face on my arms and began crying once more. It seemed the tears never moved far from me in those days, but were my constant companion in grief.

***

I think I dozed, because I felt startled by a knock. "Mum," Shanna said from behind the door. "Come quickly. Mr. Anthony needs you at once."

I sat up. It was almost dark out, close to time to dress for dinner. "Come in."

Shanna rushed in. "Here, wipe your eyes, mum. Let's get your house shoes on." She pulled me to my feet.

"What's this about?"

"I don't know, mum. Mr. Anthony is furious like I've never seen him."

Good gods, I thought. **Furious?**

What could have possibly happened?

I followed Shanna down the winding marble back stair, then down the hall past the breakfast room to Tony's study.

Furious was not the word I would use. Tony was livid: ranting, pacing as Sawbuck stood trying to get a word in. When Tony saw me, he stormed over, finger pointed. "How **dare** you do this without notifying me?"

I took a step back. "Do what? I don't understand. What's happened?"

Tony growled, stalking away.

Sawbuck said calmly, "Blitz was arrested."

The Arrest

I felt stunned. "Arrested? Why? What did he do?

Tony shouted at me. "What did he **do**? **Your** butler **shot** a Mayoral **candidate!**"

"Wait," I said. "He did what?"

"Some man went to your door, at your apartments." Tony threw out a dismissive hand. "One of the hundreds of candidates, wanting to 'meet the people'. Apparently, he and Blitz had words. I don't know what was said, but Blitz pulled out his revolver and **shot** the man!"

I'd just awakened. I felt confused. What was happening? "He **did**?"

"Now Blitz is claiming servant's right. He says **you** told him to **do** it."

"I **did**?"

"The city is fining us a thousand dollars —"

I gasped. When a penny could buy a taxi-carriage ride or a meal, a thousand dollars was a fortune.

"— and now my **cousin** is being held for attempted **murder!**" Tony threw his hands into the air and stormed away. Then he turned to point at me. "**You** did this, and **you** will fix it. I wash my hands of this **whole** thing. **You** will pay this fine. And **you** can find a lawyer for it, if you wish to defend this mess. The Spadros Family will have not **one** thing to do with **any** of it."

Sawbuck just shook his head, amused.

I felt completely taken aback, both at the news and at Tony's wrath. "Very well." I still felt hazy, as if in a dream. "Where is he?"

"Market Center," Sawbuck said. "At the station."

Blitz was **arrested**? "Let me get dressed; I'll go at once."

"Go with her," Tony said to Sawbuck.

Sawbuck had a pained expression; since he'd been shot the year prior, carriage-rides tended to jostle his back.

I said, "He doesn't have to —"

Tony acted as though I'd not spoken. "The usual contingent, plus I want Teddy and Honor with you in the station, in case this is a trap."

Sawbuck said, "Yes, sir."

I sighed. Tony wasn't going to see reason. There was no need for Ten Hogan to suffer for what I supposed I must have done. At the time, I couldn't understand why Blitz would shoot anyone.

***

By the time I got to the plain carriage, Sawbuck, Honor, and Mr. Theodore Sutherfield were already inside. Mr. Theodore looked worried.

I smiled at him. "Never fear; we'll get through this."

The carriage set off.

"Thank you, mum," Mr. Theodore said. "This whole business has our Ma fretting something awful." He glanced aside. "Not to mention Mrs. Mary."

"I imagine. Please let them know that I'll pay whatever this costs him."

Mr. Theodore let out a relieved laugh. "Good to hear; I don't think that between Ma and the six of us we'd be able to come up with a hundred, much less a grand."

Hmm, I thought. Blitz had five older brothers, all from different fathers. Blitz had mentioned once that his own father had died during the first Diamond-Spadros war, but the men who'd sired his brothers had to be around somewhere. Would they not help?

But once I considered the matter, I felt surprised. "Doesn't my husband pay better than that?"

Mr. Theodore gave a start of surprise, then looked pained. "A wife and children are expensive, mum. And none of us are that good with money."

I'd have to make sure Blitz took care to put something away. I couldn't guarantee I'd be around to protect — or provide for — his family forever.

***

Somehow, word had gotten out about my trip there. I suppose the Queen of Spadros quadrant appearing at the Market Center police station must have been the news of the hour. When we arrived, dozens of reporters stood round shouting in the lamplight, kept back by Tony's men.

I went up the steps, police ready to open the doors, and was confronted by a wide, semi-organized chaos. The room was large, lined with doors, and had an open second floor with a high domed roof. An ancient chandelier hung in the center. Men sat typing, trundled carts past full of baskets carrying envelopes, papers, files. On the second floor, more men sat typing, walked along the deep brown banisters, stood discussing.

"Mum," a man said. "This way."

I'd been gawking like some tourist! Feeling chagrined, I followed the man — a Constable, by his uniform — across the front of the wide room and to a door.

Faces alarmed, Sawbuck and Mr. Theodore hurried ahead to check inside before allowing me to enter.

When I looked inside, I shuddered.

The room was gun-metal gray, windowless, and cold. It reminded me of the area Jack Diamond had me trapped in on the night of the fire.

Blitz Spadros sat huddled in an armless metal chair of the same color behind a metal table to match. He didn't seem to be hurt, but his hair was disheveled, his clothes, rumpled.

Relief washed over him when he saw us. "Thank gods you're here. I don't care what he's calling himself. I swear it was him."

Hesitation gone, I went to the chair across the table and sat. "Tell me what happened, Blitz. All of it."

Sawbuck took a step forward. "No. Don't you say another word. Not until we get you a lawyer."

Blitz looked from him to me, eyes wide.

Sawbuck turned to me. "They're listening to us right now. But they can't once a lawyer gets here."

I took a deep breath, wanting to shake Sawbuck and Blitz until they told me what was going on. But of course, Sawbuck was right. "Very well. How soon can Mr. Trevisane get here?"

Sawbuck let out a laugh. "Were you not listening? Mr. Anthony has washed his hands of the matter. This is your problem, Mrs. Spadros. You must fix it!"

I didn't want to do this. "Get Doyle Pike." I called out to whoever was listening. "I designate Doyle Pike as lawyer for my man."

Sawbuck shook his head. "Hoo, boy. You think Mr. Anthony was angry before ..."

"What does my husband have against Mr. Pike, anyway?"

"Not here," said Sawbuck sternly. "We can discuss that later."

I glanced at Honor. "Make sure they're getting him."

Honor nodded and left, shutting the door behind him.

I said to Blitz, "How's Mary?"

Blitz glanced at Sawbuck, who nodded. "Scared. She wanted to come, but I told her to stay put."

Mary was having a difficult time with her latest pregnancy. And now this. "I'm sorry, Blitz."

Blitz opened his mouth to speak. Sawbuck said, "No! Do not. Say. Another word."

Blitz looked disgruntled.

I turned to Sawbuck and Mr. Theodore. "This looks to be a long night. You two best find some chairs until Mr. Pike deigns to arrive."

***

We waited and waited. And waited. Finally, Honor went out to get four dinner wraps from the bistro down the street, and we ate in silence.

Three hours later, a Constable came in. "Mr. Pike wishes to speak with Mrs. Spadros."

I followed the Constable to the front desk, Honor trailing behind.

There were less people in the huge room now, but it was still fairly busy. Mr. Pike stood beside the counter as if he owned the place.

Doyle Pike was probably the best defense lawyer in the city. He was lean, in his middle eighties, and very rich.

I didn't know why Tony hated the man so. But Mr. Pike had saved my life once before, and I felt confident he could help Blitz as well. "Good evening, sir. Thank you for coming."

Mr. Pike scrunched his face up in one of those "are you trying to pull a fast one on me?" sort of looks. "I'm only here because you're the Spadros Queen. But if you want me to do anything for you, we need to talk."

I glanced at the man behind the counter, who suddenly decided he had pressing business elsewhere. "So talk."

"I always did like you: you get to the point. So I'll do so as well." He leaned forward. "You owe me money. And I'm not doing one thing for you until I get it."

I still owed him about eight hundred dollars. I didn't have the thousand for the fine, but between several years of rent from my apothecary's shop and the take from the artists who rented the upper room of my apartments, I had saved up that much. For an instant, I felt annoyed: it'd take almost everything I had. "Done."

Mr. Pike's eyes widened. "Well, that changes matters. What sort of trouble have you gotten yourself into this time?"

I shrugged. "I was told my butler shot someone."

"Hmm," said Mr. Pike. "Why aren't you letting the miscreant hang?"

Really? "First off, he's my husband's cousin, and my Queensman. Second, he's claiming servant's right. He says I told him to. Which I don't understand." I shook my head. "In any case, I heard that the man he shot was a Mayoral candidate? So ..."

"I see," said Mr. Pike. "You want someone discreet." He snorted. "I'll need ten dollars a day —"

I gaped at him. "Ten **dollars**?"

"Plus expenses. The first week up front. Now. And I want the money you still owe me in the bank by noon tomorrow, or you can find your scoundrel a new lawyer."

The man was insufferable. "One moment." I returned to where Sawbuck and Blitz sat. "Ten," I said. "Do you have any cash on you?"

A quiet laugh burst from him. "How much is the old rat charging?"

I leaned over to whisper in his ear. "He wants seventy up front before he'll even come in here."

Sawbuck reached in his pocket and pulled out a billfold. In it was an impressive stack of tens, which he proceeded to count off. "Don't tell your husband I gave you this."

I laughed. "It's a loan, nothing more." The artists renting the room above the stairs by the hour paid well, plus the apothecary's rent ... I'd almost be out of money, but Ten would get repaid.

He grinned.

Blitz watched the exchange, horrified. "I —"

Sawbuck's head tilted, his hand shooting up beside his head to point towards the ceiling. "Remember what I said? Not a word."

Blitz groaned, resting his head upon his arms in a dejected fashion.

I returned to the front counter. Mr. Pike hadn't moved. Honor stood by, looking bored.

Mr. Pike pocketed the cash as if it had been seven pennies rather than a thousand times that. Then he turned to the man behind the counter, who'd been staring in awe at the exchange. "I want the prisoner — and his file — in the lawyer's room. Now."

The man jumped up like he'd been goosed. "Yes, sir."

"Now we'll get to the bottom of this," said Mr. Pike. "You can go on home, if you wish —"

"No," I said. "I want to stay with him. He's my servant, and it sounds as if I might've gotten him into this mess. Besides, my husband is wroth with me, and —"

Mr. Pike chuckled. "Not likely to get much sleep either way. Very well, you can stay. But let the man tell his own story. And encourage him to tell the truth. I can't do much once he starts lying to me."

The man behind the counter returned. "He's ready, sir."

I followed Mr. Pike down a long corridor and to the right, where a finely-laid room awaited. The chairs were polished wood with cushions of soft, brass-bound leather. The gently oval table was of the same fine wood. A manila file full of papers sat on the side closest to us. Blitz sat on the other side, a guard beside him.

Mr. Pike said to the guard, "Leave us."

Once the man left, I told Blitz, "This is Mr. Doyle Pike. He saved me in the trial, and he's willing to help you. You can speak here. But you must tell him everything, and completely true. Can you do that?"

Blitz nodded.

I let Mr. Pike take the chair across from Blitz, whilst I sat at the end of the oval, just a bit farther away, in hopes it might give Blitz some room.

Mr. Pike opened the file and looked through it. "This says you shot a Mr. Seth Pasha, a Mayoral candidate who came to your door."

Blitz glanced at me, then nodded.

Pasha ... the name was familiar. Polansky Kerr was going by that name. Lans Pasha. And Josie used the name Finette Pasha once when she came to my apartments. At first, I thought: *perhaps this could be Joe.*

But **Mr.** Pasha?

Joe wasn't married. And the last I'd spoken to him about it, Joe had denied having any other name but his own.

This had to be an uncle. Or perhaps some cousin.

Mr. Pike spoke to Blitz gently. "Can you tell me what happened?"

"He came to the door."

I leaned forward. "Who?"

Blitz shook his head. "The man who almost killed you."

I immediately remembered the assassin in the courthouse alley.

No, Jon killed that man.

Then I recalled another alley. "You mean Trey Louis?"

"No," Blitz said urgently. "It was the man who kept coming to our **door.** I told him to go away, that he'd been told if he came here again, I was to shoot him. He laughed and wouldn't leave. So I got my pistol and told him to go. He came towards me, so I shot him." He glanced at me, then away. "I don't think he believed I would do it until I pulled the gun. If he hadn't jumped aside, I'd have killed him, and good riddance."

"Blitz," I said. "I don't understand. Why shoot this man? I don't know anyone named Seth Pasha."

"Well, that's just it," Blitz said. "He's calling himself that, but it's that man who almost killed you." He glanced away, cheeks reddening. "With the fever. Joseph Kerr."

The Candidate

Joe was **back**? And Blitz **shot** him?

I gaped at Blitz. How could this be **Joe**?

The very last time we'd spoken, Joe said he was going to Azimoff.

Mr. Clubb said Joe left the city, and I hadn't seen him since.

Why would Joe come back pretending to be someone **else**? Even then, I didn't understand what was going on.

Blitz shook his head. "I should've just shut the door on him. But he made me so angry after all he did and said the last time. It's not right."

Mr. Pike sat blinking for a moment, then said, "So you thought this man was someone else —"

"No, it's him, all right," Blitz said. "Joseph Kerr. I'd stake my life on it."

"Well," Mr. Pike said, "you might just have. You're arrested for the attempted murder of a Mayoral candidate, done in front of three witnesses, all who happen to be police Constables." He glanced at the papers again. "They say the attack was sudden and unprovoked."

Blitz looked furious. "How was it **sudden**? I told him to leave twice, then that I was getting my gun and he'd best not be there when I returned." He glanced at me, then at Mr. Pike. "Or are these Constables saying otherwise?"

"They are." Mr. Pike picked up a page. "The suspect came to the door with a pistol and then fired upon the victim without warning."

Blitz rose. "That's a bold-faced **lie**!"

Mr. Pike held up one hand. "Settle yourself, son. There are a few ways we can handle this." He leaned back in his chair. "How about we go with the *error in persona* defense?" He turned to Blitz. "You believed this man was someone else, a man your Queen had ordered you to shoot if he returned. You gave him numerous chances to leave, but not only did he not, he advanced upon you, three Constables with him. In fear for your life, you were trapped by your Queen's commands and outnumbered." He shrugged. "You defended both your home and your Queen's honor."

Blitz sat, shoulders slumped. "It was Joseph Kerr. I know it was." He looked up at Mr. Pike and shrugged. "Okay. Fine. So you want me to lie."

"Was anyone else there?"

Blitz said, "My wife and little girl —"

Fear spiked my chest. **Ariana** was there?

"— I told Mary to run. She's with child, and —"

Mr. Pike clapped his hands with glee. "Wonderful! Outnumbered, a Queensman defends his pregnant wife and child against four home invaders, then is dragged into court for it. The tabloids will eat this **up!**"

Blitz looked hopeful. "You think so?"

Mr. Pike beamed. "I know so."

"There were people in the street who saw everything," Blitz said. "One said, 'why don't you coppers leave them alone?'"

"Very good," Mr. Pike said. "We'll get them to testify."

"Wait," I said. What if it really **was** Joe? I had to see. I had to know why he left. Why he returned. And he'd been **shot!** "Do we have to do this? Surely we can talk to the man. Was he hurt badly?"

"Looks like Mr. Spadros winged him," said Mr. Pike. "Nothing some salicylate won't cure."

I thought for a minute. "If I could just speak with him, or with whoever the Assistant District Attorney is on this case, maybe we could settle this out of court."

Mr. Pike shrugged. "If that's what you want. I'll prepare to take it either direction." He stood, speaking to Blitz. "In either case, you'll have to stay in lockup." He glanced at me. "Just until we can get everyone in the same room."

***

By the time I got home, it was late. Alan told me Tony had gone to my bed, and the evening news had arrived. I brought it to my study, not wishing to wake Tony.

The *Bridges Daily* society section held a full page spread:

EXCLUSIVE STORY: CLUBB AND DIAMOND

Bride and groom tell all

A lovely photo of Lance and Gardena dominated the scene. They sat an appropriate distance apart, gazing at each other with love.

I read the story with interest, yet with more than a little horror. It told of how young Lance Clubb and Gardena Diamond defied their fathers to create their son one New Year's Eve at the Grand Ball. How in fear of their fathers, they both hid the truth. How Lance had secretly supported his son financially through the years, finally telling the truth to his father as the two Families became friends. Their joy at finally being able to marry and have the family they'd dreamed of.

Nicely done.

Mostly a lie, but still, nicely done.

They'd woven in the truth: Tony in fear of his father, refusing to marry the woman he'd dishonored himself for. His payments to Julius Diamond, forced by blackmail. Never allowed to even so much as see his son until Julius Diamond was forced to relent by the Clubbs.

The tabloids in my Queen's box the next day weren't so pretty.

The headlines went to every extreme, from

A HAPPY TALE OF YOUNG LOVE

to

DIAMOND REWARDED FOR SPINSTER'S WHOREDOM?

I hoped Gardena didn't suffer too much for that last sentiment.

Tony routinely left before I woke, so I wasn't able to speak with him about either Blitz or the evening news.

I knew Tony still had feelings for Gardena Diamond, even after everything she and her Family had done to him. And he adored his little son. To see his firstborn given to the Clubbs — who hadn't even publicly acknowledged him as Patriarch — must be galling.

But he'd said little to me about it.

After transferring the money to Mr. Pike's bank account, I returned to the Market Center police station.

Mr. Pike and I went to a different room this time. Much larger, it reminded me a bit of Mr. Pike's office: soft rugs, deep-stained wooden floors, a fine wooden desk and furnishings.

An older, stern-faced man sat behind the desk. A man with straight golden hair and his left arm in a sling sat with his back to me. Another much older man sat to the right of the golden-haired man, tapping him on his right arm when we entered.

All the men rose, the ones seated turning to face us. I didn't recognize either of the older men, but the man with the sling was Joe.

It was Joe, but Joe as I'd never seen him. His hair had been lightened, his thick curls straightened, his skin darkened. His eyes were more gray than green now, and the upper lids were fuller, folding over like you'd see in one of the Harts.

He could've been an "under the table" son of anyone in the city.

I peered at him. "Joe?"

The man beamed.

This was Joe. No one else in the world smiled like that.

"I'm sorry, madam. But you evidently have me confused with someone else."

I stared at him, most definitely confused. It was Joe. He spoke with Joe's voice. He moved and smiled like Joe. But for some reason, he felt it important not to say so. "Okay, I'll play along. What is it you want?"

Joe drew back, glancing at the other men. "I don't want trouble with the Families. I only wanted to meet the people I wish to serve as Mayor."

What was he playing at? "Why do you want to be Mayor?"

"Why, to improve the city, of course."

What was his angle? "Do you want an apology? Is that it? Make my man crawl after I wouldn't see you?"

Amusement flashed past Joe's eyes, then he quickly recovered. "Madam, I assure you, I've never had the pleasure of meeting you before now. But an apology and some reimbursement for my doctor's visit would go a long way."

The older man beside him said, "Mr. Pasha —"

Joe held up a hand. "Now, now ... there's no need to make an ordeal out of this. The Spadros Queen has come herself to apologize for her man's behavior. That's got to count for something. And I'm sure a dollar to pay the doctor wouldn't be too much to ask. Then we can get back to the business of becoming our next Mayor."

The man — who I'm assuming was Joe's lawyer — seemed ready to grumble, but relented. "Very well, sir."

I glanced at Mr. Pike, who shrugged. I said, "Might I speak with Mr. ... Pasha, is it?" I glanced at the others. "Privately?"

The man behind the desk said, "So we're settling this amicably?"

Joe's lawyer said, "It seems that way."

"Very well," said the man behind the desk. "I'll notify the Court." He made a dismissive gesture. "You're welcome to collect your man and discuss anything you like elsewhere. I have work to do."

I almost laughed. "Mr. Pike, see Mr. Spadros to my carriage. This should only take a minute."

Joe's lawyer and Mr. Pike left Joe and I standing in the hall.

I had to ask; I might not get another chance. "Where's Josie?"

His manner became guarded. "She's safe." He glanced aside. "Don't try to see her, Jacqui. She's — she's not ready."

Okay, I thought. There was a lot I didn't understand. But I didn't have much time. "Pasha, huh? This has to be your grandfather's doing."

Joe nodded. "He registered us when we were small." He looked away, shaking his head. "Why did he let us stay in the Pot all those years?"

"Hmph," I said, feeling disgruntled. "**Mr.** Pasha?"

"Yeah." Joe sounded defensive. "I got married. So? You said you didn't want me."

"Hmm." I did say so. Some days, I regretted it. But not that day. I ran my thumb along his cheek, expecting his color to wipe off on my glove. But it didn't. "Where did you get all this done?"

Joe grinned. "You can get almost anything you want done in Azimoff."

Joe got married. "Congratulations. Anyone I know?"

"I don't think so," Joe said. "A widow. She has a son. I've known her for some time."

Why would he marry a widow? And I just didn't see him as a father. "Why are you running for Mayor?"

Joe's manner became earnest. "Someone has to!" He pointed down the hall; Mr. Theodore stood at parade rest at the end of it, watching us. "Just look outside, and —"

"I know about your grandfather. What he's done."

Joe took a step back. "Then you know why I'm running for Mayor."

I looked in Joe's strange darkened face, his strange changed eyes. *He got married.* "I liked you better the way you were."

He shrugged.

"There's been allegations against you. You and Josie."

Joe gazed placidly back, unconcerned. "What sort of allegations?"

"Crazy things. That you're in with what your grandfather's doing."

He gave me his beautiful smile, so full of life and freedom. "People will say anything to pull others down. You know that."

Even in his changed form, the way he made me feel ...

Gods, I loved him.

Then I sighed. Joe got married. This ... whatever this was between us ... was over. It had to be over. I turned away. "Good luck, Mr. Pasha. I hope this brings you whatever you're looking for."

I left him standing there and returned to my carriage.

Blitz sat inside. "What happened?"

"I don't know what Joe's play is here. But he did this on purpose. Came to the apartments, I mean."

Blitz nodded.

Had all this just been to show he had power over me? To force me to come to him? To make Blitz look the Fool? Was he that petty?

It'd been a reckless, ill-advised play. What if Blitz had killed him? "If he comes to the apartments again, shut the door on him. If he approaches you on the street, walk away, no matter how he tries to provoke you. If he lays a hand on you, shout for the police. Shout for our men. I'll tell them to watch over you." I leaned forward. "Under no circumstances are you to give anyone cause to accuse us."

Blitz looked hesitant, then nodded.

"Something's going on here I don't understand." Did Joe think he didn't look good enough? I never thought him to be vain, not like that.

Blitz had leaned forward, elbows on his knees, staring at his hands.

Now I knew why Joe went to Azimoff. And that he opposed his grandfather.

But why change his appearance? So he'd look more like the Four Families? It seemed to me he'd be considered less trustworthy if anyone found out he'd done so, not more.

Patricia Loofbourrow

The Shame

When we arrived at the apartments, Mr. Theodore went home. I brought Blitz inside, to the delight of Mary and Ariana. Blitz held Ariana on his lap. Mary insisted I sit, and went to the kitchen.

I sat across the coffee table in one of their armchairs. Even in the heat, sitting in my apartments felt pleasant. "It's nice to be here again."

Mary handed me and Blitz glasses of cooled tea, and sat beside him. "Thank you for bringing him home."

I smiled at her. "My pleasure." Then I thought of what Mr. Theodore had said. Should I speak of it here?

Blitz said, "What is it?"

"Oh. Perhaps this is much too nosy, but your brother said something strange: that between the lot of you he'd not be able to get a hundred dollars, much less pay that fine. Does my husband pay so little?"

Blitz laughed. "Ah, yes. Teddy." He put his hand to his chin. "I shouldn't say this, but, well ... my brothers have their flaws. Like anyone, I suppose." He hesitated.

"No need to say," I said quickly.

Blitz snorted. "It's no secret: Teddy likes to gamble. He's over at the little casino as much as he's out front."

"Oh," I said. "Too much, I take it."

Blitz shrugged. "He pays his bills and feeds his children, so it's no concern of mine. But I do wish he'd save some for the future."

"So what's your flaw?" If I were to be nosy, I supposed I should be entirely so.

86

He seemed to honestly consider the question. "I tend to be distrustful, suspicious even. And I have to be reminded to consider the good in things." He smiled fondly to himself. "My Mary helps with that."

I felt touched at his love for his wife. "If those are all your flaws, sir, then you're a lucky man."

As I returned to Spadros Manor, I considered the matter in regards to myself. I knew what people had said. Blitz had called me reckless, and I suppose back then, I was. At the time, though, I could see little into my own self, and make less of an accounting.

When we're young, we think we know all there is to know, call everyone else fools for not seeing it, acting boldly upon it.

How little did I know.

***

Tony had canceled his afternoon meeting, and asked if we might spend tea-time out in the gardens.

Even though the sun was low in the sky, the day was sweltering. The shade of the arbor seemed only slightly cooler. Why did he want to come out here?

I glanced at little Millie. She was well out of earshot, but curtsied low at my glance.

Tony sat watching me as we ate. "Something troubles you," he said. "What is it?"

I realized I hadn't told him what happened over the past twenty-four hours. So I did. "Joe obviously wanted to get my attention. He got it, for what that's worth." I shook my head. "I don't know what to say."

"I'm sorry," Tony said. "It must hurt that he chose someone else so easily."

A wave of grief hit; tears came to my eyes. I felt angry with myself. "You were there. I told him to go. I have no one to blame."

Tony said quietly, "I wouldn't have married someone else." To my surprise, he reached over to take my hand. "Not even Miss Gardena. Not even if she wanted me." He let go and leaned back, looking towards the gardens. "I know what it's like to be so besotted with someone you can't see reason, even when the truth is in your face. Even when everyone — including them — is shouting it." He slumped forward to rest his elbows on his knees, his face in his hands. "The way she looked at Master Lance at the meeting ... she's never looked at me that way. I —"

"Oh, Tony," I said, feeling grieved for him. "I'm so very sorry."

He let his hands fall in front of him with a shrug. "I have no one to blame but myself. If it were not for the Dealer's mercy in giving me a son, I'd despair even of life for the horrible choices I've made in this matter."

Being reminded of little Roland made me smile, yet I felt sad for them both. Surely the boy didn't understand the enormity of all that went on around him just to keep him alive. To keep him safe. From everyone, even his own people. "Every day that passes brings him one more day to grow and learn." I remembered what Jonathan and Gardena had said to me about what they'd been taught growing up. "The Diamonds will instruct him well, and keep him safe. Master Lancelot has a brave and loving heart. He cares for the boy, and will give him all he needs. You'll be there to help your son prosper, to offer encouragement, connections, and to teach him the truth of his heritage." The Eldest had given me a gift when she spoke of my ancestors in the Cathedral. "All we can do is protect Roland until he has the strength and men to protect himself."

Tony nodded, seeming a bit more hopeful. "There's one thing I don't understand. Why would you go to Doyle Pike after all the times he's cheated you?"

"He saved my life." I shrugged. "I didn't know where else to turn."

Tony's face turned sour, and I knew he now regretted his refusal to help me with Blitz.

We sat quietly eating, and yet something troubled me. "Why do you hate Mr. Pike? What happened between you?"

He sighed. "I hoped never to see that man again. Yet he seems to continually follow me." He shook his head. "I was just a boy, really, and had been told I was a father and a Diamond enemy all in one day. I couldn't go to Roy: I felt terrified of what he might do. So I asked someone on the street who was the best lawyer." He let out a bitter laugh. "I can't believe I was so stupid! If the man had recognized me, I'd probably be dead now."

I saw where this was going. "And the lawyer was Doyle Pike."

"When he heard of my troubles, he fairly cackled!" Tony's shoulders slumped. "I think he did try to help, but I should've known nothing would come of it. And then I was trapped. Not only was I being blackmailed by Miss Gardena's father, but by him as well."

An astonished laugh burst from me. "Wait. Doyle Pike's been blackmailing you?"

"He did. Nigh on ten years. And he tried blackmail to get the money you owed him from me after the trial. I said I'd not pay. It was your debt and you claimed you would pay it. I also told him that if he spoke one word about my son, I'd send my father after him. If he survived, I'd have him up on blackmail charges, and add incitement to murder." He glanced away. "After I told my — Roy — about Roland, I told Pike I didn't care what he said." He looked at me. "Tell the world if he liked. Yet he's not said a thing." His eyes grew distant. "I wonder what's changed."

"You stood up to him," I said. "And something about him is different since the trial."

"Yes," Tony said.

"His wife's death must have affected him also."

"Oh?"

"Yes. Back when the trains stopped running. He tried to get her to Azimoff, but the Clubbs — well, that man running the station — impeded his way. He got her there too late."

"Good gods," Tony said. "Well, that would affect anyone."

Yet I helped him. Without my intervention, Mr. Pike's wife might never have been allowed to leave.

Had Doyle Pike regretted his blackmail of Tony? Wondered if he'd been wrong to antagonize the Families? Thought Tony might have been part of impeding his wife's treatment? "This is complex."

Tony's eyebrows raised. "I don't understand."

I sat there pondering this, staring towards the table. "During the trial, Mr. Pike didn't believe me. On any of it." A bitter laugh burst from me. "I'm sure he thought me guilty. Until ... what was it? I told him I'd not let them kill me when I'd done nothing wrong. That the men who did do this stood mocking. His attitude towards me changed. He changed." I looked up at Tony. "He still doesn't trust me, not really. He demanded the rest of his money —"

"Oh?"

I shrugged. "About eight hundred. But ... I don't know. I can't explain it." I laughed, not intending to. "But I think he's been re-evaluating his life's choices."

Tony tilted his head, eyes wide, then nodded. "As should we all."

I sighed. "I regret so much in my life I don't know where to begin."

Tony smiled a fake smile, taking my hand. "Begin with your son. Daisy tells me you've not visited Ace for some time. He asks for you."

I don't know why this surprised me. "Why should he care about **me**?"

"You're his mother, that's why —"

"Every time I see him, I think of how I caused him to suffer. I can't stop weeping." I shook my head. "That can't possibly help."

Tony let go of my hand, then leaned over to place his upon my arm. "His life is not all suffering. He's a good boy. He's learning to speak, to play, to walk." He rose, taking my hand. "Come see."

So I let him lead me to Acevedo's rooms, those rooms which used to be Roy's, where Roy had been tortured by his mother. But I pushed the image of Roy's pain-stricken face from my mind, willing myself to smile.

Acevedo had two small strangely-made canes, by which he toddled across the room on his good leg. The canes had an addition to the top, which ended in a strap which curved around his forearm.

Daisy sang as he went to her, and cheered when he threw his arms — and canes — round her. She glanced up. "Look! There's Mama!"

He turned to me, beaming.

I knelt before him, feeling truly touched. "Oh, my! You have another tooth! And look at how fast you go!"

"Mama!" He hobbled across the room to me, right as he reached me throwing his arms wide.

The canes poked me on my sides, came round to hit my back, but it was nothing, really, compared to seeing my boy almost run. "Oh, my baby," I sobbed. "You're such a good boy. Such a very good boy."

Ace pulled back. "No cry, Mama." He patted my shoulder, his canes dangling. "Happy!"

I smiled at him. "I **am** happy. I'm **so** happy. You're doing so **well**!"

"Mama," Ace said, "kick ba." A ball the size of a man's fist sat in the middle of the room, and he tried to kick it as he balanced on his canes. He managed to kick, but toppled backwards.

I let out a little scream, terrified to see my boy fall.

He landed hard, but rolled over with a smile.

Daisy said, "Uh — oh!" She went to him, helped him up. "You kicked it this time! Good job."

He beamed proudly at her. Then he said to me, "Kick ba!"

I glanced at everyone. "You want me to kick the ball?" We didn't have balls back home like this — we kicked rocks in the Pot sometimes, just for fun. But in this place, even showing an ankle was scandalous; women didn't do sport here.

"Mama," Ace said sternly. "Kick. Ba!"

I laughed. "Very well." So I lifted my skirts just enough to gently kick the ball towards him.

"Guh-jaa, Mama." Ace still stood next to Daisy, and he kicked the ball at me, falling back onto her a bit. "Kick ba!"

So we kicked the ball back and forth for some time, Tony watching, as the afternoon sun painted the landscape golden outside the windows.

It was one of the happiest days of my life.

***

After Ace tired and his hip began to hurt, Daisy got him his medicine and put him to nap before dinner. Tony went downstairs. I went to my rooms.

My boy was doing well.

I hadn't dared to hope he might do well.

I wanted him to do well, yet it frightened me. I didn't want to lose him.

I sat at my tea-table sobbing, not even sure why. I hated to see Ace in those canes, when he should be running on grass, playing with other children. I hated to see him in that horrible room that used to belong to Roy. I felt terrified sometimes to even be near him. I didn't want anything to happen to him because of me.

But I made myself think of his sunny smile, his joy at kicking a ball.

Him feeling the need to comfort me.

I felt ashamed.

What was **wrong** with me? I'd been able to smile through the years of not consenting to marriage with Tony. After years of beatings and humiliations by Roy. Yet when my boy was doing well, I'd made him feel like he needed to comfort **me**!

After all he'd gone through, my abandonment and neglect, my wishing him dead in the womb — he still loved me. He still cared about me.

I cried for so long I must have fallen asleep, because I woke to Shanna shaking my shoulder. "Time to dress for dinner, mum."

***

During dinner, I said, "I'd fancy a turn in the gardens after our meal. Would you join me?"

Tony looked curious as to what I might have to say, but he nodded.

Alan gestured to a maid, who hurried out, and soon several maids moved through and out to the veranda.

Our meals were often silent. With Alan Pearson at his post beside the doors to the preparation room, Chef Monsieur carving the meats, several of Alan's brothers waiting table, and the occasional maid bringing something up from below, we could never speak freely at table. Vents above and below made the house comfortable, but also brought our words to ears we might not even know.

The conversation became more lively when we had company, but those days were few and far between. With my husband's mother Molly kept captive upstairs in a guest room since her revelations over a year earlier, we'd not given a formal dinner at our home in some time.

Once dinner was finished, Alan pulled out my chair whilst Tony came round to help me rise (quite unnecessary, but tradition). Tony and I went out to the gardens. Clear votives had been set, candles burning along our path. Men walked in the distance, the moon faintly illuminating them.

Tony had put some of Mr. Hart's men to patrolling the far meadow. Those who looked more like Spadros men patrolled the block out front.

Our gardens had a long oval path of packed earth running well beyond the length of the house. A path from the stables ran in at the far end to our right. Another path at the second turn stretched out to the meadows. Between the two lay an arbor with a tea-table. A lit votive had been set upon the table. Three chairs were there. We sat.

Tony leaned his cane upon the table's edge. "What troubles you?"

I shrugged. *Many things.* "Roy's journal. Have you considered what might be in it?"

Tony shook his head. "I hadn't considered it at all. The ravings of a madman, perhaps. Little more."

I wasn't sure. "I only hope he didn't write anything that our enemies might use against us."

Tony shrugged. "As I told Mr. Hart, we'll know soon enough."

"That's my concern. Why steal it? If it contains something to harm our Family, we should know beforehand, so we might plan our play when the information's revealed."

Tony blinked, giving a slight frown. "What do you suggest?"

I took a deep breath, feeling shaky, and let it out. I knew he wouldn't like this. "Who might know what lies in there? Master Bresciane and your mother come to mind."

Master Seven Bresciane, otherwise known as the Knife Man, had been Roy's right hand man. A feared man, but so far, a truthful one.

Tony nodded slowly, eyes narrowing. "And?"

"I know you said I must not speak with your mother again. But —"

He laughed. "You wish to anyway."

"Only so you don't need to." I straightened. "I am prepared. I promise you, whatever she says, I will not allow her to upset me."

"Thank you for consulting me." Tony sat quietly for a moment, then said, "I will agree only if you tell me why you really want to see her."

I felt taken aback. "Do I need another reason?"

"I know you, Jacqui, much better, I think, than you know yourself. You seek information by any means, and wouldn't bother with her unless you believed there was more than one thing to be gained from it."

I pondered this for some time. "I've often wondered how we lost the aristocrats. If what Miss Gardena and Master Jack said at the meeting is true, we lost them when they were children." I looked up at him. "Perhaps even before Roy ever found me. The business with 'Old Pasha setting things straight'."

Tony nodded.

"So I did wish to see what your mother thought of that. Because I can't believe it was only my being drunk, or not seeing them, or even me being a Pot rag, that would cause them to abandon us."

"Don't refer to yourself in that way," Tony said. "You're not like that."

I shrugged. "It's what they say. They see me as some cheap dirty whore dressed up as Queen, who —"

Tony hit the table. "Stop it!" He looked truly angry, but then his eyes grew moist, and he spoke quietly. "Please. Stop. I can't bear to hear this, least of all from your mouth." He took my hand, peered into my eyes. "You are **so** much more than where you were born, where you were raised. More even than who your ancestors were."

I shook my head, thinking of the Eldest. He had no idea.

"You are as worthy to be Queen as I am to be King, perhaps more so." He let go of my hand, looked away. "And if anyone disputes that, to Hell with them."

I felt surprised: Tony didn't often use such language.

He turned to me. "You may go. Get anything you can from her. I'll speak with my father's man." He nodded then. "You're right, of course: we must know what might be there, before we're surprised with it."

I felt rather pleased with myself. Maybe Tony did love me after all.

As we returned to the Manor, I began to plot. I might not get many more chances with Molly Hogan Spadros, and she'd try anything to sway me to her favor. What did I want?

I needed information about the city, about the aristocrats, anything that would help us know how to fight them.

Knowing her, she'd never give up information without a price, even if it meant the lives of her family. But what would she want in return?

Most things, I couldn't give her. But by the time I got to her rooms, I had some answers.

The Queen

Two guards stood in front of her door, one of Tony's men and one of Mr. Hart's. Molly's maid sat with some mending beyond the door, rising to curtsy low when I approached. I spoke to Tony's man. "I've been sent by my husband to speak with her."

He opened the door for me. "Yes, mum."

Molly Hogan Spadros sat in front of her dressing-table, brushing out her long raven hair. When she saw me in the mirror, she smirked. "The Death Card approaches!"

I'm sure she thought this would rattle me. But I never took on the Queen's mantle, neither in my mind nor heart, and I no longer cared what Molly thought of me. "So now we are two."

This seemed to disturb her. "What do you want?"

I gestured to the brush in her hand. "May I?"

She shrugged.

I took the brush and began on her hair. Perhaps me acting as her maid would make her feel superior enough for her to let down her guard. "How would you like it?"

She didn't meet my eye. "It doesn't matter. I get no visitors here."

It was hot on the upper story, the windows locked on the outside by Tony's command. I drew her thick curls, much looser than mine, away from her face, then braided them atop her head. "How did the aristocrats come to hate us so?"

Molly snorted. "When did they ever **not** hate us?"

I put down the brush. "What do you mean?"

"Perhaps you don't recall your lessons."

I smiled: she had no idea. But I let her continue.

"When the first Acevedo Spadros took the city, he stripped the aristocrats of their power. He took their lands in the countryside to give to his men. He allowed their homes in the city center to lie in ruins. Then he took their country homes when it pleased him." Her tone turned vindictive. "And my Vedo's grandmother — the first Acevedo's wife — she was a conniving, manipulative bitch!" She made the sign of the Board, crossing her arms to grasp her shoulders. "Thank the gods she died before my boys were born."

I felt taken aback. "Why do you say that?"

Molly shook her head, a sour look upon her face. "She looked pleasant, made a show of religion ... but scratch the surface and everything was about her and what she could get for herself. It was her second marriage, you know. I wouldn't have put it past her to have killed her first husband so as to get his inheritance."

"Oh," I said, quite surprised.

"I feel truly sorry for Vedo's Ma. She was a lovely woman. The poor thing couldn't wait to get out of their home. Her cousin was the first to court her, and they eloped. She had the wedding the very instant she could find a Dealer who would believe she was of age."

"My word." This explained quite a bit.

"Well, of course, it was a terrible scandal. The entire family came round to bring them — well, her husband Caballo Roman in particular — back into the deck. His father was high in the Business by then, and took their elopement as a personal affront." She sighed. "The other mistresses spoke of it all the time."

I stared at her reflection. The **other** mistresses?

Molly let out a laugh. "Oh, yes, they all had them. Vedo used to bring me along to parties with his men." She glanced away. "But Mrs. Liza drank altogether too much, even when with child, and often caused a scene." Molly took a deep breath, let it out. "I don't think the aristocrats ever saw us as anything but wild and unprincipled."

That made sense. "What about your Mr. Acevedo?" This would be Roy's father — and, as it turned out, Tony's. "How did they see him?"

She shrugged, let out a breath. "Vedo was a ruthless man." She sat silent for a moment. "A strong man. But he wasn't one for social niceties. Nor was he overly intelligent." She hesitated, then spoke quickly. "Don't get me wrong. He was smart in the Business. It was what he thought truly mattered. I don't think that to his dying day he understood that the aristocracy really ran the city. And they hated him."

I began to see what had happened. "So Mrs. Maria's disappearance —"

"Was entirely blamed on him. The rumors! Vedo couldn't understand it." She laughed. "He never loved his wife: it was wholly arranged. But he found the idea of him killing **her** utterly absurd! He had no idea anyone blamed him until he saw it in the tabloids. He never paid much attention to her once Roy came along, so he assumed she'd found someone else." She shrugged. "He did look for her, but only to kill whoever she'd run off with, as was his duty."

And Roy had the social graces of a rock. Tony marrying a Pot rag probably only confirmed their decision to overthrow us — likely made decades ago — to be the correct one.

I drew up a chair and sat beside her. Now the real questions. "You're no coward. And you were friends with Julius and Rachel Diamond. You had to eventually learn about Master Jonathan's claim. Why did you not get me out of here? The truth, now."

She looked away. "Even as a child, Tony loved you. He was attached to you. He spoke of nothing else. If you'd just disappeared, it would've hurt him deeply."

"And?"

She faced me, her manner fierce. "And nothing. Your mother hated it, but she couldn't do much about it. She eventually came to think as I did." She fell silent.

"Which was?"

"I thought it'd be good for you to be trained in the Business. Particularly Roy's side of it. For when we got you free. You could one day become the Lady of Diamond, the mother of a Hart heir. If you played your Hand as well as I believed you could, the information might become useful to you."

"So you wanted me to spy against your own **husband**?"

Molly shrugged.

I just peered at her, unable to fathom the workings of her mind.

"So what did you really come here about? Tony cares nothing about these things."

"Oh! Thank you for reminding me. Apparently Roy kept a private journal. Mr. Hart says it's gone missing."

Molly raised her eyebrows.

"Would you happen to know what might be in it?"

"I didn't even know he kept one," Molly said. "So I can't help you there." She leaned back, hand to chin. "But it's interesting that someone might take it."

"Tony wants to learn what's in there before we're surprised by it."

Molly snorted. "No, **you** want to learn what's in there." She shifted in her seat. "My son's capable enough, but your thoughts are different as night and day." She crossed one knee over the other. "I've helped you. Now you help me. I want to see my grandson."

I shook my head. "Tony will never allow that, and you know it." I rose. "But I can have a bottle of your choice sent up here."

"Hmm." Molly sounded surprised. "Two bottles. Merlot will do."

It'd be kept by the guards and poured for her into paper cups, but hopefully that would suffice.

I turned to go; she said, "One of these days you're going to need me."

Two could play this game. Without facing her, I shrugged and left.

The Rival

As the days passed, and my baskets filled, my mind became clearer. I could sit, walk, play my piano, and yet not weep.

I even went to an event, something one of the few aristocrats still with the Spadros Family had put together. Honor and Mr. Theodore went with me, as did Shanna. A luncheon, and the long list of speakers ended with a Mayoral candidate, a man named David Korol.

I'd welcomed the chance to hear one of Joe's rivals for this election speak, and as I'd recalled hearing this particular man's name mentioned before, I listened with interest.

An ordinary-looking man: straight brown hair, skin a bit lighter than mine, brown eyes. A bit taller than Tony and perhaps a decade older, with an expressive face and a pugnacious stance. A working man, for sure, his voice clear and strong through the microphone before him. "For generations," said Mr. Korol, "we've had the opportunity to live under the Mayoral system. As our Families have made the streets safe again, brought us free from the terror of sudden violence, new aspirations have come forth. Schooling for our children. Protections for the elderly, so that those without friends or family might end their days free from the terror of starvation and death in the Pot." He looked at me. "I believe the first Acevedo Spadros wished the same, which is why I welcome our city's Queen today."

How dare this man try to ingratiate himself with me?

Everyone looked to me and applauded; I forced myself to smile.

"We can do better. We can **be** better. One day, we might even rule ourselves —"

Shanna, standing behind me, gasped.

" — create a true republic. Just think! Representation from the common folk of each quadrant in the way things are run."

I stared at him, shocked that he would say such things in front of one of the Families.

"We have more power than we know," Mr. Korol said. "Our ancestors did not throw off the yoke of the Kerr Dynasty to have their children enslaved to four others."

The room went dead silent, and everyone turned to me.

Did I agree with him? It came very close to what Thrace Pike had said to me the night I went to hear him speak. I surveyed the man up on stage and shrugged.

I almost laughed at the way jaws dropped around the room. In their eyes, the gears turned. I could see them recall my origins, my homeland. Their speculations as to what my thoughts might be on the matter. I nodded to Mr. Korol, recalling Tony's speech to the quadrant after we'd rooted out his rebellious men. I spoke clearly, making sure all heard. "My husband and the Spadros quadrant aim to be enlightened as well as secure." I smiled at him. "We welcome all forms of theoretical discourse, sir. Please continue."

Mr. Theodore, standing behind me and to my left, snorted quietly.

Mr. Korol drew back a bit, evidently surprised at my reaction. Then he bowed low. "Our Queen is gracious." He took a deep shaky breath, as if he'd expected not to be allowed to continue. "Well, um," he glanced at the small pad in his hand. "Our city faces many challenges, the first being the plight of the slums. The Dealers do their best, but we need jobs, care for the streets, fair rents and wages —"

As I listened to him go on, I recalled what Tony said: *We rule here at the sufferance of the aristocracy.* Would they allow ideas like this to continue?

They might. They wanted the Four Families gone, and this fellow did too. I could see it in his eyes, the passion he had for true self-governance.

Then he said something which startled me. "We must get to the whole, entire truth of our history to be able to make these changes. Move forward. The only solution, my friends, is truth!"

The only solution is truth. As the room burst into applause, I remembered little Ariana singing those words. And I watched as he waved to the crowd, as he left the stage and took his seat. If people on 33 1/3 Street were saying these words often enough for a two-year-old to know them, his candidacy was a strong one.

I didn't know what Tony — or the other Families, for that matter — thought of this man. But Tony needed to be aware of what he was saying.

After all was done (as I thought might happen), Mr. Korol was presented to me. He bowed low. "Thank you for attending."

I did not extend my hand. "My pleasure."

"I had to arrange this," he said. "Once I'd heard Mr. Pasha was given a private audience, I couldn't allow his influence to go unchecked."

"Mr. Pasha, sir?"

He chuckled, spoke low. "Surely you didn't think the issue with your," he glanced at Mr. Theodore, "Queensman would go unremarked."

So he knew of Blitz, and of his family. Who was this man? "You have remarkable resources, sir."

Mr. Korol smiled: I could see why men followed him. "A motivated man can do much, mum. And I wish to make a change entire —"

That was what Etienne Hart had said, up in the meeting with the other Inventors atop the Opera House after the trains stopped. *What's needed is a change entire.*

" — surely this city of ours deserves better."

I had to get out of here. "It was a pleasure to meet you, sir, but I must be off."

***

After tea, I went to Tony. "Who are our candidates for Mayor?"

Tony listed off a few names, but no one that I knew.

"And ... we're actually trying to win, right?"

Tony smiled at me as if I were a child. "Of course. Why would you not think so?"

"Because I don't see any of these names in the papers. I don't see them being endorsed. I've not been invited to their speeches. It worries me."

"Why? Just like before, with Mayor Badugi, we tell the people who to vote for, and they vote."

"But what about with Mayor Freezout?"

Tony chuckled fondly. "His winning was part of our plan. So Roy could beat him in front of everyone." He nodded sagely. "Everyone knows not to cross us."

Yes, they feared Roy. But did they fear Tony? "I don't know if it's that simple." I took a breath. "I just came back from a speech by one of the candidates, a Mr. David Korol."

"Yes, I know. And?"

"The things he's saying are being repeated out by my apartments. And something he said just now ... it was the same thing Mr. Etienne said after that meeting with the Inventors."

His eyes narrowed. "So?"

"It's obvious the Red Dog Gang wants the Bridges Strangler to win. You and Jon both thought so! We must do more to stop him."

Tony laughed. "A man saying something you don't like doesn't mean he's the Strangler."

"I didn't say that." Why would he not listen? "Ask Mr. Theodore, then. Ask Honor, even. They heard it all. This man is dangerous. His ideas are dangerous. He might even be with the Red Dog Gang. And people are following him."

Tony closed his book. "What do you suggest?"

I didn't know. "Maybe have our men give speeches? Or go round and meet people?"

Tony snorted. "Jacqui, these are Family men. They've risen up through the streets. Everyone already knows them." He gave me a warm smile, like you would a child. "Don't fret yourself; it's all been planned. A man from each quadrant will win enough of the vote to qualify, around 20-30 percent of the total vote, then we'll have a run-off. Just like usual." He returned to his book. "Mr. Badugi was our man, so it's Diamond quadrant's turn this time for their man to win." He let out a soft laugh. "We might have a few holdouts. But we go to the non-Family homes and let them know we're watching them vote. They know what'll happen if they don't toe the line."

I shook my head. "I have a bad feeling about this."

Tony patted my hand. "I'm just glad you felt well enough to attend." He gave my hand a soft squeeze, then returned to his book. Then he

)h. I almost forgot. I have your bank statement! For some
as in my mail instead of Mr. Howell's." An envelope lay
olded again upon the table beside him, and he handed it to
me. "Your apothecary man Mr. Pok-Deng paid his rent. And even after
paying Mr. Pike, you have a nice amount saved!" His tone was fond. "I'm
very proud of you."

I had maybe eighty dollars in there, and I still needed to pay Ten his
seventy back. But something inside loosened. "Thanks. I have tried."

"It's good for you to have your own wealth," Tony said. "I don't ever
want you to feel trapped here."

I didn't. "But —"

"I mean it, Jacqui. You are free to go or stay as you choose." He took
my hand. "Remember that."

I knelt before him. "I stay because I love you, Tony. That's all." I kissed
his hand, lay my forehead upon it, eyes burning. "I wish to all the gods
you could love me again, like you used to."

Tony sighed, withdrew his hand, and when I looked up at him, he'd
gone back to reading his book.

I rose and left, not understanding anything. I suppose if I had, things
would've turned out much differently.

The Location

The next day, Tony called me to his study. He sat behind his desk, and to my astonishment, all four of the Inventors stood there before him.

Our Inventor, Piros Gosi, now wore a charcoal gray tweed suit a bit too large for him, and a pair of silver-rimmed spectacles. The Clubb Inventor, Lori Cuarenta, was an attractive woman of half past thirty, with the pale skin and freckles of the Clubbs, along with brown hair and eyes. The new Hart Inventor, Liu Madiao, was a short thin man about my color, with a shock of unruly black hair which stood on end despite evident attempts at pomade. Diamond Inventor Themba Jotepa was the youngest, just past twenty and dark as a Diamond.

I'd met three of the four so far, but I particularly liked Inventor Jotepa. From what I'd seen so far, the man was both brilliant and insightful.

I felt surprised to see them there. Chairs had been set out as before. Why had Tony made them stand? I curtsied low. "Welcome."

Tony glanced at me, then gestured the chair beside him. "Please, everyone. Sit."

So we did.

Tony said, "To what do we owe this honor?"

The Inventors looked between themselves. Lori Cuarenta spoke. "Mr. Spadros, we've come to an impasse that we hope you and your wife might be able to help solve."

Tony nodded soberly, yet he sounded surprised. "How might Spadros quadrant aid the Inventors' Board?"

Inventor Cuarenta said, "After careful thought, we have surmised that the issue with the heat plaguing the city must be due to a problem with the ventilation systems of the dome."

Tony nodded, yet I could tell he didn't understand.

"There must be windows of some sort," Inventor Jotepa said, "to allow hot air to escape. Much as vents in the roof prevent the temperatures in an attic from rising too high."

Tony said, "I see."

Inventor Cuarenta said, "We chartered a zeppelin to survey the dome. Of course, we can't possibly survey every part of a dome 600 miles across. But we reasoned the windows were most likely to be near the center of the city, over the city proper."

"That makes sense," Tony said.

"But we've encountered a problem. The city proper is over a thousand square miles, and of course with the sloping nature of the dome itself, this adds a great deal to the search." She took a deep breath, let it out. "Yet with these windows shut, even upon close examination it's nigh upon impossible to tell where exactly they are."

Tony leaned forward, and I could tell he felt annoyed. "And I can help ... how?"

Inventor Cuarenta's voice shook. "Sir, your beloved former Inventor, Maxim Call, believed that the Dealers had some knowledge of these matters." She glanced at the other Inventors, and they nodded. "They've refused to see us." She turned to me. "We'd hoped you might be able to speak with them."

I felt surprised. "Me? Why?"

Inventor Madiao said, "We believe there is still some link between the Dealers and the Cathedral. Perhaps with your connections there —"

I felt grieved. "I have none. The last time I went to the Cathedral, I was told not to return." I'd been rebuked, called their enemy. But I didn't want to say that here, not to them.

The Inventors reacted as one, as if pushed back by some unseen force.

Inventor Cuarenta said, "I see."

I felt their eyes on me. "I'd go again, if I thought there'd be any hope of a welcome."

Tony stood, so the rest of us did as well. "Perhaps if we all went to the Dealers directly."

Inventor Jotepa said, "An excellent idea."

Tony gave a thin smile, not looking at the man. "Let me show you to the parlor. It'll take time to prepare my carriage."

I gaped at him. "You want to go now?"

He didn't look at me. "I think these good Inventors have waited long enough." He gestured to the door. "Please, everyone, come with me. I'll have refreshments set up for you."

Inventor Gosi said, "That's very kind of you, sir."

So Tony told Alan to fetch cooled tea with chipped ice. We got the Inventors settled, and went to change into clothes for the street.

I had Shanna select my best summer walking dress, a pale gray linen trimmed in sage green.

Once all was ready, we went to the closest poorhouse, the one by the Gap. I'd have liked to have seen the newest poorhouse, which was several miles south of this one, but since Tony had already given instruction to the driver, I had no choice in the matter.

The poorhouse hadn't changed much since last I saw it: a long, squat structure of gray stone with a roof to match. Tony's men had apparently gone ahead: several of the elderly Ladies stood out front to meet us.

Their deep green robes were well-worn, faded to a hue closer to the sage in my dress than the forest green of their counterparts. One of them approached, apparently in frightened awe of so many dignitaries. "How might we help?"

By his demeanor, Tony had spoken with this woman before. "Blessed Lady, we come in peace. We seek any advice your people might give us as to locating the ventilation windows in the dome above us."

The woman's eyes widened. "I know of no such thing!" She glanced back, and the others seemed equally mystified. "We'd be happy to speak with our superiors on the matter."

Tony, myself, and the Inventors glanced at each other: the Inventors merely shrugged. Tony bowed low. "That would be most helpful."

A curious crowd had begun to gather. The Dealers returned inside.

Tony said to the Inventors, "Well, I won't keep you. You'll be informed of their reply the moment they do so." He smiled at them. "My regards to your Patriarchs. Have a safe trip."

The Inventors nodded and smiled and soon we were all on our way.

Yet I wondered at us going to bother these old Ladies in the first place. Could they really have known anything of importance about the workings of the dome?

The Labels

A few days later, Duchess Sophia Whist returned for an audience. "My Queen, I have considered the matter we spoke of last time." She drew a paper from her handbag.

I gazed at her. The woman's hands shook, and she looked even paler than she normally was. "You may speak to me on any matter without fear of harm to you and yours."

She took a deep breath, color returning to her face. "Well, mum, I believe it to be ... um ..."

"Yes?"

"Well, mum ... Mr. Roy."

I nodded. "What about Mr. Roy?"

Her voice shook. "Well, um, he was ... um, quite fearsome. Callous. Rude. Many thought he could be even ... well ..." She gave me a frightened glance. "Mad."

"I don't know," I said quietly. "Perhaps he was."

She blinked, evidently surprised by my answer. Then she recovered, grasping her paper more firmly. "He wasn't well-liked, mum. I had just come out, um, for my debut, when his mother disappeared. Most thought it to be the work of his father, but I heard whispers that he ..." She gave me another frightened glance, then said, "had his own mother **killed!**"

I nodded. Only a few days before his murder, he confessed to me that he'd tortured and killed her in the months after his wedding to Molly. "And what of —" I almost said, "the Queen Mother," but Tony had stripped her of her title. "Mrs. Molly?"

The woman's face went white. "S-she t-tried, mum. Truly she did. People like — liked her. She —"

"She's not dead. She's resting upstairs right now."

The woman took a deep breath, hands shaking. "Yes, mum."

Did people think Tony had **killed** her? "I'm glad to hear that people like her. What happened when she tried?"

"Well, mum," she said, seeming more at ease, "people have eyes. She was a beaten woman. No amount of makeup or stories could hide that." She let out a breath. "Some of us begged her to go to the Dealers. We even offered to bring her to them. B-but she seemed afraid to. It only made them hate Mr. Roy more."

"I see." People didn't trust this woman anymore, she'd told me that. Anything she repeated would be taken as Family propaganda. But I supposed it wouldn't hurt. "You may tell anyone you wish of our talk today." I leaned forward. "Mrs. Molly betrayed both her husband and her son, our Patriarchs. More than once, I might add. She has received fair punishment. And in his vast and gentle mercy, Mr. Anthony has allowed her to live. She's well-fed and in comfort." I smiled to myself. "I had a bottle of wine sent to her just the other day."

"Yes, mum."

It took all the self-control I had not to drink the other one myself. "But she's tried to get word to our enemies, even since her confinement!"

Duchess Sophia sat back, mouth open. "Why?"

I scoffed. "Who knows why she does what she does? In any case, she's well. More well than she deserves."

I saw the gears turning in her eyes, and I realized I'd said more than I should. I hadn't intended to place blame upon Molly for Roy's treatment of her, but how much of it had been spawned by him learning of her betrayals? "Rest assured, she's both safe and well, in rooms reserved for our guests upstairs. Why, even Patriarchs and Inventors have slept in those rooms!"

"Yes, mum."

I wasn't sure she believed me. But I couldn't risk bringing her up there — no telling what Molly might do or say in order to escape. "Is there anything else I should know?"

"No, mum. Thank you for your trust in me. If I learn anything at all, I'll bring to you at once."

***

When I consider it now, I left the boxes in the basement untouched for far too long. At the time, I feared going down there, feared that the information might upset the balance I'd created in my baskets of the mind. For several days, even the thought of going downstairs to face the boxes there felt daunting. So much information!

But Tony became more distant and angry with each passing day. I couldn't let him think I ignored my duty.

One day, I gained the courage to bring Shanna and Daisy down to help label the boxes.

The sheer number of boxes seemed incredible. How could there be so much information on these people, yet no proof of what they were doing?

Acevedo toddled round the table on his canes giggling as we labeled each box with the Family the box had come from and a number.

When the labelling was finally done, I felt I might be able to handle this. But I still didn't dare open any of them.

Acevedo raised his arms, the canes dangling on their armbands. "Mama, up."

Laughing, I picked him up with both arms, as settling him on my hip usually hurt him. I turned him to face all the boxes, kissing his cheek. "See? Look, how pretty!"

Of course, we weren't done, not by any stretch of the imagination. Each box had to have its contents labeled by Family and box number, entered into a ledger with a description of what it held. It would become useful if I — or anyone who might assist me — found something important, so we might recall where it came from or how it connected to everything else.

And the servants really couldn't help. Shanna and the housemaids had their own work to do. Daisy was too preoccupied with watching Acevedo and keeping track of his schedule to do much more than move a box. And my little son wanted nothing more than to sit on my lap, play ball with me ... which although I loved, made doing anything useful rather difficult.

When Mr. Howell came by to collect my Queen's box later on, I asked him, "Did my husband speak with you about finding me an office?"

Although he'd come into my study, he seemed clearly uncomfortable there. "I did, mum. But I've not found anything in Spadros quadrant I'd feel good about."

"Really? Why?"

"One had neighbors I'd distrust with your safety. Others have passages in secret we've not been able to fully explore. Another seemed good, but isn't defensible." He sighed. "I hate to say it, but many of the buildings in Spadros quadrant just aren't suitable."

"Keep looking," I said, trying to be encouraging. "I trust you'll find something."

Secretly, I thought the man over-worried. Not always a bad thing, when I knew people intended me dead.

The Menace

It was almost time to dress for dinner when Alan knocked upon my study door. "Mr. Anthony wishes to see you in his study."

"Oh." What could Tony possibly want to speak of now? "Thank you."

He bowed and left.

So I went down the hall and knocked.

"Come in."

Tony stood in front of his desk, a tabloid in hand. The front page read:

SPADROS QUEENSMAN ATTACKS!

I realized my mouth was open, and shut it. "Why wasn't this in my Queen's box?"

Tony let out a breath, shoulders drooping. "I asked your secretary to have anything on the matter brought to me directly." He threw the tabloid on the desk, pacing about. "The article, of course, has an account from the Constables who supposedly witnessed the attack."

"This is ridiculous. Their account is entirely different than what Blitz says happened. After speaking with him, I tend to believe his version."

Tony shook his head. "This is serious, Jacqui." He picked the tabloid up, handed it over.

After an entirely erroneous version of the matter, and leaving out the fact that Joe and I had settled this amicably, the article read:

> Several of the Mayoral candidates, led by front-runner David Korol, have filed petition with the Merca Federal Union's Office of Voting Rights in Hub. They charge that fair and free elections are impossible in the current climate, and ask that

measures to protect candidate and voter rights be taken similar
to that of other city-states.

I let my hand drop to my side. "What does that mean?"

"I'm not sure," Tony said. "I'm having my lawyers investigate the
matter. I also sent word to Mrs. Clubb. She knows how these outsiders
operate much better than I do."

I nodded. This all sounded bad. "What can we do about it?"

Tony shrugged. "Short of assassination, I don't rightly know."

***

After dinner, Tony asked me to walk with him in the gardens. It was late,
the moon not yet up, and the air fairly smoldered. Not a hint of a breeze,
and I wondered why he would ask me out in such weather.

We went down the back steps and down the path to my gardens, then
turned to the right. The silhouettes of our guards — and Mr. Hart's — on
the rise in the distance, backlit by the lights of the city beyond and the
stars beyond that, gave me comfort. We should be safe here.

The servants had put candles out in low, clear glass votives along the
packed dirt path. But only to our left, leaving Tony's face in darkness as
we walked. He held my hand in his right, his cane in his left.

That he held my hand surprised me, given that he hadn't for many a
day. He'd shared my bed every night, yet pulled away from any touch.

I didn't know what was going on inside him.

The night beyond the votives' glow once our guards passed out of
sight seemed dark, menacing. As usual, I had my pistol in its calf holster.
But I wore my house shoes; I wished I might also have my boot-knife.

The arbor approached; it lay dark.

We continued past the arbor with its tea-table we'd frequented the
month or so since Tony first gave indication he wished to give his heart
back to me. Did he mean to go out into the meadow? What did he wish to
say that required such secrecy?

The path turned to the left, and left we went, along the flowers wilting
from the heat, past the turning to the far meadow, and I thought: perhaps
he just wants to walk with me.

That thought felt encouraging. For him to simply want my presence
nearby, to know someone was with him ... it seemed a good thing.

We made the next turn to the left, and a figure appeared at the far end. A man, dark of skin, standing casually hand-on-pistol.

As we moved closer, I saw clothing of brown, of dark gray. He shifted slightly, and I knew him. I smiled, and he smiled in return.

"Good evening, Mr. Theodore," I said.

Tony seemed surprised. "Why, Teddy, whatever are you doing here, and not home with your family?"

"Blitz thought she might feel better with me here."

Tony nodded. "She might."

I felt confused. "Why? What's going on?"

Tony smiled at me. "You'll see."

He led me to the next turn, Mr. Theodore following six paces behind, but casually, as if we merely strolled the garden.

We did. Merely stroll the garden. But I kept looking round. Why would Blitz send his oldest brother to make me feel better ... in my own garden? It puzzled me. It meant something was to happen which could alarm and disturb me.

It meant Tony — and Blitz — already knew what it was.

So why not tell me? What could it possibly be?

"Calm yourself," said Tony. "You have nothing to fear."

Was I so transparent?

I glanced back; Mr. Theodore tipped his cap to me.

Perhaps I was.

We made the next turn, again to our left, and the path was clear. No figures stood in our way.

With a sigh of relief, I squeezed Tony's hand, and he gave me his arm.

This simple gesture touched me so I almost began to cry; if not for Mr. Theodore behind us, I might have. And I can't say, even now, why it did.

But I felt closer to him then, safer, and I began to enjoy the stroll, the humid night air, the tiny breezes that the fluttering of my dress made.

The thought always comes to me, as it has every day of the last twenty years: *Why did I not enjoy my time with him when I had it?*

The walkway to the veranda steps came and went. So Tony had something in mind to tell me still, something Blitz thought I'd feel better about ... with Mr. Theodore here?

I couldn't imagine what it might be.

But then I began to think.

It seemed to me that Tony waited for something.

We continued to walk. Crickets chirped here and there. Up ahead, the arbor approached.

A lit votive had been set upon the table, its glow casting onto the packed dirt path. A figure sat there, hooded and cloaked.

I felt a spike of anger. Several had come to us cloaked over the years: the *Bridges Daily* editor Mr. Blackberry, Lance Clubb, his mother. But never at our arbor. Never around our table.

Tony led me to the table. The figure sat peering at the candle's flame, hands bare. A man, dark of skin, wearing black.

He looked up at us.

Dropping to a crouch, I drew my pistol from its calf holster and stood. I pointed it at him, hands shaking. "How dare you come here?"

Unbothered, Jack Diamond gave me a wry smile. "I was invited."

The Visitor

Tony snapped, "Mrs. Spadros! For shame! Put the gun down."

Jack Diamond rose, spreading his arms wide. His traveling clothes, dark brown and expensive, yet well-used and of Nitivali make. His hair, recently cut to a length much like his deceased twin Jonathan once wore. Yet Jack wore it brushed back. Several four-inch lengths hung braided perhaps an inch from his left temple. Small, deep brown beads dangled on each. "I'm unarmed." He turned to Tony, amused. "Is this how guests are greeted in Spadros quadrant?"

Tony looked angry. "It is not." He turned to me and said, "Put that gun down at once."

Mr. Theodore looked ready to laugh.

Feeling foolish, I cleared the chamber, holstered my gun. "I'm sorry."

"As they say in sport," Jack Diamond mused, "no blood, no foul."

Mr. Theodore did laugh then, and for some reason that made me feel better, as Blitz had said I would.

And I suddenly liked Mr. Theodore much more than I had. Not that I didn't like him before. But he seemed in that moment not just a guard, not just the oldest brother to Blitz, but a real person. A man of middle age who dressed in tweed, read the newspaper every day, and liked to gamble. A man with a wife and children waiting at home.

Being delayed by me.

"Very well." I crossed my arms, annoyed with Jack for coming to my home, sitting at my table without my leave. "What do you want?"

Jack's hands flew to his chest. "Me? Nothing. As I said, I was invited." He gestured to the chairs. "Shall we?"

Tony, Jack and I sat, making an equal-side triangle. Tony rested his cane upon the edge of the table. For a short time, we peered at each other.

Tony said, "I asked you here because I wish us to work together —"

I blurted out, "**What?**"

Tony held up a hand. "We **must** work together! I am sick and tired of this feud. Of my wife's nightmares. Of anything that stops us from finding the villain that stalks our Families and destroying him." He pointed at me and at Jack. "You will work together. Is that clear?"

Jack surveyed me archly. "I have no objection."

But I did. He looked too much like his twin Jonathan. My ... Jon.

I couldn't look at him without grief washing over me.

Just being at the same table with this man, knowing he'd vowed to kill me ... torture me ... it made my skin crawl. "You renounce your threats?"

The look Jack gave made me think he heard my thoughts ... or perhaps saw them on my face. "I ... I never truly **meant** them. As I told you in the factory." An instant of dismay crossed his eyes. "Did you not believe me?"

"I don't know what to believe. For a decade, you publicly wage war against me. Now I'm supposed to take your word it was all fakery? What better way to destroy me than to be invited to my home?" I glanced at Tony, whose face revealed nothing. "To be 'forced' to work with me?"

Mr. Theodore stood by perhaps three paces off, just close enough to be lit in the candle's glow, his face also revealing nothing.

Jack Diamond leaned back, glancing away. "You may believe me, or not. Work with me, or not." He leaned forward then, placing his arms on the table. "But I will do as I said I would, with or without you: prove Polansky Kerr IV and his kin are scoundrels and traitors to the Families they swore to serve in exchange for freedom from the Pot." He glanced at Tony, then me. "Are you with us in this?"

Us?

He left unsaid that which I felt sure Tony was thinking: *Or are you so besotted with Joseph Kerr that you would impede our bringing Joe's grandfather to justice?*

"I'm with my husband, of course," I said. "But I'm not convinced Mr. Polansky is any worse than the rest of you. And I don't believe his grandchildren share in Mr. Kerr's crimes." I leaned forward, pointing at him. "That I intend to prove."

"Fair enough," Jack said lightly. "How might we proceed?"

What was he doing? Why was he really here? "Surely you don't think to just waltz in and —"

"That's exactly what will happen," Tony said. "All the information is here. Mrs. Clubb believes in you, but she also believes you can't do this alone. And I agree." He let out a breath. "I can be of little use: I'm trying to run a quadrant." At this, he nodded at Jack Diamond. "He's going down the same lines of inquiry, so I asked him to help." He gave me a small thin smile. "In return, we've agreed to keep his secret. So you have to be discreet. No more weapons, no more accusations, and no more **outbursts!** Is that clear?"

I felt exasperated with this man. "What am I supposed to call him then? Hmm?"

Jack rose, his words falling into a slow, heavy Nitivali drawl. "Mr. Hector Jackson, Esquire, at your service, ma'am. A simple country solicitor, here in Bridges for my young cousin's wedding." He bowed low. "I aim to be of whatever assistance you and yours might require."

I stared at him, mouth open, trying my best not to laugh. "Is that really what they sound like over there?"

Jack turned to Tony; the accent vanished. "When shall I return?"

"At your convenience," Tony said. He turned to glare at me. "By then my wife should have learned some courtesy."

***

Once Jack left (by way of the stable gates), we returned to path in front of the veranda steps.

Tony rounded on me, furious. "Why are you acting like this?"

"I don't trust him. I don't believe him."

"Why?"

"He was my first suspect in David Bryce's abduction. Did you know?"

"I thought you'd cleared him of that."

Millie stood on the veranda by the door to the dining room. I wasn't entirely sure I trusted her, either. But Tony had promoted her, not me. "His mother said he wasn't the one who came to them before the boy was taken. That doesn't mean he wasn't involved." I lowered my voice. "I found the boy in his Party Time factory, or had you forgotten?"

Tony spoke softly. "Jacqui ... you were the one who told me he couldn't have done all that. That someone had betrayed him, let those scoundrels into his factory without his knowledge. Jon and I spoke at length about this after Master Jack faked his death. He wasn't involved." Tony glanced away, then back. "I don't know how to get through to you!"

Years of nightmares, the memories of Jack screaming hate at me, his rage — true rage — at the Grand Ball ...

My heart pounded, the lights felt too bright. "That was one thing I could never speak to Jon about. I could tell, even though he never said a word, that he'd take Jack's side."

"There's no side here. Yes, Jon loved his brother. But do you really think if Jack meant you harm, that Jon wouldn't stand with you?" He stopped, as if he was going to say more but decided not to.

I felt as if he'd stabbed me. I turned away, not willing for either of these people to see me cry. Jon loved me. But he loved his brother. My enemy. "Please don't make me work with this man."

Tony laughed, so softly I could barely hear it. "Can you do this on your own?"

When he put it that way ... "No."

"You'll be in your home, under guard by your own men." His hand fell warm upon my shoulder. "He wants to help."

That sparked anger within me, and I flung his hand away, turning to face him. "What better way to impede us, to learn what we know, than to volunteer to help? Get inside our walls, see our —"

"Wait," Tony said. "You really think he's with the Red Dog Gang, after all this time."

Did I? He'd claimed to have been investigating them. Investigating Polansky Kerr IV. "I don't know," I said. "But he knows I've been the main one looking into the matter." I took a breath, trying to keep my voice from shaking. "He shows up at our meeting above the Grand Ballhouse, but only to throw out the one piece of information which is sure to upset and distract: Jon's feelings for me."

Tony looked hesitant.

"It's too ... too obvious. It's what the Red Dog Gang has done since the beginning: use distraction and harm to keep me from learning the truth about them."

"In that case," said Tony, "perhaps the best thing to do is to keep him close at hand."

Why did Tony want this man in our home so badly?

Tony said, "I'll have him followed by men who don't know who he is. We'll see what he does, who he speaks to." He took my chin, raised my face to look in my eyes. "He wants to be here. We may as well use him for our benefit."

***

That night, Tony's words haunted me. *He wants to be here. We may as well use him for our benefit.*

This wasn't like him at all.

Tony had changed: he'd become hard, calculating. I didn't know why.

***

Early that next morning, after I'd dressed but before breakfast, I went to Acevedo's rooms. Daisy had my little Ace dressed already. Alan stood beside Ace's tea table setting breakfast plates for them both.

Ace shouted, "Mama!" He tried to climb from his chair to come to me.

I went to him. "My dear boy." I hugged him. "What have we here?"

"Beffiss," Ace said.

"Oh, how lovely!" I looked up at Alan. "I look forward to it."

Alan said, "Might I bring a plate for you, mum?"

"I can't stay," I said.

"Very well," said Alan, sounding remarkably like his father, and left.

"Go on, eat," I said to Ace. "I want to speak with Miss Daisy."

I brought her aside. "A Mr. Jackson will be coming to visit most frequently. But unless Mr. Anthony commands it, you are never to allow this man to so much as catch a glimpse of my son." I peered into her eyes. "Do you understand?"

"Yes, mum," said Daisy. "You fear him."

I took a deep breath, heart pounding. "I don't know why he's here or what he hopes to learn, but I'll not have my son become part of his plan."

She quickly nodded. "I'll guard your boy with my life."

A carriage went past, and Ace stiffened in fear. "Daisy?"

A flash of jealousy: he called for her, not me!

Daisy said quickly, "All's well, my love."

I took a deep breath, heart pounding. Him calling for her was normal: she'd been there through all his pain, all his fears. "There's one more thing: he must become accustomed to the carriages. There may come a day where we must leave in a hurry, and he mustn't cry out."

Daisy nodded, face pale. "Yes, mum. I'll bring him to the stables first. All children like horses."

I turned to Ace, smiling. "Miss Daisy's taking you on an adventure!"

He beamed at me.

I left feeling sad, disturbed, lonely. None of this seemed right. But since the attack, this was how it was, and I had to make sure my baby was never, ever put into harm's way again.

***

In my Queen's box that morning — right underneath all the letters — lay a Diamond tabloid. The front headline read:

YOUNG DIAMOND RUNS WEEPING — TO SPADROS!

My first thought was: so Mr. Eight Howell knew about Roland. Tony must have told him.

My second thought: someone at Alexander Clubb's graveside service had spoken of the boy's most private, grief-filled moment ... to a tabloid.

This shocked and angered me. Was nothing sacred?

The article held all sort of speculation. Who was this boy? Why had he been at Alexander Clubb's private graveside memorial?

And it brought up the rumors of Tony's frequent trips to Diamond, the rumors of his affairs there. How did a Diamond child know Anthony Spadros this well? Had Julius Diamond been in secret talks with the Spadros Patriarch?

I shook my head. Someone at Mr. Clubb's graveside was false. Whoever printed that had no consideration for the boy's safety.

The only good part of this was that somehow, still, no one had learned the true name of Roland's father. And I feared what might happen if anyone did learn of it.

***

Jack Diamond arrived well after luncheon in a private, medium-gray Diamond-quadrant carriage, sporting white draft horses and gray leather tack clasped with steel. The horses marked him as Family; the carriage marked his status — a distant cousin, perhaps, or someone who'd married-in. No one to warrant special attention.

We'd asked Alan to have the men out front stand watch, and inform us when Mr. Hector Jackson arrived.

Jack climbed from the carriage as a man of fifty might: slow movements, particular, even courtly — so different from his usual animated form. Of course, he looked much younger, as the dark of skin often did. He wore dark brown Nitivali-cut traveling garb, a black Stetson, and a set of round false spectacles trimmed in gold.

Alan and the men out front stared at him as if they'd seen a ghost.

Tony and I met him on the front porch. Tony appeared amused. "This is Mr. Hector Jackson of Nitivali," he said to no one in particular. "He's here in Bridges for Miss Gardena's wedding, and has kindly offered his help with our papers below."

Jack tipped his Stetson, his words slow and precise. "Well, sir, I'm much obliged to be of service."

Alan still looked alarmed. He blurted out, "Isn't Miss Gardena's wedding some months away?"

Tony snapped, "Mr. Pearson!"

"Now, now," Jack said. "Young men do say whatever comes to they mind." He turned to Alan. "Yes, sir, it surely is. But it's been many a day since I visited my cousins in Bridges, and I took a hiatus from the practice of law to come here." He smiled broadly. "They say a long vacation does a man good."

Alan gulped. "H-has anyone t-told you how much you look like M-master Jonathan?"

Jack laughed. "Many a time, sir!" He shook his head. "I only wish I could've had the pleasure of meeting the young man."

"Yeah," said Alan. "He was a good fellow. That he was. A real good one." He seemed downcast. "He and Mrs. Spadros were fast friends; he was here many a day."

"Ah," Jack drawled. "Fast friends. I do wish I might have seen it." He tipped his Stetson to Alan, then removed the hat and turned to Tony. "Might we begin?"

"Of course," Tony said. Then he turned to Alan. "Pray speak with the staff. I'd not like Mr. Jackson to be questioned at **every** turn whilst here."

Alan snapped to attention. "Yes, sir. At once, sir." He held the door for us to enter, then closed it behind us and hurried off.

I almost laughed. "You do draw attention," I said to Jack, "even in your present form."

Jack smiled broadly, hat in hand. He gestured to the hat stand; Tony's top hat hung there. "May I?"

Tony twitched. "Of course, sir — forgive me."

I could tell that Tony was more than a bit annoyed with Alan for his lapses today.

Jack hung his black Stetson upon the stand. "Don't be too terribly harsh with your men, sir. I get this reaction nigh upon everywhere I go, at least here in Bridges." He grinned fondly. "It seems your Master Jonathan was well-loved."

Tony took a deep breath, nodding, his eyes far away. "That he was."

I'd watched this with amazement. Jack's charade was consistent, believable. He had to have spent quite some time in Nitivali. Why?

"Let me show you to your rooms," Tony said.

"Thank you for the hospitality, sir," said Jack. "But that won't be necessary. I'd be happy to make the trip. There's so much to see and do."

Tony nodded slowly; it was clear he didn't understand. "Then let me at least offer some refreshment. Tea, perhaps?"

Our housekeeper Jane Pearson rushed in, took one look at Jack, and gasped. "My Alan was right!" Then remembering her manners, she curtsied to the floor.

"Hmm," Jack said. "Coffee, if you have it. With heavy cream. The more the better."

Tony laughed. "Let me give you a tour." He turned to Jane. "Coffee with cream for Mr. Jackson, tea for our Queen. In the workroom downstairs."

Jane, who had just risen, curtsied low. "At once, sir."

Somehow Honor and Mr. Theodore had appeared beside us.

So we made the rounds of all, ground floor and downstairs.

Tony and I had undertaken a huge argument after breakfast on the matter. Tony agreed at last never to allow the man upstairs, nor to ever indicate where our little Acevedo slept.

When we got to the basement room filled with boxes, a tray with tea and coffee sat next to the thick blank ledger I'd asked Alan to buy for this.

"Splendid," Jack said as he sat. "I do so love a good coffee."

"Then all you need do is ask. Be at ease, sir; the layout of the Manor is such that no one can listen here." Tony turned to Honor and Mr. Theodore. "This is my footman, Master Skip Honor, and my Queen's personal guard Mr. Theodore Sutherfield. They have been apprised of your particular situation, and are here to provide whatever you need."

So Mr. Theodore was my personal guard now? I almost laughed.

Jack seemed perfectly comfortable with the situation: no guards of his own, deep in the heart of his enemy's Manor. He sipped his coffee. "Excellent!"

I sat; Tony left.

Honor and Mr. Theodore stood across the hall facing us.

I surveyed the boxes of information all around us, heart pounding. This was too much like the search we'd done for people who might have wanted to harm Jonathan, when he went "missing." At Jack's behest.

As he drank, Jack peered at me, his dark eyes unreadable. Finally, he put down his cup. "Well, my dear, where might we begin?"

Honor came then, taking the cups and tray to set them upon a small table across the hall I'd not noticed before.

As far as Jack's question, I had no idea how to answer. I'd avoided coming into this room stuffed with information for so long that I'd almost forgotten what lay in it. I sighed, pulling the thick blank ledger towards us. "I suppose the first thing to do is to fill this."

***

124

Beginning at the stack of labeled boxes at the far left wall beside the door, we went through each piece in each box. Honor or Mr. Theodore would bring us a box. I'd select an item, affix a label to it, and summarize its contents aloud. Jack would then inscribe the item's contents and the number on the box which held it into the ledger.

At first, I couldn't see how some of the information was relevant to the Red Dog Gang. Receipts, notices, pamphlets. It was mind-numbingly tedious work, but Jack didn't seem to mind it at all.

"Fast friends." Jack seemed downcast. "I'm truly sorry for your loss."

Was he trying to upset me? "Not now," I snapped. "Besides, you already said that. After the meeting."

Jack flinched, but said nothing.

Honor looked at me sideways, as if wondering what was going on.

I'd have to talk with him later.

"I've brought much of what I've gathered," Jack said. "The documentation about the companies."

I nodded. "Then I suppose we may as well add it to the pile here."

Jack gestured warily to his breast pocket. "May I?"

I suppose he didn't want my gun pointed upon him again, and I felt a bit embarrassed at my rash response the night before. "You may."

He brought out an envelope and handed it to me. "A diagrammatic summary. If you require the original files, I can have them sent."

I had an instant of joy, immediately tamped down. I did so love diagrams. Yet I refused to give this man one inch of approval.

The information was much as Tony had said. Mr. Polansky had extensive holdings, in an impressive array. One company might oversee many others, who each oversaw as many of their own. Foodstuffs, warehouses, buildings, companies for insurance and investments. It spread across the entire city.

When had Tony been meeting with Jack Diamond? I sniffed, tossing the sheets back. "I don't think that will be necessary."

He accepted the papers as if a gift. "Then I will enter these into the ledgers as well."

To my surprise, he put them into Tony's boxes, which had been placed in such a way that on our current schedule we'd enter them last.

The order didn't matter, I decided. As long as we got everything looked at, I felt sure I could find what the Four Families needed.

We got through two boxes without further incident before Jack left, presumably for his hotel and dinner. He couldn't possibly return to Diamond Manor, not and keep his secret: that he wasn't dead.

As Jack's carriage drove off, I asked Honor and Mr. Theodore if I might speak with them out on the front porch. Tony lingered by the front door, clearly curious as to what I might say.

I said, "How much did you hear outside the meeting?"

Mr. Theodore gave a wry smile.

Honor raised his chin, eyes wary. "Enough. About our new guest."

I glanced at Tony, then lowered my voice so only these two might hear. "Then you must know: Jack Diamond and I have been at open war for over a decade. He has publicly threatened my life and health, more than once, in the presence of many witnesses, including Master Jonathan." I took a deep breath, feeling shaky. "I have been commanded to let that man in my presence. To work with him. But I do not trust him, and neither should you."

Mr. Theodore's eyes flickered to Tony, but neither of them spoke.

"That's all for now."

I was fairly sure Mr. Theodore would go straight to Tony, but that didn't matter. Tony knew I didn't trust Jack. As long as I pretended to, though, perhaps I might learn Jack's real motivations.

***

I had feared all that information down in the basement. I'd feared that it might upset my fragile basket system, send all the information swarming back to flood my mind.

But as it turned out, I knew where the boxes were, down in my real workroom, and to my astonishment, the information seemed to want to stay there.

Jack Diamond promised to return the next day, and so he did. At Tony's command, I met him at the door.

Tony's men, of course, were outside the front gates, patrolled the grounds. And Alan, of course, opened the door. But I felt a jolt of fear-anger-grief when I first saw Jack.

He stood calmly, hands clasped behind him. When he caught glimpse of me, he removed his black Stetson, bowing low. "Good day."

I nodded, took a step back. He'd added a cane to his disguise, cherry-wood stained with gold trim. The sight of it angered me. He'd used a wood I loved, that he had to know I loved: I'd redone the Manor in it.

And the cane reminded me too sharply of Jon.

Apparently my step back was all the invitation Jack needed: he handed his hat to Alan.

Alan said, "This way, sir."

Honor and Mr. Theodore stood several paces down the hall, hands both clasped in front of them as if twin.

I sighed. Was this to be my lot? Pretend politeness each day to a man I despised? "Would you care for some refreshment, sir?"

"You're too kind," said Jack.

Tony had given him the tour, so he made his way to the facilities closest by, beside Tony's library.

I hitched my chin at Honor and Mr. Theodore to follow him. I'd not give him the chance to learn anything about us he didn't know already.

Alan seemed perplexed.

I whispered, "I have been commanded to welcome this man. But I do not trust him. Be on your guard."

Alan nodded; his easy gentle manner disappeared.

In that instant, he reminded me of his sister Mary. She was the most amiable sort of person — until you threatened her family and home.

Once the three men returned, it struck me that the best way to tease out the truth was as Tony implied: play the gracious host.

I could do that. I'd lived in these quadrants a decade now, been the Spadros Family's "guest" for fourteen years. I'd learned how to pretend not to hate the people here. I smiled. "Come this way, sir."

It amused me the way this simple gesture stopped Jack Diamond in his tracks, his mouth open, his eyes wide. To me, this indicated that I was on the right path.

I'd learn why Jack was really here.

I'd learn who he worked for.

And then I would destroy him.

The Ability

As before, tea and coffee had been sent down to the workroom. Once we'd sat, I peered at Jack. Disarming him would be my best tactic. "How is Miss Gardena?"

At that, he gazed into the distance, with such a look of wistful fondness on his face that I felt utterly touched. He loved his sister, very much. "Busy."

I cleared my throat, tried to make my voice steady. I'd not seen Gardena for some time, and I missed her. I tightened my resolve: I would not cry in front of this man. "In what way?"

He snorted, amused. He picked up the cup with its saucer, took a drink of his coffee and rested the cup into its saucer before answering. "My dear girl, **you** may have been able to lounge about drinking the entire day, but for all purposes Dena's the Lady of Clubb. She has an enormous task ahead." He set the cup and saucer down. "Not only must she prepare for a wedding, she must woo a huge family who has every reason to hate her."

I felt surprised. "Hate her? Why?"

He leaned back, hand to chin. "Other than that she's taken any hope of their sons rising to rule the quadrant?" He shrugged, looking away, and spoke softly. "She's a Diamond! She's birthed a bastard, yet in their eyes has suffered naught for it." He shook his head. "The men are cold to her, or improper." At this, he shrugged. "Perhaps hoping to gain her charms for their own." He sighed. "But the women ... women can be vindictive."

I laughed without meaning to. Then I felt abashed. "I know exactly what you mean. I know all too well."

Jack blinked. "Ah. Yes. I dare say."

So he'd forgotten I was a Pot rag. Interesting.

"At least she has his mother's support," Jack said. "From what I've heard, that can be the most difficult."

I nodded, not really understanding. Before me on the table was an invoice for $2.53 for horse training. Our eyes met. "How did you come to be in Nitivali?"

"Ah." Jack leaned back and looked away, his elbow upon the arm of his chair, twisting the silver ring upon his left small finger. "As I told you in the meeting, I was making some investigations of my own." He twitched a bit, as if realizing something, and still not looking at me, made a dismissive gesture. "Nothing you would understand."

"Hmph," I said, feeling annoyed at his insult. "And did you learn what you needed to?"

He seemed to seriously consider this. "I'm not certain."

I leaned back, feeling smug. "I doubt your amateur questionings got very far. Perhaps you should turn the matter over to someone with experience."

Jack bristled. "Like you? We'd not be here if it weren't for your bungling."

"What do you mean?"

He rubbed the back of his neck, then leaned forward to rest his arms upon the table, face downcast. "Nothing. Forget it."

"I want to know. What have I done?"

He rose, not looking at me. "Pray excuse me; I need some air."

I said to Mr. Theodore, "Please show Mr. Jackson to the veranda."

After they left, I sat in thought for some time. Jack had learned something in Nitivali which still rankled. He blamed me — of all people — for what? The Red Dog Gang getting as far as it had?

I wasn't sure what I might have done differently. Every time I got very far, they'd do something, kill someone close to me. I put my elbows on the table, my face in my hands, all my regrets coming to mind. What could I have done?

I felt eyes upon me; Honor had been watching me, compassion on his face, snapping to attention when he realized I saw.

I sighed. "Say what you will."

Terror flashed through his eyes; he knelt. "Forgive me, mum."

I nodded. He was older than me, perhaps older than Blitz. He'd brought my tray every morning since I was a girl of sixteen. He and his lover — Tony's manservant Jacob Michaels — had sworn to me as Queensmen. Yet even after all this time, he was still afraid of me.

No, not of me. Of my position. Of who I was. Who I belonged to. What Tony and I could do to him — and his Jacob — at a word. At a whim.

I felt sad, alone, bleak. "Or don't, if you dare not."

This seemed to strengthen him. He stood. "It's only — I feel troubled to see you suffer so. Mum." He looked away. "I mean no offense."

I wondered why he thought I'd take offense at that. "None taken." Then I stayed silent, feeling he had more to say.

"Well, mum," he finally said. "It's just that so much has changed." His eyes seemed far away. "Even two years back, Mr. Roy was Patriarch ..."

My stepping from my carriage into that sea of blood upon my front garden felt a lifetime ago, yet I remember it as if it were yesterday. And before that, Roy's last words to me. Words that to my shame I dismissed, eager to be rid of him.

"... and, well, mum," Honor said. "My Ma told me nothing changes without changing everyone, even them that never hear of it." He looked down. "Like you throw a rock and the pond round the corner that can't even see it still ripples."

I felt touched. "Your Ma's a wise woman."

Honor bowed. "Thank you, mum." Then he took a deep breath. "I don't know what wrong this man's done to you, or even you to him. But he seems sincere." He shrugged, yet when he spoke next, his voice shook. "I knew Mrs. Dewey was false the moment I met her. Yet I said nothing." He swallowed, looked away. "I'll not make that mistake again."

I stared at him, utterly shocked.

"I'll take whatever punishment you give me, mum. Seeing that little boy of yours on his canes, knowing I could've at any time stopped it." He shook his head, not meeting my eye. "It'll haunt me 'til I die."

I could have, right then, had him, his Ma, his lover, all killed. Tony probably wouldn't even have objected. "I'm not going to hurt you."

"Thank you, mum."

All this time, I'd thought I could look in someone's eyes and know if they were false. But I'd had no inkling Amelia Dewey meant me this much harm for so long.

Had I been deluding myself this entire time?

***

Eventually, Jack returned with Mr. Theodore. He sat, not looking at me, and something about his stance spoke of deep grief.

What had he learned in Nitivali that grieved him so? "Mr. Jackson, forgive me for causing you pain. I spoke harshly, and I am sorry."

He gave a dismissive sort of shrug, shaking his head slightly, not looking at me. After a time, he said, "Let us continue." Other than what needed to be said, nothing more was spoken.

I felt grieved. Obviously the man went to great trouble, expense, and time to learn what he sought to, yet either had found nothing, or what he did find had upset him.

And after seeing this, I rubbed his face in his inexperience as an investigator. I'd been petty, cruel.

Why?

***

We got through the first stack on the first row by the door without further incident, making a pile of the boxes we'd catalogued in the bit of room past the table to put back once the entire row was complete. Jack left for wherever he went, and though it was still early yet, I went upstairs, meaning to look at some notes before time to dress for dinner.

Shanna had decided to bring out everything from my closets, and my clothing lay out in great piles upon my bed, chairs, tea-table, and hanging upon my doors. "My goodness," I said. "I'd sold everything when I left here. And look how much I have once more!"

Shanna giggled. "It is a right mound. I'm separating out the things you don't use anymore. Perhaps we might repurpose parts of them, or they might be given as gifts to those you feel worthy. Yuletide is coming up faster than I like."

I felt astonished at her foresight — my former lady's maid Amelia had never spoken of this. If she'd taken my clothing, well, I never noticed. "Please, continue. Perhaps I might even be of help."

Shanna smiled to herself. "No need, mum. We'll have to get you ready for dinner soon! But if you see something over here," she put her hand upon a lesser pile, "that you'd rather I kept, well —" At that, she giggled. "— then speak up!"

I went to the pile. Dresses Tony ordered for me when I moved back into Spadros Manor, which didn't fit since Acevedo was born. One that did fit had a stain which had never come out. I picked it up. "I do like this one. Perhaps we might turn it?"

Shanna took it and hung it over a door. "I'll send it to Miss Tenni."

I let out a sigh. Amelia Dewey would've done the work herself. But she was gone.

I'd ordered for everyone who'd betrayed us in those horrible days when Spadros Manor was attacked to be hunted down. Amelia's husband Peter had cut the wires to the large bell, presumably so we couldn't call for aid. Amelia knew he'd done it, and left us to fend for ourselves.

Shanna's words startled me. "I'm sorry to bring up bad memories."

I shook my head, annoyed with myself. "You've done nothing wrong."

I began moving items to create a new pile. And I found the maid's corset Madame Biltcliffe had made for me, oh four years and a half before. I laughed. I'd put my lockpicks into its upper front folds when I put it away, and later bought newer ones.

Shanna smiled warmly at me. "It's nice to see you smile, mum."

"One day I must tell you all about my business. I so enjoyed it. I've not run a case of my own in some time."

Shanna's eyebrows rose. "I imagine not, mum, being Queen and all."

I showed her the corset. "I may need this one day. And even if not, I'd like to keep it, to remember the friend who made it for me." I shook my head in astonishment. "I'd forgotten I even had this. I wonder how it never got sold at auction!"

Shanna shrugged. "I recall when Mr. Anthony had your things sent. Perhaps he thought it belonged to Mrs. Dewey."

I fingered the tan muslin. Rough material, but serviceable. I tried it on, not expecting it to fit me at all. But with all the turmoil, even though my figure had changed, I'd lost enough weight to get it round me. I chuckled to myself. "One day I might even have use for this." I handed it back to her, and she set it on a pillow. "Just think, we could sneak out on a lark."

Shanna's eyes widened. "Me, mum?" She looked as if she didn't know whether to be offended or amused. "I don't know, mum. It seems improper. For us both. And ... well, I'd not like to even pretend to go back to the days of washing pots until my hands bled."

I felt taken aback. Was this what those girls downstairs had to endure? "I'm sorry!"

Shanna curtsied quickly, looking away. "I should've said nothing. It was only the once, and I was set to sweeping and mopping for two weeks, so my hands should heal."

"Even so. No child should have to go through that."

Shanna's eyes were distant, thoughtful. "But we emerged intact." She shook her head, not meeting my eye. "I'd rather wash pots for the rest of my days than what those girls endure in the Pot." She twitched, gave me a horrified stare, then curtsied, face to the floor. "Please forgive me, dear Queen. I meant no offense upon you."

"Get up." I had no idea what to say. It was then that I understood what my Ma said to me, there in the park the day I'd seen her after so many years: *We need you! Don't you understand? Children are DYING without food, being used as whores by the hour, freezing to death in the winter.*

Shanna stood, face pale and downcast, her lashes wet.

"I'm not angry with you," I said, feeling humbled. "I was very fortunate; my mother had a patron who forbade my use." I would've said more, but I didn't know who was listening.

Shanna nodded, her face still downcast, and bit her lower lip.

All my life, I'd hated not being allowed to ascend to the position of whore, to follow the path of my friends, my family. To not have the respect of the Cathedral. I'd felt unworthy, not good enough, despised. I knew about the Masked Man's interference in my life, and I'd bitterly resented it.

That was why I'd hated Charles Hart so much when Jack Diamond told me the man was my true-born father. When I realized Mr. Hart had been the Masked Man, my mother's patron. The man who — I felt — kept me from growing up loved and happy.

But it came to me just then why my friend Poignee, once a girl who'd grown up with me, who'd played with me in the Pot, had turned so bitter. Why she and Ottilie and Treysa took money from the Red Dog Gang to steal my letters in the first place.

They'd suffered. Everyone in the Cathedral had. But through that shared suffering, they were respected, valued, a part of whatever the Eldest's plan was.

I'd forced my friends to leave their home, their family ... to go to a place where they were despised for doing the exact thing they'd grown up their entire lives being told was valuable. And I'd been the Lady of Spadros. Once I'd told Roy I wanted them there, they probably didn't feel as though they could say no.

Shanna still stood pale and frightened, as if waiting for me to speak.

So I did. "We've had very different lives. Although I've been in the quadrants ... well, I first came here at twelve, but I never really lived here until sixteen. So I suppose really, just ten years. Not that long. But I never imagined I'd be here, the Queen of Spadros." I shrugged. "In my home, we'd perhaps be friends."

Shanna took a step back, eyes wide.

 raised a hand. "I don't wish you to do anything you feel improper. What I mean is ..." What did I mean? "You may speak the truth to me on any subject, and I won't punish you. Do you understand?"

The color returned to Shanna's face, and she curtsied low. "Yes, mum. Thank you, mum."

It was then that I realized that as much as I wanted it, this woman could never become my friend. As the Queen of Spades, I'd never have a real friend. At least, not any of the quadrant-folk.

I was the highest-ranking woman in the city. To some, I was the Death Card, a woman who could kill at a glance, at the very twitch of a hand. And to top it all, I was a Pot rag: detestable, foul, something too horrible, too much for many to bear.

Jonathan Diamond hadn't cared about any of it. Jon had been a friend to me, more than I could've ever hoped for. Jonathan Diamond gave up everything, even to the point of letting Tony think he was a man-lover! Just to be close to me. Because he loved me.

He loved me, even more than his own life.

So of course, he was dead.

I took a deep breath: I didn't expect this conversation to happen, but I could use it to my advantage. "Besides, I need to know what my people say. You've helped me in this before, and I appreciate it."

In place of her sweet helping nature, a cunning realization came over her. I hated it. "Yes, mum. I can be your ears. Gladly." She curtsied low. "You do me great honor, mum."

This was the game. It had to be played. She was my lady's maid, already sworn to me. Now she would become my spy.

She likely saw the ability now to profit from me beyond what she gained from Tony, as Amelia had done for the Red Dog Gang.

How much had Amelia told them?

I turned to the pile of clothing, selecting a dress I hadn't worn in some time. "I think if something was done with this neckline, I'd like it better. The fabric chafes me."

In a flash, Shanna returned to being Lady's Maid to the Queen. "I'll have Miss Tenni look at this one as well."

I smiled at her, but I didn't feel it. Did anyone here ever speak the truth? Give their trust? Their hearts?

The more I saw of this place, the more monstrous it seemed.

At least I'd gotten to Shanna first.

It seemed that even I could learn something.

The Spy

The evening edition of the *Bridges Daily* had this report:

DREDGING SOLVES DIAMOND CRIMES

Police find secret tunnel under Diamond quadrant

I read the story with disbelief. From what the police guessed, the tunnel ran clear from the East River to the South, allowing them to dispose of bodies in the South River. Presumably, the intent of this would be — if the bodies were found — to blame Roy Spadros for the murders.

I imagined that the Diamonds were even now finding ways to block the tunnel, so the proof of it might not be traced back to wherever these bodies were coming from. But according to the forensics investigators, the angle of it ran directly below Diamond Manor!

Then I recalled: Gardena Diamond, her mother, and I. We'd been sitting at luncheon, over four years back.

This had to have been the secret Gardena had referred to, the one she never could tell me. Some enormous mechanism for digging! It would have seemed entirely ingenious, if not for all the bodies the Diamonds had sent along to the river.

Men. With all the things they could be doing to improve the city, why were they so intent on killing each other?

A dozen Diamond tabloids filled my Queen's box that day. Some calling this false, a Spadros conspiracy to attack the name and legacy of their Patriarchs. Others outraged, that the Diamonds should kill so many of their own people and blame it on others.

I cared nothing about it, only that it eased tensions between the two quadrants enough for our little Roland to live another day.

But thinking of Gardena reminded me that I still hadn't decided what to get her and Lance for their wedding present. I most decidedly needed to speak with Jack about it at his next visit.

Reading that report sent me into some thought, and after Tony fell asleep, I went to my tea-table overlooking the courtyard, a small candle on its stand to illuminate my journal.

I felt as if I wasn't digging deeply enough into Mr. Polansky's mystery. And I hadn't even begun to work towards exonerating Joe and Josie.

I had to do that before Jack found whatever it was he was looking for.

I needed more.

I'd begin with David Bryce.

I opened my journal-book and drew a line down a page's center. On the left of that page, I listed what I knew about David's abduction:

Taken during Yuletide, 1898.

In the Alley — no Signs but the Red Dog stamp upon the Wall.

Presumably seen by Eleanora Bryce and I when the Man in White and the Man in Brown carried a struggling small Form encased in Blankets to the Taxi.

Found alive January 1899 in Jack Diamond's Factory

No Signs of physical Harm. Serious Mental Distress. Will not speak.

But what were Joe and Josie doing that day?

I leaned back, going through my mind.

According to Josie, the day I found David had been the day of Joe's terrible accident. He'd been thrown from his horse, breaking his leg and arm. On the other side of the page, across from David's condition, I wrote:

Joe and Josie in the Countryside the day I found David. Joe Injured.

So I knew what they'd been doing **that** day. But I had no idea what they'd been doing a month earlier, during Yuletide.

With their grandfather at home, I imagined.

I really needed to at least find ...

Wait, I thought. Daisy used to be their maid.

Surely she would know whether they were at home that day.

I made a note on the upper corner of the page: Daisy re: J&J Yuletide.

Now I was getting somewhere.

But the next morning, Daisy just stared blankly at me. "I have no idea, mum. They left for the countryside at the start of Yule, so I went to my brother's home."

I wasn't sure what to say. How did they have money to travel to the countryside? Where did they stay? "Do you know where they went?"

She wouldn't look at me. "No, mum. They never told me much." She gave me a quick glance, shoulders hunched. "I don't wish to speak of that time, if you please, mum."

I remembered how harsh Josie was with her housekeeper Marja. "Were you mistreated there?"

Tears filled her eyes, and she didn't meet mine. "Yes, mum."

I put my hand on her shoulder. "Then we'll speak no more of it. Thank you for your help."

She curtsied to the floor. "You're so very kind, mum."

I smiled at her. "Stand up. Look at me."

Her eyes, nose, cheeks, all red.

"You hold my most precious gift. And so you have my greatest regard, more than any other woman in the city. So long as you live, and treat my son well, I will care for you. I will protect you, no matter what."

***

That day, down the workroom, I spoke with Jack about my thoughts the night before. "All this," I gestured to the boxes. "Will of course be helpful. But if the Families had any real proof of Mr. Polansky leading the Red Dog Gang, they'd have brought it to the meeting. Or at least, told us about it by now. Am I right?"

Jack seemed distracted by something: he didn't meet my eye.

"Perhaps we should take another approach to this. In my view, Mr. Polansky is a methodical man, an orderly man with definite habits. Yes?"

Jack nodded, eyes upon the open doorway.

"So there has to be more. Records, I don't know ... documentation. And ... well, Joe said —"

At Joe's name, Jack gave me a brief, horrified glance.

"— he said Mr. Polansky beat him. Him and Josie. Well, if he was unkind to his grandchildren, it only stands to reason he was unkind to his wives and children as well."

Jack's hand rested on his chin as he gazed towards the doorway. It seemed to me he was looking at Honor.

The man was attractive, to be sure.

But Jack must have been listening, because he nodded.

"Well, we know who they are. Right? One of his sons called himself Shigo Rei. He was murdered by the Red Dog Gang."

Jack looked shocked.

"He must have a family. And you've already found Ely Kerr." I leaned forward. "Listen to me: they can tell us the names of the others. They might know what he's doing."

Jack nodded slowly, still not meeting my eye. "Sounds reasonable."

"And ... I don't know. These aristocrats can't **all** be on his side. There must be some who are uncertain. If we might find even one —"

Jack let out a laugh. "That might be more difficult than you think."

I did have the few who came to see me. Perhaps they might know more of this than Jack did. "In any case, I can't go see these sons of his, nor their families. But you, on the other hand —"

Jack smiled. "You want me to be your spy." He straightened, face severe. "Aren't you concerned that my "amateur questionings" might not be sufficient?"

He was still angry; I didn't blame him. "Do as you might, sir. I know you wish to find the truth in this as much as anyone."

His eyes narrowed, and he gave me a sideways look, seeming at that instant quite like his oldest brother Cesare. "Very well."

"Oh, before I forget, there is something else you might help with."

Jack scoffed quietly.

"Do you happen to know what the bride and groom would fancy for their wedding gift?"

He laughed. "Surely you don't think **I** know of such things?"

"Well, you are her family. I only thought perhaps —"

He grinned at me. "I'm sure anything you get her will be appreciated. Although I imagine Clubb Manor would have anything the newest Clubb Queen might find needful."

I felt a bit deflated. What could we offer Gardena that she didn't already have? Perhaps something personal. "Well, thank you in any case. I suppose I must simply muddle along."

***

When Jack left that evening, he offered Mr. Theodore a ride home. As they drove off, Honor and I remained upon the front porch. And something occurred to me. "You and Master Michaels were at the orphans' Home together in Dickens. True?"

Honor seemed startled, but said, "Yes, mum."

"Master Michaels spoke about Daniel. He was his friend."

"Yes, mum. They were a few months apart, and spent a great deal of time together."

Alan stood in the doorway, but I didn't care if he overheard. "Did you know Daniel also?"

"I did, mum. He took care of us younger ones. All the older boys did." Honor swallowed, glancing away. "We all looked up to him." He nodded slowly, eyes distant. "He was a good one."

"So there's something I don't understand, and maybe you can help with that." I glanced at the street. "Does the city of Nitivali mean anything to the three of you?"

"Daniel and Jacob went to the House Servants' Academy there. It's on the northwest side of the dome. Near the North Station, if I recall."

I stared at him, mouth open. "So they lived in Nitivali for some time."

"Close to a year. I could ask if it's important."

"Not really. I only wondered why Mr. Jackson went there."

Honor shrugged. "No idea, mum. I never went to the Academy. Jacob might know more."

"No, that's not necessary," I said. "Pray continue your work."

I took my silvered case of cigarettes from my pocket and let Alan light one. Jack Diamond had said something — no, it was Jonathan who said it: *Jack has been obsessed with learning why Daniel was there that night, even to this day.*

Their father Julius Diamond had confessed to using Daniel as a spy in the Spadros Pot. Could Jack have learned something about Daniel's murder that went as far back as Nitivali? For him to spend so much time there seemed puzzling.

I stood out front smoking for a bit, then asked Alan, "Did you find that information I asked for on David Korol?"

A blank stare crossed the man's face, then he said, "Oh! Yes. I did find some things, but I completely forgot to give them to you!" Going round to the back of his station, he rummaged around in several of the baskets he had there, one after another. "Ah! Here it is." He handed me a slim folder.

"Thank you." I had maybe twenty minutes before time to dress for dinner, so I went to my study.

The folder didn't have much. David Korol's family had lived upon Market Center for three generations. None were Royalists, or even associated with them. He'd apprenticed to a blacksmith on Market Center when he was fifteen. The blacksmith had died a few years back, and now Mr. Korol owned the company, which lay a few blocks from the police station. He had a wife and three daughters, employing a half dozen men.

An owner on Market Center. A working man, with a family.

Not someone with the time to go around killing young men and boys in Spadros quadrant.

But whether he was the Strangler or not, whether he was with the Red Dog Gang or not, this man was a threat to our Family. It wasn't too far from "we want to rule ourselves" to "we want to lock you up."

The Account

After dinner, I received a certified letter:

Mrs. Spadros -

This is to give notice that your account is past due in the amount of one thousand dollars in fines to the City of Bridges.

If such amounts are not paid in full by the end of the month, you may face legal action.

Well, I thought. *This won't do.*

I didn't have the money.

I'd repaid Sawbuck his seventy dollars, but that had taken most of the money I had.

There was no way around it: I'd have to go to the person I least wanted to and speak with him about it.

***

Tony was in his library reading, and seemed in a good mood.

Until I told him why I was there. "If you can pay it for now, I'll repay you every cent. With interest. We can draw up documents, if you like."

Tony stared at me. "How-ever do you know about interest?"

So I told him about how Doyle Pike had me sign documents I could barely read, but then his grandson Thrace Pike had explained them to me. "That's how I learned about interest."

Tony slammed his book shut. "**Why** are you speaking with Thrace Pike? Isn't he the one who wrote the pamphlet against you?"

Oh, dear. "He did. But since, we have resolved the matter."

"How did you 'resolve' it?" His eyes narrowed. "Have you bedded him, too?"

I felt utterly shocked. "Him?" Then I felt revolted. "Ew! No! There is absolutely nothing unseemly about it! His wife has called on me here, and I've called on her." I tried to persuade him. "She helped with the auction!"

"So you've been completely proper with this man this entire time?"

I couldn't say that, not truthfully.

"I see. So you again have kept secrets from me. You have again gone running to our enemy —"

"Enemy?" I didn't understand. "You mean because he's the District Attorney? I've not spoken to him since he became ... Wait." Now I felt confused. When was the last time? "I believe the last time we spoke was when he was an Assistant District Attorney."

Tony sounded exasperated. "All the District Attorney's office does is to persecute us. That is the entirety of what they **do**! Can you not see that this man is our enemy?" Tony looked away for a long moment, then faced. "He tried to publicly humiliate you. He's spoken against the Four Families, not only in print, but in open court. This man would take any excuse to see us **gone**!" Tony shook his head. "And yet you allow him into your **home**? Call upon his **wife**? That **alone** could be used in court as trying to sway cases in our favor."

I felt taken aback. "I'm sorry. I didn't know."

"Well, now you do. Don't you ever see that man again."

"But his wife knows Mrs. Hart's father. The Bridges Grand-Master. I thought that maybe —"

"We could have a nice family luncheon? The Bridges Grand-Master is mad, Jacqui! I don't want Ace anywhere near him! And I certainly don't want him thinking he can sink his claws into this Family."

My heart sank. "Mrs. Hart wants so much for her father to meet him."

"Well, I'm sorry," Tony said. "I'd not let Ace see Roy's grandparents either, and for just as good reason."

I felt horrified. He thought the Bridges Grand-Master as big a threat as those who'd tortured Roy's mother into madness? "Then I'll say no more about it."

"I'll pay your fine," Tony said finally. "And you will repay me. But I'm not so far gone as to charge interest against my own wife."

***

Tony came to my bed that night, as he always did, but refused to speak with me. Soon he was asleep, but I was not.

I kept thinking about what he'd said. About Mrs. Hart's grandfather, Roy's grandparents, the things Molly and Duchess Sophia Whist had told me. I felt that if I was able to get an entire account of these people, these events, that somehow I might devise a way to stop the madness that was going on around us.

And help Joe and Josie.

And keep all the things I already had in their baskets.

It was a constant battle. But it was better than having them cluttering up my mind.

Around half past one, the front door-bell rang.

Odd, I thought. Who might it be?

I heard Alan answer the door. He was speaking with someone, there in the front hall.

I put on my robe and went to the door opening onto the stair. When I peered out, Alan stood there speaking with a police Constable.

"Jacqui?" Tony sounded sleepy. "What is it?"

"I don't know." I closed my robe tightly, put my house shoes on, and went to the top of the stair. "What's all this about?"

The Constable looked up at me, tipping his hat. "Sorry to disturb, mum. There's been a murder."

Tony stood beside me. "Go back to your rooms; I'll handle this."

So I did as he asked, but I peeked out of the door until he, Alan, and the Constable went into the parlor.

Who'd been murdered? Why did they need to speak to Alan — of all people — about it?

I sat by the door in the darkness, quite puzzled at the situation, until the door suddenly opened and Tony came in.

He laughed when he saw me. "Whatever are you doing down there?"

I got up. "I couldn't sleep. What's happened?"

Tony turned on the light, shaking his head. "Who in the world is Sir Q. Jack von Hamm?"

I went to my bed and sat heavily upon it. "My informant's dead."

Tony moved closer. "If I understand you right, then yes."

They got to her. "What happened?"

Tony sat beside me for a moment, then sighed. "You sent Alan with a flat envelope to Blitz, who mailed it to your dressmaker Tenni Mitchell. Sometime after Miss Mitchell mailed the letter to your friend, it was opened. The pages of it were lightly spritzed with water and dusted with finely powdered yew."

I stared at him, horrified. "Pages? I only sent one sheet!"

"There were three inside. Only a person who knew that this woman licked her fingers before turning pages would know that they could harm her this way."

"I didn't even know she did that!"

"Your informant brought the letter home with her and opened it at her desk shortly before tea. She fell ill in front of her family an hour later. The doctor was called, then an ambulance, but since no one knew what had happened, there was no way to save her."

"I don't understand. How did they know the letter poisoned her?"

"The police say two hard candies lay inside the package she received," Tony said. "Her son recalls them — he asked for one, but she refused to share." He let out a bitter laugh. "I suppose he was lucky. A wrapper lay upon her desk. They found the candy partially dissolved inside her. The other was still in its package. They were full of chopped yew."

Someone truly wanted her dead. Why?

"What did the letter mean?"

I put my head in my hands. "She believed there was a wildcard in Hart quadrant."

Tony gasped.

"I never was able to ask why she thought so."

"Whoever these people are, they've been watching us for some time," Tony said. "You're not to blame in this. But don't ever send letters to your informants again."

I felt stunned. How did these people know me so well? "Why would they kill a middle-aged widow on Market Center?"

"They didn't want anyone else to know about the wildcard," Tony said, as if this were obvious. "Which means that it's true." He let out a disgusted breath. "Blitz should never have sent that letter."

"Don't blame him for this —"

"I do. Mr. Pearson thought it was for Blitz. But Blitz knows better. When he saw there were letters inside letters, he should've opened the lot and brought the innermost one directly. If he'd have done that, your informant would be alive, and we'd have what information she held. Now, she's dead, and all she knew is lost forever."

Would Blitz have ever opened someone else's mail like that? I'd never thought to, much less thought to tell him to.

Tony took off his house slippers and got into bed. "I'll tell Mr. Pearson: all your outgoing mail needs to go to Eight Howell from now on. And he's not to accept any incoming mail for you but from Mr. Eight's hand." He turned away and pulled the covers over himself. "These days, it's too dangerous to do anything else."

I shuddered at the implications. Someone might try to kill me through my mail?

I lay awake until the sky began to pale, until Tony rose without even looking at me and left, until Shanna came in to open the drapes. I lay there as Honor brought in my tray, and as Shanna came in to see why I hadn't so much as gotten up to touch it.

I didn't know what to say. "Is everything I do going to end in ruin?"

Shanna laughed, but it was kind. "Oh, mum, you've fallen into melancholy again. Come, let's get up. I'll have Master Honor bring some fresh toast for you."

I got up, went about my day. But I felt as if in a dream. Would I wake, warm and safe in my bed in the Cathedral? Had this whole thing been a nightmare?

Then I stubbed my toe, and it was definitely not a dream. As much as all of it hurt, Tony had been right. I couldn't keep on doing things the way I had been.

The Director

At breakfast, Tony said, "I heard from the Dealers."

I'd been half asleep, but this interested me at once. "Oh?"

He took a letter from his pocket and handed it to me. "Yes, well, they have little to say."

> Mr. Spadros:
>
> While we appreciate your inquiry, we regret under the current circumstances, we can make no comment on this matter.

I looked over at him, unsure what the letter meant. "Is their Director still being held?"

Tony gave me a horrified look. "I believe she is! Well, no wonder they don't wish to talk to us. I'm surprised none of the candidates — or the papers — have mentioned it."

"Does she have a lawyer? Perhaps we might donate to her defense." I considered the matter. "To be honest, I'm not sure what she's being held for." Former Mayor Freezout seemed to believe the Dealers knew everything about the workings of the city, and seized their leader when she wouldn't speak with him about it.

Tony glanced at Alan. "Find out."

Alan nodded. "Yes, sir." He took a small pad and pencil from his jacket's breast pocket, making a notation.

"I should've paid more attention to this," Tony said quietly. "I'm sure many blame us for not dealing with this sooner."

***

As I was "at home" that day, Jack didn't visit.

Instead, Duchess Sophia Whist came to call. She didn't seem to have any specific request, so after the usual cup of tea, I asked, "Have you heard of a Mr. Lans Pasha?"

This was the name Joe and Josie's grandfather Polansky Kerr IV was registered under.

She got very still. "I've heard the name."

I leaned back. "Tell me about him."

"He makes a striking figure," she said. "He's well-spoken, charming. Most everyone he meets takes to him."

"And you?"

She shrugged, not meeting my eye. "He's no admirer of the Families."

"So I've heard."

I sat watching her in silence.

"He said once that once he buys most of the city, they'll have to put him on the City Council." She looked at me. "Then he can get rid of you."

"I see." This was near to what had been said of him before, except for the City Council part.

The Councilmen had neither status nor pay, but they were one way for those outside the Families to feel their voices were heard. The Council spent most of their time crafting letters to the Mayor. Most Mayors took the letters graciously, then had their Assistants call on the Families to see what they thought of the matter before throwing the letters away. "Isn't he quite old?"

She blinked. "I don't know! I suppose he must be. In his seventies?"

I leaned forward. "What if I told you I have it on good account he's past ninety?"

She drew back, face shocked. "I had no idea! So ... I don't understand. Surely he must have someone he intends to replace him. Once he turns in his cards."

"He must." This gave me pause. Joe intended to oppose his grandfather. Joe had Josie safe somewhere. If Josie was indeed Finette Pasha, as everyone was saying ... then how was Polansky Kerr running his businesses and acting as the Director of the Red Dog Gang without a financial officer? Surely he wasn't doing all this himself.

And who could Polansky Kerr have as his successor? This must be a man we'd not yet seen.

Should I confide in this woman? I might be able to use this. "The Families believe that Lans Pasha allied himself with Mayor Freezout to put me on trial —"

She gasped.

"— and to seize the Blessed Director of the Dealers."

"Good gods!"

"Who knows what's become of her there? And we all feel she was seized without reason. My husband wishes to donate in support of her legal fees."

"That's quite generous, mum."

I rose, and once she did as well, I rested a hand on her arm. "Whatever you might learn about Mr. Lans and his family would be most helpful. I fear he's not a wholesome influence for this city."

***

Jane Pearson came to my study that afternoon with a slim journal wrapped in brown leather. Jane was the housekeeper for Spadros Manor. "My Alan says you've been looking for this."

"Why yes," I said. "This is Mr. John's diary?"

"Not as such, mum. He wrote nothing of any import that I can see here." She peered at the outside as if it might tell her more. "Just notes, like a code. I don't understand it." She handed it to me. "But if it'll help, you can keep it."

"Thank you, Miz Jane. This will most certainly help."

She curtsied low and left.

I sat behind my desk and opened the little book. Behind the cover it read: WB LD.

The rest were similarly cryptic notations: a row of numbers on one page, what looked like an address — without the quadrant name — on another. It seemed more of a memory device, a way to recall things only he would.

WB LD. What could it mean?

After she left, I sat in my study, weary, the names and dates and places and faces threatening to swirl up once more. Discussing Joe and Josie's grandfather made me think of how I might prove their innocence.

I rang for Alan. "There's a journal-book upon my tea-table upstairs. Would you have it brought to me?"

"Of course, mum."

I found the page where I'd made my notes on Joe and Josie's whereabouts during David Bryce's abduction. According to Daisy, they'd gone to the countryside for Yuletide, but she had no proof, and of course, the word of a nursemaid wouldn't be nearly enough.

I wished that I would've spoken with Joe about the matter when I had him with me.

That couldn't be helped now: I had to take a different approach.

Tony had told me, and Jack Diamond had confirmed it: Josephine Kerr (or rather, Miss Finette Pasha) was the financial officer for her grandfather's company. At the meeting atop the Grand Ballhouse, Jack claimed that Josie had signed a check to pay off little Stephen Rivers' family after the boy's murder at the hands of the Bridges Strangler.

One of my theories was that this check — as well as others linking her to the Red Dog Gang — had been forged, by whoever had forged documents incriminating me. What I needed was as many of those checks as I could find, along with a sample of Josie's true handwriting.

I'd known Josie since I was born. But as far as I could recall, I'd never seen her handwriting. The messages she'd sent me up to then had all been printed cards.

Perhaps Jack could get these things for me.

The Stairs

Jack didn't visit the next day, either. Which was nice. I felt altogether too weary to spar with him.

Perhaps an hour before tea, Blitz came by the Manor. I was in my study at the time, and surprised to see him there. "You could've sent a note."

Blitz shook his head. "Is there someplace we can speak privately?"

I rang for Shanna, and the three of us went out onto the veranda. It felt like walking out into an oven. "What is it? What's happened?"

This is how Blitz told it:

Master Mike Pok-Deng, the apothecary who took over Anna Goren's business after she was murdered, went to his basement, which he'd been using as a store-room. Whilst down there, he noticed a damp spot upon the left-most wall. Upon further examination, he noted that the paint was flaking off, and the wood underneath was damp, nigh to rotting!

Alarmed, he went to my apartments.

Fortunately, Blitz had the presence of mind to speak with the man outside. "I went over to investigate. The paneling crumbled at my touch. I took off only a board or two, but ..." He lowered his voice to a whisper. "I saw stairs. Going down."

I gasped, stunned.

"I told your apothecary I saw black mold. I warned him not to go into the basement under any circumstance, and to stay with his family until we might fix the problem." He glanced aside. "I've not told anyone what I saw. Teddy's guarding the back door, and I've got my other brother Bondi watching the front."

"Your brothers? Why?"

"Your apothecary friend was murdered down there. By a woman you think was with the Dealers." He seemed quite agitated. "What if they're hiding something? Or ... I don't know, they know something's there. They might have thought your friend was close to finding it." He glanced away, then back at me. "I told them under no circumstances go inside, and don't let anyone near you. I don't want anyone else dead over this."

"Good thinking." I rose. "What do you suggest?

"We mustn't make a ruckus. I had Mr. Eight send a few of his men over too. We can go tonight with the plain carriage and just a few men, ones who won't be noticed if they're gone." He seemed to be considering this. "So no one who normally patrols out front. Let's see ... Rob Pearson, and Honor."

"Good. And let's bring some boxes with cleaning supplies. If someone sees us, we must appear to be doing work on the place."

"Well, it's gonna need work anyway. We'll have to tear some of the wall out to even get in there." Blitz made to go, then stopped. "Speaking of Mr. Howell, he said he found a few places on Market Center that could suit for your new office. They're really too big, but ..." Then he shrugged.

I nodded. "I'll speak with him about it later."

We sent Rob to help guard the shop's front door, telling him to say to any curious visitors that the building was closed for repairs. Just to be safe, I had Blitz hire some Family men who owned a roofing business to park their horse-truck out front, then go up on the roof that day to inspect it, without telling them why. Passers-by would assume the roof had leaked, and think nothing more.

I found Honor and sent him to spell Mr. Theodore. I told Honor to set up a rotation so the men might have breaks to eat and rest. Then I went to speak with Tony.

Tony was in a meeting with his men, but came out at once. "Has something happened?"

In whispers, I told him what Blitz had found. "We'll go tonight and see what the stair leads to."

Tony grabbed my arm. "Be careful. That woman has killed more than once — warn our men not to allow any woman to approach them."

"Already done."

Tony let out a relieved breath. "Good. Tell me at once what you find."

***

That night, Shanna and I went in the plain carriage to Anna Goren's old shop. Despite Shanna's misgivings, we dressed like scullery maids, our hair tied in kerchiefs, wearing masks covering our noses and mouths, and carried buckets of cleaning supplies.

The men carried boxes in after us. Entering through the back door of what used to be Anna's shop, I was reminded of the afternoon I'd hidden in her rooms.

The apothecary had set up his bedroom quite differently than Anna had: all was neat and orderly. The trap door in the floor beside his desk lay open, and light shone up from below.

Anna Goren's dead body swam before me, the look of surprise on her face, the knife-hilt protruding from her chest.

"Mum?" Shanna looked at me with concern. "Are you well?" She took my arm. "We don't have to go down there if you don't want to."

I let out a breath. "No, I must." It would be wrong of me not to see what Anna had died for.

Blitz and Mr. Theodore were dressed in gray canvas overalls, looking like any other set of workmen in the city. They'd moved the crates and boxes the apothecary had stored there to one side and taken out most of the left wall. A half-filled trash bin stood beside them, mostly rotted boards and pieces of crumbling brick.

An area behind the wall some five feet square had been swept. Strangely familiar patterns lay carved upon the red walls and raised in gold. Electric lights on the left lit the way down. "This is incredible."

Blitz pointed to an area on the wall up inside the opening. "Here's your leak. Probably a bad door seal, or a crack in the foundation." Blitz shook his head, looking around at the little room in amazement. "This could've been here a century or more." He gestured to an ancient switch. "And the lights still work!"

"More than a century," I said. "That design on the wall's Art Deco. I've seen it in the Pot, and I saw it in the chambers of the Magma Steam Generator piling under Spadros Manor. I might be wrong, but this could've been built with the city."

Mr. Theodore gasped.

I nodded. "This might've been here over five hundred years." I recalled the map on the Cathedral's ceiling. "It's in the right place."

Did I dare say it? I hardly dared to whisper. "This could be it. What the Inventors have been searching for."

Shanna and the men looked at me blankly, not understanding.

"This could be the Magma Steam Generator piling for Market Center," I said. "The one that controls the power. The ventilation windows. Everything."

The Exploration

Garish white light on one side, a golden glow coming up from the stairs on the other. Blitz was lit by both, his mouth open. "The Main Generator? The controls for the entire city? Why hide it?"

I shrugged. "Why are women from the Dealers murdering apothecaries and Inventors? Something about this place, something about what Anna Goren learned. What Inventor Maxim Call learned. They both were on the brink of some tremendous insight and right then, they were murdered. This is too great a finding to be coincidence." I turned to Honor, who'd come down, I suppose fearing some attack from below. "Send a man to fetch Mr. Anthony. But do it quietly; no one else should know we're here. And this place must be guarded well." When Honor left, I said to Blitz, "Let's go. So we have something to report when my husband arrives."

Blitz glanced at Mr. Theodore, then nodded, lighting a lantern. "Just in case these bulbs go out. Shall we?"

We descended the narrow steps, Blitz first, Mr. Theodore and Shanna behind, straight down for perhaps a quarter mile. My knees began aching after a while, and I'm sure the others felt the same, but no one complained. The ceiling was low enough to touch, if I stretched, with the same gold and red Art Deco carvings upon it.

Something important lay here, something very old, very special. I felt such anticipation I could barely hold myself back from hurrying. But we didn't know what was up ahead, what traps the builders might have set for someone coming here uninvited.

The stairs ended at an ornately carved, locked door. We looked at each other in dismay.

Blitz said, "What now?"

Then I smiled, recalling the picks I still kept in the maid's corset that Madame Biltcliffe made for me so many years ago. I turned away, fishing them out from under my bodice.

Mr. Theodore let out a laugh when he saw the picks. "A woman of many talents!"

Old picks, on an even older door. Finally, the lock clicked, the door opened, a gust of stale dry air entering the stairwell.

We never could find a lamp for the place, nor even a light switch. So we used lanterns to search.

As it turned out, it wasn't a piling.

It wasn't a Generator at all.

It was a library.

An enormous round space, a vaulted dome of a roof, bookcases running perpendicular to the walls on either side of us. Books, ancient and leather-bound, filled every case.

The floor beneath my boots felt like tile, and in the dim lantern's glow, I saw patterns in it. After a hundred yards, something appeared faintly up ahead. When we were almost to the object, the bookcases stopped.

Twenty feet past them, a map table of the Bridges of old lay in the center under a clear dome six feet across, now yellowed with age. It reminded me of those I'd seen in the Map Room at the Records Office. Bookcases radiated from the space on all sides, like we stood in the center of some giant sun.

I peered down at the tiles; Blitz raised the lantern, opening its covering to cast a wider glow. The floor held a mandala mosaic, the ancient words of my mother's people around each of its layers.

Shanna said, "What do the words mean?"

I could only pick out a word here and there. "This seems to be about the virtues of wisdom." I shrugged. "I never learned to read this language; it's only somewhat similar to that which my mother spoke to me as a child."

Blitz said, "This can't be the reason the Dealers are killing people."

"We need the Inventors down here," I said. "They may be able to figure out why this is so important."

Shanna turned her back to the table, going round it. "Imagine the number of books here!"

It was then the immensity of knowledge, of information which lay here, hit me. I leaned on the map table, feeling faint.

Then I reminded myself: it was not my duty to know all that lay here. The Inventors were well-equipped to that task.

I said to Blitz, "Might I speak with you privately?"

Blitz handed the lantern to Mr. Theodore, who ambled along beside Shanna, looking at the carvings on the ends of the bookcases. Then Blitz came to me. "What do you need?"

I didn't know why I thought to ask this at this time, but it was the one place I felt sure no one was listening, except, perhaps, his brother. "Why did you shoot Master Kerr?"

Blitz stopped, closing his eyes, not breathing. Then he bit his lip and glanced away. "I should've protected you. From him. I knew what he was, yet I did nothing. Just like when you were a child in Spadros Manor. I should've killed Master Joseph and Mr. Roy both." He led out something like a scoff, but his face held pain. "Perhaps I'd be Patriarch now. Or perhaps I'd be dead." He shook his head, turning towards the darkness. "What would it matter either way?"

"None of this has been your fault."

He stopped, barely lit in the lantern's glow. "If I can't protect those under my care, what good am I?" He walked off.

I called out, "Wait."

Mr. Theodore caught up to me, put a hand on my arm. "Let him be."

Shanna gasped.

I stared at him, surprised that he would lay hands upon me.

He stepped back, hands raised. "Forgive me." He let his hands fall to his side. "But I know Blitz. He'll deal with this best on his own."

I nodded. "Nothing to forgive." I knew men well enough; why had I tried to follow? "Let's see what else this place holds."

***

157

Mr. Theodore, Shanna, and I explored every row, which took several hours. After perhaps twenty minutes, Blitz joined us without a word, as if he'd never gone.

Rooms which had to have been for lectures: the podium, blackboard and chalk were still there. The chalk was a bit crumbly, but serviceable.

We found ancient toilet facilites which still worked. What reminded me of the door to a bank vault, which we didn't try to open. A kitchen with its cupboards bare, but that could be easily remedied. Even what appeared to be some sort of cold box, still cool.

All tidy, if dusty. Still, much better than anyone should expect.

Blitz said, "It's as if they deliberately hid it away."

But why hide it? Why have it so far below ground? "Surely whoever built the rooms overhead knew it was here. How could they not?"

Blitz glanced behind him. "That wall was old even for Market Center. If whoever hid this put a building on top, the new owners might have not have known about it. If it weren't in the blueprints for the place, that is."

I nodded. Like the missing modifications to my apartments which had allowed the Red Dog Gang to hear everything spoken there.

Voices, out in the main hall. It sounded as if they were shouting. I'm surprised anyone heard anything at all.

Blitz went to the kitchen entryway. "In here!"

We went forth along the row of books to meet Tony, who'd come down with several of his men. He was leaning upon the domed map table, gazing around, eyes wide. "Close the lanterns. Look. Up there!"

The ceiling held a steadily increasing glow, as with the coming of dawn. Even with the lanterns shut, Tony's outline was visible. I moved beside him. "This is incredible."

Tony said, "I'd heard of the technology of the old days. But this," he waved at the ceiling. "How is it done?"

I shook my head. "Perhaps the Inventors can tell us."

"Yes." Tony looked around. "If this is as old as I think it is, this might answer many of our questions."

The Owner

When the light rose enough for us to be certain it was moving with the sun rather than part of our imaginations, Tony and I started our long journey to the ground level.

Blitz left the lantern with Tony's men and came up with us, intent upon going home to bed.

The three of us labored up the long straight staircase. This felt worse than going to the top of the Grand Ball-house: there were no places to stop and rest, or to walk flat and level, even if only for a few steps. Looking for anything to take my mind off of the pain in my limbs, I asked Tony, "Have you learned anything about our visitor?"

"Nothing ... out of the ordinary," Tony panted. "He found an eatery ... he likes ... on the Spadros Promenade. Takes to his bed ... early. Reads ... every edition .. of the news." A few steps later, he said, "Visited his attorney ... in Clubb quadrant, twice now ... in as many weeks."

"Oh." I felt surprised, suspicious, wary.

What was Jack Diamond up to?

Tony stopped, leaning on his cane. "I'll let you know ... should we learn anything ... of importance." Switching his cane to his other hand, he leaned upon the glossy, black-painted banister and gazed up the stairs. "Does this never end?"

I laughed.

Once we arrived upon the ground floor, Tony ordered the entire boundaries of the building cordoned off out to the street on all sides, with men guarding the area. He also sent men to order the surrounding buildings closed and evacuated.

Using Tony's most trusted men, messages went quietly to all four Inventors. Tony then returned to Spadros Manor, and Blitz went home.

I decided not to leave my building until this treasure had been properly secured.

I didn't think it proper to sleep in Mr. Pok-Deng's bed. So I sent Shanna to fetch some of my regular clothing. I had Honor set up a cot in and curtains around Anna's former dining area, out of sight of Tony's men entering and exiting the building.

That afternoon, I got word from the Chief of Police by way of one of his young Constables, asking what the problem was about. Dozens of reporters stood behind the Constable, who was not much more than a boy, their cameras flashing.

I went out to the barricades, dressed more appropriately for the Queen of Spadros. I spoke only to the Constable, ignoring the shouts of everyone else. "An issue with water in the foundation. We aren't sure whether the ground surrounding the building is sound. Until we get someone with expertise in to look at it, it's best to be on the safe side."

This seemed to mollify the young Constable, who looked as if he'd rather be miles away. I returned inside as if the reporters weren't there.

Soon we had police standing around the area. The reporters tried to ask questions of our men inside the enclosure. Our men knew well enough not to answer, but from all reports seemed as startled as anyone to see Inventors' carriages from all four quadrants drive up, each with their own entourage of guards eyeing each other.

I unlocked the front door for them, the reporters' cameras flashing so much I could hardly see. "Welcome, Inventors."

In came the new Spadros Inventor Piros Gosi and the new Hart Inventor, Liu Madiao, each with their men. In came the Clubb Inventor, Lori Cuarenta, followed by her three maids and six white-jacketed Apprentices. And last came Diamond Inventor Themba Jotepa with all of his men.

It seemed to me that Inventor Jotepa's Family felt particularly protective of his safety. "I feel astonished that Mr. Julius has allowed you to visit so often."

He laughed. "I'm an Inventor, Mrs. Spadros, not a child. If he wishes me to move our quadrant forward, he must allow me to do so."

"Well said."

His eyes lit up. "Even if he were able to forbid me, this is a discovery I could hardly miss. The wealth of what we might learn about the city!"

A chill ran down my spine. Was that hoard of information lying far below what Anna Goren and Maxim Call died for?

I raised my voice. "Please, Noble Inventors. Please. Let me speak."

All quieted.

"Be on your strictest guard. Inventor Maxim Call and the Apothecary who once owned this shop were murdered by someone we believe is with the Dealers. Another man was attacked by this person, and barely escaped to tell the tale."

Shocked faces all round.

"The main suspect is a woman, brown of skin with eyes of bright blue. She is in her middle forties and attractive. If you see this woman, she is no friend. Shout for help and do not let her approach. She prefers stabbing in the chest with a large knife. We need lose no more Inventors."

And that made me think of Inventor Arrow. "There is another danger. We believe an outsider woman with red hair named Zia Cashout murdered Inventor Montgomery Arrow. She has a strong accent, and consorts with a very good looking brown-haired man named Frank Pagliacci. Do not allow either of them to lure you away. They are to be considered armed and extremely dangerous."

Inventor Cuarenta's eyes narrowed. "What interest do Dealers and outsiders have in our work?"

I shook my head. "I don't know. But I wish no further deaths here." I gestured to them all. "Now let's get you out of sight of these reporters."

***

I decided not to brave those stairs again, letting Rob Pearson show the Inventors and their men the way.

I came to feel glad I did: an hour later, Chief of Police Geofrey Schwimmen arrived at the barricade, demanding to see me.

I had the men escort him into the shop area.

He was a portly man, of an average height, with thinning white hair. He wore gold-rimmed spectacles and was dressed for the street, yet carried himself with an air of immense self-importance.

I surveyed this man, who I suspected was on the take from Polansky Kerr. Mr. Hart had been sure of it. "How may I help?"

"Well," he said, "I'd like to know why, when my city is hot as the Fire, all four of our Inventors and their men are inside this shop instead of fixing the matter."

"A fair question." I glanced outside the large plate window, at the many reporters outside the barricade, who had their camera-men hard at work. "There's an issue with the building that needs their attention."

"Poppycock! What could possibly be wrong here that a good construction-man or architect couldn't fix?" But he did look round, then, and test the floor a bit with his shoe.

I didn't know whether I could trust this man. I probably couldn't. But I had to give him some answer, or he might decide to go down there himself. And I couldn't let him do that: I didn't know who he reported to. "The area is full of rot and mold, sir. Undermined by water damage. But we've found some documents that the Inventors need to see."

Chief Schwimmen scoffed.

"It might not sound like much, sir. But the Inventors believe these documents might help solve the heat problem."

He crossed his arms, and his eyes narrowed. "Very well. But I want regular reports. You tell them that. I'll not have them lollygagging about when there's work to be done."

I almost laughed. A Police Chief, giving orders to Inventors? "I'll relay your message."

"Hmph," said he, and turned to go.

I escorted him out to perhaps ten feet from the barricades. The reporters immediately began shouting questions:

"What's happening here?"

"When will we get a report?"

"Why were the surrounding shops evacuated?"

"Are people in danger?"

I, of course, ignored them all. Tony had asked me not to tell anyone anything, so I'd try my best.

Master Pok-Deng stood off to my right, trying to get my attention. When the police tried to push him back from the barricades, he shouted, "This is my **business**! My **home** is in there!"

Honor stood to my left, so I said to him, "Bring the apothecary to me," then I returned inside.

Master Mike Pok-Deng was a slender, energetic man close to thirty, with an expressive face and keen mind. He looked round the inside of his shop as if it might fall upon him at any instant.

I said, "There's nothing to fear, sir."

He seemed most agitated. "I don't understand. You close my shop, send me away, evacuate the surroundings, then tell me all is **well**?" Then he seemed to recall who exactly I was, and gave a little bow, touching his forehead as he did so. "Forgive me, mum. My entire family's savings is in this shop, and I fear for my goods."

I thought as much. "I give you my word: nothing will be harmed. But I may need to find you a new building. Upon Market Center, of course."

He took a step back, face alarmed. "Is the matter that dire?"

I took a deep breath. What should I say? This could never go back to being a working shop, not with the treasure which lay underneath. "The matter is serious. You will not be able to stay here. That's all I can say."

Master Pok-Deng pondered this for a moment. "But I have hospitals and clinics all over the city awaiting their pharmaceutical orders." He looked at me. "I've received numerous messages even this morning on the matter. What shall I tell them?"

I hadn't considered this. "Tell them the orders will be delayed."

He flinched. "If the delay is too long, they'll go somewhere else."

This was my building; I needed to make this right. "Prepare a list of those orders which can be delivered now. Then another of those which need only packaging. I'll get you some help with that." Surely the Inventors didn't need **all** those Apprentices down there. "We can't have the city go wanting, not when there are hospitals in need. Once things have calmed, you may be able to work on the orders in progress for a few hours a day, just until I can find another place for you."

He let out a breath. "Thank you. This was more than I expected."

This amused me. "Why? Because I'm a woman?"

His eyes widened. "Because you're a **Spadros**. You lot care little for us here on the island. I feared ... well, I feared that I'd not be treated fairly."

I nodded. "Well, sir, this is my building, not theirs. I'll make sure you're taken care of."

He seemed astonished. "You mean, your husband allows you your own **property**?"

I laughed. "All this time, you thought your rent went to my **husband**?"

"Well, not at first. Not when you lived separate. But when you returned home, I just assumed —"

"I'm sorry to disappoint you!"

He blinked, evidently re-evaluating much. Then he collected himself and bowed. "Good day."

Honor had stood there pretending not to listen. Once Mr. Pok-Deng left, I said, "Tell Mr. Howell I'd like to see those places he's found here on Market Center."

The Family

The rest of the day was spent with questions. The Inventors needed food and drink. They evidently wished to stay the night: requests came up for cots, curtains, bedding.

I felt heartily sorry for their Apprentices having to climb those stairs so often. The ones tasked to helping Master Pok-Deng with his apothecary orders were sincerely enthusiastic at having been chosen.

Over the next few days, Master Pok-Deng's orders went out. He seemed awed at Apprentices aiding **him**, which seemed to upend his view of how matters should be.

My Queen's box was brought to me there. The reactions to my continued presence ranged from alarm that I should be on the premises to suspicions that much more was going on than was being said.

One by one, the other three Patriarchs arrived, evidently curious as to what the commotion was about. I'd had curtains placed over the large picture window, if only to keep out the stares, and had Shanna make tea. So fortified, I welcomed them, answered their questions.

To my surprise, only Mr. Hart cared to make the trip down the stairs to see for himself. When he clambered back up, he was pale and sweating. "Remarkable," he panted. "But I'll not go down there again." He considered the matter. "Are you certain you didn't find a lift?"

I shook my head. "I wish we had, sir. It'd make things much easier."

Honor, who stood by the wall pretending not to hear, couldn't hide a slight smile.

Mr. Hart laughed weakly. "That it would. I'm getting too old for this."

Having made the trip myself, I felt astonished that a man of five and seventy had come back up under his own power. We sat, and he accepted tea. I said, "What news?"

"When I left, they were gathered around some old vault, full of documents." He shrugged. "I can only hope they contain blueprints for the dome, so we might fix this blasted heat."

It was decidedly cooler downstairs. "I'm sorry, sir."

"Not your fault, my dear; please forgive my complaints. It'll be very nice come winter."

I laughed. "That it will."

Shanna placed a plate of cookies on the table, curtsied, and retreated.

Mr. Hart took one. "Ah, lovely," said he, taking a bite. After a moment: "And how is our young Acevedo?"

"Well as can be expected," I said. "Making good time. He likes kicking balls around." I didn't want to reveal anything about our outing with Roland and Gardena right then, as I didn't know who might be listening. "Learning to speak. You can even understand him, most of the time."

"A smart, good-looking boy," Mr. Hart said. "And why not? With such a mother."

I felt unreasonably pleased with myself right then, as well as with my boy. "I think he favors you, except of course his hair."

"Ah, yes," Mr. Hart said. "Of course."

"And how is your wife?"

His manner immediately turned somber. "Not well. I believe she'll turn in her cards soon."

"I'm sorry to hear that." And I was. She'd told me she wanted us to be a family, intended to support Acevedo's claim to Hart quadrant. Though I'd thought poorly of her, she'd treated me well. "What can I do to help?"

"Nothing, unless you know how to stop death."

So why was he here? Did he fear the reality of her passing, as he seemed to fear all else? I rose. "Then perhaps you should be with her."

Mr. Hart rose with a sigh. "Perhaps I should." He put a hand on my shoulder. "I have only ever wanted the best for you, Jacqui. I hope someday you can come to see that."

I shrugged his hand off. "How can I? By your own words, you've hidden in your Racetrack, whilst your quadrant fell into ruin. Whilst I was mocked, beaten, and bound to your enemy." I pointed at him. "And you did. **Nothing**."

He stared at me, mouth open. "We tried, Jacqui —"

"Surely you didn't think that little plan of yours to 'send me to the Prison' would work? What an insult! Under the guise of helping me — at the last minute, I might add — you'd rather I ruin my reputation by taking the blame for what Dame Anastasia did. And now you think I should **thank** you for it?" Feeling truly angry, I pointed at the door. "Go. Take care of your **wife**! For once in your life, stop running from your problems and do something **useful**!"

He shook his head, scowling. "I've never been one to beat my children, Mrs. Spadros. But your insolence is almost more than I can bear."

I scoffed at him. "I'd be glad to see you try." I turned to Honor, who looked ready to faint. "Pray see the Patriarch out."

The nerve of that man! I felt glad to see him go.

Honor came to me paler than usual. "Did you need anything else?"

"Get a carriage." I was tired of being here, tired of listening to useless old men. "I want to return to Spadros Manor."

***

Jack Diamond visited the next day, and as usual, we set up the ledger and boxes and began to go through them. Jack drank his coffee as we worked in relative silence. Finally, he said, "I hear you've been busy."

I laughed. "Indeed. Oh, and I won't be here tomorrow; I have an engagement."

Jack nodded. "Very well." He took a sip from his cup. "As you've been preoccupied, I took it upon myself to look into those invoices Mr. Hart claimed were forged. From your trial?"

"Yes, I recall."

He set his cup down. "They're curious, to say the least. Black cloth? Wigs? Horse training? Well, horse training makes the most sense of the lot, if it weren't for the fact that the Racetrack has its own trainers."

"I didn't know that."

Jack nodded. "Did any of this make sense to you?"

I let out a breath. "I believe the wigs were to disguise that woman calling herself Black Maria."

"Ahh," Jack said, leaning back. "I remember this 'Death Card' woman. You mentioned her at the meeting."

"I did." Should I tell him this? "And, well, they used the cloth to impersonate our men. False livery."

Jack put his hand to his chin. "I see."

I felt confused by his manner. "So what about the horse training?"

Jack glanced at Honor and shook his head slightly.

"I don't understand. What aren't you telling me?"

Jack leaned forward. "Do you recall anything to do with a horse? Anything unusual?"

My mind instantly went to the horrible accident. "The Red Dog Gang covered a pothole with cloth. It was a deep one. It was a trap. They shot our driver. The carriage fell into the hole and went on its side. One of our horses was badly injured and had to be destroyed."

"Was there anything unusual about this horse?"

"We'd loaned it to — wait. You're not saying **Josie** had anything to do with this?"

Jack shrugged. "You tell **me**. I presume you're referring to Miss Josephine Kerr? Or I should say, Miss Finette Pasha?"

"Yes," I said. "She came to us after Joe's accident out in the Hart countryside. Joe's horse had been injured and she asked to borrow one of ours for their carriage. She seemed to pick one ... at random." I'd spoken to the stable-boys after the accident — the horse turned out to be their favorite. The younger boy, Tommy, had been devastated. "We visited the Racetrack for our anniversary, and one of our horses went lame. Josie had our horse brought there, let us take it home." I shook my head, recalling what Tony had said: *It would've been better if it had stayed with them.*

"Do you recall the horse's name?"

"No, I don't think I ever asked." For some reason, this grieved me.

Jack nodded. "I spoke with the trainer. When Mr. Hart refused to pay, the man went to Mr. Polansky —"

"Wait. Why go to him?"

"Mr. Polansky had set it up."

I rose. "Where is this trainer? I must speak with him."

Jack laughed. "I have him somewhere the Kerrs will never find him. I also got an affidavit in triplicate, each sworn and notarized. I have copies in three separate places, so even if we have a spy in our midst —"

I sat heavily. "You don't trust me."

"**No. I don't** trust you!" He scoffed. "I'm not stupid enough to tell you where he **is**! They're watching your every **move**! If I told you, you'd go to him to 'confirm his story,' and he'd be dead like all the rest."

I felt as if he'd stabbed me in the heart. "What did he have the horse do? The one he trained."

Jack leaned forward. "To lie on its side when a gun went off."

I stared at him in horror. Honor and Mr. Theodore both looked stricken, as if they'd not heard this part of it, and I remembered the blood. The horrible cries the animal made. How Honor had been forced to shoot the poor thing.

I thought I might be sick. "I can't believe this. Mr. Polansky wouldn't **do** this."

"Now do you believe Miss Josephine to be innocent?"

"She **hates** Tony. She didn't even want to be there! She was only there on her grandfather's behalf ..." I stopped, unsure, heart pounding.

"I was there the day the forgery expert testified," Jack said. "The invoice was forged by a woman. Could this —"

I hit the table with my fist. "**Why** are you so against Josie? She's done you no harm whatsoever." My hand hurt. "That Fed of theirs, Zia Cashout. Maybe she's been trained in forging."

Jack seemed unperturbed. "Perhaps. But I have a question for you as well: why do you defend them?"

I stopped, struck by the question. Jack could never understand. But if he did, perhaps he'd stop tormenting them. "They're my only real family."

"What do you mean?"

I sighed. "My people in the Cathedral have turned against me. The Pot is in the hands of that woman calling herself the Death Card. The closest thing I have to a brother keeps telling me not to come home." I felt ready to cry. "I have no one **but** them."

Jack said nothing, just sat watching me.

"I've known Joe and Josie my whole life. No one here understands me; they see me as either their Queen or a filthy rag. But with them, I can be myself." I pictured Joe's smile, Josie's golden curls. The time she kissed me. My cheeks grew hot; my heart beat faster. "I feel safe with them. I —"

Jack's dark eyes burrowed into mine. "You love them,"

It was the one truth I had in all the world. "Yes."

Jack looked away. "Then we'll speak no more about it."

I had a chance, though. "If you'd get me one of those checks, and a sample of Josie's handwriting, then —"

Jack laughed. "You don't have the handwriting of your best friend?"

"I don't. It's odd; she only ever sends printed cards." I shrugged. "I always thought it an eccentricity. Or perhaps she thinks that's how you uppers communicate."

Jack looked amused.

This annoyed me. "In any case, no. I don't have either. If you might be so kind?"

He leaned forward. "If it will show you who this 'family' of yours really is, I'll do anything you ask."

The Concerns

Once Jack left, I asked Alan to find out the name of the horse that had been injured. I suppose I could've asked Honor about it, but he looked so shaken that I didn't wish to.

I think, looking back, that I didn't wish to because I feared what Honor might say.

The next morning's news held several headlines of interest:

Unrest in Diamond and Clubb over upcoming alliance

Clocks stop for ten minutes due to power loss

Death toll from heat illness reaches 3000

In my view, that last one was the worst.

I disagreed with Tony's view that the aristocrats truly owned the city. The people were much more numerous. If the people came to believe that we'd lost the ability to protect them, they might turn to others for help.

Like this wretched Red Dog Gang.

***

Blitz and Mary had Ariana's third birthday tea at the river, where the breeze made the air cooler and the children could play by the shore.

So it was a merry time.

Tony didn't attend, nor would he allow Ace to accompany me, saying the place wasn't defensible in case of attack. However, he did allow Mary's mother Jane and her brothers — Alan, Rob, and the others — the day off. Blitz had his five older brothers and their families there as well, all in straw hats and cotton. I recognized a few as Tony's men.

A rough-faced blonde woman of perhaps sixty arrived with Mr. Theodore and his family, clinging to his arm as they crossed the rocky shore. This turned out to be Blitz and Mr. Theodore's mother, Ariana Sutherfield, the namesake of our little Ariana.

I'd put on the disguise Constable Hanger had liked so well, and other than Ariana's questions as to why I wore "funny hair," no one seemed to mind. In fact, Mary told me she was glad I didn't attend openly. "I wish we could just come here in peace," she said. "It's bad enough, so many Family members in one place. But if they learned **you** were here ..."

"I know," I said. "I'm trying my best to find a place for my business. Mr. Howell just hasn't found anywhere suitable for me yet." I'd paid for Tenni to alter Mary's maternity dresses so she might be able to stay out in public longer, and the one she wore looked lovely on her. "I'm just grateful to be here."

Ariana and her cousins splashed at the edge of the water as her aunts stood nearby.

"Mum, I'm sorry to bring this up now. But if you do find somewhere to have your office ..."

"Go on."

"It's just that ... will there be no one guarding the house?"

I hadn't considered it. "I don't know."

She turned to gaze out over the river.

"I won't leave you to face them unguarded. That I promise you."

Mary nodded, not looking at me.

"I tell you what: take half of any monies you get from the room rentals and use that to improve things as you see fit."

Mary seemed confused. "Improve? In what way?"

I smiled at her, amused. "Your husband can think of any number of things, I'm sure. If you wish to reinforce the doors, or the front walls, for example." I shrugged. "Hire guards if you wish. I want you to feel safe in your home."

"That's very generous." But hesitation lay behind her words. "What do you ask of us in return?"

I instantly knew: *Ariana*. Her golden curls bounced as she jumped and played with her cousins there by the water.

In all likelihood, I would never have a daughter of my own. I gestured at Ariana with my chin, feeling a great fondness for her. "Keep that little one safe. That's all I ask."

***

As usual, I met Master Jack Diamond (aka Mr. Hector Jackson) next afternoon on the front porch. He tipped his Stetson and handed it to Alan without a word.

Once past earshot, though, all pretense dropped. "Why do you have men following me?"

I continued on as if nothing had happened. "They're my husband's men, not mine."

He stopped, face angry. "I've just come from luncheon with Charles Hart," he whispered. "He says you look on him as a coward! How can you believe that?"

I glanced around. "Perhaps we might take the air, sir?"

Jack went still. "Perhaps so."

We went out to the veranda, maids curtseying as we went. I went down the path to where it began to circle around the gardens. Not facing him, I said, "And why should I not? He had every opportunity to get me out of here," I turned to him then, "and did nothing."

Jack looked incredulous. "Did **nothing**? Then I suppose you think my **brother** did nothing as well."

I didn't know what to say.

"And I suppose you think Jonathan was also a coward. And that is the **furthest** thing from the truth."

"Of course I don't think Jon was a **coward**! But what could he have done —?"

Jack rounded on me. "Exactly. What could they do, when you worked against them at **every** point!"

I didn't understand what he meant.

"They had a plan to lure you away when you were sixteen, twice. The first time, you went and bedded that **detestable** Joseph Kerr —"

"How dare you?"

173

Jack scoffed. "The second time, we planned to have your carriage diverted, so that you might steal away, sign betrothal papers with my brother. Spoilt as you were —"

"**Spoilt?** Because I bedded the man I **loved?**"

"— Jon still wanted you. But the day before the plan, you went and signed betrothal papers with Mr. Anthony."

"It was under duress!"

"We had plans to contest the wedding, saying you signed the betrothal under duress. Jon and our father would be there to speak the truth, present the pre-betrothal papers signed by your mother, and claim you. But you changed the wedding day and place at the last minute."

"**Me?** I had nothing to do with it."

Jack frowned. "Mr. Roy must have gotten wind of it, then." He took a deep breath. "My father was out in the countryside; Jon was ill and couldn't attend. Mr. Hart himself only barely got there in time. Mr. Roy met Mr. Hart with a gun, told him that if he spoke out, he'd kill you. The **last** chance you had to speak, to tell the truth in front of gods and men that you were held hostage, you did nothing."

I felt stunned. Roy had put his gun to my head and said if I didn't make everyone believe I wanted to marry Tony, he'd kill me.

"For some time, we didn't know what to do: you seemed to be in Spadros Manor willingly."

"Well, I wasn't," I muttered.

Jack shrugged. "Jon told us as much. In any case, Mr. Hart and I had a plan to get you out of the city during the trial if you lost. It was Mr. Hart's idea." His face turned earnest. "Jon explained it all. He begged you to relent, confess, go with him."

He did. I have regretted saying no every day of my life.

But that implied Mr. Hart wasn't sure of the trial's outcome back then.

At what point did the Patriarchs feel confident about it?

"My mother and Mr. Hart went to your home to beg you to go with them." He scoffed. "The King of Hearts and the Queen of Diamonds lowered themselves to visit a Pot rag's home on 33rd Street in Spadros quadrant! Did you think they only did so out of **boredom?**"

I gasped. *Oh, gods,* I thought. Was **that** why they'd come there?

"Your servants were there. Spadros servants — so they felt unable to speak plainly. But they knew Jon was dying and made one last attempt to get you out, get you —" He stopped, hands to his face, and turned away. "Get you out while they still **could!**"

Of course. It made sense. I lived separate, we had no children. What better time to do it?

And now it made sense why Jon couldn't have been told.

Jonathan Diamond was a decent, honorable man, who loved Tony as his own brother. He wouldn't want to do anything to hurt Tony, and certainly nothing to get between the two of us.

Mr. Hart must have felt as if he had to try anything — even if it went against Jon's wishes — to get me away from Roy.

But once I carried Tony's heir, it'd been too late.

Jack still stood turned away, his hands balled into fists at his side. "You make bad decisions at **every** turn," he said angrily, "and others are left to cope as they can."

Why did no one **tell** me?

I struggled to speak, grateful not to see his face right then. "I think I can manage for today, sir. In fact, I think you should go."

I walked out past the gardens to the meadow. Roy's sheep grazed there now, far off in the fields, and men tended them.

Katie used to chase them, her auburn curls flying.

They lived. She was dead.

I wandered, unable to think, unable to feel.

I'd done it. I'd done it all.

A large clean patch of grass, somehow soft and green even in this heat. I lay upon it, gazing at the sky.

The sun beat upon me, but I didn't care. I no longer cared about anything.

Why should I, when every choice I made led to ruin?

Footsteps approached. Someone knelt beside me, took my hand.

"Jacqui," Tony said softly. "Why do you lie out here?"

I shrugged. I didn't know.

He let go of my hand.

I expected him to pick me up, carry me back like he'd done before, like I was some child. But I felt him sit beside me.

He sat knees up, arms upon them, gazing off towards the Manor.

"You're going to ruin your house clothes," I said.

He let out a laugh. "As will you."

It made sense.

"Master Jack told me you argued," Tony said mildly.

The trees in the distance to my left were very green. "He was angry that we'd had him followed. He believes I should think more highly of Mr. Hart." I didn't know what to think about any of it anymore. "He was even more angry at me than you are. At least with him, I know why."

Tony put his elbows on his knees, his forehead on his fists, and sat like this for a long moment. Then he raised his head to look at me. "You want to know **one** reason I'm angry? Amelia."

I felt taken aback. "What about Amelia?"

"She raised me. You killed her. And you didn't even ask me first."

I rose up on one elbow to stare at him. "You can't **blame** me for that! I was later told if I hadn't given the order, I was to be killed!"

Tony looked away. "Well, maybe you should've been."

It felt as if he'd stabbed me in the heart.

Tony glared at me. "Whilst my mother was off sleeping with anyone she could find, Amelia was putting her body in front of Roy's fist. Until Master Jacob became my manservant, even though she was a scullery, Amelia fed me, clothed me, put me to bed." He shook his head, face downcast. "I was ashamed of it. I treated her like a servant." His head went into his hands. "She served you for years," he said bitterly, "yet you ordered her death out of fear for **yourself**?"

I sat up. "No. She betrayed us. Whilst you and Roy and Ten fought for your lives, whilst John Pearson and our newborn son were pierced with bullets, she and her husband cut the wires on the large bell and left us to die. She told me how much she hated and despised me before she left."

I took a deep breath. "Roy made his instruction completely clear on what should happen if he should fall to those who betrayed us. He even taught me the exact words to say, should the day arrive and you couldn't speak them."

Tony didn't move.

"Would you rather have had Peter and Amelia escape to our enemies so they could try killing us again?"

He shook his head.

I tried my best to keep my voice from shaking. Why was he doing this? "Mr. Eight Howell visited with a box full of jewelry of the dead. One of many, taken from those who betrayed us. The ring Peter Dewey just gave her sat atop the pile. A new ring, of real gold." I turned away, feeling bitter. "They'd been paid to betray us. They expected us to be soft. They expected you to be soft. Not to chase them down. Not to find them."

Amelia needed to go into my basket in the closet, and Peter, too. They were dead, their children scattered, and it was my fault. Honor had seen it. Why had I not? "I grieve them. Amelia especially. But Roy Spadros commanded me to rule if you were unable, so I did. Instead of waking to find your people gone, your son and I dead, yourself captured, and your home overrun — if you lived to wake at all — you now have a secure quadrant." I rose wearily. "I could have left you to die, but I didn't."

I'd have been hunted down and killed if I had left, but perhaps that would've been better for everyone.

I began walking away.

Tony said, "Wait."

I stopped, not turning to face him.

"I was wrong," Tony said. "Forgive me. I owe you my life."

I didn't move. His words had left me angry and hurt. "Mr. Spadros, you must decide what you want. Because the next time they aim at us, I may not survive." I walked to the Manor, and didn't look back.

As I took the steps up to the veranda, it came to me: *this is why my brother lies dead.*

Mr. Hart had told me not to breathe a word of our connection. Yet Mrs. Hart had come to me, in my own parlor in Spadros Manor, and spoken of it all. Mr. Hart, myself, my grandmother, and Inventor Etienne.

Mrs. Hart trusted us. She trusted our people.

And Amelia had been false, all along.

Had Amelia reported on my conversations even then? Had the Red Dog Gang known that the secret was out? That Mr. Polansky's blackmail had been broken? That Hart and Spadros might ally one day?

Millie held a door to the dining hall open. I went past and inside.

If the Red Dog Gang really believed that an alliance between Spadros and Hart threatened them, then why kill the men determined to stop it? By killing Roy Spadros, they took away the alliance's main impediment. Etienne Hart had also vowed to stop it, fearing we wanted to take his quadrant. Yet they killed him, too.

***

Somehow, the evening news had gotten wind of Tony's offer to the Dealers to contribute to their Director's legal fees. The biggest news item, though, was that their Director hadn't asked for a lawyer at all!

I remembered the middle-aged woman who'd spoken with Mary after her first pregnancy had ended in a misdeal. What was this woman doing?

The morning paper's editorial column was filled with speculation about Tony and the Dealers. The responses were varied:

"As cold and calculating as his father. What is the Spadros play?"

"Finally, a Spadros who honors the Blessed Dealer!"

"Those who turned a blind eye to our Ladies locked behind uncaring steel should cower in shame. Morality has found a champion!"

David Korol sent in a lengthy letter, in which he said, "The city breaking with the Families in this matter is misguided, but encouraging. Although they seek to rebel by imprisoning one of the Dealers without the consent of the quadrants, the fact that they are at odds with our oppressors is a good sign."

I wasn't sure I either agreed or understood, but it was interesting.

A tabloid editorial, on the other hand, was downright ugly:

"Perhaps the Spadros has repented of his perversity and wishes to return to the Dealer's light. Now cast off the Pot rag, so we might cleanse the city of its shame and bring a true Queen to lead us."

The editorial was signed Mr. Boris Snodgrass.

I called in Alan. "Do you know who Boris Snodgrass is?

He let out a laugh, quickly recovering. "I'm sorry, mum. But didn't you know?"

"Know what?"

"Well, that's the Bridgers Grand-Master. Since you had Mrs. Hart here, let her up to see the little Master, I just assumed —"

"Thank you." When he went to leave, I held up a hand. "Wait."

So Mrs. Hart's father wanted to play it that way, did he? I circled the editorial and closed the tabloid, handing it to Alan. "Bring this to Mr. Anthony's study, if you will."

"Yes, mum."

Since no response that was both suitably harsh and unable to be traced back to me came to mind, I'd let Tony deal with this.

***

Duchess Sophia Whist visited that day with more to say about Polansky Kerr. "I considered what I've heard over the years. I feel his biggest concern is about the city. I heard him speak once about the state of the bridges, the roads, even the dome itself."

I nodded.

"He seemed worried about Bridges falling into disrepair, the way Narni did." She looked away. "I must admit, the situation with the trains, and, well, this heat ... it's only added cards to his deck."

It made sense. If the Families were to reveal we had no understanding of or even way to repair our city, the results could become catastrophic. It was only Lady Luck on our side that had kept us ruling as long as we had.

The Expedition

The next day at breakfast, Tony seemed in an unusually good mood. "I wish to undertake an expedition. All of us."

I said, "Oh? Where to?"

"Out to the countryside," said Tony. "Where we went when you were so sick."

I felt perplexed. "You mean the cottage? Why go there?"

He smiled. "Because it has cows, and roses, and a certain small boy liked it."

"You want Ace to meet him."

Tony leaned back, evidently pleased with himself. "I do."

Very few even knew of the place, not even my driver. "I trust you have the security arranged."

"I do. Certain men were persuaded to come out of hiding in return for being protected in the future. They, and those they love."

"Oh." Tony, blackmailing people? "If you're certain."

"I am. I value those I love more than anything in the world."

"And Mr. Jackson's been informed?"

Tony smiled. "I will inform him today, in the most general of terms."

But Jack didn't visit. Tony sent Sawbuck to speak with him.

He's probably still angry with me, I thought.

So I spent the day catching up on all my Queen's work. Answering mail. Doing my exercises from the Memory Sheaf. Playing ball with Ace. But all the time, I considered the things Jack had said.

Mr. Hart thought I'd married Tony willingly, been in Spadros Manor willingly, when I was **eighteen**? I was still a frightened child, just trying to survive long enough to someday go home. My one rebellion had been my investigator business, and even that hung upon a thread at times.

I think I truly would've gone mad, if it hadn't been for my nightly fantasy of loving Joseph Kerr.

I hadn't done that mental scenario in some time, and now, after what the reality of it became that horrible afternoon, I never would again.

***

We left before dawn the next day, bringing Acevedo still asleep to the carriage so he might not feel afraid.

The man who took me home after I was so ill was there by our plain carriage, older and more hunched. Several other men I didn't know well, but who I recognized as Tony's men, took positions on horseback alongside us.

To my surprise, several plain carriages sat there. Two plain carriages went ahead, another behind, each leaving us at certain points after we passed into the countryside. A man and woman resembling us, with a small boy and blonde nurse accompanying, rode inside each. No casual observer would know which carriage held us.

Acevedo woke several hours into our trip, crying in bewilderment. Daisy consoled him, pointing out the lovely sights.

We stopped then, to allow us refreshment and breakfast beside the road. Poor little Ace shrieked and thrashed in fear when we brought him back to the carriage, but there was no use for it — we couldn't stay there any longer.

After a time, he went to Tony's lap to huddle there for some time, then to Daisy's, then to mine.

Soon we turned off the Main Road onto a dirt track going off into the woods, hills looming in the background. Two of our horsemen stayed behind to ensure we weren't followed, and to erase the carriage-tracks, lest someone see our detour and became curious.

Acevedo perked up then, peering at the forest, something I realized he'd never seen. But then the carriage jostled, and he cried out, grabbing onto Daisy.

"All's well, boo," she said soothingly.

I chuckled. "Boo?"

Daisy shrugged. "Something my grandmother said to me." She looked wary. "No offense intended."

Tony glanced at her, then out of the window.

And I recalled what he'd said once: *My nurse wasn't nearly so kind to me.* "No offense taken," I said. "It's good that you feel kindly towards him."

She blushed, smiling to herself. "I do." She reached over to smooth his wavy hair. "He's such a good boy."

Acevedo beamed up at her through his tears.

The love they had for each other touched me. I so wanted my boy to feel safe, and cared-for, and most importantly, loved.

***

We arrived around noon, I for one hesitant to see the cottage again. But the tongueless, thumbless servants were gone, the cottage cleaned and repainted, and it really did look lovely. Gardena Diamond, her nine-year-old son Roland, and their men waited for us.

Gardena shared the dark, dark skin of her brother Jack, with raven pencil-curls and a lovely figure.

Gardena's son looked very much like her, apart from his skin, which was a bit darker than mine. Roland's hair, whilst black like them both, hung in loose ringlets. His deep brown eyes were shaped like Tony's, and he had Tony's chin.

I went to him. "My, how you've grown! Did you get to see the cows?"

"Not yet," Roland said. "I wanted to wait until Daddy arrived."

I called Daisy over, had her set Acevedo before him. "Master Roland, this is your brother Acevedo. Ace, this is Roland."

Roland crouched, so their faces were at the same level. "Rollie. That's what everyone calls me."

"Hi, Wa-wee," quoth Master Acevedo.

Roland beamed. "I'm your big brother. And I shall take very good care of you."

We looked at cows, horses, and pigs. All were unused to people after being left alone for so long, and shied away until we brought food for them. Roland showed his brother flowers, trees, and how to dig in the mud for worms. To my surprise, a pond lay nearby, and men brought out lines from the carriage so Roland and Tony might fish.

Tony had never gone fishing before! I could see that Roland was proud to show off his skill.

Soon a nice fish sat in Acevedo's lap. He touched it as it wriggled and gasped. When the fish stopped moving, Acevedo burst into tears.

"Aww," said Daisy, "it's okay. We're going to eat it."

Acevedo looked at her as if she were some horrible creature, then began sobbing. "No! No eat fiss!"

Roland smiled at him fondly. "He'll get over it. Hey, Ace, want to learn how to make a fire?"

This interested Acevedo at once. So to the shock of us all, Roland built a fire! When everything was ready, he opened and cleaned the fish, and soon it sizzled in a pan.

Gardena said, "I didn't know you could do all that."

Roland smiled proudly. "Grandpa showed me."

Gardena beamed at us. "My father does love his fishing trips."

Our men brought the picnic we'd arranged for the day and set it out for us. We sat under a canopy, upon blankets and pillows, taking in the beauty of the day. Tony grinned at me from across the canopy. "A nice family luncheon."

I laughed.

The fish was delicious. Acevedo wouldn't even taste it.

I said, "Aren't you hungry?"

"No fiss," he said, taking a definite bite of roll.

Roland grinned. "More for me."

Eventually, Acevedo's curiosity overcame his sorrow, and he hobbled over on his canes to beg some fish from Roland's plate.

Ace seemed to like it.

Roland somberly watched his little brother eat. "Grandpa says everything dies. We can use death for our purposes, or not. But it doesn't change the facts of the matter."

I had never imagined Julius Diamond to be a man of such depth. "What else has your Grandpa taught you?"

Roland jumped up. "I can skip rocks. Look."

He actually got the rock to skip three times, so of course Tony had to try as well. Acevedo toddled between the two of them on his canes, picking up pebbles and flinging them into the water.

Gardena said, "Look at them." She glanced at me. "I'm serious. Look at them. It's what you always wanted. For us to be a family."

I wanted you to be a family with Tony. The thought didn't give me the pain it once had.

But she was right. This amused me. "A very secret family, to be sure."

She laughed. "It'll always be so. But sometimes secrets make things more special."

"Dena," I said softly. "Do you need anything for your preparations?"

"I think not." Then she laughed. "Between my mother, my sisters-by-law, and all my aunts and cousins, I've hardly had to do a thing."

I'd had no one with me for my wedding. I suppose Molly did the preparations, because I'd been locked away, only brought out for public viewings and photos.

But this reminded me of Jack. "I suppose you know of our visitor."

She didn't speak for a moment. "I do."

"What happened? He's obviously been in Nitivali some time, but it upsets him to speak of it."

"Hmm," she said quietly. "It's complex." She smiled over her shoulder at me. "And has little to do with you."

"Oh. Forgive me; I don't wish to pry."

Gardena looked at the lake. "He doesn't wish you harm. On the contrary; he would very much like to help you find the truth."

I nodded, not really understanding. Every time we came within a few feet of each other, he seemed to be angry, distressed, disturbed. And it frightened me.

Still facing the lake, she said, "Jacqui, I must tell you something. But I fear you wont like it."

My heart started pounding. *Oh, gods,* I thought. Had Tony betrayed me with her again?

"You recall Master Kerr. Joseph Kerr."

I felt surprised at what seemed to be a change of topic. "Of course."

"Cesare's oldest son adored horses when he was small. So we brought him to the Racetrack for his birthday. We all went: Rollie, my brothers and their families. This was ... it was Kumkani's fourth birthday, so ... it had to be the summer you were on house arrest during the trial. When everyone was searching for Master Joseph and Miss Josephine."

Gardena seemed quite hesitant, so I nodded, hoping to encourage her to speak.

"My father had insisted on securing twenty rows of seats near the back. There was a canopy set up and everything." This seemed to amuse her. "Much larger than this one. But we were quite far back. It was early in the day, and there were very few people there." She paused, her eyes far away, as if remembering. "We'd just finished luncheon and were having cake. A loud commotion came from over near where one places bets. Master Joseph stood perhaps ten feet away, struggling with several men in Hart livery who tried to hold him. But he won free, and ran."

My mind reeled. "At the racetrack?"

"Yes. Several women rushed after the Hart men, calling after him."

"Several ... **women**?" It made no sense.

She looked sad. "Yes. Five that I saw." She paused. "I'm sorry."

How could it be? "Are you sure it was him?"

She laughed. "I don't think I've ever seen another man like him." She shook her head. "It was him. His voice, his motions, his face. I saw him clearly." Her shoulders slumped. "I'm so sorry."

Five women. At the racetrack. When I thought him to be dead. "And Jonathan was there with you?"

She nodded quickly. "He was."

I felt confused. "Yet he never said a word!"

"He told me not to."

I gaped at her, astonished.

"He didn't wish you to be hurt." Gardena looked downcast. "So much was happening back then. I think Jon feared making you feel even worse."

This made sense. "So why tell me this **now**?"

"I heard Joseph Kerr had returned." She sat up straighter. "I wanted to warn you. I don't believe him to a good person, Jacqui. He hasn't been true to you —" At this she hesitated, looking down. "— and I'd hate for you to connect yourself to him again." She turned to face the lake. "Jon and I were entirely shocked to see Master Joseph at the Racetrack with those women, particularly since you'd told us he wished to leave the city with you." She shook her head. "I think he might've been caught if my father had told his men to make chase as well." At that, she snorted. "My father said he'd not do a thing to aid Tony, that he'd gotten a taste of his own medicine."

"He said that?"

Gardena nodded. "In front of everyone." She turned her face away. "It was humiliating."

"I'm sorry."

She shrugged.

I took her hand. "You made a mistake. And you've suffered for it. But you don't deserve to suffer forever! And you certainly didn't deserve your father treating you that way."

She sighed. "Thank you for saying that." She gripped my hand, hard. "You don't know how much that helps."

I hugged her. "Like you said, we're a family now." I pulled back, smiled at her. "Us outcasts have to stick together."

She laughed at that. "I suppose you're right."

***

We stayed until the sun dipped below the horizon, not wishing to spend the night there. We got home late; I felt bleary the next morning.

And it came to me: Rachel Diamond overheard Gardena speak of killing her grandfather, that day we met in the Diamond Women's Club for luncheon.

Oh, dear, I thought. I imagined that there had been some words about that situation. Or had Mrs. Diamond decided not to speak of it?

I pictured Gardena saying: *this has little to do with you* ... and I laughed.

The Conference

Whilst we were at the cottage, the Inventors had held a news conference, which to my surprise, I only learned about in the morning papers.

The conference was about the discovery I'd made (at least they had the courtesy to mention me), which they were calling the Ancient Library.

"It is clear," the Clubb Inventor said, "that the Ancient Library is a pre-Coup facility, hidden underground for at least a hundred years. Its construction is clearly consistent with those buildings created before the Coup. In it are books, documents, and artifacts dating back to the founding of the city."

The Inventors brought forth photographic images of items in the Library, which lies deep below Market Center. One item of great interest was the original charter to the city, thought lost.

Diamond quadrant Inventor Themba Jotepa spoke about the original charter. "Even upon cursory reading of this document, it's clear that everything we knew about the history of this city is based on falsehood."

When questioned about this statement, the Diamond Inventor said, "The original charter for this city, signed by the Founders, the Inventor King, and the Southwestern Tribes, was more consistent with the charter for the Republic of Tollkeen than anything we have today. We have compared this original with the copy of our charter in the Mayor's Office. We have also contacted Hub; they agree that the Mayor's copy is the one they received June 21st, 1400 AC. The only conclusion one might have is that someone — most likely the Inventor King himself — betrayed the original intent of this city."

A two-page spread was devoted to the text of the two documents, the original on the left and the current "official" charter on the right.

The whole thing was entirely shocking. The Inventor King betrayed the very people who helped him build the city?

The next days' tabloids were filled with theories of all sorts. The range of the theories really surprised me, most either denying the truth or blaming the Families for it. I'd planted a fake document to discredit the city. The Inventors were lying about the Inventor King, lying about the charter, in league with "outsiders who want to destroy our way of life."

Some historian pointed out that Inventor Jotepa was in error: it would've had to have been the first Benjamin Kerr who submitted the false documents. The Inventor King, Benjamin Kerr II, the first Benjamin's grandson, had not yet been born.

A letter to the editor of the *Bridges Daily* even claimed that the Families learned about the false documents even then and banded together to overthrow the King, then hid the news from everyone

The next day, a different writer claimed (in great detail) that this was absurd: the Four Families hadn't even been formed yet.

I read this editorial with interest, not knowing the history of the time that well.

Apparently, the Spadros Family had only owned a small portion of the Southeastern Pot of Gold, and was one of many such groups there. The Clubbs of Justice had been indentured farmhands out by the Zeppelin Station, and didn't form a Family as such until well after the Coup.

The Diamonds had been an assortment of peaceful homes scattered throughout the city until Caesar Diamond — the man Jack's oldest brother Cesare had been named for — took power during the Coup.

And it sounded as if my own ancestor, Charlie Hartmann, had been little more than a boy.

Despite Sawbuck going to speak with Jack Diamond, he didn't visit that day, nor the next. During that time, I did more of my Memory exercises, sent out messages (through Mr. Howell, of course) to my informants with questions about Joe, Josie, and Mr. Polansky, and played with Ace a great deal.

Ace was such a delight: from the waves in his dark brown hair to his bright smile to his zest for life, even though he must often have been in pain. I feel so grateful for that time I had him with me. I only wish it would've been longer.

A few days after our trip to the cottage, David Korol gave a speech at dawn. Even at the early hour, the event was attended by hundreds. I went to hear him speak, keeping myself veiled, far at the edge of the crowd, and never leaving my plain carriage.

"Even our **charter** is a lie! We were **never** supposed to be ruled by criminals. The people who worked so hard to raise this dome wanted us to live in a garden paradise without masters or servants, all equal under the Dealer's Blessed Eye. You see now how knowing the truth frees us?"

He cast a hand out over the crowd. "I don't say or even think that we can make the changes we so desperately need overnight. But how can we learn to live, make progress in our futures, when even the pennies we do make are taken by thugs," he began to pound his lectern with each word, "who can't even keep us **safe**?"

I felt his gaze, though I was far enough to not see him clearly.

"The Families watch us even now. Will you let them rule us forever? Or will you vote to move our city forward to join the rest of Merca in freedom and honesty?"

People turned to peer at me; many wore blue armbands. Then I saw that Mr. Korol did as well. What did it mean?

I shut the curtains and took up the speaking tube. "Drive on."

When I got home, Mr. Howell emerged from my study.

He looked embarrassed. "Forgive me my lateness, mum; I had some family matters to tend to."

"No, I needed to speak with you." I brought him into my study, keeping the door open. I heard Honor take position just outside the door. "Tell me about these places you've found on Market Center."

"None are suitable. I mean, they could be split into two, I suppose. But they're all quite large — more shops than anything else."

"Give Master Pok-Deng the list and have him select one. Tell him to make an offer on whichever suits him best, and I'll pay for its purchase."

Mr. Howell's eyes widened. "Are you certain?"

"He won't be able to return to his shop, and I'm not even sure he'd be safe there if he did. People now know he's living in a building I own, and I want nothing to befall him. If he makes the offer rather than me or you doing it, that will reduce the danger."

He nodded. "Well played. I'll see to it today."

"Oh, one more thing. Does the Family have anything on David Korol?"

"Don't think so." He hesitated. "May I speak frankly?"

"Always."

"It's a risky play. One that could backfire. Not sure we oughta try that this late in the game."

It was the first of September. The election wasn't until November. But he seemed to know about these things better than I did. "Just find out where he goes. What he does. Whether he has any connections here in Spadros quadrant."

"What are you thinking?"

I lowered my voice. "One of our theories is that the Red Dog Gang plans to put their man in the Mayor's office. Our most likely candidate is the man they've done so much to help. They even hanged a man to cover up his crimes."

Mr. Howell blinked, taking a step back. "You can't be serious."

"My husband thought it. Master Jonathan thought it as well. We don't know who, but any man who appears too popular for no real reason is suspect in my book."

He let out a small laugh. "He does speak well. And he's got plans the people enjoy." He stopped, as if realizing who he spoke to. "Not that I'm voting for him, mind you. But ... you hear things."

"Keep hearing things, sir. Let me know what you find."

***

Jack Diamond again did not arrive that day. I was in my study going over my Queen's box — the usual heap of mail, events to consider, and the tabloids Mr. Howell thought it necessary for me to read.

The power had gone out in half of Diamond quadrant the night before. Well, half of the area in the city proper: the outlying areas seemed to have been unaffected.

Why had this not been in the morning news?

Though the *Bridges Daily* had seemingly missed the bid, the Diamond quadrant tabloids were full of it, from every angle. Wild theories, calls for the Inventors to stop the investigations into the Ancient Library, which some thought "wasted precious time," and anger at the city itself for not bringing in experts to consult on the matter.

One editorial read: "We have young, inexperienced Inventors, most new at that, who have focused on the irrelevant whilst we all suffer."

I thought it bordered on disrespectful to say such, but the tabloids seemed to be allowed to publish anything these days. I wished for the original *Golden Bridges*, which at least had some sense of decorum.

But that led me to remember Major Blackwood, and the Army's lawsuit. Morton's murder, and the Feds.

The Army and the Feds had been suspiciously quiet. Were they planning to move against us? Or were they secretly in the city now, stirring trouble?

And where was Jack Diamond? He couldn't **still** be angry with me!

But he'd left no word with either Alan or Mr. Howell.

There was no help for it: I might have to work on the boxes myself from now on.

***

The next morning, the *Bridges Daily* had this headline:

GRAND ANNOUNCEMENT FORTHCOMING

Clubb and Diamond Joint Press Conference

The article was a terrible tease, speaking of a scheduled announcement upon Market Center later that week. Tony mentioned it at breakfast: "All the Families are invited. I think we should attend."

From what I'd seen so far, that meant that Tony had already made all the arrangements.

I was right. That afternoon, my dressmaker Tenni Mitchell brought over a beautiful gown just like one already in my closet, only pale green. When she was fitting it, I asked, "Do you know anything about the blue armbands people are wearing?"

She laughed around a pin in her mouth. "They're selling as fast as I can make them." She took the pin and made an adjustment in my bodice.

"What do the bands mean?"

She stopped, looking away. "I believe they indicate the admirers of David Korol." She laughed. "A funny name."

"Why so?"

"Forgive me, mum. My Ma studied with the Dealers before she met my father." Then Tenni sighed. "She married for love, not that it got her anywhere. But she taught us the cards. The meanings of names, and such. David Korol means 'King King'."

This threw me back to Jack had said in the meeting: *None of these companies — or even the owners — are named Kerr, or anything close to it. Most are variations of King, Ruler, or Monarch, in other languages. It's clear they want their true power to be disguised.*

"Very good, mum," Tenni said. "Let's get this off you, and I'll have it back here tomorrow."

***

Why Julius Diamond decided to have a press conference at noon, I'll never know. The day was already sweltering when we left the Manor, just after breakfast.

On the way, I saw a crowd of Bridgers on the side of the road handing out pamphlets, which made me recall Mrs. Hart's father. Tony was looking at them, too, so I said, "What did you do about that editorial?"

He stared at me blankly for a moment, then laughed. "Oh, that. I had Master Bresciane pay the Bridgers' Grand-Master a visit. I understand he now knows the consequences of further indiscretion."

I gaped at him. Master Seven Bresciane was the Knife Man, Roy's trusted confidante, a master, shall we say, of removing the tongue. "You **threatened** him?"

"**Me**? I did nothing. I sent an old family friend to call on another." He shrugged. "Mrs. Hart **did** say she wanted us to contact him, did she not?"

I felt horrified. I felt ... afraid. But I also felt proud. Tony'd thought of a solution that had never even crossed my mind. "I'm glad that's settled."

Tony snorted. "That depends on him. But if he continues on this path, he chooses his reward."

Once we arrived at the square upon Market Center, we were surprised to see that covered stands had been erected in a hexagonal shape. One side had been set up head-high as a stage, also covered to shade from the sun. The side directly opposite the stage had a doorway for people to come and go, which I thought wise: it allowed for packages and bags to be inspected for guns and sniffed for bombs. We were directed to stairs, which led to our seats.

The Four Families each had their own private seating, a Family on each side, on a level with the stage. Tony had brought Sawbuck and all his main men, who followed us up and also sat, giving us two seats space on all sides.

The air under the awning was only slightly cooler: heat radiated up from the cobblestones on the street below. Reporters crowded the floor, along with people from all parts of the city.

Right at noon, Rachel and Julius Diamond, followed by five of their sons and their families, entered from one side. The men all wore black linen suits with white shirts.

At the same time, Lance Clubb and his mother Regina, along with Lance's sisters and their families, came in through the other, the men all wearing golden suits and the same white shirts. The women all wore black and gold silks, which really looked lovely once they stood together.

Jack Diamond was nowhere to be seen, but I hadn't expected him up there. He was pretending to be a distant cousin, not a Family member.

I peered at the Clubbs. Which of them had told the papers of Roland's rush to his father at Alexander Clubb's gravesite?

Two microphones had been set up a few feet behind the edge of the stage, a pace apart. Lance Clubb went to one, Julius Diamond went to the other. Mr. Diamond spoke. "It is my great privilege and honor to make an announcement." He gestured past his family.

Gardena guided Roland to stand between his grandfather and his soon-to-be father, then stepped back a few paces, closer to her family.

Julius put his left arm around Roland's shoulders; Lance put his right arm around Roland's shoulders as well.

Julius said, "Diamond and Clubb quadrants are pleased to ally. With the marriage of my daughter to the Clubb Heir, we wish to introduce you to Roland Diamond, who will legally be known henceforth as Master Roland Lancelot Clubb."

Startled murmurs throughout.

I whispered to Tony, "Did you know of this?"

Tony scoffed.

Lance moved slightly right, letting go of Roland to speak into the microphone. "I wish to announce that I have chosen Master Roland, my true-born son, to be the Clubb Heir."

Gasps, and the murmurs grew louder, people looking at each other, at Gardena, at Roland.

Julius drew Roland in front of him, placing his hands upon his grandson's shoulders. "I declare Master Roland Lancelot Clubb to also be Diamond-born —"

The crowd began booing.

"— and an Heir to the Diamond Family."

People began pointing, shouting. Fists were shaken.

A sudden movement, from in the crowd; Lance's eyes widened.

A man shouted, "No Spadros-loving Clubb bastard shall ever rule us!"

As he spoke, a pistol rose from the press of reporters, held by a dark-skinned hand ... pointed up at Roland's head!

Tony gasped in horror. "No!"

The microphones fell as Lance leaped upon Roland, knocking the boy to the ground right as the shot fired.

Utter silence.

Then a woman screamed, "He's killed our Patriarch!"

Blood spread over the center of Julius Diamond's white shirt. He looked down, then at the crowd, face surprised. "Oh."

Then he collapsed.

"Oh, gods," said Tony.

Calls for a doctor, calls for the police. Rachel Diamond fell to her knees, howling over her husband's body.

Lance and Gardena carried a screaming, fighting Roland away from the scene as the crowd converged on the shooter and proceeded to beat the man.

Then gasps: the crowd drew back. A large knife protruded from the gunman's upper abdomen.

Cesare paced and raged. The other Diamond brothers stood huddled together with Cesare's wife in shock, clutching their own wives and children around them. The rest fled or rushed to help, as was their wont.

I sat there, stunned, as Julius Diamond's blood spread over his shirt, then upon the stage.

I never thought the man would die naturally. But this? At the prime of his life, when he'd finally gotten his daughter settled, when he had so much to live for?

It just seemed wrong.

Tony was pulling on my arm. "We have to go, Jacqui. We have to go. Before the police arrive."

The police weren't here? I thought they'd be all over this.

But I let Tony lead me away.

***

The whole way home, Tony sat beside me, head in his hands.

I felt so grateful young Roland was alive, and it seemed, unhurt.

But I wanted answers.

Who did this? More importantly, who stabbed the gunman? The only reason to do so would be to ensure the man didn't speak of who sent him.

And in an event sponsored by the most distrusting Family, with the best security, how did either of those men get in there with weapons?

The chain of matters seemed entirely suspicious. Could this possibly be just the acts of two hate-crazed men? Or was this another plot by the Red Dog Gang?

First the attack on our little Acevedo, then the murder of the Hart Heir, now this. It terrified me. The best way to end the Four Families — if that was what the Red Dog Gang truly wanted — was to kill our Heirs.

Cesare and his brothers had to be warned: they and their children were likely to be next.

When we arrived home, Tony immediately called for a fresh rider. I stood beside Tony as he wrote the letter, as he went over it aloud:

> To Cesare, Diamond Patriarch
>
> Diamond Manor
>
> The Spadros Family denies any involvement whatsoever in the heinous murder of your beloved father and Patriarch Julius Diamond.
>
> Spadros Quadrant offers any and all assistance you require in this time of anger and grief.

Anthony, Spadros Patriarch

Spadros Manor

I thought the message well-done. Tony never allowed anyone to write his words for him, as some other Patriarchs had over the years. In it, he both immediately acknowledged Cesare and offered his aid, something the Diamonds had never done after Roy's murder.

That had to mean something.

Because if Julius Diamond hated us, well, his oldest son Cesare hated us even more. And we didn't need another war right now.

The Acknowledgement

Tony's letter received no reply. But then we didn't expect one.

The death of three Patriarchs in two years had left Bridges in shock. My Queen's box held nothing that whole week but tabloids expressing grief, anger, and bewilderment. The topics ranged from wild speculations on the motives of Roland's would-be assassin to a sober assessment of Bridges politics, decrying the violence aimed at a child. There were dozens of articles about the Diamonds and their Patriarchs, the chain of investiture, and about Cesare's oldest son Kumkani, a boy of eight, who was now the Diamond Heir.

I quickly had condolence cards made up; an entire afternoon was spent signing and addressing them. I sent these to everyone I could think of: Mrs. Rachel, Cesare's wife Mrs. Furuta, Gardena, Roland, plus a whole list of women Mr. Howell said were wives of high-placed members in the Diamond Family.

Our horsemen were kept busy; it seems Tony had done the same. Fortunately, Sawbuck and Mr. Howell were keeping track, and the cards from us to the same household or street were both sent at once.

Mr. Hart returned from the countryside, giving a press conference at the same spot where Julius Diamond was murdered. However, it was noted in several papers that the security was in some ways far more stringent than for the speech the Diamonds held.

One tabloid even described it: "every rooftop, every street, every window to every room within sight of the area was taken over by Hart men in groups of five. A sniper, two to watch the sniper's back, two to watch the sniper himself."

Well, I thought. That sounded impressive.

Mr. Hart used a microphone. Reporters were kept out of pistol range. Apparently, even a zeppelin was filled with Hart men to fly over the area, to look for suspicious activity.

In the midst of this, Mr. Hart spoke:

"Hart and Diamond have been and remain strong allies. Through our grief and dismay, we stand calmly together, resolute against those who hate our way of life so much that they would target children. And we urge you to remain at peace in this terrible time. Much has happened, but each of your Families is committed to keeping you and your children safe."

According to the report, he stopped, then continued on:

"I have spoken to your Patriarchs. We have nothing but the greatest concern for the smooth and orderly running of the city. We want you to prosper. We want your lives to be free from care. We stand together through these dark times, and will come through even stronger for it."

I thought it well-done, surprisingly so. Perhaps my father had taken the seriousness of his position — or my words — to heart.

***

The next day, the Inventors emerged from the Ancient Library's depths to give a press conference of their own. They'd found information about the dome's ventilation system. They'd also located a map of the location of the windows within the dome.

Again, Clubb Inventor Lori Cuarenta was the main speaker. "This discovery gives us hope that the cause of the dreadful heat plaguing our city can be resolved soon."

To everyone's surprise, she was met with thundering applause. Editorials praised the Inventor, saying, "Our most senior Inventor gives an admirable performance, showing great promise despite the disadvantages of her sex."

A rather backhanded compliment, to be sure, but still better, I dare say, than none.

So that week, a team of balloons, with daring aeronauts both professional and amateur, was sent into the heavens to examine the dome.

This interested the populace at once, and despite their grief, sales of spyglasses skyrocketed, the better to get a glimpse of the work.

Tony had a Telescopic Magnifier crafted in silver, similar to my magnification spyglass but much larger, with special shields so as to dim the glare of the Sun.

He and Acevedo spent many a happy afternoon peering up into the skies once the Sun had passed behind the buildings. Through the glass, I could see little but the Sun glinting off of the supports, just thin strands of light at this distance. But Tony claimed that he could see two balloons and once, even a small zeppelin.

I suppose the city needed the distraction. Diamond quadrant had all but shut down in their preparations for their Patriarch's funeral. Between the fierce heat and the sorrow, the news filled with clashes between households, deaths due to heat exhaustion, suicides.

Our only hope, it seemed, was that the Inventors — or at least, the aeronauts — might find the ventilation windows to our dome soon.

***

Jack didn't visit until twelve days after his father's murder, and his visit was brief — I only heard of it later. He'd personally brought an invitation to the funeral and reception, which was to take place the next day.

Well, I thought. *That was a near thing.*

But then I remembered the turmoil around Roy's funeral and recalled the Diamonds had been in the midst of planning a wedding. I marveled they'd been able to arrange everything that quickly.

Fortunately, we still had our mourning garb, and it fit well enough.

Tony and I were uncertain whether to bring Acevedo. Was he in more danger at the funeral, or at home?

Finally, we decided that as the Spadros Heir, Ace had to be present. We'd bring Daisy, who could take the boy out should he need tending.

The invitation allowed us to bring three men. Sawbuck, Honor, and Mr. Theodore were assigned to guard Ace and Daisy. I'm sure Sawbuck would have much preferred to guard Tony, and it showed. But Tony insisted. "My son is my life. You're the only one I trust in this matter."

Sawbuck seemed surprised at the acknowledgement, but he never balked at guarding the boy again.

The Procession

I contacted my dressmaker Tenni that night, who brought over three sets of child-sized mourning garb. Fortunately, one fit reasonably well. She spent an hour taking up the hems and cuffs, and the next morning, my little Ace looked splendid. I patted him on the head. "You'll make a fine showing today — the most handsome boy there."

Ace beamed up at me.

Since his reaction to the carriage on the trip to the cottage, I'd had Daisy practice going to the carriage with him several times a day to get him used to it. It was a good thing, because dozens of reporters had arrived outside Spadros Manor. Kept at a distance, with our snipers on every rooftop alert for danger, the reporters still got many photos of Ace toddling along the stone walkway on his crutches between us.

He didn't like sitting on the bench seats, though they were padded in velvet. So he stood, toddling from one of us to the other the whole way.

***

When our carriage approached Diamond Manor, all the buildings were draped in black. It looked as if the entire quadrant was there.

To our surprise, Cesare Diamond met our carriage, dressed in the finest mourning garb I'd ever seen. "You have your son to thank for this," he said at Tony, then stalked off, leaving us unsure which way to go.

The young Diamond man from the meeting atop the Grand Ballhouse came forward and bowed. "I'll show you to your seats, sir."

Tony nodded at him, and we followed. The young man moved apace; when I glanced back, Daisy had scooped up Acevedo, crutches and all, and hurried to join us.

The stands and seating were much the same as for Jack Diamond's "funeral." Yet the scene felt chaotic. Many layers of Family men had arrived from all four quadrants, and it was clear from their stances that they each wished to be the closest to their Patriarch.

Tony sent Honor to stay with the carriage and left Mr. Theodore at the base of the stands. Sawbuck followed us up to guard the end of our row, eyeing the burly (but not nearly so tall) Clubb man there, who'd glared at him when he thought we weren't watching.

The covered seating for the Four Families was almost full. We were placed in the front row with the other Family heads, Tony sitting beside Mrs. Clubb.

The young man who'd led us there presented a cushion for Ace.

I felt touched. "Thank you!"

The man looked embarrassed at me speaking to him, but bowed and backed away.

I sat beside Tony, putting Ace between Daisy and myself. I said to Ace, "Is the seat good?"

Ace beamed up at me. "Yeah, Mama."

Feeling moved, I leaned over and kissed his forehead. "I'm so happy."

There was a long funeral procession, much as we'd done for Roy. White flags, with Holy Symbol of the Diamond Family embroidered in black upon them went first. The white and silver coffin lay upon a silver-wood cart drawn by white Diamond horses with silver tack.

The skin of a golden animal had been draped over the coffin. I leaned over to Mrs. Clubb. "Do you know what the skin signifies?"

She didn't look at me. "That he was a King."

Cesare and his wife Furuta, both dressed in black, wore the white ceremonial robes and crowns of their Family trimmed in black and silver. The diamonds in their crowns flashed as they walked hand in hand behind the coffin-cart.

"I don't wish that on anyone," Tony said softly.

I recalled the agony of Tony's walk behind Roy's funeral cart, mere days after almost dying, and took his hand.

To my surprise, he didn't move his away.

Mrs. Rachel Diamond, Gardena holding her arm, went next, then Gardena's brothers and their families. Her brothers wore black and white beaded bands which went straight across their foreheads, and white capes without adornment which reached to the ground. The women's hair — Gardena, her mother, her sisters-in-law — were completely wrapped in black, with beaded white lace binding it.

It took over an hour for the parade of Julius Diamond's men, now sworn to Cesare, to pass. Groups of men came past singing; the Diamonds in the crowd sang with them. One walked alone, a man holding a microphone and small speaker on a wheeled stand walking backwards in front of him as he spoke out poems in a language I didn't know. Hordes of others followed them.

The young man who'd seated us now came with an envelope for Tony. "For the meal," was all he said.

I felt surprised. "Won't your Patriarch be on his way ...?"

The young man smiled. "He'll be buried at the Manor. It's where he was born."

I wondered at them not making the procession through their entire quadrant, as they'd done with Mr. Alexander, or at least out to their Country House, as we'd done with Mr. Roy. But perhaps they did things differently here.

"We'd be glad to join you," said Tony.

So we rose when the other Families did, followed the young man (whose name turned out to be Flannery Hook) to our carriage, and set off.

Acevedo seemed so awed by all he'd seen that he didn't protest once.

In the carriage, Ace said, "Papa?"

Tony smiled at him. "What is it?"

"Go home?"

"Not yet. We'll eat first."

"Okay," Ace said.

I'd thought perhaps they'd secure a hall somewhere.

It was more like a stadium.

Huge lines of tables laden with giant pots of food sat along the walls, each table devoted to a sort of food or drink. At the back wall, three chefs stood upon a raised area, creating small portions of sliced meat from what looked like an entire cow, roasted whole.

The center held round tables and folding chairs a-plenty. Diamond ladies high and low entered behind us, their servants burdened with huge platters trailing them. The crowd was immense; compared to this, Jack's "funeral" was a tiny affair.

"Come," Flannery said. "We have a room for the Families to dine in private." He glanced at Daisy, then at Tony's men, who'd gotten out behind us. "The nursemaid may enter, but there's not room for the men."

Tony turned to Sawbuck. "Keep an eye on things down here."

Sawbuck did not look happy, but as no other Family men were allowed up either, he stationed himself near the bottom of the stairs with the rest.

The steps went up to a spacious room overlooking the main floor. Large glass windows tilted backwards displayed us to the crowd.

All the Four Families were represented there: Mrs. Diamond and Gardena, Lance and little Roland close by. The five oldest Diamond brothers, with their wives and children. Mrs. Regina Clubb was there, with seven of her daughters and those of their husbands who still lived. A woman in her thirties a bit darker-skinned than me sat in a corner, a satchel with a stuffed toy protruding on the seat beside her. I thought: *this must be the Diamond nursemaid.*

Kitty Clubb of the Dealers did not attend.

Mr. Charles Hart arrived alone.

Jack was nowhere to be seen. And I hadn't seen him at the procession.

Had his news atop the Grand Ballhouse, his seeming betrayal of his Family ... had it been too much? Had he been disowned?

I could see Julius Diamond doing something like that, but it bothered me that Mrs. Rachel would go along with this. Perhaps in her grief, she'd never thought to specifically invite her youngest son.

The back of the room was filled with a similar array of food and drink as lay below. The main part of the room had comfortable armchairs upholstered in white and silver, with tables of dark polished wood.

When Gardena saw us, she came over. Roland took one glance and hurried up behind her.

Ace beamed. "Wa-wee!"

Roland got on one knee and rested his head on Acevedo's shoulder. "Oh, Ace," he sobbed. "I'm so glad to see you."

Little Acevedo seemed perplexed. "Why sad?"

Roland kissed his little cheek, and hugged him once more. "My grandpa's dead."

"Oh," Ace said, not understanding. "I sowwy."

Roland smiled at that, moving back to wipe his cheeks with his sleeve. Then he wiped under his eyes with both his hands, wiping them on the backs of his trousers. "It's okay." He got up and rested his hand on Ace's shoulder. "Let's get something to eat."

"Yay!" quoth Acevedo, and the two went off.

Daisy glanced at us. "I'll look out for him." She followed them.

Roland hadn't so much as looked at his father.

We'd watched this all, I for one touched to see the two boys and their love for each other. I turned to Gardena. "I'm so very sorry for your loss. This whole thing is horrendous."

Gardena's eyes went red, and she bit her lip, glancing away to compose herself. Finally she took a deep breath. "Thank you."

I held her, listening to her cry.

I didn't know what her relationship with her father had been. Contentious, from what I'd seen. But just from what I'd gone through after Peedro's murder, I thought I might know a bit of what she felt. "It's terribly difficult," I murmured, patting her back. "This might sound trite. But ... time does heal much."

Gardena let out a laugh, then nodded, drew back. "I'm sure I've completely ruined my makeup." Then she twitched, glanced around, and curtsied low. "Dear Queen."

I shrugged, gesturing for her to rise. "No matter." Then I smiled at her. "You'd be just as beautiful with none."

I glanced back at Tony, who stood awkwardly by, trying to look anywhere but at us.

I moved close to speak in Gardena's ear. "Where's Jack?"

She pulled back, head down. "He feared to come." She shook her head. "His deception truly angered my parents. He went to the first day of the wake. Cesare told him not to return. That he was unwelcome."

"Cesare?" I felt astonished. "How could he?"

Gardena let out a breath. "Like it or not, he's Patriarch. And even at the best of times, my brother is slow to forgive."

Surely Cesare must know of Jack's visits to Spadros Manor. I wondered what he thought of them.

Cesare should have been at the meeting atop the Ball-house — there was much he might not know. But there was nothing to be done about that now.

Gardena said, "Have you eaten?"

"Not as yet."

She took my arm. "Then come; it's quite good."

It smelled good: roasted meat, a thick stew, another dish that looked like a mix of cooked pumpkin and corn. There was something Gardena called "summer salad," but reminded me of Ace's porridge that had been cooked until it could be diced cold, then mixed with spinach. It looked strange, but was tasty. There were fried foods, both sweet and savory, a rice dish with chicken and vegetables, and mashed sweet potatoes.

After filling our plates, we followed Gardena to a table far to the back of the room, where Roland, Daisy, and Ace already sat eating. "It's our way to eat the meat first at funerals," Gardena said. "But you may do as you wish."

This amused me. "Will you join us?"

She glanced around. "Since we're out of view."

At this, I felt sad. "Only if you wish to."

She sat.

Roland looked up at her. "I'm sorry to cause trouble."

I said, "What do you mean?"

He looked miserable. "If I hadn't gone to hug my Daddy at Mr. Alexander's funeral, they wouldn't have killed my Grandpa."

Gardena and Tony, faces horrified, both said, "No!"

Gardena set her plate upon the table and knelt beside her son, taking his hands in hers. "My sweet, this is not your fault. That bad man killed your Grandpa, not you. Oh, come here." She hugged the boy as he cried.

"They tried to kill Ace," Roland said. "They tried to kill me." He pulled back, glancing between his mother and father, his cheeks streaked with tears. "**Why?**"

How could I say this? "They hate us," I said. "They want us gone."

Tony quickly said, "But we love you. We won't let them hurt you. I won't let them hurt you, not if I have anything to say about it."

I said, "And you'll have Master Lance and your Mama and all your Family with you."

Ace looked at us without understanding. He gently patted Roland's arm. "No sad, Wa-wee."

Roland hugged Ace, sobbing.

Gardena rose, going round to lay hands upon them both, squatting down behind them. "Rollie? What troubles you so?"

Other than his beloved grandfather being shot in front of him? Perhaps she didn't realize what that would do to him, inside.

Roland sat up, not looking at her, and shrugged.

Gardena spoke gently. "Come on. Tell me."

"I'm supposed to take care of **Ace**," the boy said. "How can I help him, when I'm not even in the same **quadrant**?"

"Oh, sweetheart," Gardena said. "You see here? Your Daddy, and Mrs. Jacqui, and all your Daddy's men, are at Ace's house to protect him."

"Yes," I said. "There are even men outside his rooms, day and night, so no one can get in and hurt him. And Miss Daisy is in his room all night long to make sure he's okay."

Roland considered this a moment, then sniffled. "Okay."

"Besides," I said. "It's not your job to take care of him. That's our job, because we're his parents."

Roland looked at me, nodding somberly.

Gardena kissed his cheek. "So be at peace, my love. Eat."

We all sat there picking at our food — except for Ace, who ate as if he'd never tasted anything so wonderful.

The Relationships

Eventually, the boys went off to congregate with the other children, Daisy trailing behind. Flannery took our plates, and we got up so others might have the table, rather aimlessly walking about.

No one spoke with us for some time. Then Mr. Hart approached, giving a slight bow. "Good day to you."

"Good day," said Tony, his eyes fixed on his sons. He did not bow. "I hope you're well."

Mr. Hart shook his head. "I've known Julius since he was born." He sighed. "Such a tragedy."

"Indeed," said I, but I was thinking more about Roland than Mr. Julius.

Mr. Hart glanced in the direction of Tony's gaze. "I see young Acevedo is winning over the crowd."

In the far corner, Ace held court with a toothy bright grin.

I'd felt hesitant about Ace going off on his own, even with Roland and Daisy to look after him. But the other children, instead of bullying or teasing, were all smiles.

I felt touched. My baby was **loved**!

"This bodes well," Mr. Hart said proudly. "Smart and winsome both."

Tony watched with longing, and I felt sad for him, recalling the lonely life he'd led. No brothers, not allowed friends. Even his own cousin Sawbuck, who loved him, was forced to call him "sir."

Perhaps this was what caused Tony to distrust me, to push me away.

Tony said, "Can I get either of you a drink?"

I felt so glad that Diamond quadrant didn't allow alcohol. "Water, if you will."

Mr. Hart said, "The same."

Tony nodded and headed off.

"My dear Jacqui," Mr. Hart said softly. "I hope you're well."

I shrugged. "I dislike seeing anyone die." I felt bitter. "I've certainly seen enough of it in my time."

"That grieves me, Jacqui. You must know ..." He lowered his voice even further. "I regret our conversation on Market Center. I've been told of your conversation. With your visitor." He hesitated. "Surely you see I've done everything I could to keep you safe."

I snorted. "You want me to believe that twenty-six years ago, Polansky Kerr was such a threat that the Hart Patriarch had to succumb to **blackmail**? That any time up to now you couldn't have just **killed** him? Told everyone that he was **lying**?" I struggled to keep my voice from shaking. "Or was I just expendable?"

"No! Good gods, no." Mr. Hart put his hands on his hips under his jacket, looking away. Then he took a deep breath, facing me. "I have no excuse. I was weak. I was afraid. I was desperately in love. You'd not yet been born, and I'd only just rebuilt my quadrant." He gazed towards the floor. "It may seem strange to you; it'd been a decade and a half since the Bloody Year. But after seeing my entire family murdered, for a long time ... I was changed."

Tony stood a few paces off, holding three glasses of water, a question in his eyes.

I took a glass from him, drank it. "I would go to the Fire before I let Acevedo live like I did."

"I offer no excuse," said Mr. Hart. "I've wronged you. But I love you, Jacqui. I always have. I still believe there was nothing else I might **do**! Not and keep you **alive**!"

I couldn't look at him. "Perhaps you should've let me die then."

Tony's voice was filled with compassion. "Oh, Jacqui ..."

Now Tony decides to care about me? I turned away. "Forget it."

Then the sound of Acevedo's little canes came clattering up. "Mama!"

I turned, knelt before him, feeling moved. "My boy." I kissed his forehead, then gestured up at Mr. Hart. "This is your Grandpa."

Mr. Hart knelt, offering his hand. "It's an honor to meet you."

Confusion came over the boy's face. "You no dead?"

I chuckled fondly. "No, sweetie, it was Rollie's Grandpa that died. This is **your** Grandpa."

"Oh," Ace said, clearly not understanding.

Mr. Hart stood, amused.

Roland approached, hanging back a bit when he saw we weren't alone.

"Wa-wee." Ace patted Mr. Hart's leg. "Gampa!"

Tony said, "Mr. Hart, might I introduce Master Roland Diamond."

Mr. Hart smiled at Roland, offering his hand. "Honored to meet you."

Roland shook hands. "And you, sir."

"Wa-wee," Ace continued. "Gampa!"

Roland looked down. "Yes, I see your Grandpa." He laughed, his face showing he understood his little brother's confusion. "Ace is funny."

I said, "How so?"

"When we got to the buffet, he didn't want any meat. It's our way to eat the meat first at funerals, so I asked him why." He giggled. "Remember when he didn't want to eat the fish?" He kept giggling, so much that he could hardly speak. "He thought that since the fish was dead and we ate it, now my Grandpa is dead, and —"

"Good gods," Mr. Hart said, clearly taken aback.

The rest of us laughed.

Ace looked embarrassed and hurt.

I squatted beside him. "Come here." I took him into my arms. "I know this is all **so** confusing." I kissed his hair. "Even if you don't understand what's going on, we still love you."

Ace put his head on my shoulder.

Roland said, "I told him we only eat animals. Not **people!**"

Mr. Hart said kindly, "You did well, son."

Roland held out his hand. "Come on, Ace — let's look over the hall."

Of course, Ace couldn't take Roland's hand, not and use his canes. But the two went to the large windows and peered out over the crowds.

Tony said to Mr. Hart, "Is that wise? To have the Families on display like this?"

Mr. Hart chuckled. "It's well-crafted: the glass is slightly darkened, and the angle of the glass is such that it's difficult to look into the doings here." He lowered his voice. "Your boys are safe, sir."

Tony glanced at him, startled. "Well, of course."

I looked across the room. Cesare Diamond stood, fists on his hips, glaring at us.

Now Diamond Patriarch — for the second time, as it were — Cesare was half past thirty. Very tall, very dark, and reasonably handsome.

I hadn't expected for him to come to us, even though that would've been polite. But I'd passed it off as him grieving his father. But why did he glare at us so openly?

Our eyes met, and his face turned stubborn, fierce.

Tony looked in the same direction and sighed. "Things can't go on like this." He shook his head. "Perhaps it's time to face him."

Mr. Hart said nothing.

I took Tony's arm and spoke softly. "I've had some dealings with Mr. Cesare. It might go better if I went along."

To my surprise, Tony nodded somberly.

We crossed the room, many eyes upon us, and I watched as Cesare's face turned wary, then confused, then hesitant.

Tony said to him, "Our condolences, sir."

Cesare nodded.

Tony said, "Might we speak privately?"

Cesare's eyes narrowed, and he hesitated. After a moment, he gave a slight nod. "Come."

We followed him to a door nearby, which led to a windowless room.

Once we'd closed the door behind us, he faced us. "Say what you will."

Tony had a peaceful stillness to him, his gaze inward. "I have apologized to your parents, but never to you." He looked up at Cesare. "As Miss Gardena's oldest brother, you had to have felt the greatest burden of her actions —"

Cesare looked outraged. "**Her** actions?"

Tony stood his ground. "**And** mine!" He stopped then, face twisting in anguish. "She suffered for **years** as a spinster, when **all** she wanted was children. For **years**, I let my fortune, my **life** be wasted under blackmail, put myself under the terror of both your father and mine, let my little son live his childhood without a **father**. **I** did this." He swallowed, glanced away. "**Yes**, I was dishonorable to bed your sister, even though she came to me." He took a deep breath, let it out. "Deeply so. It was **wrong**, and it was wrong not to marry her when she came with my child." He shook his head, not looking at any of us. "I was foolish, and reckless, and cowardly." Then he faced him. "You have reason to hate me. But in your entire life, have you done **nothing** dishonorable?"

Cesare gave me a quick glance. He knew I knew he'd run away, leaving his friends to die at Roy's hand when he was a boy. But he didn't know whether I'd told Tony.

Tony straightened, face calm. "If we are to be enemies, then so be it. But like it or not, we share two people we love."

Feeling touched, I blinked back tears.

Cesare glanced at me, a question in his eyes, then at him.

Tony spoke mildly, fatigue in his eyes. "I don't wish you harm. I don't wish your family harm. As I told your father, we face an enemy that wants us all dead." He took a deep breath. "I need you. The Four Families need you. This," he gestured into the room, "this feud has to end. None of us can stand alone and survive."

Cesare didn't move, simply staring. Perhaps he was re-evaluating his life's choices. Perhaps he simply needed time to come to the decision.

But eventually he sighed, and nodded, and stuck out his hand. "You are my nephew's father. Like it or not, that makes us brothers."

The Goodbye

We returned to the room, all eyes upon us, with little to say after that.

Eventually, it was time to say goodbye. Tony and Acevedo and I left the still-full hall with the other Family heads and returned to our carriage.

It was a short drive to where Julius Diamond was to be buried. No one walked the streets outside Diamond Manor; the crowds were held back at the ends of the block by Diamond men. But instead of people, carriages filled the space from curb to curb.

"I don't like this, sir," Sawbuck said once we alighted to the street. "If we're ambushed, there's no way out."

"All will be well," said Tony. "Stay here."

Tony, Daisy, Acevedo and I were led onto the Diamond Manor grounds through a side gate. Blood-red carpeting had been laid upon the packed dirt path. After a walk far out to a fenced, cleared area past a wide meadow, we joined dozens of others around Julius Diamond's gravesite.

We watched as the officiant from the Dealers read the rites. Then we moved back, as we had at Alexander Clubb's funeral, to allow the family their time.

The Diamond family was large: old and young, cousins galore. An older man read aloud about Julius Diamond's life. One by one, others spoke: of kind things he'd done, what they'd learned from his life. There were loud cries of sobbing, wails of grief, men and women I didn't recognize throwing themselves upon the closed casket to embrace it.

Julius Diamond had seemed gruff, irascible, harsh. From what I'd seen, he hadn't been a particularly good father. But these people — his family — they loved him.

Finally, all stilled. The white and silver coffin was lowered, and white flowers were thrown into the grave.

Today, Roland didn't run to his father, only stood clutching his mother's hand, staring into the open grave, face angry, streaked with tears. I held Tony's hand, yet he had eyes only for his son.

The poor child! To lose both his grandfathers suddenly, without warning. And to see Julius murdered in front of him! I couldn't imagine what the boy was going through.

But then perhaps I could. My best friend Air, falling after Peedro Sluff shot him, his dark eyes too big for his little face going blank and cold. The blood streaming around him.

I felt so much grief that I couldn't help crying too.

We stood there until the crowd began to disperse, as the distant cousins, the main men, the neighbors and friends, all drifted to their carriages. The older man who had spoken first began to speak more softly, and the Diamonds' close family gathered around him.

We turned to go. I hadn't known until then how very near he was.

An upright marker of white stone, a plot ringed with silver, the grass upon it short and green.

JONATHAN COURTENAY DIAMOND
JULY 4 1872 AC — APRIL 5 1902 AC
76TH KEEPER OF THE COURT
DIAMOND HEIR
BELOVED SON,
BROTHER, FRIEND

I found myself clinging to the stone. "Oh, Jon! My poor Jon!"

I don't know how long I sat there and wept. My Jon, so full of hope in his short time, who only ever wanted to live.

And now he lay here, dead. It seemed so unfair.

I heard Tony say quietly, "I'm taking her home."

Someone had planted daffodils upon his grave, but the leaves had withered and dried in the summer's heat.

You really couldn't keep daffodils down, though; they rose again, every spring.

So much like my Jon. He'd never let anything keep him from doing what he wanted. Even dying, he got up, barely breathing, and carried me to where we had a chance to be found, at the cost of everything.

He loved me!

How I wish I would have left with him when he begged me to.

I felt Tony and little Acevedo close by, their hands warm upon me. Ace patted my shoulder. "Okay, Mama."

I turned and hugged my baby, who Jon died to save. "I'm okay." I pulled him onto my lap, canes and all. "This stone is about a very good man. When you were still in Mama's tummy, he saved your life."

Ace's eyes grew big. "Oh." Then he looked up at me. "Where he go?"

"He died, and his family put him here." I patted the grass.

"Oh," Ace said.

I kissed my baby's wavy brown hair. "You would've liked him."

Acevedo and I sat upon the grass as I told my son about the man who saved his life. How Jon liked lamb, and tea with milk, and how he always wore the latest fashion. How he loved to paint birds in watercolor, and all the things his duties as Keeper of the Court. How when I used to live at my apartments, we'd watch sunsets together. How he sent me encouraging letters every day that he could and gave me pressed daffodils at the New Year.

The whole time, Tony stood watching Jon's headstone as if he wished to memorize it, his eyes and nose red.

We were never allowed at Jon's funeral. But that day, as the shadows lengthened on the three of us there alone in the Diamond Family cemetery, I feel like we finally said goodbye.

The Decisions

Tony didn't speak the whole way home; he just sat across from me, staring out of the window.

As Ace slept in Daisy's arms, I thought about what the death of Julius Diamond might mean for the city. What had the man seen in his life? What knowledge had he gained?

His relationship with his sons seemed rocky at best. Had he passed along enough for Cesare to be able to govern?

Maybe Jack would know.

Why had Cesare forbidden Jack to attend? Had his relationship with his parents been that bad? I remembered how his mother wouldn't look at him at the meeting atop the Grand Ballhouse. Did she blame him for the deterioration of Jonathan's condition after Jack "kidnapped" him? Jon's injuries when he'd been pushed out of that carriage on Market Center?

That might very well be the case. No one might ever have told her that Jon went along with it. Certainly Jon wouldn't have — he'd been trying to keep Jack's secret.

But there might be more to it. Perhaps Jack feared being recognized, his identity challenged. Surely his own family would know that there was no cousin of theirs named Hector Jackson living in Nitivali.

I smiled to myself. It was an audacious plan, to be sure.

The carriage pulled up to Spadros Manor; Honor opened the door.

Tony said, "It's good to see you smile." Then he got out of the carriage before I might reply.

I handed Alan my hat, went upstairs to my bedroom. Before I reached the top, Alan said, "Mum? I have that name you wanted. Of the horse?"

"Hmm? Oh, yes. Just put it on my desk. Thank you."

Shanna helped me change into my house clothes. Re-did my hair.

When I went to my study, the door hung open.

Tony, still dressed for the funeral, stood in the midst of the room. His back was to me, and he didn't turn at my approach. "I've never really looked at this room."

I wasn't sure what he meant, so I said nothing.

"I see it now: the people you most love are here. Around you." He sighed then, turned to me. "Yet I see nothing of Joe, or your friend Josie."

I felt confused. "I have no portraits of them."

Tony went to the framed daffodils. "Jon gave you these."

Grief came again, yet this time, muted. "Yes."

Tony gazed far away. "I have no portraits of my brothers. Only glimpses of their pain. Anger. Death."

Roy, the man who for decades he thought of as his father, fighting for his life one last time. Little Roy Acevedo, Tony's older brother, who by John Pearson's account, Tony had adored. Tony had witnessed Roy murder the boy.

And lastly, young Pip Dewey, once our servant, then for a time, our master, now gone to Paris, it seemed, forever.

"I thought I loved you —"

I felt as if he'd stabbed me in the heart.

"— loved you more than life itself. Yet that time at Master Jonathan's grave has taught me something I'll regret until the day I die."

My heart was numb. "What is it you regret?"

Tony sighed, face downcast. "That I never loved you the way Master Jonathan did." He glanced at me. "He swore he never touched you ..."

I shrugged. "He asked me to kiss him, there at the end." I didn't look at my husband, only seeing Jon. "I did it out of friendship, out of pity, thinking perhaps he'd never been." Grief hit me hard then, and I squeezed my eyes to hold it back. "He knew he was dying: I saw it in his eyes." I needed a rug of some kind on these gray stone tiles. Perhaps a green one. "I told him I loved him. And then I realized I did. I did."

Tony nodded. "You were right to say so. It was well-done, no matter what anyone might think."

I felt such relief: all this time, I'd feared Tony's reaction if I told him.

As much as I wanted, I couldn't keep from crying. "I don't blame you for not loving me. I'm glad you don't any longer." I swallowed, my throat burning. "Everyone who loves me dies."

Tony took my arm. "Don't say that." He took a deep, shuddering breath. "It's not that I don't love you. I do. I — I — I want you, more than anything." Then he let go, turned away. "But everything I've done has been for the wrong reasons. Has led to disaster."

"Even Acevedo?"

He laughed, but it was bitter. "To bring a child to the world, only to become an assassin's target." His voice dropped to a whisper. "Both my sons have faced death because of my folly."

"Why do you say that?"

"You were right about the alliance with Clubb: it was too soon, against Mr. Alexander's wishes, done to please myself. Lance and his mother agreed to it, but I could feel their hesitation." His voice turned bitter, sarcastic, cynical in a way I'd never heard from him. "Yet I kept going, feeling in the right. Feeling ... strong." He bit his lip, staring up towards the ceiling, face anguished. "My son almost **died**!" He turned away, gasping for air. "In his worst moment, I wasn't beside him. What kind of father **am** I?"

I thought about Peedro Sluff, about Charles Hart. Roy Spadros. "A good one. You care about him. You try your best to be in his life." I thought about our trip to the cottage, how Roland, rather than running to see the animals as most children his age would do, had insisted on waiting for Tony to arrive. The boy had grown, well beyond his short years. "He loves and respects you greatly."

Tony ran his fingers through his hair, clutching it at the nape of his neck as his face twisted in anguish. "But what kind of life can he possibly have?" He let his hands fall. "We're being hunted, Jacqui. One by one." He shuddered. "It's not even a fair hunt: we're being toyed with, allowed to be moved freely to our deaths. I can feel it in my bones."

The man who shot at Roland didn't seem to be toying with anyone; he wanted the boy dead. Only Lance's quick action saved him.

"It makes me doubt every decision," Tony said.

I could surely relate to that.

Tony peered into my eyes. "All I want is peace. For you. For Ace. For this city."

I nodded. "What you did with Mr. Cesare was a good start." I took his hand. "I felt proud to stand with you."

He gave a small smile, cheeks coloring. "I didn't know if it would work. But I had to try."

I felt eyes upon me: Alan stood in the open doorway. "Sorry to disturb you, sir, mum. But Inventor Jotepa is here to see Mrs. Spadros."

I could tell Tony was annoyed — by the intrusion, at himself for not telling Alan we weren't "at home," by someone coming to call right after we'd been to a funeral. I said quickly, "Thank you. Put him in the parlor. I'll be there momentarily."

Alan bowed and left.

I turned to Tony. "We can't very well turn away an Inventor."

Tony had a wry smile on. "Especially the Diamond one."

"True." I patted his arm. "Let's continue this later. On the veranda?"

Tony seemed weary. "Yes. That would be good."

Inventor Jotepa had been sitting on the sofa, dressed in mourning, and rose when I entered. "Forgive the intrusion, mum."

"Please, sit," I said. "Would you care for some tea?"

"No, thank you, mum."

We sat there for a moment. Finally, I ventured, "I'm very sorry for your loss, sir."

He nodded solemnly. "Thank you. As strange as it may sound, I didn't know Mr. Julius well. I wasn't there for my cousins' announcement, so the news came as quite a shock." He lowered his voice. "I'm only grateful the boy escaped."

I nodded. "Indeed." Why was he here? Why hadn't he gone to the dinner, or to the graveside service?

He smiled. "I'm sure this seems terribly strange, me being here instead of at my family's side. But I was chosen, so here I am."

I took a deep breath, heart pounding. Had something happened at the underground library? Had someone been killed? I tried not to let my voice shake. "What must you tell me?"

His dark eyes widened. "No, nothing's gone amiss. On the contrary! All is well. I come from the Inventors' Board. To bring you a proposal."

The Proposal

This surprised me. "A proposal? Of what sort?"

"The Inventors — or it would be more precise to say the Inventors' Board — would like to buy your building."

I didn't know what to think. "I see."

"We'd like to set the upper area as a museum, whilst gaining access to the library below. Extensive work is needed to install a lift, open up the stair to the surface, and so on."

I felt stunned. "I never imagined such a thing."

"Well, upon hearing of your discovery, Inventor Cuarenta contacted Hub straight-away. We've received funding and permission to proceed."

"My word." These were Inventors. Could I accept their money? "This is too much. I'd prefer to make it a gift to the city."

The young Inventor laughed. "Inventor Cuarenta thought you might say so. But the Inventors' Board **cannot** take favors from the Four Families. We mustn't be beholden to anyone, not even to you."

Is **that** what they thought? That I'd concocted some sort of play against the Inventors' Board?

Then I began to consider: I still owed Tony a great deal. "What might you wish to pay for my building?"

"Two thousand dollars," Inventor Jotepa said.

Two thousand dollars would pay what I owed Tony and then some.

You're at your best when you think, Tony had said some time past.

And I recalled my deal with Doyle Pike even farther back. "I'll take a thousand, if I might receive half of the proceeds from the museum ticket sales." The income from this could profit little Acevedo's grandchildren.

Inventor Jotepa laughed. "A shrewd play!" He rose, so I did as well. "Our lawyer will send the papers for you to sign. If I might have your bank information, I'll have the down payment transferred today."

***

After I gave the information to the Inventor and he left, I went to Tony, who sat at the table out on the veranda, and told him of the Inventor's offer. "I can pay you back everything, either tomorrow, or the day after."

He said nothing for some time, just looking out over the gardens for so long I thought perhaps he hadn't heard me. Then he shook his head. "Keep it. You owe me nothing more."

"I don't understand. What's changed?"

He sighed, still not looking at me. "So much that I'm not sure where to begin. But ... Oh, I don't know. Perhaps I never knew what it was to truly love someone."

This made no sense to me. "Well. Thank you."

He sounded weary. "I didn't lie to you, Jacqui. If you want to leave, you can. I'll pay for your ticket to anywhere in the world."

That hurt. "Why do you keep saying this? You claim you love me. Why push me away?"

He rested his arms upon the table, head down. Then he looked up at me. "Because I don't know why you're **here**."

"I'm here because I want to be. Because I love you. Because I love our little son." I whispered, hoping the servants might not hear. "Because I have hope that one day you might love me again, and that I might one day be well, and give you more."

Tony looked startled.

"Sons. Daughters. Children to love."

Tony put his face in his hands. "Do you truly love me?"

"I do. Why would I lie?"

"Then what about Joe?"

I shrugged. "What about him?"

Tony turned away. "I want us to be a family, Jacqui. But until you know the answer to that question, there's nothing for us to talk about."

***

Tony's words utterly shocked me. So much that I got up, went back to my study, and for a while sat at my desk, numb. I honestly wanted to understand why Tony would say such things. Yet to my shame, I did not.

A folded piece of paper sat on my desk. I opened it, glancing at it only to see that it was Alan's handwriting. *Oh, yes, the horse's name*, I thought, then locked it in my top desk drawer.

The next day, after morning meeting, I went to my study, intending to apply myself to the question of Joe and Josie's innocence. When I got to my study, some mail lay atop my Queen's box. The formal proposal from the Inventors for me to sign. A letter from Master Pok-Deng with the details of the shop he'd made the offer on. I made a notation on that for Mr. Howell to have the premises inspected for soundness and vermin, and put a deposit on the place.

I was about to open the next letter — from one of my informants — when I heard ... giggling!

What was going on?

I left my study to investigate; the sound came from front stairs.

At the bottom, Mr. Hart's man Chipmunk stood leaning on the banister gazing at my little Ace.

Acevedo was five steps up!

I felt terrified, angry, but I did my best to speak calmly. I didn't want to startle Ace, do anything to cause him to fall. "What's going on here?"

Chipmunk pointed to Ace. "He's doing well, don't you think?"

Ace looked over his shoulder, beaming. "Up stair, Mama!"

I trembled in fear, my heart pounding so I could hardly speak. "Good job!" Then I whispered to Chipmunk, "What the hell are you doing? What if he should fall?"

Chipmunk gestured with his chin at my boy, who continued to make his way along. "He's gone to the top already. Twice." He gave me a smile which I'm sure was meant to be comforting. "We'll start down the stairs once he's got better balance." He put his foot on the step. "I'm coming **after** you!"

Ace giggled, using his canes to go to the next step.

Chipmunk said, "Mr. Charles spoke with your husband about this, and he agreed: one day, Master Acevedo will be the Spadros Patriarch. He can't be swaddled and carried forever." He turned to Ace and took another step. "I'm gonna **get** you!"

Ace shrieked and laughed, taking one step, then another.

I took steps to be at Master Chipmunk's level. Why hadn't Tony told me about this?

Chipmunk was young, but he spoke in all seriousness. "Ace is my little cousin. My own blood. And even if he were not, I'd never let him fall." He crouched down, pretending to creep up the steps. "I'm gonna get you!"

Ace laughed, and his little cane slipped on the carpeted edge. I shrieked in fear, but Chipmunk was there, grabbing the boy from behind before his face hit the step. "Have your cane firm, young master, before you put weight on it."

Ace said, "Okay, Ih-muh." He smiled up at me. "Okay, Mama."

I sat beside him, putting my hand on his arm. I felt close to tears. "I'm so glad you're okay."

He spoke most definitely. "Up stair, Mama."

"Can I go upstairs with you?"

"Yeah."

So we went up the stairs, he off to his rooms and I to mine.

I sat on the side of my bed, feeling humbled, shaky.

Mr. Hart had seen what I had not: my baby would be Patriarch one day. It seemed too much to even imagine.

The Disdain

I'd cleared my Queen's box by the time Jack Diamond arrived. It was only then I realized that for the past few days I hadn't once thought of, nor even dreamed of him. I passed it off as to the depth of my fatigue.

Alan had shown "Mr. Jackson" to the workroom, and our coffee and tea were already set out.

Face startled, Jack bolted to his feet when I entered, mildly jostling the table. "Good day."

"My condolences for your loss, sir."

Jack didn't answer.

We both sat.

I didn't particularly want to see him. "To be honest, I didn't expect you to return."

Jack hadn't looked at me. But at this, he gave me a quick glance. "I gave your husband my word. I intend to keep it."

I straightened, raising my chin. "I'm sorry you feel obliged to endure my presence, sir. Particularly since you feel I'm your enemy."

Jack leaned back, surprise upon his face. "I never said that."

"You didn't have to. You said I — I worked against the Families at every point. I've disrespected both Mr. Hart and your mother. You believe I even worked against you and Master Jonathan. I'm a spoilt Pot rag woman, who ... who," I recalled what he'd said when he captured me. "Consorts with detestable men, whose word can't be trusted, and who makes poor decisions at every turn." I took a breath to keep my voice from shaking. "No, you didn't say the word. But you need say nothing more. Your utter disdain for me speaks loud and clear."

He didn't meet my eye.

My eyes stung. I wanted nothing more than to leave. But I gritted my teeth and stayed. This was **my** house, and by the gods, I'd not leave him here alone in it. "But since my husband has commanded I work with you, I shall do so."

Jack nodded, seemingly staring at the table.

Finally, he said, "I was able to get a copy of Mr. Kerr's bank records."

I stared at him, astonished. "How?"

He smiled to himself. "My spinster teller was most forthcoming."

This angered me. "Flirting with the poor woman, giving her cause to hope, only to get something that could cost her her job? For **shame**!"

Then I thought: *he got the information. At least we might use it.* I leaned forward. "What did you learn?"

"Well, on their own, not much. He takes in huge amounts on a regular basis; equally huge amounts leave, likely siphoned to his other enterprises to avoid Family fees." He shifted in his chair. "But there are smaller deposits and withdrawals that I find interesting. If we could link any of these to the known expenditures of the Red Dog Gang, might that be proof enough?"

I nodded. "It might." Then I considered the matter. "Did you bring that copy with you?"

He leaned to his right, glancing warily at me. "If I might?"

I snorted, gesturing to whatever he had under there. "Be my guest."

Jack produced a deep brown soft-sided leather case, perhaps fourteen inches tall, such as one might use for traveling. Laying it upon its side, he brought out a two-inch thick leather presentation folder of dark green, clasped with brass. Unclasping it, he opened the folder.

The information had been neatly typed and single-spaced: dates, amounts, who the payments were to, who signed the checks. It went back years. Decades. I looked quickly through the pages in astonishment, then closed the folder and clasped it. "This woman really cares for you."

He scoffed. "Hardly."

Unbelievable. "Well, would **you** do all this for some stranger? Even if it might cost you your job?"

He considered this, face becoming more uncertain as the time passed. Then he looked at me, face stricken. "What should I **do**?"

I laughed at the absurdity. "How should I know?" I leaned back. "What are your intentions towards this woman?"

Jack gave me a blank stare, shrugging.

This angered me. I leaned forward, pointing. "You need to make this right. And if this woman loses her job, you will answer to **me**."

He seemed entirely taken aback. "Of course."

I picked up the folder. "Now, how shall we enter this?"

***

We worked for some time in relative silence, speaking only when need be. But then Jack said, "I spoke to Mr. Polansky's family."

I set down the page I'd been holding. "What did you learn?"

He leaned back, hands folded behind his head. "They tried to hide it, but none of them care for the man, his children especially. From the sound of it, they're entirely estranged."

That could be useful. "Anything else?"

He leaned forward, placing his arms upon the table. "Master Ely Kerr told me the most. It's as you thought: Mr. Polansky is abusive, harsh, and cruel. Or at least this is what Master Ely told me."

I wondered how much booze Jack had to give the man to get that much from him. I was honestly surprised Joe and Josie's father still lived. A drunkard, alone on the streets of the Pot. "Did he know anything about the Red Dog Gang?"

"Oh," Jack said. "I forgot to ask. Although if Master Ely is as forthcoming with others as with me, it might be for the best. I'd not wish another assassin in my rooms."

This took me aback. "Do you mean to say you believe the Dealers are in league with the Red Dog Gang?"

He leaned back, crossed his arms, looking towards the open doorway. "I have no idea what to think." He sighed, letting his hands fall to the table. "I've faced more people wishing to kill me in the past four years than in the seven-and-twenty before."

***

The rest of the day was uneventful; as usual, an hour before dinner, he left, taking the bank records with him, as he wished to read them further.

The next day, Jack Diamond didn't visit, nor did he send a reason as to why. In some ways, it was pleasant: I didn't need to deal with him, nor take time from my work, nor forego time with my son.

But he'd given no indication that he planned not to visit, and after his words the day prior, I hoped nothing had befallen him.

I was in my study sometime well after luncheon but before tea, when I heard Tony enter through the front door. This was odd — normally, Tony would never be home until almost time to dress for dinner. So I wondered what had happened.

Perhaps an hour later, Alan called me to Tony's study. He sat behind his desk. I went in, curtsied. "How may I help?"

Tony snorted in amusement, but his words held barely restrained rage. "Sit down. Something's happened that you might want to know about."

Puzzled I sat across the desk from him.

"You should not have sent your man to investigate David Korol."

Something in his voice terrified me.

"He's made complaint to the Feds. Between that and the attack on Mr. Pasha, Hub has ruled that Bridges must have election oversight."

"What does that mean?"

"You have no idea what you've done, do you? It means we — the independent city-state of Bridges — is in danger of being reduced to a Protectorate."

"I don't understand."

His voice dripped with sarcasm. "You don't, do you? Our election will be entirely supervised. **Everyone** must vote. Even **women**!" He stood, leaning over the desk onto his hands. "Even **servants**!" By this time, he was shouting. "Even the **Pot**!"

I felt stunned.

"And this will be enforced. By the Army." He took a deep breath. "That means no double-voting. No Family going door to door to confirm the vote. An independent tally." He shook his head, turned aside. "This changes our entire play, six weeks before the election."

"I'm sorry. I didn't think —"

"No, you didn't. You never do." He threw a hand out towards the door. "Just go. Get out of here. I don't want to see you."

I went back to my study, unsure what else to do.

This man David Korol was bold, cunning. More so than I was.

Then something occurred to me. No mid-card on Market Center knew how to contact the Feds! I didn't even know how to do that, and I was the Spadros Queen.

He had to have had help. Could David Korol be the man that Polansky Kerr was backing for Mayor?

Could David Korol be — or know — the Bridges Strangler?

I'd put things off long enough. Whether Jack still wanted to help or not, I had to find out what this plot against the Families was all about. I needed to get to the cause of everything.

I rung for Honor. "There's a large basket in my bedroom with a large binder atop it." I'd brought the binder home with me one day from my apartment, oh, a few months after Peedro Sluff's murder, intending to read it, and never gotten around to doing so. "Would you bring it to me?"

"Yes, mum."

I was still well-behind on my investigations into Joe and Josie's whereabouts when David Bryce was taken. I hadn't done my memory exercises that day. But I felt determined that nothing would keep me from reading Peedro's binder, in its entirety.

The Book

Honor came in, set the basket in the exact opposite corner from the dress Madame Biltcliffe had made for me, bowed, and left.

The basket was so full. Why was it so full? I gazed at it, trying to recall what I'd put there. The letters Ottilie, Poignee, and Treysa had stolen from me. The pamphlet about olden days, with the Hart mark upon the front illustration. What else?

I felt disturbed that I couldn't remember. What else was I not recalling?

Eventually, I retrieved Peedro's large binder from atop the basket.

Clearing my desk, I opened the binder and began to read.

I'd not really read the thing, just quickly surveyed it that day we went to clean Peedro Sluff's back rooms after he died. But now, I started from the front, and began to read each item.

The first was a tiny news notice of the opening of his liquor store. On the same page, a society column, several months later, about Roy and Molly's attendance at a Midsummer party, given by an aristocrat who was now dead.

I remembered that party. The food was strange, the drink was strange. Everyone said things I didn't understand, and glared at me when Roy and Molly's backs were turned. Evidently, they'd brought Tony, which I didn't recall, and in the paper, listed me as "their young ward."

The words were underlined. So even then, Peedro had wondered why Roy wanted me.

I felt so tired. The past two weeks had been awful, and I'd not slept well, even for me. I closed the binder, lay my head on my arms.

I woke with a start.

I'd had a dream ... something about John Pearson's book.

I felt groggy: it took me a moment to recall where I'd put the thing. Once I found John Pearson's book, I held it, pondering what the book, the dream might mean.

John Pearson was a private, secretive man, with no time or place to actually be in private. He had his post — which wasn't exactly private — and his rooms.

Maybe something in Pearson's rooms could help. Anything.

We needed some edge, some information that would point us in the right direction, give us help of some kind against Polansky Kerr.

Alan stood at his post, writing in a ledger. He looked up at my approach. "Yes, mum?"

I waved his father's book. "Did your mother tell you about this?"

"Yes, mum. Although I've not read it."

"I need to see your father's rooms. Would you arrange it?"

He hesitated, glancing away. "Yes, mum. One moment." He held up a hand. "Please, wait here."

I leaned upon what was really a lectern, built into a counter of shiny painted black wood. It had seemed too much to ask Alan to change the post his father'd had worked at for so long to match my renovations of Spadros Manor.

After perhaps twenty minutes, Alan returned, moving to the wall behind his station to ring the bell for "uppers coming downstairs." He turned to smile at me. "This way, mum."

I knew the way full well, but I let him lead me as if I were entirely new. The pretense gave a sort of theater to the event. My maids, sculleries, waiters, all along the way bowing or curtsying.

Mrs. Jane stood at the door to her rooms, curtsying low. "Please forgive the mess, mum."

What I saw looked spotless. "Nothing to forgive. Thank you so much for seeing me."

In the doorway, I surveyed their front room. Portraits. On my left, a bookcase that came to my shoulder. A sofa covered in black cloth on the far left. A longer one in front of me, a small table and lamp in the corner between them. A thick picture-book on a low coffee-table.

Close to my right, a coat and hat rack, a short cabinet with a small candelabra and more portraits atop. Doors in the far right corner, to what had to be the toilet-room and the back bedrooms.

This front room was the size of my bedroom. John and Jane Pearson had raised six children here. "Let's see the back."

I'd guessed correctly: the corner's right door led to a very small toilet and bath. The door straight on led to a narrow hall. The door across opened onto what had to have been their boys' room: the bunks, three high on each side, were still there. Books and boxes lay neatly piled upon the top left bunk.

The room down the hall had been Mary's: it still smelled of her, after all these years. Floral and pastels, an ancient vase of flowers long dry.

Both rooms had doors to another narrow hall, which held one door in the center, to the room shared by their parents. This room ran across the width of both.

A four post bed lay in the center, its back to the far wall. Small dressers stood upon each side to the corner. A wardrobe on each wall, just past the bed, with racks for hats and coats upon the walls beside me. All neatly laid out: I could immediately tell which side Pearson had used.

It looked as if nothing of his had been touched.

Then it came to me: WB LD. His side of the room was on the left. I turned to Alan. "Please move your father's dresser aside."

Alan glanced at his mother, who nodded, and they carefully moved the dresser all the way out so it stood in front of the bed. They did it well; as far as I could tell, nothing was disturbed. Alan bowed, gesturing to the empty spot where the dresser had once been.

I went past him; both stared at me.

WB LD. Wall behind left dresser.

I peered at the wall, which was made up of the same paneling as the back of my closets. Now I knew why Pearson always found my hiding places: he'd done the same thing.

I dropped to sit on the floor tailor seat, and putting the book aside, I began to test the paneling.

Jane said anxiously, "What are you doing?"

"I think he may have hidden something here," I said. "If not, I'll bother you no more."

I could hear her curtsy. "It's no bother, mum, I —"

I raised a hand to stop her. "Hush." I'd felt something move, as I'd pushed in with my left hand.

Using both hands now, I slid the paneling up. Behind it was a thick, leather-bound book of dark gray.

A noise from behind: several of the servants stood at the door.

Jane shouted, "Begone, you!" She chased after them. "How dare you come into my rooms and stand watching!"

I had a bad feeling abou this. "You must dismiss all of them."

Alan said, "But mum —"

I set the thick book upon my lap. It was quite dusty. "Hire from Dickens if you must. But I guarantee you one of them was in the hire of our enemy." There was no reason for them to be there if they weren't, and they likely were right now going to whoever paid them to — "Wait. Question them first. Get Master Bresciane to help. They might've been paid to do this by another. We must find out who that is before they flee."

Alan nodded. "Right on it." He rushed out.

Another book, almost as thick, sat behind the empty space where the first had been. With some difficulty, I pulled it out, then slid the paneling shut. I knew how cunning, how thorough, how driven Mr. Pearson had been. If anything had endangered Tony or Roy, anything at all, he would've sniffed it out.

Pearson knew as much as anyone about the city. What went on in it.

This was our chance. As far as the plot against the Families went, this information could help us solve everything.

***

I took the books to my study's toilet room. Standing at the sink, I wiped them down with my handkerchief and some water, so as not to soil my desk. As the outsides were quite dirty, this took some time. Once that was done, I dusted off the edges and moved beside my desk.

I shook the first book, pages facing the floor: nothing.

The portrait of an elderly woman fell out of the second book. Dark hair with streaks of white, and her eyes ...

She reminded me very much of Roy.

Alan appeared in the open doorway, panting. "Mum, one of the servants escaped. One of the stable-boys. Tommy."

I barely remembered the boy. He'd loved the horse we'd lost. Honor mentioned he and Master Jacob had tucked Tommy and his friend Listy into bed at night when they were small.

I shook my head, feeling discouraged. "We should've spoken to the boys more about why Peter Dewey left." We'd had that meeting. They knew to be wary of the Red Dog Gang. Of Frank Pagliacci.

But I'd ordered Peter Dewey killed. The Red Dog Gang had to have brought in someone we hadn't mentioned to befriend the boy, to use the boy's grief and bitterness against us.

Alan sighed. "That was my job, mum. Not yours."

"But this is my household. I —"

Alan shook his head, one hand upon the doorpost. "No, mum. Begging your pardon, mum, no. I don't wish to be out of line. But this is my fault. You mustn't blame yourself for this."

I stared at him, mouth open at his courage. "Well, then, contact my husband's men. Tommy has to be found alive. Question the men out front first — someone may have seen which way he went." I sighed, feeling weary. "Maybe we can follow him to his master."

"That sounds good, mum."

Off down the hall by Alan's station, The Telephonic Telegraph rang.

That line went to the doctor's office, then to my apartments!

Alan hurried out of the room.

I locked the books and portrait in my desk, then went into the hall. There was no reason to make a Telephonic Telegram to Spadros Manor unless it was terribly urgent.

Alan stood by the device, the receiver to his ear, his face terrified and pale. "Thank you. I'll tell her at once."

I ran to him, heart pounding. "What's happened?"

He turned to me, tears in his eyes. "Ariana's been shot!"

The Friends

My mind raced, my heart pounded. "What?" She was just a tiny child. How could this happen? "Oh dear gods, is she —?"

"No." Alan's eyes were wild. "But she was hit by the gunpowder, on her arm and the side of her face." He took a shuddering breath. "That was Dr. Salmon's nurse. The doctor's probably there by now."

I grabbed his arm. "Get a carriage and we'll go."

He rushed to his desk and pulled a bell cord, one of many beside his area. He stood panting. "It'll take at least a half hour to prepare the horses and carriage."

Tony came out of his study. "What's wrong?"

I ran to him. "Ariana Spadros was shot at. I don't know by who, but she's hurt!"

Tony stood there, blinking for a moment. "Very well." He took my arm, moving me towards Alan's post. "Get dressed. Mr. Pearson and I will help the boys with the horses. Meet us out front. We'll go together."

Alan said, "Sir, there's something I need to tell you ..."

Tommy had fled. I was only wearing a house dress. I ran up the stairs, shouting for Shanna.

As I went, the large bell rang. By the time I returned downstairs, Tony, Alan, and Tony's carriage were out front, along with twenty men on horseback. Once I got in, the carriage took off at a full gallop.

It was just before tea-time; the streets would normally be choked with people coming home from work. My guess was that more horsemen had gone along our path to clear the roads, because we managed to arrive at my apartments only an hour later.

The door to my apartments stood open. Spadros men swarmed the area, sidewalk and street. I jumped from the carriage and ran up the steps. "Blitz? Mary?"

Alan pushed past me, looking in all directions.

Sawbuck's voice came from behind. "They're gone with the doctor."

I turned to face him, not understanding.

Alan rushed out of the door.

Sawbuck said, "Dr. Salmon said he needed more supplies, and a place to work. And his nurse."

I stood there, men going to and fro around me, unable to think. Ariana was **shot**?

Tony came in and said to Sawbuck, "Show me where it happened."

Sawbuck led us to my old bedroom. Plaster, boards, pieces of ancient quilt batting, toys, and crowbars lay strewn around a torn-up gap in the floor, perhaps four feet on a side. A support beam ran through the midst of this area. Two of the boards laying beside it had parts of a blast hole, as if made by a shotgun shell. A similar hole lay in the ceiling.

So someone had shot up ... from **below**?

Underneath the floor was an open living area, deep enough for a man to comfortably stand in, lit by a lantern one of Tony's men carried as he moved past.

The Red Dog Gang had been spying on me ... under my **floor**?

I stumbled to a chair by the tea-table, sitting just in time. Mr. Howell had **thought** the Red Dog Gang had another way to spy on me here. Gods! Poor Ariana! "How were they under my **floor**?"

Sawbuck sighed. "They were under the whole house! It's really a wonder no one heard anything." He drew a piece of wood from his pocket — a knothole, with small screws underneath it. "This is what they used to look. They'd screw it into the floorboards, tight, and with the floor laid so close-knit, you'd never tell the difference." He returned the knothole to his pocket. "We found a clever little gadget down there, like a spyglass but for peering round corners." He put a hand to his chin. "They're smart, no doubt about it. The floors down below are carpeted, and there's no hinges on anything. Everything's covered in thick fabric. Nothing to squeak or clatter."

"Ariana had to have been talking to them," I said. "She must have seen an eye in the floor, like Tenni did in the wall." I felt shaky. "She kept saying her friends were in here." I looked up at Sawbuck. "We thought she was talking to her **dolls!**"

Sawbuck shook his head. "They must have sent a new fellow under there. Her talking to him probably unnerved the man." He shuddered. "But why shoot? If he hadn't shot at her, we might have never known this was there." He pointed towards the back of my apartments. "There's a tunnel that comes out way over on the other side of 32nd. That place is abandoned, too."

How could this have happened? "Where'd Master Alan go?"

Tony said, "I told Teddy to take Mr. Pearson to Dr. Salmon's office." He let out a small laugh. "I don't think the man heard either of us in his rush to see his niece." His face grew pensive. "I don't much blame him."

Yes. It was too close to what had happened to our little Acevedo.

Yet Ariana was Mr. Theodore's niece as well. "Take me to her."

Tony peered at me solemnly, then nodded. He clapped Sawbuck on the arm. "Good work, Ten."

Tony took my arm, drew me outside to the carriage. Barricades had been set up, the police and a few reporters kept outside them. Our carriage passed through without stopping.

Dr. Salmon's office hadn't changed since we'd last been there for Acevedo's last x-ray. The office was old, but well-dusted, and in good condition. Chairs lined the walls of the front room; Alan and Mr. Theodore sat in two of them.

Blitz and Mary stood in their midst, rushing over when they saw us. Mary said, "I knew you'd come."

I said, "How is she?"

Blitz said, "Alive. Dr. Salmon said he'd get as much of the gunpowder out of her face as he could, but —"

She still might be scarred. "Oh, gods," I said. "This is my fault. I should've considered —"

"Stop," Tony said sternly. "This is not your fault. None of us considered anything like this, much less that the man hidden underneath would shoot at a **child**!" He shook his head, face disbelieving. "It's a wonder she's alive."

Dr. Salmon stood by the far door, wiping his clean, wet hands on a towel. "She said she stepped on her doll. The man scared her. When she stepped on her doll, she fell, and there was a loud noise that hurt."

She slipped on a toy. That was the only reason she still lived.

Mary said, "Can we see her?"

Dr. Salmon nodded, stepping aside to let us all pass. "I gave her a bit of ether, so she's groggy."

Ariana Spadros lay in bed, bandages covering her right cheek and the underside of her lower right arm. When Mary rushed to her daughter's bedside; Ariana stirred. "Mama?"

"I'm here, baby," said Mary. "Just rest now."

"Mama, he was different. He sang the same song, but he was scary."

"What song, sweet pie?"

She tried to sing it. "The only solution is truth."

"Wait," I said. "The man underneath sang it?"

Ariana looked up at me. "Yeah."

I turned to Tony. "That's his slogan. David Korol."

Tony took my arm and pulled me from the room, into the hall. "I know. But you can't question her **now**! Besides, it means nothing."

"Nothing? But it proves —"

"It proves **nothing**!" He let out an exasperated breath. "Jacqui, I promise you. When she's well and rested, I'll speak with her myself. I'll have her sit with a police artist and get portraits of the men." He snorted. "Whatever she could've possibly seen through a knot-hole into a darkened room. But we can **not** start making accusations of Mayoral candidates unless we have some actual **proof**!"

"But she said —"

He raised a hand. " What we have is the word of a three-year old girl, under ether, of what she thought two different men said. That's all." He let his hand drop to his side. "And what if these men meant to frame Mr. Korol? Did you consider that?"

I had to admit I didn't.

"I know you wish your man to win —"

Did he think this was about **Joe**? "It's not that —"

"— we each do. But let it at least appear to be a fair fight. Otherwise, we risk turning the city even more against us than it already is."

***

It took several hours to get Ariana home. First, she was sick after the ether, which spoilt her bandages, which then needed changing. She cried the whole time.

By the time she was able to be moved, Tony had left, and with him, his men who'd been keeping the streets clear. We still had the carriage Mr. Theodore and Alan had brought, but the way back was slow.

When we arrived at my apartments, Mr. Theodore and I went in first. The debris had been cleared and the men were out of the house, but the hole still remained. I locked the door before I let the rest go in.

By the time I got everyone inside, Ariana to bed, and returned home, it was past time to change for dinner.

Tony met me in the hall. "How are they?"

I shrugged. "It can't be easy, knowing assassins and spies lay under your very floors."

"I've instructed dinner brought to my rooms," he said. "Shanna's waiting in yours."

"Thank you." I was hungry, having entirely missed tea-time.

Shanna got me changed, I went to Tony's rooms, and we had dinner.

Tony was silent for most of the meal. Finally, he said, "I think we've been going about this the wrong way."

"How so?"

"What benefit was gained from these recent events? Until we can determine what Polansky Kerr wants, I don't think we can solve this."

I pondered his words, the tone behind them. "You think Ariana was deliberately shot."

Tony snorted. "Someone who's planned a play for decades and had it in motion for over four and a half years would hardly send in a man unreliable enough to reveal the entire operation because a little girl said hello." He took a drink of water. "No, he was sent there to cast the final card and announce their victory."

"By killing a child?"

"You said it yourself. It's this Director of the Red Dog Gang's way to distract, upset, and alarm so we won't take some action, find some piece of the plan." He looked away. "I only wish I could conceive of what his plan might be."

I shrugged. "Getting rid of us is all I can imagine."

Tony shook his head. "It's more than that. Amelia was in this house the majority of her life. At any time, she could've brought in a bomb —"

"Rocket would've smelled it, though."

"Well, yes. Or slit our throats in our sleep —"

"She wouldn't have done that. She loved you."

He snorted. "Until it came time to prove it. Then she fled." He shook his head. "That's just one; many more were here, each with access to the house. By all rights, we should be dead. The fact that we aren't suggests to me that this Red Dog Gang doesn't want us dead. At least, not yet."

The Alarm

Exhausted, I went to bed, and when I woke, the curtains were still shut. I went to the window: it was late morning.

I rang for Shanna. "Why did you not wake me?"

Shanna curtsied low. "Mr. Anthony told us not to, to tell everyone you were not 'at home' today. He said you needed your rest."

Perhaps I did. "Very well; I need my tray, my paper, and my bath, in that order."

As she rushed off to find Honor for my morning tray, I wearily got into my robe.

I put my elbows on the table, rested my forehead upon my fingers. I had so much to do. I was hours behind in my work, after missing an entire day for the funeral and another for Ariana's injury.

I think I dozed for a moment, because I was startled awake by Honor's knock. He brought the tray in and left without a word.

Tea and toast, paper and personal mail, a note from Blitz. I opened the note first:

> Someone found out about my daughter. Reporters are everywhere, and the police are asking questions. They're threatening to cite us if we don't speak with them. Howell's men are holding them back so far, but they need help. He sent a man to your husband but wasn't given a reply.

I got up, rang for Honor, and returned to my seat. After Tony's reaction to my going to his rooms, I didn't dare go inside, even if I knew he was there.

And by this time, he could be almost anywhere in the city proper.

I stared out at our gravelled courtyard, at the servants moving around, not really seeing them. My head hurt, and the sun seemed too bright. Why would Tony not help Blitz and Mary?

"You called, mum?" Somehow Honor stood beside me.

"Yes." I felt befuddled, still asleep. "Where's Mr. Anthony?"

"I don't know, mum. I could ask Mr. Pearson."

Yes. Alan would know Tony's schedule — but hadn't the man Mr. Howell sent gone to Alan in the first place? "Send for him, please."

Honor glanced to the right. My bed had been made, and my house clothes lay draped upon it. When had that happened? The sounds of Shanna starting my bath in the next room came forth. Honor said, "When would you like to see him?"

"What time is it?"

"Almost eleven, mum."

"Very well. Noon will do."

Honor bowed and left.

Eleven!

I smeared butter on a piece of toast and took a bite. It was cold, unappetizing. I took the piece from my mouth and drank some tea.

I drew the curtain to block out the sun. I had to think.

Blitz should know what to do, what to say. Mr. Theodore lived right there, in their neighborhood — surely he would've gotten his brothers together to help. Alan would have rung the large bell, sent everyone, if his sister and niece were in real danger.

I opened the letter: it held all the signs of forgery.

I felt like crying, both from relief that the alarm had been false, and in anger at myself. How could I have been so stupid? This could've been any number of traps, ambushes, or confirmations handed to our enemies.

But I had stop. And I had to think. How did the Red Dog Gang get hold of a letter from Blitz to know his handwriting?

Shanna said, "Your bath's ready, mum."

Now I had to figure out what to ask Alan.

When he arrived, I told Alan that I wanted no luncheon, and to bring the salicylate: tea had helped very little for my headache.

241

He seemed concerned. "You've eaten nothing today. Would you like me to call for the doctor?"

I did feel rather unsettled at the stomach, but I passed it off as nothing.

"Mum, did Shanna not open your curtains?"

I'd asked her to close all the curtains, and the room was lit only by the glow around them. "She did — but the light pains me."

Alan drew back. "Then the doctor should see to you, mum, before you take anything. My Ma would say the same."

The thought of Jane Pearson in a fury amused me. "We wouldn't want your Ma to be annoyed with us, now, would we?"

He smiled to himself. "No, mum. We surely would not."

***

I lay upon my bed, a cold cloth on my forehead. Shanna and Jane stood beside me as the doctor looked me over.

Dr. Salmon pronounced the matter a migrainous attack. As I'd never had one before, he thought it possibly the aftermath of the blow to the head I'd gotten the day before Acevedo was born.

I was to rest and eat as I might, and he grudgingly allowed the salicylate. "If your stomach becomes disturbed further after taking it," he said, "then you should stop." He turned to Jane. "If she has no appetite, bring her broth." He glanced at Alan, who stood in the open doorway. "Notify me on the Telephonic if she can't keep liquids down."

I hadn't vomited, but Dr. Salmon seemed more concerned with my lack of eating than by anything else.

Jane curtsied low. "Yes, sir."

Tony didn't come by until after tea-time, and then after changing into his house clothing and coming by way of his rooms. He quietly pulled a chair beside me and took my hand. "I hope you're feeling better."

Was I? My head still hurt, but I'd been able to keep down broth, and felt more rested. "I think so." I squinted up at him. "Where were you?"

He bent to kiss my hand, and petted it. "On Market Center. Work on your building goes apace. And the Chief of Police wished to speak with me about the matter."

This seemed amusing. "I imagine."

"We'll give a statement tomorrow." He loosened the upper button on his shirt. "Hopefully this will take people's minds off the heat."

I snorted. "They'd be able to sell tickets down there just for the cooling effects alone."

He smiled to himself. "True."

"What must I do? To help."

He kissed my hand, eyes shut. "Rest. The world will turn without you for one day."

And so it did. The next day, I was able to eat, and although the light still bothered me, my head hurt much less than before. The third day, I returned to my study, eager to do something useful.

Peedro's binder still sat as I'd left it, my Queen's box set atop it.

I sighed. I wanted like anything to keep reading the binder, but I'd let others do the duties which were rightly mine for far too long. So I set the binder upon the basket — now next to my desk — and got to work.

***

That evening, we received a special edition of the *Bridges Daily*. I'd never seen the headlines so large:

WAR!
Wild Men Attack Multiple Domes
Feds Call For Aid

I read the article, scarcely believing my eyes.

Wild Men had broken into the domes at Nitivali, Dickens, and Potter, stealing food, animals, weapons. Mining camps throughout the North were under attack. The ruins of Zion and Narni had been stripped, the repair crews in both domes murdered. The Army had been tasked with patrolling the train to the Tollkeen steamer after reports of sabotaged tracks and robbed passengers.

The Army urged men to enlist. The Feds hinted at conscription.

Whilst the tabloid headlines were strangely quiet on the matter, the next day's editorial sections of the *Bridges Daily* were not. "What business have we with foreign wars?" was the most common remark. "I'll not send my sons off to die for those who care naught for us," was another.

A few, though, spoke of our duty as citizens of the Merca Federal Union. "We might one day be in need. Who might come to our aid, if we fail to go to theirs?" That sentiment was roundly mocked in future editorials. For example, one fellow said, "If men fail to build properly and secure what is theirs, they deserve the thief in the night. Our dome is well-made, and we have no need of outsiders to come 'save' us."

***

According to the morning news, Mr. David Korol had spent the entire day prior making speeches. The main headline read:

KOROL ATTACKS

> Best-bet Mayoral candidate David Korol gave a spirited speech in front of the Mayor's Mansion this morning, and another in the late afternoon.
>
> The first focused upon the Four Families.
>
> "An old man, a bastard, a cripple, and a child. This is what we have for the future of this city."

This shocked me. Roland and Ace were living, human children, yet he spoke of them as if they were dogs!

> "Is this what you want? Will they keep us from this war the Feds have drawn us into? Or will your sons and brothers and fathers be forcibly taken to far-off lands to die?
>
> "This is not the only concern. Are these 'Families' even going to be able to keep the peace here? One heartbeat separates the strength of Hart quadrant 'standing beside us' from a rudderless ship, a quadrant in chaos, without Heir or destiny."

Hmm, I thought. If David Korol were with the Red Dog Gang, then he should know of my connection to Mr. Hart. Or perhaps they didn't trust him with that information.

> "Many of you are old enough to remember the gangs that ravaged our city in the days before the Four Families. Yet I fear that the time of the Families is waning. We need strong leadership to carry us into the future."

David Korol no longer cared who he offended.

As I read on, I felt horrified.

> His second speech targeted fellow candidate Mr. Seth Pasha.
>
> "Who is this man? Why does no one know him, yet so many follow? Why does he refuse to consent to photos, or to have his

244

portrait drawn? What is he hiding? You can ask anyone — my family has been on Market Center for fifty years. I have played in these streets, worked on this land. Yet where is Mr. Seth Pasha from? What neighborhood claims him? What quadrant claims him, for that matter? Men speak of him as if he were the Floorman himself, yet none can say more than he's the best man to win.

"If he's a better man for this position, then why? What do so many see in him? What are his plans for this city? I challenge this man to a debate, in full view of the world, on the real, substantive issues facing our city.

"Beware the glamor of a quick smile and a slick tongue, my friends. This man plans to lead us for life — we'd best have knowledge of what sort of man wishes to do so."

Fear gnawed at me: David Korol couldn't be allowed to win!

The Arrangement

Jack visited that day, went downstairs, drank his coffee, never meeting my eye. All outwardly seemed as usual.

Yet I felt a sense of agitation and unease in him. Something had happened. "I hope you're well."

He quickly glanced towards Honor and Mr. Theodore, as he often did, then back towards me and shrugged.

After several minutes of silence, Jack ventured, "I heard about your servant's child. The injury." He glanced at me. "Is she well?"

What do you care? "She's alive. For the rest, it's too soon to tell."

He nodded.

We were almost finished with the Clubb boxes. I took out a sheet. "A listing of people coming to the Hart-Clubb lowers' bridge." I scanned the list; Josie had asked to see Miss Cheisara Golf, and been refused.

Jack began writing in the ledger.

I recognized the name: Cheisara Golf was Regina Clubb's grand-daughter, and now my dressmaker Tenni Mitchell's paramour. But this sheet was dated well before they began their association, before my former dressmaker Madame Biltcliffe's murder, before even little David Bryce's abduction. "September Second of Eighteen and Ninety-Eight."

Jack finished writing, then held out his hand. I handed the page over, feeling uneasy and not knowing why.

He looked over the sheet. "Any idea as to what this is about?"

"I don't know." I needed to speak with Cheisara about this. "What did Joseph Kerr say to you at the Grand Ball after you pretended to attack your brother?"

Jack seemed surprised at the question, but then to consider it seriously. "Something to the effect of 'calm yourself, sir' ... I don't recall his exact words." He sat still for a moment, eyes narrowing. "I must admit I let my play-acting overtake me; even Jon thought I meant to attack him."

For some reason, this made me laugh.

But that meant my suspicions had been true: Joe **did** lie to me about what he'd said to Jack that night. What else had he lied about?

Jack said, "I learned something the other day."

I peered at Jack. "On what topic?"

"The day you were abducted. The day before your son was born and my brother died."

This interested me at once. "What did you learn?"

"The warehouse had been abandoned for some time, but it was owned by none other than Polansky Kerr."

I stared at him, stunned.

"One of his many companies, that is. But that's not the most interesting thing I learned. That warehouse lay empty for decades. But a little over three years back, a company that collected scrap metal was tasked to bring in its entire inventory —"

A shock went through me.

"— and place it in a very specific arrangement." He drew a tattered page from the breast pocket of his jacket.

I'd been struck upon the head. I'd been sick, in labor, bleeding heavily, and in great distress. But my mind gave me the answer. "Yes, that was the pattern. At least, the amount I saw." Yet that he had the page surprised me. "Where did you get this?"

"The foreman gave this to me. He didn't even ask for any pay for it — he and the company's owner had been paid triple the going rate for their wares. Yet his company's store of metal was still not enough." He leaned back, looking again towards the doorway. "Three companies' wares lay inside that warehouse. That was the price for my brother's death."

That day has never left me — Jonathan bearing me from that terrible place, how terribly pale his face, his lips. The lostness of his eyes as he asked me in desperation to kiss him.

"Do you still find the Kerrs innocent? Or must I give you more?"

This angered me. "Did you learn who **paid** for this metal?"

Jack scoffed. Yet he shook his head.

"Anyone could've gone into any abandoned warehouse in the city and done this. It proves nothing." I thought back to what Tony had said. "And what if whoever did this meant to frame Mr. Polansky? Did you ever consider that?"

He shrugged, not meeting my eye.

"Why would he imprison his own grand-daughter? I found her there. I saw her, sitting in filth, her wrists rubbed raw by the chains. Do you think he meant for her to be scarred for life?" It seemed absurd. "There are so many easier ways to kill someone. I just can't see the point of it."

Jack sighed, shaking his head.

What did he want from me? "What are you not saying?"

He did meet my eye then. "I wish nothing more than for you to see what kind of creatures you love so well. But I promise you, I am telling you everything I can."

I felt truly offended. "**Creatures?** Is **that** what you think of me and my friends? Oh, yes, we're just Pot rags. We must be capable of **anything!**"

Jack shook his head and rose. "I apologize for upsetting you, Mrs. Spadros. I believe it's time for me to go."

He'd barely been there an hour, but I rose as well. "You may stay or leave as you wish."

But he no longer looked at me, and left without a word.

***

Jack did not visit the next day, nor the day after, so after my Queen's duties were done, I went down and did the work I could on my own.

I grumbled to myself the whole time. The nerve of that man! He was insufferable, haughty, too full of his own importance by half.

Honor and Mr. Theodore stood in the hall as usual, simply watching.

And these papers — most of them made no sense to me. Receipts, invoices, listings of all sorts.

But then I began to see a pattern. Why did the Clubbs and Diamonds refuse Josie entry so many times? Why did she keep going to the bridge if she knew they wouldn't see her?

The next page was another listing: a chart of entries and exits for the Diamond-Hart lowers' bridge. I looked over it, then filed it with the rest.

But I didn't truly read it. If I had, I think things might have turned out very differently.

***

On the third day of Jack Diamond's absence, Tony burst into my study shortly after luncheon, without even knocking. "I have an idea." He sat across my desk. "Mr. Jackson has secured an invitation to an aristocrats' Fall Equinox ball at Countess Victoria's — and it appears most of the ones who failed to come to our Grand Ball will be there."

I sat back, astonished. "And you wish to attend?"

He beamed, and it so reminded me of my little Ace. "I've made all the arrangements. Just imagine their surprise, their alarm!" Tony seemed giddy. "Mr. Jackson will arrive first. We'll show up late, unannounced. They can't possibly refuse us entry. It'll be a clear sign that we know what they're up to!"

"Whatever shall we do there?"

"Watch their reactions. See what their connections are. See who comes to us, and who draws back." He rubbed his hands together. "This will be spectacular!"

I could see several issues in this plan. "What does Ten think of this?"

"He always has concerns about my safety. But I'll have one of the footmen — Honor, I suppose — be my taster —"

A shock of fear. Honor, my Queensman, put into danger?

"— and I'll bring ten men to guard the premises. That should be enough." He shrugged. "I doubt there'll be any trouble."

I felt uncertain. "I ... If this is what you want."

"I do. I have to see these people, have them see me. They have to know that I know what they're planning!"

"Even though we don't."

"Well, not exactly. But all I need to know is that they want rid of us. And I won't go quietly."

This seemed bold. "Very well. Is the event tonight or tomorrow?"

"Tonight. Even if someone here is false, these aristocrats won't have time to react. Not properly."

"But won't they become suspicious of —" I hesitated, not knowing who listened. "Mr. Jackson?"

Tony laughed. "He assures me he's gone to several other functions without anyone being the wiser. It was his idea, and a good one."

I nodded slowly, unsure of what this meant. Could Jack have some trap set for us there? "If this is what you wish, of course."

I didn't really want to attend. But if we could learn something, then it would be worth it.

The Cover

We dressed for dinner as usual, with Tony requesting I wear green. I chose a finely-made linen lawn the color of new grass — which even I had to admit set off my hair nicely — and my best jewelry. Tony had on his best suit, with a vest woven in medium green and black.

During the first course, he called for Honor, handing him a list.

Honor read the list, glanced at me in surprise, then said, "At once, sir," and left through the servants' entry.

By the time dinner was through, Honor had changed from his usual footman's garb, and now wore Spadros livery. He brought out the tiara I'd worn at my wedding, silver with black stones.

"Put it on," Tony said.

I'd not seen it since the wedding, but Tony never sent it to me for the auction. Why, I'd never learned.

Tony and I left Spadros Manor through the front gate. Twenty of Tony's men were on horseback, all in Spadros livery. They stood beside Tony's carriage of the Patriarch: shining piano-black, with his crown and Holy Symbol raised in real silver. When I glanced at Tony, I realized he had a pin on his lapel which matched this exactly.

When had he had this made? Why had he never before worn it?

Honor helped us in, then moved to his post at the back of the carriage.

Sawbuck and Shanna already sat inside. I recognized Shanna's dress as one of my pale green discards. The shade didn't suit me, but on her it looked lovely.

I recalled Tony's anger at Tenni wearing my clothes and wondered what Tony thought of my lady's maid now doing so.

Sawbuck said, "Well, this should be interesting."

As we set off in the darkness, Shanna gave me an anxious look, as if she'd not been told where we were going.

I shared Sawbuck's misgivings: this seemed far too dangerous, stepping into the serpents' lair, as it were.

But I was Queen. What would Mrs. Clubb do? "This is for the best, Ten," I said. "If we can learn the cause of their actions, it will be well worth it."

Sawbuck gave Tony a quick glance, then nodded.

The ball was at a small mansion on 190th, well past Spadros Castle — almost to the Diamond betters' bridge. By the time we got there, it was after ten, and I don't know which of the footmen standing at the front gates was more surprised. One bolted inside as we disembarked; the other, face fearful, opened the gates. Up ahead, the front door opened; the butler stood there gaping.

Tony led me straight inside as if invited. Honor, Ten, and Shanna were close behind.

Their butler moved quickly ahead of us to their main hall.

The guests were in the middle of a dance. A waltz — the musicians were very good. It both amused and saddened me to have the music stop, the dancers turn in a mix of surprise, horror, fear and alarm to curtsy and bow as we moved into the room.

Jack had not been dancing. He held a wry smile upon his face and his cane in his hand as he bowed.

We went to our hostess, the Countess Victoria Welli Von Schafkopf; Tony stopped in front of her. "Good evening."

Although Countess Victoria bore my former friend Dame Anastasia a passing resemblance, the woman was old enough to be Dame Anastasia's mother. Skin that perhaps was alabaster in her youth was now lined into a perpetual sneer, unsoftened by too much makeup. Hair white, in a style out of fashion forty years ago. The dress she wore was costly, but from a long-past age, with too much jewelry and that of a lesser quality for her rank. Antagonizing the Spadros Family had not served her well.

She stared at Tony, mouth open. You could've heard a pin drop.

Then she blinked, swallowed, and curtsied low. "Patriarch."

Tony said, "Please forgive our lateness, Madam: our invitations only just arrived."

She took a step back, her face going even paler. "Uh ... welcome!" She gestured to the butler, who looked ready to faint. "Secure proper seats for our — guests, please."

I smiled. *She couldn't bring herself to say "King and Queen."*

Some high-backed seats were brought in and set in front of a floral display — in the corner.

Tony gave her an even, unblinking gaze, his public emotionless mask firmly in place.

Countess Victoria took a step back. She looked around the room, eyes wide, and from her face I could tell she was desperately trying to come up with an actual spot to put us in.

Once her eyes returned to Tony, he smiled, not keeping his amusement hidden. "Thank you." He turned to me. "Let's take our places."

He took my hand as if we were being brought to the highest seat in the land, leading me past people frantically getting up to push in their seats so we might pass between the tables. He led me proudly, head held high, to the chairs in the corner.

Our servants followed.

Before sitting, Tony turned to Countess Victoria. "I'll need seating for our two personal attendants. And," he gestured at Honor. "All food and drink shall be handed to him first."

She reacted as if slapped: first outraged, then fearful, then ashamed. She curtsied low. "Yes, sir." Turning to her butler, who stood there with his mouth open, she said, "See to it."

He bowed to her. "At once, my Lady."

Tony refused to sit until two chairs — of regular make — were brought for Shanna and Sawbuck, who sat beside us, one on each side. I sat to Tony's right, as usual.

Honor stood behind and between me and Tony, and although his face was entirely correct, I could tell he tried very hard not to laugh.

Tony leaned back in his chair, crossing his legs ankle-to-knee. "Well, this should be interesting." He gestured to the musicians. "Begin."

The conductor glanced at Countess Victoria , who nodded. Although the music began, everyone seemed much too preoccupied with looking at us than either eating or dancing.

Two waiters came forth bearing a narrow covered table, just long enough to cover the four of us. Maids quickly set up napkins, utensils, cups, flowers. Behind them, more waiters with full plates.

Tony raised his hand. "A saucer and utensils for my taster."

The waiters evidently hadn't been told of this, because they looked shocked, embarrassed, angry.

But Honor grabbed the saucer off Sawbuck's tea cup along with Sawbuck's knife and fork and came round to take selections from each plate. He stood by, eating, then smiled at the waiters. "My compliments to your Cook."

This broke the mood, and the waiters were all smiles.

When Honor didn't fall over dead, Tony also smiled. The food was placed. Tony waved off the sommelier. "No wine. Tea will do for now."

Honor chuckled as he wiped Sawbuck's knife and fork on his napkin and handed them to him. "I could get used to this."

Sawbuck hadn't seemed too pleased with his things being taken this way, but at this, he relaxed. "Until you get poisoned."

Honor shrugged, amused. "Well, there is that." He poured a bit of tea from each cup into Sawbuck's, tasted it, then stood watching the show.

And a show it was: whilst the music continued, very few danced. Most gathered themselves into groups, their faces ranging from cunning to fear-stricken to disdainful.

"Make note of who is here, and who speaks with who," Tony told me.

I nodded, for once grateful of my ability to do so.

Because I knew all these people. I'd had dealings with them many a time over the years. And it struck me that they didn't yet know what I could do.

Since I'd begun Mrs. Clubb's teachings, the baskets of my mind had filled. My mind had cleared, to the point that I had room for even more.

Many — the fearful, for certain — would believe that if they stayed out of our notice, that we might forget they were even there.

But I would not. I could not, even if I wanted to.

The exact view the moment we walked in displayed before me — everyone who sat, all who danced, their names, families, connections, and petty insults over the years coming to mind.

I reviewed the room now, comparing the names to when we'd arrived.

Several had left, possibly to alert their masters. Fortunately, Tony had brought the extra horse-men to follow whoever did so and see where they next went.

He really was getting good at this.

With a blink, I put them all in a basket in my mind, right in the center of Tony's study. "Done."

Tony shook his head in astonishment. "Remarkable."

I grinned at him, took his hand. "Why thank you, sir." I leaned over to speak in his ear. "Your horse-men will already be busy."

He gave me a glance of surprise, then nodded. "As I imagined."

Still holding my hand on the table in full view of everyone, he began to eat, and I loved that. I loved that he acknowledged me. I loved that he was left-handed and could.

I leaned over once more. "You shouldn't consider yourself unworthy. Never think that."

He smiled to himself, color going to his cheeks. I watched from the corner of my eye as people whispered, glanced at each other. At me.

I recalled what Jack had said about the way Gardena was being treated, and I wondered what it would take for these people to see me as who I was — besides being a "Pot rag." Besides being the subject of so much speculation, so much hate. Was it even possible?

Apparently, Jack's persona didn't dance. He'd been circulating around the room, speaking with one group or another, finally coming to our table. He bowed, and spoke quietly to Tony. "A pleasure to see you."

I imagined Jack would have much to speak of at our next meeting. "And you."

Jack froze, anger radiating from him.

Tony said, "Anything interesting going on?"

Jack gave a fake smile, taking an easy step back to lean on his cane, and went into his Nitivali drawl. "About what I'd expect, sir. Lovely evening to you." He continued on his way.

Tony took a bite. "This is marvelous. He came and went without so much as a notice."

I'm sure they all knew by now of his visits to Spadros Manor. I wondered what they thought. "Something troubles him."

Tony nodded.

The food was good. As I ate, I surveyed the room.

People were beginning to lose their desire to congregate. They began to dance, to sit, to relax.

Tony stood beside me, holding out his hand. "Care to dance?"

His cane still leaned against the table. Honor moved quickly to pull out my chair as I took Tony's hand and rose. "If you feel well enough."

He nodded. "I do. But I must show them I am." He grinned. "There must be no doubt of my health here."

I took his arm. "Then let's do this."

Another waltz had begun, for which I felt grateful. I didn't know all of the new dances, and I'd not had time to learn.

Tony didn't dance often, and never with anyone but me. But when he did dance, he was spectacular.

I looked up at him as he swept me around the room, and I felt such gratitude. He could've refused to take me back after all that had happened. He could cast me out even now, and no one would fault him.

But he was here, and close by. His hand lay upon my back, and I loved him. I wanted him.

And I knew he wanted me. His pupils were wide, his cheeks flushed, his lips parted as his eyes gazed into mine.

Maybe tonight, I thought. *Maybe tonight he'll put aside whatever it is that troubles him, and love me. Maybe tonight he'll let me love him.*

But then he looked away.

The dance ended; he led me to our table.

I said, "I think I'll get some air."

After consulting the nearest footman, I went out to Countess Victoria's veranda, which was well out of view of the street. To my surprise, Jack Diamond already stood there at the railing between two slender pillars, both hands upon his cane, gazing into the darkness.

He jumped a bit, as if startled, then turned as I approached and bowed.

"Forgive the intrusion," I said. "I merely wished to smoke."

He gave a tense laugh, not meeting my eye, then made an expansive gesture, keeping to his Nitivali drawl. "Be my guest."

I chose a spot to his right, keeping a pillar between us. I felt rather than saw Honor appear in the doorway, some five yards behind.

The lights of 192nd shone past the trees in the distance. The moon was unlit, the stars silent. I lit my cigarette, feeling melancholy. Then I remembered my manners. "I hope you're well."

Jack didn't reply.

Something in his laugh ... something in his manner. I turned towards him: he stood head down, eyes tightly shut, gripping his cane so hard his knuckles were my color. I felt alarmed, glancing back at Honor, then at Jack. "Sir? Are you well?"

He let out something like a gasp, then, and his knuckles regained their color. "I cannot answer this." He shook his head, not meeting my eye. "Forgive me for alarming you."

I went to him. "You're distressed." Then I thought: *could he be ill?* "Should I call for the doctor?"

Jack began to laugh bitterly, turning away: his accent disappeared. "If only this might be solved by a doctor's care."

I felt perplexed. "Is there a way I might help?"

He scoffed. "You've done more than enough already."

"How have I offended you?" I began to feel afraid. "Has something happened? What have I done?"

"What have you **done**? Oh, this is rich," Jack said quietly. "I see it now. You use us all — myself, your husband, your servants, even Jonathan, who loved you beyond reason. You use us for your own schemes, not caring who is harmed. Then when you're confronted, you feign ignorance. The poor, pitiful, innocent Pot rag who's being **so** tormented."

"What? How dare you?"

He scoffed at me once more. "How dare I? I came to you offering help!" He gave a small shake of his head. "But I will do so no longer."

"But why?"

He shook his head. "I've spoken to so many people: your butlers, your servants, your friends. To see what kind of woman my brother died for ... " At this, he squeezed his eyes shut.

Feeling grieved, I laid hand upon his arm, wishing to offer comfort.

But he flung it away. "Begone from my sight! If it weren't for you, my brother would still be alive."

Suddenly, I had no thoughts whatsoever. Turning, I walked away.

"Wait," Jack said. Remorse lay in his voice, but I didn't want to hear it. "Mrs. Spadros —"

I went past Honor, past everyone, to Tony. "I wish to leave."

"Very well." Tony gestured to his men.

All the way home, Jack's words rang in my mind.

You use us all.

If it weren't for you, my brother would be alive.

If it weren't for you, my brother would be alive.

If it weren't for you, my brother would be alive.

Tony said, "What happened? Is something wrong?"

I shook my head, unable to think, to breathe, understanding in that instant what Jack said to me. *I cannot answer this.*

Something had happened, something I'd done, or that Jack thought I'd done. I wasn't even sure what it was.

But it was terrible. And I didn't even know what I'd done!

If it weren't for you, my brother would be alive.

I feared that no matter what I did, all this — my marriage, my child, my quadrant, my city ... everything, just like my Jonathan's life, would come to ruin.

The Summons

I spent the next day in melancholy, though I did my best to complete my work. The whole time, Jack's voice rang in my ears.

If it weren't for you, my brother would be alive.

I didn't know what he meant. I didn't know what I'd done. But he believed it, as surely as a man might believe anything.

The thought that I'd done something that led to Jon's death weighed on me. It wouldn't let me go. I had to do something.

Just after tea, I rang for Alan. "Would you have Blitz visit?"

"I'll summon him, mum."

"Oh, and before you go: what have you told our guest? He mentioned speaking with you."

Alan froze. "You said he was untrustworthy, mum. So I told him nothing of our operations, manpower, or defenses."

"But I take it that the matter of me came up."

He stood blinking, pondering, I guessed, what exactly he'd said. How much of what he'd said he might tell me without harm to himself or his family. "It did. But I — I told him nothing." He focused on me. "What did he say?"

"What did he ask?"

"Nothing, mum. We merely spoke of the weather, of how you'd redone the house. He inquired of Master Jonathan, mum. He wanted to know him better. Did I do wrongly? He does look so like him, that any man might be curious."

"No, all is well. Did the two of you converse on anything else?"

"I don't know, mum. Let me think on it."

I let him send for Blitz, not even knowing what I'd ask him. Somehow, Jack Diamond had learned something from them, something terrible enough to turn him against me. I needed to know what it was before I allowed him in here again.

About an hour later, I sat in my study, wanting to work but finding myself unable. The front bell rang, and I heard Alan answer it.

Some time later, Alan knocked. "Your husband requests your presence in his study."

All but one of Tony's chairs had been moved aside. Our Inventor Piros Gosi sat across the desk from Tony, rising when I entered.

I curtsied low. "You summoned me?"

"Yes," Tony said. "The Inventor was kind enough to come here with an update on the ventilation."

I stood there, not knowing where he wanted me to sit, until I realized he wasn't going to offer me one.

The Inventor looked confused for an instant, then stepped aside to offer me his seat.

I wasn't sure what to do. I glanced at Tony, who nodded. I should leave an Inventor standing?

Tony gestured to the chair. "Please," he said to me. "Sit."

So I did, unsure of what was going on.

Tony said to our Inventor, "Please continue."

It was evident that Inventor Gosi wasn't sure what was going on either. He kept glancing from me to Tony and back again. "Um, sir, we have located all seventeen of the ventilation windows. They are, as we surmised, stuck shut, allowing no air to flow from the city."

Tony said, "I see."

"So we face a dilemma. We can find no latches, and the documents in our Ancient Library say nothing about the means of operating them. We have but three choices."

Tony frowned slightly. "Three?"

Inventor Gosi bowed, just a bit. "We could, of course, allow things to continue as they are. During the depths of winter, the city will eventually cool. But this will bring heavy rain and serious flooding, particularly in lower Hart quadrant, along with a long-term risk of mold and algae accumulation. This could cause more illness and crop failures."

Tony let out a breath. "Not a good option."

"No, sir. The other two choices are almost as dangerous. We could break the windows —"

I gasped. Break our own dome?

Inventor Gosi nodded. "Not an ideal choice, particularly since these windows are larger than most of our balloons. We don't as yet have a way to keep the pieces from falling upon the city."

I said, "So what's the third choice?"

"Pry the windows out — somehow," the Inventor said. "If we could attach the windows to dirigibles, that might give us a way to lower them without injury to anyone below." He sighed. "First, we must find a way to pry them out."

I considered this. "You'd have to evacuate the people directly below each window, just in case the window falls. But if you spread stout netting underneath the area as you were prying, that might help."

"Good idea," Tony said. "Can it be done?"

The Inventor considered this. "We'll have to recruit more airships, and hire weavers to create this net. Probably two nets: one of an enormous strength for the window, and a finer net underneath in case any tools or men should fall."

Tony said, "That sounds wise."

"Thank you, sir. But this is going to be a massive, expensive, weeks-long undertaking, involving all four quadrants. This is why I came to you."

Tony nodded. "I will speak with the other Patriarchs, and with the city-men. I trust they'll agree that your third option is the best."

As we were walking Inventor Gosi to the door, the door-bell rang: Blitz stood there.

Once the Inventor left, Tony said, "Blitz, why are you here?"

Blitz looked to Alan, then to me. "I was summoned."

I could tell Tony was upset, but not why. So I said, "Might we go out to the veranda?"

Tony gave a quick nod, and we went through the house and to the veranda. The minute the door closed, Tony turned on me. "Why would you summon a man whose wife was seven months with child?"

I felt taken aback. "Jack — Mr. Jackson is upset by something. I don't know what, but he said he'd spoken with my butlers —"

Blitz froze.

"— and I wanted to know what was said."

Tony shook his head. "We do not have **time** for this!" He put his hand on his face, turning away. "He was supposed to visit today. Why has he not returned?"

"I don't know! That's what I was trying to find out!"

Blitz said, "Maybe I should go —"

Tony said, "Just stop. You've done harm enough."

I didn't know what was happening. "What has he done?"

Tony let out a disgusted groan. "Blitz, go home. Stop speaking of our business to outsiders. Just ... leave. Both of you. I have too much to do."

He went into the house, leaving me and Blitz there.

Blitz said, "I believe my cousin no longer wishes to see me."

"I'm sorry. I don't know what's going on. How are Mary and Ariana?" I felt more than a little ashamed that after everything that happened, Tony didn't even ask.

Blitz went to open the door for me, but Millie opened it instead. Blitz turned to me. "They're well as can be expected."

We went through the dining room, past the breakfast room and down the hall towards the front door. "Please give them my regards."

Blitz nodded at Alan, then said, "I will, mum."

I watched him go, thought about him and Mary, Lance and Gardena, and at that moment I knew what to get Gardena for her wedding.

***

A few days later, after Tony had gone wherever he went, I was in my study. A knock came at the door. "Come in."

Tony's manservant Jacob Michaels entered, leaving the door wide open, and bowed. "Might I have a word, mum?"

I wondered what this might be about. "Certainly."

Master Jacob was a short man, older than me by quite a bit, yet he could be mistaken for much younger. He had a reticent air to him most days, but today he spoke plainly. "I wish to join the Army."

This was surprising. "Whatever would you do there?"

He stood blinking for a moment, then said, "With my training, I'd likely be set as manservant to an officer."

I scoffed. "Don't be a fool. I don't release you, and I suspect my husband wouldn't either. You're sworn to the Family." I leaned my elbows on my desk. "Why do you want to go?"

He seemed taken aback. "I grew up in Dickens, mum. Until I was sold to Mr. Roy. And then I lived some time in Nitivali for training. So I have friends there. One of my friends who trained with me is in the Army. Another is a zeppelin under-pilot." His eyes grew distant for a moment, a slight frown on his face. "He sent word he's been summoned. I suppose the Army must wish him to fly one of their fighting ships."

I had no idea such ships even existed. "I don't wish to raise your hopes. But if you're determined to go, I'll speak with my husband. I doubt he'd say yes; we're short-staffed enough as it is."

He shook his head. "No, mum. It'd anger him that I came to you first. I'll speak to him myself."

I don't know what came of his talk with Tony, but Jacob never left. Which, as it turned out, was probably for the best. Many who went to that war never returned.

The Desire

Lance and Gardena's wedding hadn't been postponed by her father's murder. So on the first of October, we dressed in our finest and set off across the betters' bridge to Diamond quadrant and their wedding hall.

When we arrived, masses of crowds were being kept back by Diamond Family men in black suits with golden roses upon their lapels. Closer in, men dressed in the white-and-silver livery of Diamond stood watch. Servants, obviously: no Diamond gentleman would wear all white, especially now that Jack Diamond was "dead."

But there were others: men from all four Families standing guard, both inside and outside the hall. I recognized a few of Tony's men coming forth to greet us as we pulled to a stop. Each of these Family men from all four quadrants had been carefully screened, their families down to their third cousins brought to a huge garden party in Clubb quadrant, "for their protection." We wanted no incident here.

The hall was vast, draped outside in white and gold. As we arrived, a narrow golden carpet atop a wider white one led up the steps and into the hall, the stanchions white with golden chain. Inside, giant bouquets of white carnations, yellow orchids, white daffodils with golden centers, white and yellow daisies, and baby's breath hung at the front, with smaller ones at the end of each row. Small strands of fine ivy draped down from each bouquet. Candles lit the area up front on all sides.

An enormous tapestry of the Blessed Dealer, embroidered in white and gold, hung at the far end of the hall from floor to ceiling. Flowers massed around it.

The seats were draped in same gold, with the Holy Symbols of the Clubb and Diamond Families intwined embroidered upon the backs of each chair's drapings in white. Two half-arbors of white and golden roses arched over each side of the front of the hall as far as the tapestry, with ribbons of white and gold entwined.

"This is beautiful," I said, without meaning to.

"It is," said Tony.

I should have done more to help, I thought. But would the Spadros Queen have been welcome in Diamond quadrant?

A golden-haired young man, somewhat shorter than Lance, came to us. "Right this way."

Though we arrived — as requested — right at eleven, the hall was near-empty. Evidently, they'd chosen to seat us early. We passed row after row of empty chairs until we came to a set of black stanchions bearing thick gold-and-white rope. These lay perhaps eight-tenths of the way to the front, with two paces laid bare on either side. The young man unlatched the rope, allowing us to pass.

The first two rows we encountered were full: elderly aunts, distant cousins, family friends. On the right were Diamonds, on the left, Clubbs.

Everyone rose and bowed or curtsied as we passed. The third row contained three larger, more elegant empty chairs to our left, beside the center aisle of the otherwise full row. A soft black cushion already lay in Ace's seat; he smiled when put upon it.

The six rows in front of us were completely bare.

Sawbuck and Daisy took position at the far end of the row by the wall. Sawbuck's face showed his displeasure at being forced to stay so far from Tony, but there was nothing for it.

A full orchestra wearing gold and black, composed of both Clubb and Diamond musicians, played soft, pleasant music in the balcony behind us.

Next, Charles Hart was brought in to sit across the aisle, in his own elegant chair.

Ace's face lit up. He began waving and shouting, "Gampa! Gampa!"

Mr. Hart, obviously startled by the boy declaring this in front of everyone, smiled sheepishly, giving the boy a surreptitious wave.

Oh, dear, I thought. How do you tell a child this young about secrets? "Hush, my love," I said gently, and he settled.

Fortunately, the noise of the crowd drowned out most of it, although those around us began giving us — and each other — calculating glances.

"Perhaps we should've left him at home," I told Tony.

Tony had his public mask firmly on. "No matter," he said in my ear. "People pay little heed to the whims and words of children."

One of the Clubb women had turned to look right at me. I laughed softly, face coy and knowing, as if Tony had made an intimate joke. I winked at her, and she twitched, turning away.

Tony chuckled to himself and leaned closer. "I wonder what our hostess will say to that one when she makes her report."

"Heh," said I. "That could be amusing." Mrs. Clubb knew full well that this matter had to be kept secret, but I imagined she'd spend much of this day and possibly most of the next stomping on rumors.

The hall filled behind us. Yet as time went on, various members of the Clubb and Diamond Families were brought in to sit ahead of us, the Clubbs on the left, the Diamonds on the right.

Which I thought odd, but I'd not been to many weddings in my day. Each time, each group stopped to pay respect to us and to Mr. Hart before moving to their seats. Cesare's wife Furuta held Roland's hand as they walked past.

Ace yelled, "Wa-wee!"

Furuta and Roland nodded to him soberly, then left.

Ace looked up at me, ready to follow him. "Where Wa-wee go?"

"Hush," I said to Ace. "He'll sit up front with his auntie."

"Oh." Ace had no aunts, so the word must have confused him.

Then came the Clubb sisters and their husbands who still lived, along with their many children and their husbands. My friend Karla Bettelmann, one of Mrs. Regina's grand-daughters, smiled at me when she and her husband passed us.

Then the Diamond brothers and their families were escorted in.

We all rose as the Queen Mothers came down the aisle arm in arm, smiling, but both looking a bit bereft. When they reached the front of the hall, they kissed each other's cheeks before being seated.

Then the Clubb Patriarch and bridegroom, Lance, strode in. Tall with thick golden hair, he wore a suit the color of the midday sun, with wide lapels striped in white and gold going straight from his shoulders to the hem of his jacket. Around his waist was a band of gold brocade on white. Eyes entirely forward, he moved past us to his place up front to wait for his bride.

And then there she was. For a moment, I couldn't breathe.

Her cheeks glowed, her eyes only for Lance. Dressed in a creamy color just missing a golden tan, Gardena Diamond held a bouquet of gold and white tulips. Gold brocade on white peeked out from each of the folds. Her raven curls were held back by a tiara of gold, heavy with diamonds.

She walked beside her oldest brother Cesare, who wore the same black suit and golden rose in his lapel as the rest. Gardena's dress was most proper, yet cut low, and as she walked past, Tony let out a quiet sound close behind me, somewhere between a moan and a sigh.

He still, after all was said and done, desired her.

Not that I blamed him: she was stunning. But it made me think — and feel — what we missed, the love I so wanted to share with him.

I said nothing. This was their day, not mine.

Mr. Hart peered at us from across the aisle, eyes narrowed.

Had Tony been staring at Gardena in an unseemly fashion?

That concerned me. If Mr. Hart had noticed it, others might have too.

As Cesare gave Gardena Diamond's hand to Lance Clubb, we all sat.

I hadn't even noticed Kitty Clubb ten paces behind the couple, entirely clad in the forest green silk of the Dealers. Only her face showed to us: as pale as her younger brother's, with a scattering of freckles.

Kitty climbed the steps after passing between the bride and groom, and turned to face them. She raised her face and hands to the sky. "Our beloved, both in this life, the lives past, and the lives to come, welcome." She lowered her hands, gazing out over the crowd. "We meet here to celebrate the joining of these Holy Hands into one."

She spread her arms to encompass Lance and Gardena. "In the beginning, the world had form, yet the people, no breath. Our Blessed Dealer gave the Holy Hands to Her people, and they breathed their first. Taking the hand of the Floorman, She directed Him to minister to these new souls with food and drink and fire. Thus the people lived long, and prospered, and brought forth more in their image."

The people said, "Amen."

"This is the Grand Play given to us by the Holy Mystery, the One who constructed and planned all we see: the joining of Hands, in bodies female and male, to engage in the Sacrament of Love. In this way, we spread upon the world the vast number of all possible Hands, both High and Low, to bring forth the Dealer's love."

"Amen."

She smiled at her brother Lance, and then at Gardena. "These two, by the grace of the Dealer, were dealt Most High, and given their Hands to in turn deal forth love and happiness to their lessers, and by the will of the most Blessed Dealer, new life."

"Amen."

"Who gives this woman to be wed?"

Cesare had stood two paces behind and directly between them. At this, he stepped forward. "As Patriarch and kin, I willingly present my precious and beloved to the Sacrament."

Kitty nodded. "And who vouches for this man, that he may be allowed into the Holiest of Holies?"

The entire Clubb side stood. "We his people do so swear."

Not wanting to be caught out, I started to stand, but Tony stopped me. "This is for his people," he whispered.

Not a single person across the aisle had risen, not even Mr. Hart.

The Clubbs sat.

Kitty turned to Gardena. "Have you a gift for this man?"

From a small bag on her wrist, she produced a ring.

"Place it upon your chosen and repeat after me: I, Gardena Rachel Diamond, do swear by the Dealer that this marriage is entered freely and in good will. That I gladly take on the duties and joys of womanhood, in full understanding and without reservation. I vow to love and honor, cherish and protect this man, until the day I turn in my Cards."

Gardena repeated all.

Kitty then turned to Lance. "Have you a gift for this woman?"

He had his ring in his pocket.

"Place it upon your chosen and repeat after me: I, Lancelot Alexander Clubb, do swear by the Dealer that this marriage is entered freely and in good will. That I gladly take on the duties and joys of manhood, in full understanding and without reservation. I vow to love and honor, cherish and protect this woman, until the day I turn in my Cards."

Lance repeated all.

Kitty said loud enough for all to hear, "By the blessing and might of our Most Beloved Dealer, I pronounce these two Hands joined as One. May this union prosper, bringing forth abundant and healthy life. Joy upon all who tend and encourage this Partnership. Cursed be anyone who dares tear it asunder." She beamed, raising her hands high. "As a full and ranking representative of the Dealers for the Independent Domed City-State of Bridges, may I present Mr and Mrs. Lancelot Clubb."

Applause, music, and, of course, much kissing by Lance and Gardena, then they came past us hand in hand. Gardena looked radiant, beaming at her husband.

Tony sighed. "So it's done."

As the rest moved behind them, front row first, I turned to him, took his hands in mine. "She's happy."

He nodded, not looking at me.

I kissed his cheek, feeling sorry for him, then turned to Ace, who'd been patting my leg for attention. "As soon as it's our turn, my love. Then we'll go eat."

"Yay!"

When it came our turn to go, Daisy came round and scooped Ace up into her arms as he giggled, canes and all. She walked in front holding him, whilst Sawbuck walked behind us.

As we passed the back of the hall, Jack stood in the last row on the Clubb side. He'd not shaved since last I saw him; he wore dark spectacles and an eye-patch on the left. He nodded to us as we passed.

I didn't like Jack being there. He had perfect right to attend his sister's wedding, but I still didn't trust his motives. And now he'd seen my son.

***

After that, much like every other time we did anything formal, we made a slow parade past the thousands who'd stood outside hoping for a glimpse of the wedding party. Diamond and Clubb men stood guard, ever watchful for anyone intending mischief.

Tony spent the entire time staring out the window, which didn't surprise me.

We were set last in the line of Patriarchs. Given the current political climate, this didn't surprise me either. After an hour, the crowds thinned, and we made our way to a much smaller hall than that given to Julius Diamond's funeral meal.

Round tables lay on either side of the room, with a cleared area in the center. To the right of this cleared area lay a jazz band. To our left, maids were setting up drinks. Since we were in Diamond quadrant, I could only assume they were more like fruit juices than anything stronger.

The bouquets had evidently been brought over, because they now stood in the corners. The smaller ones lay upon each table. The half-arbors that had been in front now stood in the center of the room, arching over the cleared area.

Flannery Hook again appeared beside us. "This way, if you will."

We were brought past the tables to a raised area similar to the arrangement we'd seen at Morton's funeral luncheon. A rather long table, decorated in white and gold, sat in the center. Two smaller tables sat on either end, the one on the left draped in black and silver, the other in red and silver. We were brought up a short flight of steps to the left.

Daisy set Ace in his chair, which was next to the white and gold table. He said, "Where Daisy?"

Tony sat next to him. "She'll sit downstairs with the other servants."

"Why?"

Tony smiled at him. "Because that's how it's done."

Ace seemed perplexed, but said nothing.

I was seated next to Tony; Daisy curtsied and left.

Sawbuck apparently wasn't interested in luncheon. Instead, he stood at parade rest at the bottom of the steps, facing the crowd.

The stern, dark-haired gentleman Mr. Hart had introduced me to at our ill-fated meeting with Etienne Hart had taken a similar position at the other end of the raised area. Mr. Tong Tau Ershiwu was his name, if I recall. He nodded soberly at me.

Through all the times I'd met with Mr. Hart, I'd only seen Mr. Ershiwu that one time before. Perhaps he wasn't as obsessive about Mr. Hart's safety as Sawbuck was about Tony's.

The room filled up, then on some signal, everyone rose. Lance and Gardena came in and through the crowd, passing behind Mr. Hart to sit in the middle. Mrs. Diamond, Mrs. Clubb, and Roland followed, Roland sitting beside Ace.

I wondered how safe it was for the two boys to be seen together like this. If you ignored their coloration and hair, they looked very much alike.

That is to say, Roland looked much more like Tony than like Lance.

But I figured that Mrs. Clubb must know what she was doing.

Cesare and his wife Furuta came in last, sitting between Gardena and Mr. Hart. Mr. Hart sat alone at his table, which looked rather empty compared to the rest.

Great heaping platters of food were brought to us: smoked fish and roasted corn, thick stews and small round loaves, beef and lamb, cooked greens and pickled cabbage.

The room buzzed with conversation. Lance and Gardena hardly had eyes for anyone else. Roland and Ace chattered at each other, with it mostly Roland explaining to Ace about what just happened. The rest of us ate in relative silence.

It felt peaceful, even with being on display as I was, there at the end of the table. Clubbs and Diamonds sat freely together in the tables below us, moving about to make introductions.

Two quadrants that could not be more different had become one, from opposite sides of the city.

When the waiters finally took the plates away, I felt as if I couldn't eat another thing. Ace gnawed at a piece of lamb, wide-eyed, as Roland told him a story involving several of his older cousins.

I nudged Tony, who had alternated between staring at his plate and staring at Gardena the whole time. "Look at those two."

He jumped, just a bit. "I'm trying not to."

"Look at your **sons**. Look how they love each other."

He smiled then, color coming to his cheeks. "They do. I'm glad."

The music began, and Lance brought Gardena to the dance floor. To my dismay, Tony's eyes followed her.

If he kept looking at Gardena like this, I felt sure there would be a scene, if not from her brother Cesare taking offence, from her husband

Lance doing so. "And now that he'll live in Clubb, they can visit whenever we like."

"True."

Mrs. Diamond nudged her oldest son, and Cesare got up, making his way to the dance floor. The two mothers grinned at each other.

I leaned over so as not to be overheard. "We won't have to worry about Cesare getting in the way."

He laughed softly. "That will be an improvement."

"So after Cesare dances with his sister, then with his mother, and Lance with his, will you stop this moping?" I gave him my best smile. "I'd like to dance tonight too."

He sat quietly for several minutes to the chattering of his sons as Mrs. Diamond and Mrs. Clubb went down to dance with theirs. He finally said, "I'd like that."

So I motioned Sawbuck to fetch Daisy, and when she returned Tony and I danced.

I knew how to keep a man's attention. Each time he lost focus, I'd touch his face, his shoulder, low upon his back. His pupils were huge, his cheeks flushed.

But we had nowhere to go. We had eyes on us continually. And I couldn't keep him like this forever. "I very much look forward to tonight."

Tony closed his eyes for a moment. "Yes."

I moved close, to speak in his ear, my clothes brushing against his. "I wish time moved faster."

"As do I."

I glanced over at Sawbuck, eyes wide, *I need help* on my face. He took one look and nodded, disappearing into the servant's door.

Tony pulled on my back, pressing me to him. "Oh, gods, Jacqui, I want nothing else. But where?"

Sawbuck was beside us, tapping on Tony's shoulder, and he spoke loudly. "Sir, please come with me."

Tony looked at him, dazed. "What?"

Sawbuck seemed amused. "A situation, sir." He gestured at me with his chin. "Both of you, come with me."

I took Tony's arm and followed Sawbuck. All eyes were upon us as we went out of the side doors onto what looked like a long porch which went around the building. Large bushes obscured us from view of the many reporters encircling the place.

Sawbuck opened a door painted the color of the wall, and we followed him in and down a short, dark flight of steps. Another door lay just to our left; it opened onto a smallish coat closet, about the size of my bath, which was practically empty.

"Oh, Ten," Tony said as he turned on the light. "You are a lifesaver."

Sawbuck gave me a wink and turned his back as we went inside.

I felt sad for Ten, shut out of the place he most longed to be.

But then Tony had his jacket off, pulling, pulling me towards him. Then he swept me from my feet, set me on the floor. We began kissing, and I wanted him.

He loosened his belt, unfastened his fly, raised my dress ... and then he stopped. "What am I doing?"

I grabbed his arm, desperately hoping to feel him press against me again, to feel the warmth of his body inside mine.

But he threw my hand away, shaking, face white. "No. This is too much ... too much like ..."

I sighed. Like with Gardena. In a closet, only to be discovered, humiliated. "Tony ... my love ... no one will discover us. Ten knows. He's standing guard."

"No." He shook his head. "How can I trust you? If we do this, will you just leave me? Betray me again?"

I sat up, offended. "No. I won't." Then I saw him straining there under his thin cotton pants, and stood, shaking my head. "This is ridiculous. I'm your wife, not your bed-maid. If you can't love me —" I threw my handkerchief at him. "Take care of your own damn problem."

Bitterly disappointed, I went to the door. Ten stood there, a startled look on his face. I rolled my eyes, scoffed at the whole absurd situation, and returned to the steps.

I wanted a smoke, but I mostly wanted to be alone.

Body aching, heart heavy, I wandered along the outside of the building, guarded by railings, to the wide veranda overlooking the gardens in the back. Tony's men standing guard outside the building followed at a discreet distance.

I felt sad. I felt numb. I felt lonely. Cigarette in hand, I pondered all that had happened.

Tony didn't mean to punish me. He wanted me, but ... he didn't trust me. He feared to open his heart to me.

I didn't know what to do to change that.

Something had happened to Tony the night Gardena seduced him. He'd been hurt, perhaps too badly to bear, by being found as he was, by being shamed and threatened. But instead of being repulsed by her, he'd turned his hurt into obsession.

Because this had gone beyond merely desiring someone.

Whatever was wrong with my husband, it wasn't something I could fix, and that frightened me more than anything. I didn't know what he wanted. I didn't know what **I** wanted.

I didn't know how much longer I could go on like this.

A voice, from behind: "Might I join you?"

I didn't even have to turn to know who it was. I lay a hand upon the white railing at the veranda's edge. Did I want to see him? What would he do? Did it matter? "Very well."

I felt rather than saw him move beside me, a pace away.

Jack said, "It was wrong for me to blame you."

I couldn't look at him. I bit my lip, eyes stinging. "I'm sorry Jon's dead. I'm sorry that man of yours is dead." I swallowed the lump in my throat. "All I ever wanted was for your brother to live."

Jack spoke softly. "I know."

I saw Jon's pale lips, his ashen face, as he lay dying. Because of me. "I loved him so much. There are days I wish nothing more than to join him."

Jack gasped. "No."

I shook my head, eyes upon the railing before me. "What keeps me here — the **only** thing that keeps me here — is finding the men who hounded him to his death, looking them in the eyes, and killing them." I turned away. "I think you want the same."

He didn't answer.

I didn't face him. "You were right to be angry. If you are truly here to harm me, I only ask that you let me take my vengeance first." I turned to look in his eyes; he glanced away.

I spoke softly, not wishing my men to hear. "Then afterwards, you may do as you wish, sir. I deserve every blow."

He reacted as if I'd slapped him: he recoiled, hurt and astonishment upon his face. "You have my intentions **entirely** wrong. My brother **loved** you! It would be an affront to his **name** if I were to do **anything** other than," he glanced away, biting his lip, and took a step back, his manner cooling. "Ensure your safety."

I stared at him, surprised. What was he hiding?

I lit my cigarette, took a drag. "It seems we both want the same thing." I held out my hand. "Help me learn why they wanted Jon dead."

He took my hand. "Gladly."

***

Jack left then. Feeling shaken, I finished my cigarette and went inside. People were still dancing, eating, talking.

When I re-entered the room, most were dancing. Gardena sat at a table full of Diamond women — her aunts and cousins, from the introductions. They all rose and curtsied, then each decided they needed to be elsewhere. I almost laughed.

Gardena patted the chair beside her. "Sit."

So I did. Tony and Mr. Hart were over at our table making paper gliders out of the seating cards, and the boys were trying to fly them.

"I'm glad he's doing better," Gardena said.

I sighed.

"But you're not."

"Don't mind me, Dena. Or him. This is your day, and I'll not have **either** of us spoil it for you."

She gave a fake smile. "I don't know what's going on between you, and I don't want to. But Mr. Anthony will no longer be calling upon me."

"What?"

"Of course, he can see our son as often as he wishes. But even Mr. Lance has noted how your husband looks at me, and —" at that, she laughed, "— I don't wish Mr. Anthony to be cursed by the Dealer."

Gardena wasn't any more religious than I was. "That **would** be unfortunate."

She sobered quickly. "It'd be more unfortunate should Cesare decide to shoot him."

"Indeed."

"Cesare said that if he were his actual brother, he'd whip him for appearing at a wedding in such a state. Well, he said more, but it was rather rude."

"Please convey our apologies to your brother. And your husband." I let out a breath, feeling unsure what to say next.

"It's not your fault. He **knows** better. And it's not the first time, either."

"I don't understand."

"At the Queen's Night dinner party. Jon was furious with him for not taking care of these matters **beforehand**!" She twitched, as if remembering who she spoke to, and looked embarrassed. "Having seven older brothers makes one much too outspoken."

I shook my head, remembering how pale and sweaty Tony looked when he emerged from his library. "Not at all. You could say I had dozens of them. Brothers. Not that any would go to a ball or dinner or wedding. But I think I understand."

Gardena looked relieved. "My mother would've had them whipped if she knew what they said around me. But it's helped ever so much."

I didn't understand, but I nodded anyway.

Then I thought I should ask: I might not get another chance. "Why is your mother treating Jack so badly?"

Gardena's face fell. "I asked her the same thing and got no answer." She bit her lip. "It's hurtful; I always felt the closest to him, more so even than with Jon. My mother and I argued about the matter. I had to insist on him being there, or she would've forbidden him."

"She **would** have? But he's —"

Gardena held up a hand. "I know. I know." Her hand dropped; she fell silent, hesitant. "I have a thought about this."

"You may share it, of course, but only if you wish to."

Two Clubb women came over and curtsied low. "My Queen, we don't wish to intrude, but we must go."

Gardena held out her hand, all smiles. "Thank you so much for coming. We truly appreciate your regard."

They turned to me, curtsied, and left.

Gardena lowered her voice. "Being so ill, Jon spent a great deal of time with my mother. I feel that they had a relationship much closer than she ever had with Jack."

And then when Jack walked in at the meeting to feel that joy, to have her hopes raised, then bitterly dashed ... I nodded. "I think I understand."

"She won't see him. She won't look at him. I do believe — well —"

"That she wishes Jon had walked into that meeting." And that Jack truly lay dead.

Gardena nodded.

What a blow! To gather the courage to return when you believed your own father might have ordered your death, then have your mother turn away? "I can't fathom it."

"I have trouble myself," Gardena said. "He tries to speak lightly of it, as he does everything else. But I know it must pain him."

I saw a new side to my old enemy. I wasn't sure what to make of it, and yet I didn't want to speculate as to his motivations for then coming to us to offer help.

I think that back then, I didn't want to pity him. I didn't want to let myself feel anything for the man.

Sawbuck had said this a few years before:

For an investigator, if you take a liking to someone, you seem to do very little real investigating.

More than myself could be harmed if I chose wrongly. I would never let an assassin come close to my little son again.

The Threats

Karla Bettelmann and her sister Cheisara Golf sat a few tables over. I said to Gardena, "Would you care for something to drink?"

"No, thank you," she said.

Lance came up then, and she held out her hand to him.

I rose, curtseying. "My congratulations."

He nodded to me with a smile, then focused on his wife, so I retreated to Cheisara and her sister. They both rose and curtsied, along with the other women sitting there. Karla said, "Would you care to join us?"

"I'd be honored," I said.

A new song began. At that, several of the gentlemen standing around moved to escort their ladies to the dance floor, and I took a place beside Karla. "I hope you're both well?"

"Quite," Karla said. "How may we help?"

I grinned at her. She was ever the one to get to the point. "I must admit I'm glad to see you both here. I know so few people in the room."

Cheisara smiled softly. "I'm sure you'll know us better over time."

I wasn't certain how to reply, so I said, "I'm sure."

Suddenly I had several questions. Not only about Josie and why she'd kept requesting to go into Clubb quadrant, but about Morton, not to mention who might have spoken to the press about Roland. But I wasn't sure any of those would do to ask here.

Karla said, "Since our father's death, I'm afraid we're kept out of most any news. If that's why you're here."

I felt taken aback. "Can't I sit with my friends?"

Cheisara glanced at Karla. "My sister meant no offense. We feel honored that you'd call us friends."

My heart sank. Not even Karla thought of me as a friend? "Very well." I had to consider how to phrase this. "I felt curious about an item your grandmother sent." That should tell them the importance of this matter.

Karla glanced around: no one stood close enough to hear. "Go on."

"Are either of you familiar with a Miss Josephine Kerr?"

They both froze.

Cheisara glanced at Karla, who nodded. "Yes, we know her."

I leaned back. "What can you tell me?"

Karla looked at her sister. "Would you like to tell this, or should I?"

Cheisara shrugged. "Miss Josephine and our young cousin, Miss Calcutta, spent a great deal of time together. Our aunt and uncle thought that Miss Josephine would be a good influence on her, but Miss Calcutta grew ever more wild. My uncle even had to engage a duel! Alas, the scoundrel never arrived to duel him, and no one's seen or heard from our cousin except for an occasional letter ever since."

"My word." I recalled hearing this story before. "Ah. Yes. Miss Tenni told me of this."

A laugh burst from Karla, and she turned to Cheisara. "I **knew** you shouldn't have told her!"

"Forgive me," I said. "I'd only inquired after Miss Calcutta after seeing her parents from afar at an event. Miss Tenni meant no harm."

"Well," Karla said. "In any case, her father told the guards not to allow Miss Josephine into the quadrant. We had nothing to do with it."

I nodded. "Thank you for telling me. I only wished to understand the situation better." I wondered why Mrs. Clubb had sent the page to me in the first place. Whatever might it have to do with the Red Dog Gang?

Ah. We'd also asked for information on the Kerrs. She likely thought to help me know more of Josie's movements during the time around David Bryce's abduction. But that page was from months before. Maybe it was sent by accident? "How terrible! So you still have not seen your cousin in all this time?"

Karla shook her head. "No, and it worries us all." She gave a thin smile. "But that's nothing we need assistance with — pray put it from your mind."

I remembered when Tony's little sister Katie ran off. I could only imagine the fear for her safety, the worry as to her situation. "If there's any way we might help, you have only to ask."

Karla nodded slowly. "That's very kind of you."

I owed Karla Bettelmann a favor already, and I'm sure she was saving it up for some rather large request. But no matter. I rose, and so did they. "It was lovely to speak with you."

After that, since the entire room had watched me sit with Karla and Cheisara, I made the rounds of the room. As Queen, I was expected to do it, so I played the part, meeting dozens of Clubb and Diamond women and sitting with each group to chat for a moment or two. After an hour or so of this, I returned to my seat up on the stage and listened to Tony and Mr. Hart play with the boys as I watched the dancing.

What was Josie's interest in Calcutta Clubb, of all people? And why would Josie allow a young girl to meet up with a scoundrel?

***

We stayed until well into the night, when those of us left sent Gardena and Lance on their tour of Clubb quadrant. It was an immense secret where they were to stay for their wedding night. But since there weren't too many hotels in the Clubb countryside (apart from his mother's, which — at least to me — would be decidedly out of the question), I imagined the reporters had them all camped out.

But the happy couple drove away in Lance's carriage, waving and smiling. We collected everyone and started for home. Ace slept the entire way; Daisy was dozing.

Tony said, "What did we get them? I saw the invoice for the expense."

I felt amused. "I ordered a set of blank books, for her to record the doings of her children."

Tony looked startled. "Children?"

"I recall Master Jonathan telling me she wished to have at least a dozen. She can buy more books on her own if she wishes to."

For a long moment, Tony just sat there, appearing entirely astonished. Then he leaned over. "I must speak with you when we get home." He gestured with his chin towards Daisy.

I nodded. She guarded our son with her life, but that didn't mean we wanted to speak of anything personal in front of her. And I presumed it was personal, or Tony would've left it for the morrow.

So we rode the several hours in silence: through Clubb, then across the river and through Spadros. Acevedo must've been exhausted: he didn't even stir when Daisy took him from the carriage.

After Tony and I went in the front door, I turned to him. "Where might we speak?"

He looked tired. "On the veranda." He looked round at Alan. "No, in our rooms. I fear we've kept these good people up much too late as it is."

I nodded.

Alan said, "Should I call for your servants?"

Tony said, "That's not necessary. Good night."

"Good night, sir."

Tony offered me his arm. We climbed our grand staircase, curved and carpeted wood. Tony stopped at the top of the stairs, his hand upon my door. "How do you feel?"

I didn't honestly know. "I'm well."

He nodded and opened the door, turning on the light. My bed lay there to view.

We took a few steps into the room, bringing my tea-table into view. Tony said, "Would you care to speak first, or undress for bed?"

I considered this. "Let's speak." If this became heated, I could always call Shanna to undress me.

Tony gestured to the tea-table. We sat.

After all that had happened, what could he possibly have to say to me?

"I wasn't merely being polite," Tony said, "out there in the hall. I want to know if you're well."

I scoffed. "Tired of this," I waved my hand around me. "Of it all. Of this farce of a marriage."

Tony flinched.

"**None** of that needed to happen. I have **begged** you to bed me, here in this very room. Did you ever think **I** might have desires, too? Or is it only ever about **you**? You never once even **inquired** after me, whether I was **well**, what I **wanted** —"

"But —"

"Did you know that Cesare Diamond was threatening to call you out? That Gardena was afraid he might **shoot** you?"

Tony froze, face white, giving me a frightened stare.

"Lance Clubb saw you lusting after his bride. If he saw, half the people in the hall did. I wouldn't be surprised if it was in the tabloids tomorrow."

Tony looked utterly humiliated.

I leaned forward. "What is it that you actually **want**? Huh?"

Tony put his face in his hands. "I don't know."

"Do you even **want** a wife? Because if not, give me the tickets you threatened me with and I'll go. And you can duel Lance or whatever you think you need to do to bed Gardena, and I'll find someone who actually wants me."

Not that Gardena would ever bed Tony. She loved Lance, and Tony had made himself a Fool in front of everyone on her wedding day.

Tony peered at the table for a long time. Crickets chirped outside. "Mr. Hart threatened me."

"He ... he **threatened** you?"

Tony shook his head, eyes still upon the table. "He called me a child. He said he'd take you and Acevedo to his home and secure an annulment rather than allow you to ... to waste your youth this way."

Mr. Hart said **that**? To **Tony**? What had made Mr. Hart so angry?

"He said he didn't care anymore. Not even about the scandal."

Scandal would be an understatement. That I'd been forced to marry Tony when the city's beloved Keeper of the Court had legitimate claim — and Tony had persisted in the matter once he knew the truth — would likely turn anyone else not in the Family who was still on our side against him. And it would probably lend credence to the rumors that Acevedo was actually Jonathan's son. Tony would lose his heir, his wife, and much of his quadrant in one blow. "You never answered my question."

Tony twitched; that frightened stare returned to his eyes. "I don't want you to **go**! I've ... I've been s — so afraid of ..." He stopped, took a deep breath. "When I saw you and Joseph Kerr there in your study, I felt as if you ripped my heart out. For a while I wished to die."

I felt entirely taken aback. He wished to **die**?

"Ever since then, I've gone round and round, trying to find some reason, some meaning, some way to bring sense to it all." Shame crossed his eyes. "I cannot **help** but love you. Though — though you destroy me again and again. I feel like I'm dying inside. I don't know why you're **here**." His head drooped. "It can't be because you think me worthy."

In the silence, I didn't know what to say.

"Please don't leave me."

I took his hand, feeling too much grief to even speak. He wanted me to stay. So why did I have the urge to get up and run?

We sat there, silent, and then I began to think. He wanted me here, even though he didn't know why I was here. Even though me being here terribly frightened him. He didn't believe me when I told him I loved him and Ace. Why wouldn't he believe me?

It had something to do with Joe.

Joe was married. He'd hurt me again and again. I told him I didn't want him, in front of Tony.

Why could I not stop thinking of Joseph Kerr? Why did I feel drawn back to him? A pit formed in my stomach. "There's something wrong with me."

Tony sighed. "At last you see it."

This surprised me. "Oh?"

He made a sound, deep in his chest, like a laugh, yet it never made it to his lips. "Everyone sees it but you."

"Oh." Everyone saw it but me. "Then what is it?"

Tony turned to me, taking both my hands in his. "Don't you see? If you don't know, then nothing I say will help. You'll only become angry." He took my hands and kissed them, then let out a sigh of relief, laying his cheek on my hands. "I never thought this day would come."

I snatched my hands away. "You treat me like I'm a **child**."

He shrugged. "If I were to give you the answer, that would be treating you like a child, too ignorant to find the answer alone."

I considered this. "I will stay. But you must tend me. It is my right as your wife."

He nodded solemnly. "I will."

***

I didn't bed him that night: I felt too angry, too unsure of what I wanted, to do much more than hold him. But at least he let me do that.

What could I **do**? What did I **want**? What did everyone **else** see that I did not?

All the faces and voices and scenes came from their baskets that night, and I let them. Like I told Jack, I deserved whatever they had for me.

I was in my bed in Spadros Manor, alone, under the covers yet fully dressed for dinner. A loud ruckus came from downstairs.

Jonathan Diamond burst into my rooms, flinging himself onto my bed. "Oh, gods, Jacqui — I'm so glad to be home."

Suddenly we were in bedclothes, in each others' arms, kissing with passion, his hand upon my back pressing me against him. He rolled atop me, entered inside me. I pulled him close with all my strength, again and again, legs wrapped around him as he thrust himself deep inside. I loved and wanted and needed him so desperately.

Right as I gasped and moaned and shuddered in my deepest fulfillment in years, Jack's deep, deep voice said, "I love you."

With a shriek, I woke in horror, utterly revolted, flailing myself back to the headboards.

Tony had gone; from the sliver of light between the shut drapes, it was barely dawn.

After a moment of panting, my heart pounding, confused and stricken, I laughed, feeling foolish. The whole scene was absurd.

Jack was a man-lover.

Jon was dead.

"Mrs. Spadros," Rob said from the other side of my door. "Is all well?"

I said, "Just a dream."

I sighed, drawing my knees up to hug them, tears overflowing. *Oh, Jon,* I thought. *How I wish ...*

I shook my head. It would never happen. Jonathan was dead. I had to play the hand I was given. Somehow, somehow, I had to face the future without him.

The Challenge

The *Bridges Daily* sat atop my Queen's box the next morning. The paper's top story:

CANDIDATE ACCEPTS CHALLENGE

Korol Versus Pasha In Open Debate

At a press conference yesterday afternoon, Mayoral challenger Mr. Seth Pasha agreed to debate top Mayoral candidate Mr. David Korol at the Charlemagne hall upon Market Center.

These were Mr. Pasha's comments: "As Mr. Korol hides here upon Market Center, I have gone door to door throughout Bridges, speaking with the people of this city, listening to their concerns. I plan to not only bring you evidence of how I might personally benefit this city as its Mayor, but of my blueprint for moving this city forward in the future. Whilst Mr. Korol speaks of the truth, I offer the entire truth. Not only about my background and qualifications for this post, but about our so-called 'best bet' Mr. Korol."

When asked for comment on these remarks, Mr. Korol said, "If anyone has cause against me, my door is always open. I have endeavored to run an honest race. If he wishes to dig up some fanciful dirt, let him sling it. Any man doing so only spoils his own coat."

The debate is set for two weeks from today. Tickets for indoor seats go on sale next Monday at the Charlemagne. Free outdoor seats with loudspeaker broadcast of the speeches within are first come first served.

This sounded exciting. I felt impressed by Joe making such a speech!

Tony brought it up at breakfast. "This is something I'll need to speak with the other Patriarchs about, but I think it'd be good for us to attend."

"I'd have thought you'd want nothing to do with this." I glanced at the servants pretending not to overhear. "Because of who might be there."

Tony seemed amused. "I have no fear of what anyone might say about this Family. I've heard it all."

Yet I noticed he watched me throughout the meal, as if gauging me.

The day progressed as usual: "Mr. Jackson" came to visit, for once in a better mood. "I read about the debate. It should be interesting."

"Do you plan to attend?"

"If I can get tickets. They really should have secured a larger hall."

"I'm sure my husband can get one for you."

He held up a hand. "No need. If the hall sells out, the outdoor speakers should be quite sufficient." Then he relaxed, smiling. "In any rate, I can't be seen as taking Spadros favors."

Ah. Yes. Anything we did would be remarked on, and I felt certain that Jack's visits here had been noticed, particularly after our visit to Countess Victoria's ball.

"I felt surprised at Mr. Pasha's remarks," Jack said. "From the little I know of him, they sounded ... well ..." He seemed to be casting about for what to say.

I nodded. His words were an echo of my thoughts earlier. "Different for him, to be sure."

"Yes." I wondered if Josie was writing his speeches for him. That wouldn't have surprised me one bit.

Jack leaned forward, arms on the table on either side of his coffee cup. "I was most interested in what **you** thought about what he said."

Hmm. "I'm not sure what to think. I've done my own investigation of Mr. Korol and could find nothing untoward about the man."

Jack leaned back, his hands still on the table. "I wonder what Mr. Pasha's learned, then."

I felt uneasy, then, uncomfortable. Not with Jack, but with my own thoughts. My own feelings.

Why would Joe cast aspersion on this man? Why do it now? I always thought Joe to be better than that.

Jack sat quietly, unmoving, just watching me.

I'd be shredded and in the Fire before I spoke a word against Joseph Kerr to Jack Diamond. But I didn't want to say or even think about what I felt right then.

Jack spoke softly. "What do you wish to gain from all this, Mrs. Spadros? What do you really want?"

I thought back for some reason to the conversation Tony and I had the night before.

Something is wrong with me.

I'd wanted to prove Joe and Josie innocent of David Bryce's kidnapping. I still did. "I feel as though ..." Could I reveal myself to this man? I wasn't sure he wished to hurt me any more. But could I tell him how uneasy I felt, how afraid and uncertain I felt, how my inner self screamed at me about something vitally important, but I couldn't understand it?

No, I couldn't.

I took a deep breath, sat up straighter, pushing that all aside. "I wish to repair this rift between us and find the truth about Polansky Kerr, as my husband has commanded."

Jack's face turned amused, and he put his hand to his chin. "Well, then, we best get started."

***

When it was time for bed, Tony and I went to our respective rooms to be changed into nightclothes as usual, then as usual, Tony returned to my bedroom. Once Shanna left, he came to me, took my face in his hands, and kissed me.

I hadn't expected this at all. But I did enjoy it. I wrapped my arms around him, pulling him close.

When he released me, I said, "What's this?"

He had his public face on, emotionless and cold. "As you and half of Bridges has reminded me, no matter how I may feel about it, I have a duty as your husband. I am here to do my duty."

I laughed, thinking: this must be some joke. Then I saw he was serious, and I drew back. "Why do you speak so? Do you not want me?"

His face didn't change, but his eyes dropped, his gaze considering. "I do. And as Mr. Hart reminded me, I am a fully capable man of seven and twenty, and should not deny myself the pleasure of and rights to your person." He stopped, as if he was going to say more, yet decided not to.

I stepped back, mouth open. "Mr. Hart said **that**?"

Tony looked away. "He said many a thing to me." He turned his head to face me, yet didn't meet my eye. "Shall we begin?"

I stood there, confused, stunned.

Tony peered at me, head tilted, and caressed my cheek, tucking a strand of hair behind my ear. "I've not let myself truly look upon you for many a day." His hands went under my arms, slid slowly down my ribs, my waist, my hips. He moved his hands behind, pulling me to press firmly onto his body. "You are **most** beautiful."

He'd never been like this before, ever, and something about it stirred passion within me. I hugged him, kissing his neck, his ear, as his hands went up and down my back.

He turned us as one, pushing me onto the bed, his hand going between my legs, then his body.

He was skilled, he was gentle, he always was. But there was a force to him that night, as though he'd become a different person altogether.

I admit I was quite incapable of much thought about the matter.

We lay there after, bathed in sweat, and Tony touched my cheek. "Did I do well?"

I could hardly move, I felt so spent. But I took his hand. "You did. You always do."

He got an amused look to him, though his face barely changed. He reached over to grasp the side of my waist. "You are mine, Jacqui. Not his. Mine. And I shall tend you, as often as you wish it, 'til the day I die."

The Fall

The rest of the next two weeks I pondered the change in Tony. What had caused it? Why now? What did he really want?

Each night, Tony came to my bed, asking me what I wanted from him. Most nights, I bedded him, others we simply lay close. On those nights, he'd ask about my thoughts, my day. But he'd say little of his, turning the conversation back to me each time.

And each day, Jack Diamond arrived to offer his assistance. He asked no more questions, simply did his duty as well. Moving boxes, retrieving pages and folders, writing what I asked of him.

But our conversations nagged at me. I didn't know what I wanted. I didn't know what I was missing. And as much as I searched the inner baskets of my mind, I couldn't find the answer.

During this time, an announcement came from the Inventors that after much discussion with the Patriarchs, Diamond quadrant was to have the first ventilation window opened.

This partially explained where Tony had been recently, as well as why he hadn't spoken about it.

Zeppelin flights were canceled for three days so that the Aperture might be closed, to prevent excessive air circulation at the instant of the window's opening. Diamond homes below the massive window and for five blocks around it were evacuated. Cesare Diamond offered his men for help with moving, and those who had no family they could stay with were offered rooms at one of the many fake Country Houses they had scattered across the quadrant.

They accomplished this with surprising ease, and I wondered at it. When I mentioned it to Jack, he chuckled. "Our people are trained in discipline and order. Are the Spadros so unruly?"

Good grief, I thought.

"No offense meant," Jack said quickly. "Forgive me: I see I've disturbed you."

Even in truce, we repelled each other. I almost laughed.

That evening before dinner, I brought Ace and Daisy out to look through Tony's Telescopic Magnifier. Tony had placed a covered stand holding a book through which he made notations as to the locations of the ventilation windows. Even so, it took us some time to find the group of balloons below the window in question.

The Inventors had offered extensive documents and maps for the *Bridges Daily,* which I consulted as we peered into the heavens.

"The Inventors have launched a dozen large balloons capable of holding six to support the edges of the stout net," I read, "with one man in each. The finer net will raise next, being held with six balloons around it and the most intrepid reporters aboard." I looked at Daisy. "This sounds most impressive."

Daisy shuddered. "To go so high above the ground!"

Seeing how this dismayed Daisy so, I returned to reading silently. Fearing the weight of the windows, three airships used in tourist runs over the city were attached to each of the corners of the window. Then dozens of workmen were suspended aloft to attempt prying the window free from the dome.

I could see little of this, although Daisy claimed she saw a cluster of dots in the area. Ace amused himself by running after Rocket, who had come over, presumably to see what we were doing. Rocket took my boy's attempts to chase him in stride, and was careful not to knock Ace over.

The black pit bull terrier had a slight limp, and more white hairs in his coat than I'd remembered. But he bore Ace's pettings and hugs with equanimity until Tony emerged. Then Rocket bounded to greet him.

Ace went to chase Rocket, shouting, "Papa!" along the way. Then he slipped, and fell. I ran over, fearful that he might be hurt.

Tony reached Ace first, kneeling before his crying son. "Are you hurt? Or did that scare you?"

Ace sat thinking, the tears forgotten. "Scare me."

Tony patted Ace's back. "The grass can catch your foot! Up we go."

I felt touched. I felt grateful he wished to try for more children. As Ace toddled off once more, I said, "You're so good with him."

Tony smiled to himself. "I suppose I merely consider daily what might help him be stronger. He has a long road ahead, and he'll need every bit of strength he can muster."

***

It took two days and nights to pry the ventilation window off, and to everyone's relief, it did not fall. The moment the window opened became evident: at once, a stout wind swept upwards from the city, knocking a few of the workers from their posts. They fell safely into the fine net, for which I'm sure they were quite grateful.

Due to Inventor Cuarenta's caution, the Aperture was able to be re-opened a day early, which made everyone happy.

The group of aeronauts rested a day, then conferred to make plans for the new window's opening. Once the next section of the city was evacuated, up the airships went, and the city followed their every move.

The day before the debate shone clear and bright. The air already seemed cooler, and as I began my Queen's work, I felt a sense of hope for the future.

If Tony was right, no matter what the outcome of this debate, the Family man running for Mayor would win. Joe would lose: I'd come to terms with that.

But I did have hope on another matter. We couldn't touch Mr. Korol whilst he remained a Mayoral candidate, but once he'd lost, we could have him properly investigated in Ariana's shooting.

It was after luncheon. I sat in my study. Alan came in with a pale face and a paper in his hand. "Mum, a special news."

I took it from him.

CANDIDATE DEAD

Shot from carriage

Mayoral candidate Mr. David Korol has been shot dead outside of the Charlemagne Hall as he and the other candidates waited for the doors to be opened for the debate rehearsal this morning.

A carriage full of men bearing pistols shot the candidate as they drove past.

Also shot was the wife of Mayoral candidate Mr. Seth Pasha, who had been standing close by.

"Good gods," I murmured. Joe's wife was **shot**? The paper didn't mention whether or not she'd survived. "We must deny involvement, and send condolences to the families."

Alan took a folded paper from his pocket. "Too late." He brandished the paper. "Our informant in the Courthouse just wrote. The District Attorney is seeking a warrant to arrest everyone."

I felt confused. "What do you mean, everyone?"

He peered at it, then me. "All members of the Four Families, and anyone associated with them." He let his hand drop to his side. "They think we killed Mr. Korol. They want to arrest everyone."

The Distrust

I couldn't believe it. "Why would Thrace Pike do such a thing?"

Then I remembered what he'd said the night he'd laid hands upon me on Market Center almost five years earlier:

I will not surrender. If your husband, or your father-in-law, or whoever sent that mob wants war, then war I will give them ... I will see this city restored to one where law, not crime families, rule. Where people can move about their city safely, not limited by checkpoints and retribution. Where everyone has an equal say and a man can advance in life with honesty, not crawl in servitude to some trumped-up self-appointed monarchy.

I thought I finally understood. Thrace Pike had pretended friendship as a way to gain my trust until he might jail me with the rest. "The scoundrel! He's as bad as Freezout!"

I hurried towards Tony's study.

Alan said, "Mrs. Spadros, wait —"

Reaching the door, I burst in.

Tony stood in the middle of his study, his men staring at me. Tony said, "Do you never knock?"

Heat rushed to my face, and I curtsied low. "Sir, the city —"

"I know." Tony turned to his men. "You've got your orders."

The others left. Tony said, "Well? What's so important as to disturb me in a meeting with my men?"

"I didn't know you were in a meeting." I felt embarrassed. "I didn't know you knew."

"Oh, yes, and I'm just the Fool, sitting around slack-jawed until you bring me your commands."

The bitterness in his voice took me aback. "I don't think that at all! Alan — um, Mr. Pearson just brought in the news, and —"

His words were smeared in sarcasm. "You thought I didn't know."

"No. How could I?"

He shook his head, letting out a breath. "I have my own informants. My own men, in every corner of this city. I know what's going on."

I took a step back. "I'm sorry." Then I had a terrible thought: *they might come here.* Images of police entering, searching the Manor, ransacking the place, entered my mind. "Should we prepare to leave? What will you do?"

Tony gave a soft snort, smiling to himself. "I considered what my father would've done."

"What? No, Tony, please."

Tony began to laugh. "You really think so little of me. I don't plan to **kill** anyone! But this city needs to consider what will happen if we fall. The Four Families run this city, Jacqui, as much as your Joe Pasha and his lackeys might wish otherwise. And we will not go quietly." He took my arm and drew me outside his study. "The next time you want to see me, at least have the courtesy to knock."

I stood there, stunned.

Joe had mentioned some animosity towards the Clubbs, long back when we were teenagers, but that was because they refused to let his ancestor, the first Polansky Kerr, leave the city during the Coup. Surely Tony couldn't believe that Joe, of all people, would try to disrupt the entire city! Why else would he want to become Mayor, if not to improve things? From his position, he could rebuild the Pot, help the poor, coordinate fixing the city's infrastructure. All things he'd actually spoken of in his speeches. "You think Joe wants to get rid of the Four **Families**?"

"I do."

I sighed. "You are so angry at Joe for giving me womb fever that you've lost all reason."

Tony turned to me. "You speak of reason. Very well: who benefits by David Korol's death? Not the Feds. They've gone to great lengths to ensure fair elections. Why kill the people's choice?"

"Wait," I said. "Surely you can't think Joe would —"

"He wouldn't even bat an eye."

I shook my head. "This is ridiculous."

Tony took hold of my upper arm. "Just once, **use** that mind the gods gave you."

I tore my arm from his grasp and stormed away. How **dare** he?

I went to Alan. "I need a message brought."

Alan blinked. "Very well. By Mr. Anthony's orders, all your outgoing mail is to go to Mr. Howell."

Hmm, I thought. If I sent it to Mr. Howell, he'd surely open it.

"Should I call for a Memory Boy?" Alan hesitated. "Or should I call one of your men?"

I didn't need Tony to know of this. "Find Honor. I'll be in my study."

I went to my desk and wrote:

> I'm sure you've heard of the warrant.
>
> Please help. My husband accuses you of being with our enemies.
>
> Mayoral candidates here seem to have great power. Anything you might do to stop this could dissuade him.

But where would Joe be? How might I send him this?

When Honor arrived, I asked him, "Is there a place where Mayoral candidates gather? Where I might be able to contact one?"

Honor shrugged. "If you need me to, I can find out."

Honor was a day footman. Not many knew him as one of my men, other than him riding with me on my carriage from time to time. "What do you know of disguise?"

"Nothing, mum. I've never had cause to."

"Very well. I need this to reach a man named Pasha. He's a Mayoral candidate. Do you know someone who might be able to help?"

Honor considered this. "Is he a gentleman?"

So far as I knew, Joe owned no property. He had no title or wealth. "Sadly, no."

"Well, then Jacob isn't likely to know how to reach him."

We'd contacted Lance Clubb through his manservant earlier in the year. Tony's manservant Jacob Michaels had known the man from a pub where the manservants gathered.

Honor seemed hesitant. "Mum, forgive me, but isn't this the man Mr. Blitz shot at? This seems unwise."

How might I find the man?

Then an idea came to me. "One moment." I took out another envelope, put the first inside it, and addressed it to Mr. Paul Blackberry, the editor of the *Bridges Daily*. We'd known each other since I was five; he'd know how to reach Joe. I sealed the envelope. "Bring this directly to him."

Honor took it, bowed, and left.

If anyone might help, Joe could.

***

That night, riots began in every quadrant, on every street. Fires burned. Stores were looted, homes wrecked, both high and low. Signs were torn down. Carriages, destroyed. Men wielding bricks and cudgels shouted, "You can't take our Families from us!"

Curiously, the only buildings damaged were those **not** owned by Family Men.

While this went on, peaceful marchers converged upon the government buildings, to convene candlelight vigils there. Men and women with their babies held posters saying, "We love our Family," "Keep our city safe," and "Stop destroying our quadrants."

Evidently, the Acting Mayor wasn't at all prepared for this — for several hours, the quadrant's rioters remained unchecked. The quadrant's police (only armed with nightsticks) fled when the mobs approached.

Groups of Constables upon Market Center with pistols in hand tried to cross into the quadrants to help secure them. But Tony had sent our Acey-Deuceys — the most violent of the young men of Spadros, Roy's enforcers-in-training — to man the Spadros bridge.

Not a Constable survived.

At that, the other groups were withdrawn to secure Market Center. When riots began upon the island, the gun battles were fierce, with the Constables no match for the hardened Associates from all four quadrants who'd been sent there. The Constables fled to the Mayor's mansion, and the mobs followed.

The wrought iron fence around the Mayor's mansion was torn down before the Constables managed to drive back the crowd, killing many and chasing off the rest. Some signal, from who, no one knew, and the bulk of the attacks stopped as if on cue.

At least, that's how the *Bridges Daily* put it.

The next day, the cleanup began. Family men went to help each of those who had lost property ... with gentle reminders that it could have been much, much worse.

That evening, Joe held a press conference upon the steps of the Courthouse. The next morning, copies of his speech filled my Queen's box. According to most of the papers, the huge space in front of the Courthouse steps was packed so full not an empty spot remained.

They say his eyes were full of tears as he spoke, a small boy by his side. "My innocent wife was murdered by violent scoundrels, leaving her little son as my only hope. But hope is not lost. I vow to end — I will end — this mindless violence, and restore a true and lasting peace to this city."

I now regretted sending that letter to him. He'd lost his wife! In my fear for myself, I'd sent not one word of condolence or comfort.

One of the tabloids had an unauthorized and grainy photo of the scene, taken from far off. But even with that poor quality, the little boy's face and eyes confirmed my fears. This was the child Jonathan Diamond had taken me to see, the one he claimed had been sired by Joseph Kerr and abandoned.

His mother's face as she sat in her window-seat, ringed with reddish curls and streaked with tears, swam before me. She had found Joe, or he'd found her, and now she was dead.

Who would **do** such a thing?

Tony thought Joe did it. But why would Joe murder his own **wife**? It made no sense.

For the Families to kill these people made even less sense. We didn't kill civilians, for one thing. And the Families had it all set up for their man to win. Why disrupt their own process to kill a man who had no chance?

***

Late that night, I woke to find Tony gone and voices in the front hall. By the time I got my robe on, Alan was knocking at the door. "Mum, your husband wishes to speak with you in the library."

I put my house shoes on and went down the front stair after Alan, curious to see what the commotion had been about. For Tony not to wish to wait until morning to speak frightened me. Yet the house was otherwise quiet: no wakening of the servants, no bustle of preparations to flee.

I found Tony in his pajamas and robe standing, hands behind him, facing the large portrait of the first Acevedo Spadros which hung over the unlit fire.

When the door closed behind me, I said, "What's happened?"

Tony didn't turn. "I am the fourth man since the Coup to have charge over this Family. Yet my line has stretched back over a thousand years."

I felt too frightened to speak.

"I don't know why I didn't realize it sooner," Tony said. "I wanted so much to believe that you loved me. I needed to believe it." He dipped into his robe's pocket then faced me, a sheet of paper in his hand. And his eyes ... he looked dead inside. "Yet with all that has happened, all you have told me, this shouldn't have been a surprise." Tony took a step towards me. "You will not see, nor speak with, nor send word to that man again. Or leave, and don't return." He tossed the paper at me, which fluttered to the floor, and walked out.

I picked up the page and sat to read. It was the letter I'd sent to Joe, with a notation below it:

> I thought you should be aware of this.
>
> Paul Blackberry,
>
> Editor, *Bridges Daily*

I felt humiliated. I felt betrayed. I felt frightened. I felt dismayed.

Tony could only see this as disrespect of the highest order. Proof that I'd lied about trusting him, loving him, believing in him.

I felt glad that the letter hadn't reached Joe — it would've only hurt him as well.

But now I was in a terrible situation that I had no idea how to solve.

Words wouldn't fix this. No action could, either.

I sat there, in the library, just sitting, until the sun rose and Millie came in to do the dusting.

The Connections

The morning news held all the information about David Korol — his family, his beliefs, his assassination. His picture stared back at me.

If he **were** part of the Red Dog Gang, what did his death mean? Had he displeased them somehow? I couldn't think of how. Perhaps his zeal for truth and self-governance went too far, upset the very aristocrats who'd backed him.

***

Later that day, Inventor Jotepa arrived just after our morning meeting, asking to speak with me. He handed over a closed portfolio a bit larger than a sheet of paper but an inch thick. "Inventor Cuarenta got a message from Regina Clubb that we should send you this. I happened to be on my way to meet with Inventor Gosi, and so ..."

I took the portfolio from him. "What is it?"

"This is a translation of what we've found so far about the Kerr Dynasty's plans in the event of a coup. I gather you've been investigating the recent unrest in the city?"

This surprised me. "Yes, I have."

He shrugged. "She thought this might help."

Once the Inventor left, I brought the packet to my study, setting it aside to look over once Jack got there. I had a lot of Queen's work to do before he arrived.

Jack arrived as usual, an hour after luncheon. He'd returned with the bank records, and he seemed pleasantly surprised by my own acquisition. He turned the unopened portfolio over in his hand. "I don't know why, but I feel this could be very helpful." He moved his partially-drunk coffee aside, an air of excitement in his movements. "Let's see what's inside."

Inside lay a thick sheaf of paper, bound in a similar way as my Memory Sheaf. But it was evident that this had been copied using an Automated Mimeograph — it still smelled of the process. The front read:

DYNASTIC RECOVERY

Jack began to read, and not for the first time, I was struck with the depth and quality of his voice. With a start, I realized I hadn't been listening to what he was saying.

"... in the first generation born after an overthrow, the prime purpose must be to rebuild lost wealth. No matter how meager the resources, make all attempts to leverage it to gather a store of funds, goods, and properties. These will form the basis of your plan to retake the city."

I felt stunned. "Good gods."

Jack closed the sheaf, his finger keeping the place in it. "So contingencies had been set well before the Coup." He returned to his place and continued to read. "It is vital to form a large group of associates with utmost loyalty, willing to die for your cause. These can be friends, other organizations, and those unpleased with the current regime. However, the most stable means of producing the required manpower will be ties of blood. Many will be lost in the coming battle, so prepare yourself for that eventuality."

This was horrifying. "So sacrificing your own children."

"And grandchildren, from the sound of it." Keeping hold of the sheaf, Jack took a long drink of his coffee and continued. "The second step can be accomplished during the first, depending on the initial resource base and the skill and speed of sufficient means to engage in bribery —"

"What?"

Jack laughed, shaking his head. "This is masterful. That is, the Families could learn from the author."

These quadrant-folk were all alike.

He returned to reading. "No matter how horrifying the offenses of your ancestors' deeds, it is human nature for there to be many who wish for 'better days.' It is vital to cultivate those persons and groups ready to aid you, if only given a focus for their zeal. Your goal then must be to utilize those men to locate spokespersons and presses ready to give voice to your return. Start small; the longest stair may be climbed one step at a time. Never forget: over-extension can be fatal. You will have but one chance to regain what is yours." He closed the sheaf, shaking his head. "Polansky Kerr has performed the tasks here, word for word."

"Well, this only proves it! He's been doing this for decades."

Jack nodded. "Biding his time, gathering his men? Yes. This is suspicious. But it's not proof. This ..." He stood then, gesturing around the room. "This has the proof we need, if we can only connect these bits into one. We must find evidence of an offense against the Families, something that no one can gainsay. There are many men in this city gathering wealth, and it's no crime to do so."

I sat pondering for a moment. "Were you able to locate copies of those checks Finette Pasha signed?"

He hesitated. "Why do you need them?"

"Well, if I can get a sample of Josephine Kerr's handwriting, I can compare it to this Finette Pasha's. I can also examine the check to look for signs of forgery."

Jack leaned back. "You still believe her innocent."

This irritated me. "I do!"

He brought out Polansky Kerr's bank records. A silver bookmark with black cord had been placed about a quarter of the way through the sheaf, and he opened to the page, turning the book for me to read. "I found this last night."

A third of the way down was a notation:

HORSE TRAINING (SHADOW): $2.53

Jack turned to Honor. "What was the name of the horse that you had to put down? After the carriage incident?"

Honor blinked. "I believe it was Shadow, sir."

I sat there, unable to believe my ears. In fact, I wouldn't believe it. Jack could've coached Honor on what to say.

Alan had given me the name, put it upon my desk. Where did I put it? I stood. "One moment, please."

Mr. Theodore, Honor, and Jack only stared at me. My servants stared at me as I ran down the hall, past the kitchens, up the stair to the dining room, then past the breakfast room to my study. I fumbled for my keys, opened my desk drawer.

The folded piece of paper still sat there. I opened it.

Shadow.

I ran to Alan's post. "Did you speak with Honor about this?"

"I'm sorry, mum. About what?"

"The horse's name. Where did you learn it?"

His face fell. "Tommy, mum. It was his favorite horse. Listy's too." He took a deep breath. "There's something else I must tell you. They found Tommy, mum. Dead. The Strangler."

I felt grieved. Numb. "Thank you for telling me."

I walked back downstairs, passed by Honor and Mr. Theodore to stand in the doorway. "I've seen that price before."

Jack looked puzzled. "Where?"

"Here, in these boxes."

I didn't need all the boxes, just the ones we'd looked through so far. I took a deep breath, focused on the price. Where was it?

The whole world became silent.

And there it was. "Hart. Box 13, file 27." I gestured with my chin. "If you might?"

Jack's eyes widened slightly. Then he nodded. Honor and Mr. Theodore had to move some boxes to get to Box 13, but soon it was on the table. Jack pulled the sheet out, handed it to me:

INVOICE

OPEN STAKES TRAINERS

2107 CRIBBAGE RD, HART, BRIDGES

TRAINER: VICTOR EVERHEART

CUSTOMER: CHARLES HART

SPECIALIZED COURSE

HORSE TRAINING: $2.53

There were some terms and conditions, but at the bottom it read:

NAME OF HORSE: SHADOW

HORSE TO DROP UPON HEARING A GUN SHOT, STANDING AND RUNNING

Below that lay a signature that I supposed was not Charles Hart's. I'd never seen the man's handwriting, but it did have the stops and starts shown at my trial to indicate forgery.

That Mr. Hart had turned this request down made sense: he bred race horses, not circus ones. "So how, I wonder, did this payment end up in Mr. Polansky's bank records?"

Jack said, "That's the question. If you notice, the date on the invoice is quite a bit before the date here on the payment."

I sat heavily. "Mr. Hart refused to pay. So the trainer went to Mr. Polansky for the payment."

Jack said gently, "Because Mr. Polansky set it up in the first place."

The screams of that dying horse after it'd been dragged by the carriage have never left me. "Good gods." I felt ready to cry. "And a Red Dog card lay there."

Jack's eyebrows raised. "What? Where?"

"By the horse. It must've had a card on it." Where did that card come from? "I saw it on the ground, beside the horse's body."

Honor's gaze went inward, as if remembering. Mr. Theodore stared at me in horror.

Jack leaned back in his chair. "I'm not sure that we'll find better proof than this."

So it was as I'd feared: Mr. Polansky Kerr was the Director of the Red Dog Gang. He had to be.

Everything now made sense. Joe running for Mayor made perfect sense. Why **else** would he run, if not to stop his grandfather from tormenting me?

But for Mr. Polansky to do that to a **horse**! An innocent gentle beast, eager to please its master, only to have its training used in the most horrible way possible.

Joe had been right: his grandfather **was** a monster.

Mr. Kerr had to be the Hart wildcard. Yet for some reason, he didn't want us to know it. Otherwise, why kill my informant?

I stood. "We need to bring this to the Patriarchs, and then to the city."

Jack had risen when I did. "The Patriarchs first." He chuckled. "My brother Cesare won't be happy to see me, but I can do that."

"We best leave the originals here." I turned to Honor. "I want this room locked and all keys to it brought to me. There must be a round-the-clock guard here, two men."

Honor nodded. "Yes, mum."

We had the proof. We had the proof!

We had the invoice, the name of the horse, the bank statement showing the payment from Mr. Polansky's account to the trainer, and the affidavit from the trainer himself.

The card on the ground beside that poor animal swam before me. I felt sick at the thought of it.

So now we knew our enemy: Mr. Polansky Kerr.

Tony had been right not to trust him.

We returned to the front porch. Mr. Theodore said his farewells and went down the walkway and home.

But then I realized something. "Mr. Jackson, I believe you and Master Honor here have a mutual connection. A man named Daniel?"

Honor's jaw dropped in surprise. Then he put the answer together. "We do!"

Jack looked just as surprised.

I smiled at them. "See if Master Michaels is available. I believe the three of you have much to discuss."

The Parting

The next day I went to my apartments. To my surprise, Blitz and Mary were in the front hall: they'd just received a letter from the Memory Guild.

"She's not a Memory Girl," Mary said. "But they're going to send a tutor for her!"

"Wonderful," I said. "I'll be happy to pay —"

"No, mum," Mary said. "For free!"

I felt astonished. "However did this happen?"

"They think she might do well in the Tinkerer's Guild," Blitz said proudly. His nose reddened. "I can't believe it. My little **girl**!" He shook his head in amazement. "We're to give her tools, or anything else she wants to work with. They said she will know her path."

I took a step back, remembering Anna Goren and her love of knowing. Of understanding. "Let's see who they send. But bring her with you. Show her your work." I glanced at Mary. "Both of you. When she's older, I'll find an herb-woman to teach her. See if Dr. Salmon might show her his medicaments."

Mary nodded. "She has an appointment next week for her arm."

"Good." Ariana'a face had healed, but there were still some red and swollen marks upon the underside of her right arm. "Bring your letter. If he has questions, he can use the Telephonic Telegraph to speak with me at the Manor."

Mary curtsied. "Yes, mum."

I hugged them both. "This is too wonderful." After I let them go, I said, "I won't be coming here openly anymore. It's just become too dangerous."

Blitz said, "But where will you go?"

In a moment, the pieces came together. And I knew. "I'm done with my investigation business. As long as I'm Queen of Spadros quadrant, no one will ever trust that I'm impartial. That their concerns won't reach my husband's ear. That I won't use them in some Family game." I sighed. "I'll find a place for my things, and let you know. But you can take down my signs. Tell Mr. Howell he can get some real renters here now."

Blitz nodded soberly. "I'm sorry."

"Don't be. This has been a long time coming." I smiled at them. "I have income from here. And once I get Mr. Pok-Deng settled, I'll have his rent once again. Plus the revenue from the library tours. So I have an income, a good and independent one. Just not one I ever imagined."

***

The day of the election was a shambles. Some were too frightened of the Army men to approach the buildings. Hundreds of women and servants were too frightened of what their husbands or fathers or neighbors or masters might do if they tried to vote to approach the polls. On Market Center, the Army commander told men that they wouldn't be allowed to vote unless they brought their women; many went home instead.

The Clubb candidate was attacked, and almost killed. One election hall in Diamond caught fire, another had a water break. A cart full of ballots in Hart quadrant overturned in the mud.

But not all was lost. Joe — or I suppose I should say, Seth Pasha — won the election for Mayor. I don't know what he did or didn't do, but the rumored warrant against the Four Families vanished into thin air.

When I heard the news, I felt so relieved. Someone I knew had become Mayor, someone who grew up in the Pot, a man who would never intentionally harm me. Maybe we all had a chance to succeed.

Because right then, I was utterly convinced of one thing: Joe couldn't be the Bridges Strangler.

So that meant we'd won. We'd stopped whoever Polansky Kerr and the Red Dog Gang had appointed to become Mayor from winning. We now had a chance to find the fiend and destroy him.

Yet underneath it all, I felt uneasy. What did Joe know about running a city? And where was Josie?

They were both in terrible danger. If the Red Dog Gang had been dealt a true setback, then Joe would become their next target. And I couldn't bear the thought of anything happening to him.

After he took on the seals of the city and of the Merca Federal Union, his little son beside him, Joe said, "We've won. We have overcome so much. But this is only the beginning. Our next job is to root out the evil which has terrorized us, pitted us against each other, and destroyed so many lives. The Bridges Strangler and those who have backed him must be brought to justice."

The cheers were so loud I had to hold my ears.

"My first act as Mayor will be to appoint a special task force to do just that. Anyone with information about the Bridges Strangler should come forward to cooperate with the investigation." He put his arm around the boy's shoulders. "We can and will make our city safe for our boys. We must! Here is our future."

Tony had his arms crossed, his face set, refusing to look at me. On the way home, he said, "You are not to enter into any of my rooms uninvited. You are not to come to my study uninvited, nor to my meetings. Ten will inform Mr. Howell of anything you have need to know."

"I can't attend meetings with you anymore? Why? What have I done?"

"You really don't understand?" Tony turned away, breathing heavily, with small shakes of his head. Then he turned to me. "For the first time since my ancestor gained control of this city, the Families have lost it." He tapped his chest. "I'm the one who's taken the blame."

"How can they blame **you**? The Feds —"

"Would never have come if your man hadn't shot Seth Pasha —"

"**My** man? Blitz is your **cousin**!"

"— and no, it's not fair. But I'm the Spadros King. By the Blessed Dealer's mercy, I stand over all others. I rule this city. So for me **not** to take blame for the actions of my household would show yet again that I am unfit for this post, one that I have almost lost twice because of you."

I didn't know what to say. "Do you no longer love me?"

Tony wouldn't look at me. "It's not a matter of love. We **will** not survive — we **cannot** survive — when you refuse to trust me."

This hurt. "I trust you, Tony —"

He scoffed. "You say that, but at every turn, at any setback, you run to our enemies. So until you renounce the Kerrs, **all** of the Kerrs, I have no other choice. I **must** deal you **out!**"

I felt so stunned I couldn't speak.

But I now understood: without any proof one way or the other, he was convinced that Joe and Josie sided with their grandfather. He thought they were part of the Red Dog Gang.

I couldn't agree with him. I loved them. I believed in them. They were the only family of my home that I had left. I wanted to clear their names. But because of his fear, his hate for them, he feared I was with the Red Dog Gang as well.

I didn't understand how he could think this! Yet I saw now that nothing I might say would sway him.

Our marriage was broken.

All I wanted was to fix it, to somehow make him love me again, but I didn't know how.

***

It stormed for the next several weeks. Many said the city itself wept.

I don't know about that, but during that time, the Inventors finally removed all of the ventilation windows. The temperature began to cool.

Judith Hart died shortly after. Her funeral was large and well-attended, both by the Harts and the Bridgers. Mr. Hart and his grand-daughter Ferti stood silent, grief in his face, bewilderment on hers.

The Bridgers Grand-Master, Judith Hart's father, was not allowed to speak. But to Tony's dismay, the man's eyes continually went to my son. The man had no blood-right to the boy, but I wondered if he might one day present himself at our door asking to see "his great-grandson."

***

Mary had her baby just before Yuletide, a girl. Blitz and Mary named her Jane, after Mary's mother.

The snow was much lighter than usual that year and for many years after, they say due to the removal of the ventilation windows. But Acevedo loved seeing what little snow we had. I sat on the veranda with Tony on my twenty-seventh birthday, Yuletide Center, watching Acevedo toddle around on his canes, Daisy close at hand.

I loved my baby. I loved my family here, in Spadros Manor. At the time, I loved being there more than anything in the world.

But I wouldn't say things were well. Things weren't at all well.

I hadn't exonerated either Joe or Josie, and although Tony still came to my bed each night to perform his duty, he often wouldn't so much as speak to me.

I no longer went to his meetings. Honor, Jacob, and Mr. Theodore were shut out as well. Mr. Howell arrived twice each day, to bring and collect my Queen's box. He met with Sawbuck at his home for a half-hour afterwards, but wasn't allowed in Tony's meetings either.

Tony even went so far as to build a private meeting room out in the garden, on the same spot where Roy had greeted his guests some years back. The area was well-guarded, so that not even I might overhear.

I believe Tony blamed Blitz for losing the election. Tony and Blitz hadn't been close for a while. But other than a short visit from Tony to call on little Ariana, I don't know that they ever spoke again.

***

Mr. Hart hosted the Grand Ball, but it was a quiet affair, with the Harts all in mourning. Other than the Four Families, few attended.

After the New Year, Jack Diamond continued to visit a few times a week. Once, he visited during the day, yet most often in the evenings, always going into Tony's study to converse.

Neither would tell me what they spoke of. I feared that Jack had moved into Tony's camp against me. Or perhaps it was the other way round. And I wasn't sure what that meant for the future.

But I was alive. Whatever he was plotting, Jack no longer seemed angry with me. And we'd proven Mr. Polansky Kerr was behind the Red Dog Gang.

There was still much evidence to unearth. I continued to work through it as I had the time, if only in hopes of finding proof of Joe and Josie's innocence. Also, the more evidence I found against Polansky Kerr, the easier it would be to bring him down in the eyes of a city which he seemed to now own.

I still didn't understand why Mr. Polansky hated me so. But if Joe spoke true, we now had a powerful ally in our fight against him.

It wouldn't be easy. But with Joe as Mayor and the whole city searching for the Bridges Strangler, maybe now we might finally bring the fiend to justice.

One major card still remained: the woman calling herself Black Maria. Others called her the Death Card. Both these names referred to the Queen of Spades.

I had no idea who this woman was, or why she did the things she did. But I did know one thing: I couldn't let her keep calling herself this, not if I wanted my Family to be safe. By using those names, she claimed Spadros quadrant. She was a direct threat to my life, my rule, and my son, in a city which didn't want me here in the first place.

So I had to find her, and soon.

I knew where she was: my old homeland, the Pot.

I knew who backed her: the aristocrats, Polansky Kerr.

I knew her associates: many thousands of men, women, and children from my old street gang, the High-Low Split. And Frank Pagliacci, who I felt certain was the Bridges Strangler and by all accounts, her consort.

I'd let Joe and the city go after Frank. I planned to go after her.

This Death Card's machinations had ruined my city, my quadrant, and my home. She'd been part of killing my brother and my friends. She'd injured my husband and crippled my child.

And at the time, I wanted nothing more than to have this all end with her lying before me, dead.

~~This ends Chapter 11 of the Red Dog Conspiracy~~

The Death Card:
Part 12 of the Red Dog Conspiracy
Releases March 2026

Acknowledgments

My thanks go to Julian White, Hope Gerhardstein, and Lenka Trnkova for beta reading *The Jack of Diamonds.*

Thank you also to my street team, The Commission, without whom this book might not have made it into your hands, and to Andy Loofbourrow, who has given me the time, space, and backing to have a writing career.

Special thanks to my Patrons, whose monthly financial support makes this series possible:

Julian White

Melissa Williams

Laura Prime

Michaelene Alston

Danielle Barnes

Rachel Heslin

Phoebe Darqueling

Carl Poellnitz

Follow the Red Dog Conspiracy on Patreon

patreon.com/red_dog_conspiracy

About the Author

Patricia Loofbourrow is the NY Times and USA Today best-selling author of the Red Dog Conspiracy steampunk noir crime fiction series. She has been a professional blogger, author, and editor since 2000 and began writing novels in 2005. Her first published novel, *The Jacq of Spades*, released in 2015 and has sold over 23,000 copies worldwide.

A native of southern California, Patricia Loofbourrow has lived in central Oklahoma since 2005 with her spouse and three children. You can see all her books (and learn more) at pattyloof.com.

Note from the Author

Thanks so much for reading this far! If you like this series, please leave a review where you bought this.